THE MORTAL BLOW

Lady Fan Mysteries Book Five

Elizabeth Bailey

SAPERE
BOOKS

THE MORTAL BLOW

Published by Sapere Books.

11 Bank Chambers, Hornsey, London, N8 7NN,
United Kingdom

saperebooks.com

ISBN: 978-1-913028-33-6

Chapter One

Despite the fur rug covering her legs, the chill seeped into Ottilia's bones. Her husband's breath was misting as he grumbled his dissatisfaction against the rattle of the coach, the chink of harness and the steady clopping of hooves. She lent only half an ear, drowsy with the rhythm and fatigued by the length of the journey.

Lord Francis Fanshawe's monologue ceased and he leaned a little to peer into her face. "Are you even listening to me, Tillie?"

The sharp note made her shift in her seat. She looked round, caught the frown and gave a little sigh. "You've said it all several times, Fan."

"Oh, I'm boring you, am I?"

She brought one gloved hand out from under the warm rug and set it against his chest. "Don't turn on me, Fan, if you please. It was not my notion to join the family for the Season."

He let out a defeated breath, caught the hand and held it. "You could have told Mama you are not yet well enough to leave Flitteris."

"What, lie? I am perfectly well now. Besides, I owe it to Sybilla. She took time to come to Weymouth for me."

The Dowager Marchioness of Polbrook had been instrumental in jerking Ottilia out of the doldrums after the disastrous end to her pregnancy the previous summer. The seaside trip had been her husband's solution, drawing her in to help solve a particularly grisly murder. She had relished the intervening months of quiet content at their home, with its undemanding pace of life. But if truth be told, she was ready for a little more interest. She was guiltily aware that Francis knew it.

"You need not dissemble. I saw how your eyes lit when Mama's summons came, you wretch. You were bored to death."

She let out a gurgle, but clutched his hand nevertheless. "Not bored, dearest. Just beginning to itch a little."

"Well, you may scratch to your heart's content," came the acid response. "The whole business promises a debacle of the first order."

This was undeniable. Randal's decision to bring his new marchioness and her now legitimised children to town had sent Sybilla into a predictable rage.

"Stealing poor Candia's thunder," she wrote, "when the child has been obliged to wait a year for her debut already. Harriet is furious and I don't blame her. How will it look, I ask you? Could he not have waited? It is all of a piece and I must have you here, Francis, to lend support to your niece."

"What the deuce she thinks I can do I really don't know," Francis said, for the umpteenth time. "She only wants me there so she may vent her spleen upon me instead of raking Randal over the coals."

"She will not, Fan, because I shall intervene. I won't let her rub you raw, I promise."

He drew her gloved hand to his lips and pressed it there. "Thank the lord for you, my dear one. Though I am minded to hire a house instead of staying at Bruton Street. How will that look, if you please?"

"Well, we can hardly stay in Hanover Square. The place will be crowded out, what with Giles in residence as well as Violette's two children."

"No, and I don't wish to listen to my nephew's complaints either."

"Giles is betrothed to Phoebe now, remember," she soothed. "I should imagine he will spend little time at home."

"But Mama is right, you know. There is bound to be a deal of talk with Candia staying at Harriet's for her come-out instead of the family home."

Lady Dalesford was bringing Candia out along with her own daughter, and Ottilia knew she had confidently expected a free hand without the interference of her elder brother and his scandalous marriage to his erstwhile mistress a bare year after his first wife was horribly murdered. Gossip was inevitable and Ottilia made no attempt to gloss the matter over.

"Just so. And therefore I think it will be of help to her, and to Candia, to have us there to smooth the waters."

Her spouse gave one of his wry laughs. "You'll smooth the waters, Tillie. I am more like to muddy them further."

She was about to answer in kind, when a warning shout from the box and an abrupt lurch changed the pace of the coach, throwing the words out of her head. Francis let out an expletive and Ottilia's attention snapped in.

"What's to do?"

He was leaning to look out of the window. "Ruts in the road belike."

But the carriage slowed and drew to a standstill. Ottilia heard muffled talk from above. Coachman Williams and the groom Ryde on the box? Then came the sound of boots hitting the ground.

Francis let down the window just as Hemp Roy's dark features appeared outside it, coming from behind where he had been travelling in the rear seat.

"What is amiss, Hemp?"

Ottilia's steward poked his head into the aperture.

"There's a woman standing in the middle of the road, milord."

"Alone?"

"That is what Ryde seeks to find out, milord. It may be a trap."

"Make way, Hemp. I'm getting out."

The steward drew back but lifted his hand. "No need, milord. I am armed. I will go."

With a riffle at her breast, Ottilia saw he was holding a serviceable pistol. He disappeared towards the front before Francis could protest.

"Why a trap, Fan?"

"Footpads." Her spouse was making himself master of his own pistol, tucked in the holster on his side next to the window. "A common trick. The woman may be a decoy to get everyone away from the coach." He cocked the gun and opened the door.

"Then had you not best remain here, Fan?"

"Don't fret. I'm getting out, that's all. You stay put, Tillie."

He exited the coach, leaping down without bothering with the steps. Ottilia watched him glance this way and that, checking into the trees. The area was heavily wooded, a perfect place for concealment if highwaymen were looking to waylay travellers. She would have thought they were too close to the capital to be a target. Shifting onto Francis's side, she called out, "Where are we?"

He was looking towards the road ahead, but he glanced back. "Well past Hounslow, I think."

"Can you see the woman?"

"I can see a figure. Looks female. Standing stock-still."

"Ryde and Hemp?"

"Ryde's with her. Hemp's keeping watch between. Good man. He's checking both sides of the road."

Curiosity got the better of Ottilia and she pushed to the edge of the seat, making to lean out. Her spouse cursed.

"Ottilia, stay in! For pity's sake, will you for once do as you're told?"

She held onto the door jamb but did not move. "I've no intention of getting out — yet. It doesn't seem to be a trap."

"They may ride out on us at any moment. Get back inside!"

Perceiving he was in earnest, she made to move back into her place, but his attention shifted away as footsteps sounded.

"Ryde's coming back."

"And Hemp?"

"Seems to be staying on watch."

A flitter of anxiety for her steward went through Ottilia. He was eminently capable, but her relationship with Hemp bordered on friendship.

The groom's dour tones took her attention. "No use, my lord. I can't get her to move."

"It's not a trap then, you think?"

"A queer one if it is. She's covered in blood."

"What?"

Ottilia jumped, her eyes flying to Ryde's face as he gave a brisk nod.

"All over. Her face too. She won't talk. Wouldn't answer me. Just standing there, staring."

Ottilia took a frowning glance from Francis and made up her mind. "Let down the steps for me, Ryde."

As usual, the groom looked to his master for guidance. Francis came to the door.

"Must you, Tillie? I know you're intrigued, but it's not safe."

"Nothing has happened yet, Fan. And the woman is clearly in trouble."

She could see the uncertainty in his face, but at length he stepped back and nodded to the groom, who unfolded the steps. Francis helped her down, keeping his pistol aloft and ready.

"I'll come with you. Ryde, you guard the coach. Ottilia, wait for me!"

She had started forward but she paused at this, her eyes on the strange figure. The woman was perfectly still, her arms at her sides, positioned in the road so that no coach could pass without encroaching on the bushes either side. She must have intended it. Which meant she was indeed either a decoy or in distress. Ryde's report of the blood suggested the latter.

The horses were shifting, steam rising from flanks glossy with sweat, nostrils snorting mist.

"Can't keep 'em standing too long, me lord."

Francis, just ahead of Ottilia, glanced up at the coachman's call. "We'll be off again as soon as we can get this female off the road."

"*If* we can." But Ottilia's mind was buzzing as she passed the horses and paused at Hemp's side where he stood, eyes everywhere, pistol at the ready. She kept her gaze on the motionless figure ahead. "She has not moved?"

"Not a muscle, milady," Hemp replied.

"What in hell's name ails the wench?" muttered Francis.

"Let us find out, Fan."

Ottilia approached with caution, allowing her spouse to remain a step or two ahead. She could see the splashed red colouring the woman's gown, which looked to be fashioned of a serviceable woollen material, plain in style. Not a female of the first stare then? But no country wench either from the cut of the garment. She was hatless, her countenance streaked with blood. It was in her hair too, Ottilia saw as she neared, in thick gobs bunching the hanging locks, fairish in colour, lank and untidy.

Drawing close, Ottilia was taken by the staring eyes. They were blank, drawn inward. She would swear they saw nothing. A stupor of shock? Unsurprising, considering her condition. She looked to be young. Hard to tell under the harsh contrast of red against her pallid face.

Ottilia placed herself within the woman's eyeline and spoke with gentleness.

"What happened to you, my dear? Can we help you?"

No response. Ottilia waited a little and then tried again.

"Can you hear me? You are not alone. We are here to help you."

Still nothing. Her spouse's dry voice came.

"Dead to the world."

A flicker in the eyes. The woman's head shifted a bare inch in the direction of his voice.

Ottilia's hope quickened as the words replayed in her head. With deliberation she repeated the one she guessed had penetrated.

"Dead? Is that it? Who is dead?"

The woman flinched. Her arm rose and a finger pointed into the woods as her head turned towards it.

"Hell and the devil confound it! Here we go again."

Chapter Two

Lord Francis Fanshawe took instant command, turning towards the coach and calling out, "Ryde, with me! Bring the blunderbuss. Hemp, take care of the women." He uncocked his pistol and dropped his tone as he turned to his wife. "Get the wench into the coach, Tillie."

His wife's hand caught his arm. "If you find a body, I need to see it, Fan."

"If we find a body, we've likely got a murderess on our hands, God help us. It needed only this!"

She did not release him. "Fan, don't go off at half-cock, I pray you. You know as well as I there may be any number of explanations. I must see the scene."

Frustrated by the complication, not to mention the delay, Francis yet hesitated. There was no denying his wife's ability to read the signs better than he ever could.

"Yes, very well. *If* we find anything. *If* she isn't off her head."

"For shame, Fan. You have only to look at her. There has been some dreadful happening and she is in shock."

"Yes, and bloody to the hilt." A thought struck him and he turned back to the woman. Her arm had dropped again and she had resumed her motionless staring state. "Has she a weapon?"

Ottilia was already peering into the woman's other hand. "Not that I can see." She straightened, thrusting at him. "Go, Francis! I will attend to her."

He gave a curt nod and left her, crossing back to the coach where Ryde awaited him.

"Keep that pistol at the ready," he told the steward as he passed him.

"I will guard her well, milord, do not fear."

He would too. Hemp Roy's devotion to Ottilia had grown noticeable to all. Francis fought down the familiar twinge he knew was unnecessary and ridiculous. Tillie was his and his alone. Her partiality for Hemp niggled nevertheless. The sweating horses impinged. He called up to his coachman, "Blanket them, Williams. We may be a while yet. Hemp can assist you. I can't spare Ryde. Let's go, man!" This to his groom, patiently waiting by the roadside, blunderbuss at the ready.

Francis took a path into the woods, following the direction in which the woman had pointed, pistol in hand.

"Though if there is someone dead, we won't need weapons."

"We might, if it's highwaymen as did for him, my lord."

"We don't know it's a man, if any." Despite the bloodied female, he was sceptical of finding anything. "The body could be anywhere, if there is one."

"There's one right enough," came in a dry tone from his groom. "Bloodstains."

Francis halted, looking where Ryde was pointing his weapon at the ground. Sure enough, a smear of red was visible along the ground in a sweep of dead leaves and twigs.

"Could it have come from the woman?"

Ryde shook a grizzled head. "Flattened grass." His gaze rose, lighting further into the woods. "Felled here, belike. Might have crawled off. Looks like he left a trail."

"Staggered off more like," offered Francis, noting the intermittent splashes of blood rising from the ground to bespatter bushes. "That tree is marked. Leaned against it for support?"

Ryde moved to examine the stained bark. "Could be. No doubt someone injured went this way."

Despite his deep discontent, Francis found interest growing. Damn Tillie for being right again.

"Come on. It can't be far."

He set off at a faster pace, following the tell-tale signs, his henchman on his heels. But the inconvenience rankled. Must there be a mystery now? As if matters were not complex enough. Typical though. These things seemed to fall in Ottilia's path as if she were a bloodhound. Ha, yes. A perfect analogy and he would take pleasure in telling her so. A laugh rumbled in his chest at the thought of his wife's probable reaction.

"There, my lord!"

His attention snapped in. Ryde was hurrying ahead, pushing through the undergrowth, thankfully sparse with Spring still weeks away.

Francis caught sight of the body, sprawled on the ground, face down between two trees. In passing, he noted blood on both barks, as if the man had held to them before he fell. A man it undoubtedly was, coated and booted, but without his hat, dark hair awry at the back of his head, the ribbon that must have tied it vanished.

Ryde was already kneeling, the blunderbuss set aside, his hands in a position preparatory to turning the body.

"Don't move him!"

Primed by his wife's string of earlier adventures, Francis knew the cadaver must be checked in situ first.

"Just trying to see if he's dead, my lord."

"Feel for his pulse or his heart. Don't turn him."

Ryde shifted to the hand flung out at an angle and drew off his glove. Francis watched him set his fingers about the man's wrist. Useless. The fellow was clearly gone.

"Anything?"

"Can't feel it, my lord. He's cool."

"Dead then. Where's the blood?"

He dropped to his haunches. There ought to be a pool of blood, but there was none immediately visible.

"Underneath, my lord? We'll not find the wound if we don't turn him."

"There's none on his back?"

"Not as I can see."

Francis ran his gloved hand down the coat and lifted it to look at the palm. Nothing.

"Where the deuce did all that blood come from then?" Recalling the smears on the trees, he glanced up to find them. "What of his hands? Check that one, Ryde."

The other arm was under the body, but the groom lifted the visible hand and dropped it again. "No blood."

Puzzlement wreathed Francis's brain. A trail of blood, but no traces on the body? The devil. He needed Tillie for this.

"We'll have to turn him."

Between them, he and Ryde heaved the dead weight onto its side. The groom's brows snapped together.

"He's blooded on this side right enough. She's knifed him to pieces."

Francis leaned over to look. The man's coat was open, his shirt criss-crossed with rips and bloodied through.

"What a mess!"

No neck-cloth? Nor yet a waistcoat? The man seemed as little fit for being out and about as had the woman. His glance swept to what he could see of the fellow's slack face. Of middle years? A growth of beard on a broad jaw, thick foamy lips and a heavy nose, features as unprepossessing in death as they must have been in life.

"His face ain't blooded, my lord. Don't make sense to me. She's got it all over."

It didn't make sense to Francis either. No choice. His guts crawled with hideous anticipation, all too familiar.

"Ryde, you stay here and keep an eye out. I'll fetch her ladyship."

It had been a piece of work to get the woman into the coach. Speaking gently, Ottilia had urged her to a walk, a hand at her back. She ambled quiescently enough, but the instant she found herself at the open coach door, she whimpered, fighting all attempts to get her inside.

In the end, Hemp had picked her up bodily and thrust her in, dumping her on the forward seat and holding her there with a heavy hand until Ottilia intervened.

"Let her be, Hemp!"

"She's thrashing, milady."

"I doubt she's alert enough to escape. Release her and come out of there."

He did as she bade him and Ottilia left him space to exit the coach before re-entering it herself.

The woman was pushing back against the squabs, breathing hard, her fingers gripping the edges of the seat either side. In the dim interior it was more difficult to read her face, but the eyes were enormous. Dilated with fear? Ottilia set herself to soothe.

"We mean you no harm. We mean to help you. You could not remain standing in the road, you know. It is cold."

As if in proof of this the woman began to shiver. Ottilia took up one of the fur rugs and set it about the woman's shoulders. She would come under severe criticism from her maids for the inevitable bloodstains, but that could not be helped.

The woman clutched it about her, huddling, and Ottilia caught a dark smear appearing on its surface. Were those stains on her fingers?

"Show me your hands."

She spoke with deliberate authority and the woman at once complied, putting them out palm up so that they fell into the light from the open door. Ottilia hissed in a breath as she took the thin wrists in a gentle grip. The woman whimpered again but she did not attempt to withdraw her hands, almost as if she wished the cuts to be discovered.

There were several on each palm, oozing too much red for Ottilia to be able to see how many or how deep. Defensive wounds? Or had she cut herself in a frenzy of attack. Impossible to guess until the blood was cleaned and Ottilia had nothing with which to perform the office. But bandage them she could.

She rummaged in her pocket for a handkerchief, calling out to Hemp, on guard outside the door. "Give me your pocket handkerchief, Hemp, if you have one."

She tied her own about the woman's hand, though it failed to cover the entirety of the cuts. Hemp was holding out a large square of linen. She took it with a word of thanks.

"Her hands are a mass of cuts."

"Her hands, milady? How so?"

"As yet I have no notion. But there is undoubtedly a knife somewhere."

She was tying up the other hand as Hemp looked in.

"Is she wounded anywhere else?"

"Not visibly." Ottilia lowered her tone. "The rest does not appear to be her own. There is no seepage."

Hemp's low mutter reached her. "Too like my Tamasine."

Ottilia's heart squeezed. He rarely mentioned his unfortunate half-sister. She had hoped he was over the grief. But he need not feel this a reminder.

"She has her wits, Hemp. She is only in shock. It is not the same."

He drew a breath and stiffened. "I will stand guard, milady." He turned to face the road again.

How he hated that wound to be touched, poor Hemp. The thought returned her to the matter at hand. It looked as if the damaged hands were the woman's only wound. She tried a throw.

"How did you hurt yourself?"

Released, the woman drew her hands into her chest, holding them together as if only now she was aware of their condition. She made no answer.

Ottilia tried again. "May I know your name?"

No response. The woman neither looked at her, nor spoke, seemingly reburied in the horrors of her mind. But she had shown her hands. She was able to attend.

"Come, I am not your enemy. You may call me Lady Fan. What may I call you?"

Was there a whisper on the woman's breath? If so, it was inaudible. Perhaps the direct questions were dismaying to her?

"My husband has gone to find the dead man."

A shudder? Now they were getting somewhere. Although it would not do to send the woman into another frenzy. Better to keep her calm, even if she could not — would not? — speak.

"We will go on to London presently, my dear, and we can take care of you there. I will find you another gown and we will get you cleaned up, fed and rested. That will be better, do you not think?"

The woman's eyes rose, meeting Ottilia's for a brief instant. Her lips parted, and a low sound emerged. It sounded like a name. Pierre, was it?

"What did you say, my dear?"

The woman made a slight negative gesture and no further sound came out. She gave a little sigh and sank back against the squabs, huddling into the fur covering and closing her eyes.

At least she was accepting of a modicum of safety now. Ottilia made no further attempt to engage her, instead looking her over. She wore no wedding ring, yet her figure looked to be mature. Was she girl or woman? The gown was augmented by boots, scuffed and stained, but of good quality, as was the under-petticoat showing beneath. Hard to place her social condition, but she could not be much above twenty. How came she to be in this parlous state?

The mystery teased at Ottilia's brain and a familiar rise of intrigue began to grip.

"Milord is returning."

The warning from Hemp shot guilt into her bosom. Francis was not going to be pleased with her. To be delving into yet another unexplained death at this juncture was bound to throw him into distemper. But her interest quickened to know what he might have discovered.

She leaned out as the footsteps she could now hear brought the beloved figure into sight. She resolved to keep her reflections to herself for the present. Yet she could not withhold the question as Hemp gave place and he came to the door of the coach.

"Did you find it?"

His face gave away his dissatisfaction. "Yes, and I need you to come and see, curse it. I can't make head nor tail of it. How the deuce this female got covered in blood is a complete enigma."

Chapter Three

Ottilia was glad to know the body had been replaced just as they found it.

"From the trail, we thought he crawled or staggered here," her spouse offered, "but only his chest is covered in blood, you'll find."

Ottilia was on her haunches by the upper body, leaning to see how his head lay. "Was his face visible?"

"Ryde? You were that side."

The groom was standing off a little. "Face down he was, my lady, like this. I couldn't see no wound."

Ottilia could see none either. Not in the head as she felt through the hair. No depressions, and her fingers came out clean. She had removed her gloves, though she was cloaked against the cold at her husband's insistence. She tugged the coat collar down and pressed along the neckline above the edge of the shirt, without result.

"He's only scantily dressed, you note," observed her spouse.

"Yes, so I see."

"We looked for blood at his hands, but found nothing."

She glanced up at the stains Francis had pointed out on the bark of the trees through which the dead man had fallen. The woman's hand prints? Turning back, she felt down the arm for breaks and lifted the man's flung out hand when she found none. It was a trifle cool, but not yet cold, the skin waxy, the fingers turning blue though the nails were pale.

"I doubt he's been dead more than an hour, if that." She turned the hand. "There is a smear in the palm, but he is not cut the way she is."

"Cut?" Her spouse dropped down to join her. "What are you talking about?"

She looked across. "The woman's hands are cut about. That is her own blood and I suspect she made those marks on the trees."

"You think so? She didn't escape him back there then?"

"She left him for dead, Fan, remember? She reacted when you said the word. And she pointed when I asked about a dead man."

"Of course." He blew out a breath. "I'd forgot that. She killed him here then."

"We don't know that she killed him. As yet, there is nothing to show how he died."

"We'll turn him and you'll see it fast enough."

The curt tone rankled. If Francis was jumping to the first conclusion, so would the authorities. Vital to find the truth before they saw the woman, if she could.

She pushed up from the ground. "Turn him for me, if you please."

Ryde came to her spouse's aid. Between them, they heaved the man onto his back. Ottilia at once saw what had dictated the notion Francis had in his head.

"Ah, the matter now becomes comprehensible."

"Ha! You are of my opinion then," said her spouse, rising, one eyebrow cocked.

She had to smile. "Sadly, no, Fan."

"What then?"

She gestured across the bloodied chest. "Her gown is stained all down the front. It is likely his blood. Either he clutched her to him or she fell upon him. But as he was face down, I can't think it is the latter."

"Why not?"

"Because she would have been underneath him. The effort to throw him off, even could she have managed it, would have changed his position."

"Could she not have wriggled out?"

"From under a dead weight?"

He grunted, plainly dissatisfied. "Then let us suppose she knifed him so badly that he fell forward."

"So she might have done, but the blood would have spattered across her. She was definitely held against him. What happened after that we have yet to fathom."

"Can you fathom it?"

She shrugged, her attention snagging on the face. "I do not yet know. We may need her testimony for what actually occurred. But we still don't know that this attack killed him."

Francis threw up his eyes. "When he's cut to pieces?"

Ottilia dropped down for a closer examination. The lips were pale, though the countenance had the purplish look from his blood pooling as he lay face down. She lifted an eyelid, exposing the glassy, flattened look of death. Shifting to the chest again, she opened the coat further.

"Help me tug this shirt out, Fan."

He dropped to join her, grasping the bloodied shirt and ripping it out of the man's breeches and up his chest. "Lord, but he's badly bruised!"

"No, that is the blood collecting after death." She touched the skin and it showed white under her finger. "See. It looks livid, but it is no bruise. It makes it harder to judge the cuts, though they look superficial to me." She used a portion of shirt to wipe at the red blood, exposing several slashes, but no deep wound that could have caused the man's death.

"He did not die of these cuts."

"Then how the deuce did he die?"

Ottilia sighed at the impatient note. "Some internal malady of the heart, I suspect. The chest looks a trifle uneven, but without a post mortem it is impossible to say. A collapsed lung, perhaps."

"Would that affect his heart?"

"Severely. The air escapes and the heart cannot pump properly. The woman, if she witnessed his death, may tell us more."

"Has she yet spoken?"

"There was a murmur. Of a name, I think. It sounded as Pierre, but I am by no means sure I caught it correctly. But she is able to understand, so we must hope she will be more forthcoming in due course."

"Not if she killed him, she won't be."

The sceptical note rankled, but Ottilia was growing chilled and she had seen enough. A thought occurred as she pushed up from the ground. "Did either of you think to look for a weapon?"

Ryde stepped in. "I scoured the area while his lordship was fetching you, my lady. Didn't find a thing. Ain't come to light under him neither."

"We'll let the justices worry about that," said Francis on a curt note. "Their men will likely conduct a thorough search."

Ottilia smiled at the groom. "Thank you, Ryde." She looked at her spouse. "I can do nothing more here, Fan."

"Then let's get you back to the coach."

Relief sounded in his voice. Ottilia was abruptly grieved for him, taking on this burden in addition to the rest. She moved around the body and went to him, lowering her voice.

"My poor darling, I'm so sorry. This is wholly unfair on you."

His look was wry. "It isn't your fault, Tillie."

"But you believe I attract these things, so perhaps it is."

He returned her smile. "I admit I was thinking how you are a very bloodhound, but I can't very well blame you for this wretched woman's appearance."

"Thank you, Fan. And Weymouth was entirely your doing, so I am happy to be exonerated. Bloodhound indeed!"

He laughed but became brisk as he took over control in the way he usually did once she had done her part. Much to her admiration and relief. She was so very lucky to have him at her back on these occasions.

"We'll have to leave one of the men here until the authorities arrive. Ryde?"

The groom was tidying the body, but he looked up at this. "Best leave Hemp, my lord. He's no hand with the horses and Williams'll need me."

Loath as Ottilia was to put her steward to such inconvenience, she could not argue with Ryde's dictum. But she entered a protest, nonetheless. "Is it necessary to leave a man, Fan?"

"Unless you want this corpse to disappear."

"He's not going anywhere."

"He might, if there's a murderer other than the woman about."

"Yes, but I don't think there is."

"I thought you said she didn't do it."

"The knife attack, yes, though I suspect that was more of a fight. But if he died from some internal injury, it was not inflicted here. Or even today. It may well be days old."

"What injury?"

"A broken rib perhaps, if his lung had indeed collapsed. A jagged edge might tear into the lung, especially during an altercation such as these cuts suggest. But this is mere speculation."

She shrugged her cloak back into place and moved to check the two trees. The stains were drying, growing dark, but a fingertip touch certified their origin.

Francis was discussing with his groom the advisability or otherwise of leaving Hemp in situ. Ottilia left them to it and moved on, spying out the bloodstained trail as she went. Francis joined her in a moment.

"Ryde is covering the body as best he can."

"You'll leave it unguarded?"

"As you say, it's going nowhere. We'll mark the spot well at the roadside. Ryde was a scout in our soldiering days. He'll show the way with arrowed twigs."

She could hear the groom's activities behind them and glanced back to see Ryde laying a leafy branch across the body. Her attention was drawn back by her spouse.

"What do you make of all these bloody marks, Tillie? We thought the dead man must have made them, but if the woman was still with him…"

Ottilia looked about as she resumed walking at his side. "It grows less as we go, do you not think?" She pointed to the smattering of red spots here and there. "Her hands may have bled a great deal to begin with. She might have clenched them or clutched her garments, which would stem the flow a little."

"Ryde noticed the undergrowth was flattened along here. He thought she must have felled him at that point." He started forward, holding a stray branch out of her way. "Yes, here. Look, Tillie."

She paused, regarding the space where a number of broken twigs and bent gorse indicated some heavy object had rested there. Francis showed her the folded brushwood.

"To my mind, it points towards the spot where the body is lying, not towards the road."

"I agree with you, but it does not necessarily mean the man fell here."

"You think she did?"

The sceptical note was not lost on Ottilia. "It is possible. From her condition we may take it she was severely disorientated. She could certainly have fallen. She might have tracked back and forth, unknowing what she did. She may even have gone back or begun to move in that direction. What would you? There had clearly been a fight. The man was dead or down at least as far as she knew. She was injured. It is quite a feat in the circumstances to have found the road and waited there for rescue."

She moved on as she spoke, feeling the cold more severely, her mind roving questions.

"How the deuce did they get here, either of them? There is no sign of a conveyance, nor horses."

She threw her husband a mischievous look. "Are you reading my mind, Fan? That is just what I was wondering."

"Ha! I've got your measure, my woman of wonder. I know how you think."

She gave an irrepressible giggle. "Fiend."

He slid an arm about her as they walked, lending support as he always did. "Let's get you into the coach. If we were not so close to the capital I would have Williams stop at the next convenient inn to get you warmed up."

"No, we must make all speed, Fan. You will have to go directly to Bow Street."

"So I may, but there is scant chance their man will be able to return here before dark. I suspect they may leave it until the morrow."

"By which time the body will be crawling with maggots, making the doctor's task of reading its messages well-nigh impossible."

"It doesn't matter. They will have your testimony as well as mine and Ryde's."

"True. And the internal organs should still reveal why he died as he did." They were within sight of the coach and Ottilia's mind was shifting to the woman inside. "What is more to the point is how we can prevent the justices from taking that poor woman into custody."

"If this is not typical of you, Ottilia. Who else would arrive in my house trailing a creature covered in blood?"

Sybilla's tart complaint belied her actions as she sent her servants flying and demanded the instant attendance of her maid.

"Tell her to prepare a bath at once. Take the woman away, Teresa, and get her cleaned up." This to her startled companion, who hastened to relieve Ottilia of her burden.

The girl was leaning heavily against her and she was glad of the help. It had been difficult enough coaxing her up the one pair of stairs to the vestibule hall outside her mother-in-law's private parlour. But she was loath to leave the victim to others.

"I will come with you, Teresa, and —"

"Oh, no, you will not. You'll remain here and give me a round tale."

"Presently, ma'am. I must first —"

"Now, Ottilia. It is bad enough with Francis shooting off to Bow Street with scarcely a word vouchsafed to me. There can be no occasion for you to oversee all. Leave it to Teresa and my woman."

Recognising her mother-in-law's implacable tone, Ottilia gave in to the inevitable, releasing her hold on the woman who still had not spoken.

"Go with Miss Mellis, my dear, and I will come to see you when you are safe tucked up in bed." To the companion, she added, low-toned, "Pray be careful with her hands, Teresa. They are severely cut about."

The willowy dame, her withered cheeks showing pallid in the blaze of candlelight, glanced once at the bandaged hands and gave Ottilia one of her nervous looks.

"Cut about? Oh, dear. But…"

Ottilia saw how she shuddered a trifle at the bloodied clothes and hastened to deflect the coming question. "That is not her blood, Teresa. We don't think she is otherwise wounded than the hands. But pray tell me if you find any other source of bleeding."

Miss Mellis drew a visible breath and took a rather gingerly grasp upon her charge. "Come with me, if you please, ma'am."

"Be firm. She will go with you, but she won't speak."

The companion nodded and guided the girl towards the stairs leading to the upper floors. Ottilia watched her go, noting how she did as she was bid without argument. Either she had abrogated all responsibility to others, or she was still in something of a stupor.

"Ottilia!"

Sybilla's commanding voice called back her attention. With a sigh, she turned for the parlour and discovered a hovering maid.

"Joanie, there you are. Will you take my cloak, if you please?"

Her maid, along with Francis's valet and the bulk of their luggage, had been sent on ahead.

"I've unpacked everything, my lady," said Joanie, taking the cloak.

"Thank you, that is excellent. Pray find one of my nightgowns and a shawl and take both to Miss Mellis for our guest, if you please. Oh, and you had best lend her any lotions and toiletries she may need. There is Basilicum powder in my dressing-case which may be used for the cuts."

The maid went off and Ottilia hastened to follow Sybilla into the parlour where a cheerful fire added to the blazing light from a number of wall-sconces and candelabra placed on the mantel, the marquetry secretaire and the available surface of almost every table. Blinking a trifle, Ottilia remembered her mother-in-law's preferences.

"You must spend a fortune on candles, Sybilla."

"Never mind my extravagance, my girl. Sit, sit. Gipping will send Alice in with coffee presently, so you may just as well stop finding excuses to prevaricate."

Ottilia laughed as she took a seat by the fire, reaching to warm her hands. "I am not, I promise you." Though she could have done with half an hour's respite before being obliged to explain matters. But it was scarcely politic to say so. "I shall be glad of that coffee, however."

"Yes, very well, but get on, do. How came you to drag that female along with you?"

"It was not done by design, I assure you. But we could scarcely leave her standing in the middle of the road. Besides, there was a body to be accounted for."

Sybilla threw up her hands, delicate brows lifting over her sharp black eyes. "As if I had not guessed it! What body? Where? Is that why Francis has gone off to Bow Street? Did that woman do the deed?"

Ottilia put up a finger. "It is what the magistrates will think, but no, not to my mind. Though I believe it is his blood upon her person in the main. As to where we found the body, it was at some distance into the bushes."

As she gave her mother-in-law a fluent account of the adventure, a part of her mind was occupied with the problem of establishing the girl's identity. A matter that she rightly guessed would be at the forefront of Sybilla's objections.

"And how long, if I may ask, do you propose to house this female under my roof?"

Ottilia gathered her forces. "Not long, I hope. Once we know who she is, we can find out her direction and —"

"Foist her off onto her people while you forget all about it and bend your mind to our affairs?" Sybilla made a rude noise. "Do you take me for a nincompoop?"

A laugh escaped Ottilia. "You know I don't, Sybilla. I won't pretend to be disinterested. Of course I am intrigued. But no more than you do I wish to be saddled with responsibility for the girl, if there is someone who may take charge of her. To be truthful, my prime objective is to keep her out of the hands of Bow Street. You will admit she is scarcely in a condition to be confined, as she surely would be if we allow them to take her away from here."

"We?"

Ottilia smiled. "Come, Sybilla, you are not so hard-hearted. The poor girl is in a stupor of shock."

"That much I had deduced." An abrupt frown creased Sybilla's brow. "What do you make of her?"

"In what respect? If you mean her condition in life, her clothing is good, but not fashionable. I have not heard her voice beyond a murmur, so I can't tell her station from that."

"But you think she is genteel?"

31

"I am not sure. She is no debutante. I would guess her to be in the early twenties but she is not married. She is assured enough to give a good account of herself for she evidently fought off an attack. But to have been in the power of this man in the first place suggests she may have no real protection by way of guardians."

Sybilla pursed her lips, looking as if she considered the question. "The middling sort, then. You will have a task to find her people if she has no place in the Ton."

"Just so."

The maid Alice entered the room at this moment, burdened with a loaded tray which she set down upon a side table. Ottilia saw the coffee pot with a rise of anticipation and a good deal of relief. She needed fortifying. Her mother-in-law had not yet begun upon her own stresses and Ottilia did not dare hope to be spared. Sybilla was nothing if not tenacious. Nor was she mistaken. Sybilla began upon the subject when Ottilia had taken but a first sip.

"You are come in a good hour, let me tell you. Despite this setback. Not," she added on an acid note, "that I dare expect your attention will settle upon my no doubt tedious affairs."

Ottilia suppressed an inward sigh. "Tell me all, ma'am. Is it as bad as you feared?"

"Worse. That wretched woman is a hit."

"Violette? Well, she is a beauty."

"Yes, curse the wench. And with that accent, a positive magnet for the male element. You may imagine how Randal growls and mutters to see her so courted. If he has a glance to spare for his own daughter, you may call me a Dutchwoman."

Despite her preoccupation, Ottilia was diverted by the evidence of a brewing maelstrom. "She must be making enemies among the established belles then."

Sybilla snorted. "You would think so, but no. Half the dratted creatures must needs declare Violette's story to be romantic. *Romantic!* It appears to have escaped the public memory that she was my son's mistress for years before he made her respectable."

Which could only be to the good, if scandal were to be avoided. But Ottilia did not feel it incumbent upon her to suggest as much to her mother-in-law.

"And what of Candia? Does she take?"

"Of course she takes. She's an heiress of rank. But she's a modest child and does not rate herself half as high as she might."

"Does she feel it that her stepmother overshadows her?"

Sybilla let out a breath that sounded defeated. "She ought to, silly girl, but Harriet says she does not even feel her nose to be put out of joint. She insists, if you please, that she could never have hoped to outshine her own mother, so it is no different."

Ottilia digested this in silence. She had never met the first marchioness, whose murder had been the occasion of her entry into the family, but Emily had been, by all accounts, the sort of woman who drew men like a honeypot. Scandalous her behaviour might have been but she had been universally popular, queening it in her social circle.

"Candia is not the sort of girl to compete, do you not think? And what of her cousin Elizabeth in all this? It is her debut too."

"Oh, she is not forgotten, be sure. A pretty girl, and she has her father's brain. She will do very well."

The dismissive tone was not lost on Ottilia. It was plain her mother-in-law had less interest in her other granddaughter. She made a mental note to befriend the girl and discover how she was really faring if her mother's attention was focused upon the niece instead. Harriet had taken the girl to her heart upon Emily's death and Candia spent more time with her cousins than her own family, augmented now with a half-sister and half-brother.

"Dalesford ought to marry the girl to a fellow of his choosing," pursued Sybilla, "though I doubt he will. He dotes on the child and will no doubt allow her too much leeway in the matter. Not, I may say, that arranged marriages have proven successful in this family."

Ottilia made haste to soothe, fearing a tirade upon her elder son's activities. "Perhaps not in Randal's case, but Giles is well suited with Phoebe now."

"Now, yes."

The emphasis was just, the Polbrook heir having been all too deeply involved with the affair of the tainted Tamasine a year ago. But Ottilia had no chance to direct the conversation into a channel less provocative of Sybilla's uncertain temper.

"However, it is not only the men of the family who must needs make idiots of themselves over unsuitable women." Sybilla pointed. "And I don't mean you, so you need not take a pet."

Ottilia laughed. "I was not going to, ma'am. You very kindly approved of me at the outset."

"For my sins. I ought to have known what a deal of trouble I was admitting into our circle with you and that crusading spirit of yours."

Ottilia ignored this pettish remark, knowing full well how she was truly valued by her mother-in-law. "Are you talking of Candia? Or is it Elizabeth who has fallen for the wrong man?"

"I don't say Candia has fallen for the wretched creature, but she is too tender-hearted to hint him away and foolish enough to believe his absurdly romanticised tale of his escape from Paris."

"Ah, an *émigré* then?"

"So the fellow claims. If you ask me, he is nothing but an adventurer with an eye to Candia's fortune."

"Is he titled?"

"Nothing to signify. Calls himself a *chevalier*."

"Which proves nothing at all."

"Exactly so. But the wretch is disastrously good-looking and has a way with him. Even my fool of a daughter was taken in at first."

Until Sybilla pointed out his flaws, no doubt. "What is the fellow's name, ma'am?"

"Pierre. Pierre de Percheval."

Chapter Four

Pleading the excuse of a need to retire, especially after having drunk two cups of coffee, Ottilia managed to escape from her mother-in-law. Joanie conducted her to the chamber reserved for Francis and herself, where she relieved her immediate needs and took the opportunity to change.

"I will dress now, Joanie, if you please."

The maid had brought hot water for her to wash and was ready with a towel by the basin. "Was you meaning to go to that young miss, my lady?"

"Before dinner, yes. Is she yet in bed, do you know?"

"She were in the bath last I heard, my lady, but I can check if you wish."

Ottilia took the towel and began drying her face and neck. "In a moment. Help me to dress first."

It was plain from the maid's expression she was eager for any excuse to peep at the unusual visitor. Ottilia eyed her with amusement. "I dare say you've heard what happened? From Williams?"

Joanie became confiding. "Well, it were Hemp as told Tyler, my lady, and he told me, being as we was all at Weymouth. Only Mr Gipping were listening and I'm that sorry, my lady, but it's known all over now."

Ottilia smiled. "It makes no matter. I expected no less. But I hope I may rely on you not to pass along anything you may overhear between his lordship and myself, Joanie."

"I wouldn't say nothing, my lady. Nor Tyler wouldn't neither. Only I had ought to tell you…"

The maid hesitated and Ottilia threw her an encouraging look. "Tell me what, Joanie?"

"Well, I couldn't help but hear, my lady, as me and Tyler were helping Alice carry up the hot jugs for the bath, for 'tis all of six flights up those back stairs, and we had to go in to empty the jugs. I'd not have you think as I were listening at the door."

Ottilia hid her amusement. As if all domestic ears in the house were not flapping. "And what was it you heard?"

Joanie became confiding. "Well, it were that Miss Venner, my lady. She said as she don't need no help in looking after the lady and she tried to send Miss Mellis off, only Miss Mellis wouldn't go for as her ladyship herself said as she were to do the thing. A lot of argy-bargy there were, my lady, and that's a fact."

"Dear me. Well, I will discover how things lie when I go up."

Ottilia said no more, although her heart sank at the prospect of dealing with the dowager's dour woman. Venner was a strange woman at best, and Ottilia's earlier dealings with her had shown how difficult she could be.

It was imperative to speak to the girl alone. Her mind had been busy since the mention of this *émigré* who was courting Lady Candia Fanshawe. If she had heard aright, the name was the same as that said by her protégée. Coincidence? It might well be. But she could not ignore the possibility the girl's Pierre and Candia's *émigré* were one and the same. A tiny piece of the puzzle?

She was just putting the finishing touches to her evening toilette when her spouse entered the room. "Ah, you are back at last, Fan. How did you fare?"

He grimaced, casting a glance at Joanie, who was putting up Ottilia's discarded clothing.

She took the hint. "That will do for now, Joanie. You may finish that later."

"Yes, my lady."

The girl dropped a curtsey and headed for the door, but Francis detained her.

"Send Diplock up to me. And tell him to bring hot water."

The maid curtsied again and left. Ottilia watched her husband strip off his coat.

"Was it abominable, my poor Fan?"

He threw the garment on the bed and began untying his neck-cloth. "I saw Ingham."

"That was fortunate." Sir Thomas Ingham had been the magistrate who dealt with the unlawful death of Emily, Lady Polbrook, a little over two years before. "Was he as understanding this time?"

Francis shrugged, plainly on edge. "He took the particulars. He means to send a horse patrol in the morning. Ryde agreed to lead them to the place."

Ottilia eyed him with a degree of dismay. "Then if it is not the inconvenience of going to Bow Street that has put you all on end, what is it, my dearest?"

"Mama, of course." He flung the neck-cloth from him and threw himself down on the bed with a discontented sigh. "She caught me as I came in so I could not escape."

"She harangued you too?" Ottilia went to sit beside him, laying a hand on his. "I am quite in disgrace, you must know."

"Yes, and she blames me for allowing you to bring that female to the house."

Ottilia curled her fingers about his. "Pay no heed, Fan. She does not mean it, you know. Indeed, she could not quite conceal an interest in the mystery, though she rang a fine peal over me."

He leaned his head against hers for a moment. "I'm tired, Tillie. I've no patience with my mother's megrims."

"And hungry, my poor darling. We will be dining directly and I will engage to draw Sybilla's fire."

He rubbed her back in an affectionate way and got up. "I don't desire you to take the brunt of it, my dear one. Let me get rid of all my dirt and Diplock can fetch me a restorative."

"I will leave you to it, Fan," said Ottilia, rising also. "Sybilla would not allow me to attend to the girl and I must seize the chance to see her. Whether she will yet speak is a question, but I must try."

"Do what you will."

The weary note grieved Ottilia, but as a knock at the door produced the valet, she made no comment upon it.

The stranger was housed in a room near the top of Sybilla's neat house in Bruton Street, a Polbrook property given over to her use during her lifetime. It was adequate for her needs, but was likely a trifle overcrowded already with the Fanshawes and their retinue, never mind such a troublesome addition. Ottilia could appreciate her mother-in-law's objections, but there was no being rid of the woman until she found those who might be trusted to take her in charge.

Once she had climbed to the third floor Ottilia found the right door without difficulty for Miss Mellis was just emerging. The companion greeted her with obvious relief. "Lady Francis! Thank goodness you are come." She lowered her voice as she thrust into the hall, plainly flustered. "I have done my best, ma'am, but there is no gainsaying Venner. She has taken one of her fancies to the woman, I fear, and you know what she is."

Ottilia matched her tone. "None better. But tell me of the woman. Did you find any other wound than the cuts on her hands?"

"Those cuts! So dreadful. I cannot conceive how she did that to herself."

Ottilia concealed her impatience. "I believe she was involved in a fight. But was there any other injury?"

"None that I could see. At least no other open wound." The companion's thin features tightened. "Bruises there are, however."

"Where is she bruised?" Ottilia's suspicions were aroused by the faint colour appearing in the older woman's cheek, visible by the light from the wall sconces where candles burned. "Come, Teresa, don't be missish."

The woman's lips pursed. "If you must have it, there are marks upon her lower parts."

"Her thighs?"

"Yes." A puzzled look entered the companion's eyes. "But there are others too."

"Other bruises?"

"Scars. Old wounds, I think. Upon her back and also —" said with a prim mien — "upon her buttocks."

Startled, Ottilia stared without speaking for a moment. What did this betoken? Past cruelty? Beatings? Had there been suffering other than this recent assault? "For assault it was," she said aloud.

Teresa's embarrassed flush, still present, now deepened. "From this time, you mean? Why should you suppose she did not consent to … to…?"

The questions relating to the girl's past faded. "If she is bruised, she has been forced. Small wonder she fought the brute." Unaccustomed fury leapt in Ottilia's breast and for an ignoble moment she was glad the woman's attacker was dead. He had his just deserts. Except that it would not save the girl from a charge of murder.

"You look quite fierce, Lady Francis."

The timid note brought Ottilia back to herself with a bang. She struggled for normality. "To be truthful with you, I feel fierce. But we are getting ahead of ourselves. I must induce her to speak."

Miss Mellis looked pained. "I could get nothing out of her. And I can't think Venner will do any better."

"But she is quiescent? She made no resistance?"

"None at all. She is perfectly malleable, but she will not utter a word."

Ottilia accepted this, but her anxiety to see the woman for herself became too strong for further delay. "Do you go down, Teresa. Pray keep her ladyship from worrying, if you can."

"She is sorely beset, ma'am. And this will not help."

A certain severity in the companion's tone was irritating, but Ottilia refused to be drawn. Nodding dismissal, she opened the door and entered a scene of some disorder and little light. A candelabrum on the mantel drew her eye first to the tin hip bath still standing before a fire in the grate. Ottilia made a mental note to request Hemp to supervise its removal, which would alleviate the dowager's overburdened servants. An untidy pile of the damning blood-stained clothing lay on the floor nearby. Best have Hemp dispose of that too.

Turning her eyes to the cot bed, she found the shadowed form, lit only by a single candle on the bedside cabinet, sitting up against banked pillows, with Venner seated beside her and feeding her with a spoon from the contents of a bowl on a tray laid upon her knees. Or she had been so doing, but the spoon was poised in the air and Venner's gaze was fixed upon Ottilia in a look she recognised. Venner was a sour woman, apt to curl her lip and speak harshly.

Ottilia was not to be intimidated. She was no longer a mere companion like poor Teresa Mellis, but wife to the younger brother of the marquis and firmly entrenched in the family near two years. Sybilla's woman had no power to override her wishes. A high hand at the outset would likely serve her better than a soft approach.

"Excellently done, Venner, thank you. How is she?"

Ottilia turned her gaze upon the invalid as she spoke. There was no direct light upon her, for candles in only one of the wall sconces had been lit and she was beyond the flare of the candelabrum on the mantel. Ottilia could see well enough to note that the stranger sat with closed eyes, her hands, bandaged more efficiently, lying curled on the coverlet either side. She was dressed in the borrowed nightgown, a woollen shawl wrapped about her shoulders.

"She'll do better left alone," said Venner. "I can do all that is needful." With which, she resumed her task, ignoring Ottilia as she presented a spoonful to the woman's mouth, adopting a tone suitable to a babe. "Open your mouth, lovey."

The woman obeyed. Mechanically? She swallowed the broth but her eyes remained closed, her figure as motionless otherwise as it had been when she stood in the road. Was there any chance of getting through to her as yet?

Ottilia's gaze returned to Venner. The insolent manner was typical. Never high in the instep, Ottilia nevertheless was conscious of annoyance at the lack of any formal appellation to acknowledge her status. She would get no "my lady" from the dowager's woman. But Ottilia was made of sterner stuff than she supposed.

"Will you have the goodness to answer my question, if you please? How is she?"

Venner threw her a glance of contempt. "How should she be after what has passed?"

"You don't know what has passed, Venner, any more than I. Miss Mellis told me she has not spoken."

"I've eyes in my head, haven't I? Battered as she is, I can venture a guess as well as any. I've seen such before. There are those partial to brutish ways, as I know, but not this one."

Ottilia could not pretend to misunderstand her. For years before they quarrelled, Venner had been maid to the dead marchioness, an exacting and difficult role which had left her bitter and, as Ottilia believed, half mad with grief. She took the implication head on.

"Miss Mellis told me. Do you suppose the assault was carried through?"

A whimper from the woman told Ottilia she was attending, despite her quiescent attitude. A hopeful sign. She ignored a reproachful glare from the maid, raising her voice.

"I am glad to see you are able to eat, my dear. Presently we will have the room tidied and leave you to sleep."

No response came beyond a flicker at the eyes, which remained closed. Was it deliberate? What had she to conceal that she determined on keeping silent? But she had reacted to the implication of violation. Ottilia chose to be bold.

"Did that man succeed with you? Did he have his way?"

A shudder shook her frame and Venner's low-voiced protest smote Ottilia's ears.

"Lady Francis, how can you be so cruel?"

"Be quiet, Venner," Ottilia hissed back. "When I wish for your intervention, you will know it." A vicious glare crossed the woman's face, but Ottilia paid no heed. She had a task to perform. "Give place, if you please. She has finished almost all the broth. Ring the bell. I want my fellow Hemp Roy sent up here at once."

The dismissive tone of command had an effect. With jerky motions, and resentment in her eyes, Venner obeyed, removing the tray. Ottilia took her vacated place and set her hand on the invalid's arm.

"Who is Pierre?"

The woman's eyes flared open and Ottilia read dismay there, together with a trifle of apprehension. She pressed the arm in a reassuring gesture.

"Come, my dear, how will it profit you to remain silent? You must by now have realised I mean you no harm." The woman's hands clenched and she hissed in a breath. Ottilia gentled her tone. "Do those cuts pain you? Try to relax."

Instead, the woman brought the bandaged hands to her chest as she had done before in the coach and held them, curled as they were, against her breast. Ottilia noted their trembling, echoed in the parted lips.

"There! See what you've done!"

Infuriated, Ottilia turned on Venner, who had come up to the bed again, leaning into the woman and reaching a protective hand as if she would stroke the curling and drying hair, washed of its cloying gobs of blood.

"Leave her to me. Stand back."

The sharp tone had its effect. Though she cast a venomous look at Ottilia, the maid retired from the bedside. Ottilia caught the woman's eyes going from her to the maid and back again. She took her by the wrists, careful to avoid the injured hands, and set them down in the woman's lap.

"Do not be alarmed. It is well you have fallen in my way, you know, for I have some influence with Bow Street. I will not let them take you away." She paused, but no word came. The woman's eyes betrayed her sudden interest, wary though they were. Ottilia summoned a smile, watching her closely.

"I examined the body. I know you did not kill that man." A quick intake of breath rewarded her. "I also know he is not the Pierre you spoke of." Was there panic in the woman's eyes? "You did say Pierre? Or was I mistaken?"

Her mouth moved, as if she would form words, but nothing came out. Ottilia changed tack. "Will you not tell me your name?" A quick shake of the head. "You need not trust me with all, but it would help to be able to address you somehow." She shrank a little, her breathing erratic. But was there a softening in her look? "I am Lady Fan. I told you before but I dare say you might not remember it. What may I call you?" Still she hesitated. Ottilia smiled at her. "Shall I make up a name for you? A pretty one would suit. Let me see now…" She pretended to think.

"Meg."

It jerked out and the eyes showed immediate consternation.

"Meg? Well, that is pretty indeed. Thank you, Meg. I am happy to make your acquaintance."

For the first time in their dealings, a faint smile lightened Meg's features. Ottilia was cheered to note she could appreciate the incongruity in the circumstances. The shock was receding then. And evidence of a sense of humour was a boon.

A knock at the door produced one of the dowager's maids, as yet unknown to Ottilia. She rose from the bed.

"I will leave you now, Meg. A good night's sleep will restore you, I hope. Don't fear for the future for I mean to help you."

A whisper reached her. "Thank you."

Ottilia smiled and nodded, turning towards Venner who was standing by the wall in an attitude of offended dignity. Ottilia gave her one glance and turned her attention to the girl who had entered.

"Pray request my steward Hemp to attend me outside this room. And bring up a glass of warm milk for the lady. At once, if you please." The girl curtsied and retired, and Ottilia turned to Venner. "Have the goodness to see that Meg drinks the milk. My steward will handle the room and arrange for a truckle bed to be set up in here. I take it you mean to remain for the night to watch over Meg?"

Venner's chin came up. "It is as my lady Polbrook requested. I know my duty."

Ottilia could cheerfully have slapped her. "Meg needs more than duty, Venner."

A sneer crossed the maid's face. "You need not tell me my business. I know how to do. The poor lamb will not suffer from my ministrations."

The implication rankled, but Ottilia had no intention of taking it up. She merely nodded and headed for the door. The alien voice stopped her as she reached it.

"Lady Fan?"

Ottilia swung about, staring at Meg. She had spoken clearly and aloud, in quite a normal tone. Concealing her surprise, Ottilia moved back to the bed, meeting the woman's eyes. They were not bold, showing uncertainty.

"Yes, Meg?"

A small sigh escaped the girl. "I ... I am not ungrateful."

Ottilia softened, smiling. "I know. Rest now. In the morning, we will consider what is best to be done."

Meg's gaze became luminous and she sank into her pillows. "Yes ... thank you ... I live another day."

Then she closed her eyes, leaving Ottilia prey to astonishment and question.

Chapter Five

The veil of darkness failed to soothe. Failed to hold at bay the nightmare memories tapping at the edge of Meg's consciousness. She would have liked to ask for the candles to be left alight. But already she regretted being tripped into speech. Her rescuer was too kind. Too shrewd. Easier when she was left to the strange one. Venner? Yes, Venner. She was deft and quick, like Starkey when she took her in. She had a similar manner, harsh at one moment, gentle the next. The kindness had been grudging. A fool she had been to trust the other's softer manner, though she'd had no choice.

Choices ... what price choices now? Mere ruin was become the lesser evil now that she faced the rope. Lady Fan meant to keep her from it, if she read her aright. If she was true. If she was not another who pretended one thing and did worse. A fool to trust she was. She should not have broken her silence.

The night hours dragged as she drifted in and out of slumber. Wakefulness kept the images out. In sleep, she had no control. Faces ... blood ... a miasma of rancid breath ... running, running, through strange streets twisting into trees.

She woke panting, unknowing where she was, half convinced the whole was but a dream. A grey light produced shadows of the walls and sparse furnishings, alien, but bleak enough to mistake for her room at home. The illusion proved all too brief as memory slid back and yesterday loomed into sight with all its attendant horror.

Meg thrust it away. She would not look, dared not see. Easier to dwell in the limbo of forgetfulness, the mindless haze in which events had left her yesterday. To her dismay, she found it lifted, the protective layer gone, her mind all too clear.

She lay and stared at the dark ceiling above her head, scenes playing in her imagination. Some remnant of mist there was, for they failed to touch her, instead passing before her mind's eye. The figure of herself did not seem to belong to reality. And he, alive again, a miracle of thought that would not make him so in truth. She knew it, somewhere. Yet she could conjure him, set him in the scene, see him in motion. But feel him she could not.

Here the memory faltered, the performance failing, the actors freezing into statues, the picture going blank. Not that. No feeling. There she could not, must not go lest the screaming deep inside emerged, never to end.

On the thought her hands began to hurt. Meg stilled them, straightening the fingers. She did not want to think about the damage, nor how it came there.

"Awake are you, lovey?"

Meg started. She had not seen the figure looming over her. She blinked into the greyness and the face came into focus. The woman Venner.

She shifted away. "We'll have the shutters open, lovey, then I can see to your needs."

The figure moved to the window. A moment later daylight flooded the room, shattering the painful dark of memory and pricking hope into life. Meg became aware of physical demands, an inevitable reminder that time moved on and there was no recalling yesterday.

"How does the lady this morning, Venner?"

Ottilia, emerging from her own room across the hall, caught the dowager's woman as she came hurrying to her mistress's door, burdened with a large jug and her customary sour expression.

"I am late, ma'am, thanks to ministering to the other. You must excuse me."

She had the door already open when Ottilia spoke again. "Wait! Is she yet awake? Have you left her unattended?"

Venner looked back, contempt in her eyes. "Do you suppose I don't know how to do? She is awake, washed and fed. The chambermaid Rose is sitting with her."

Before Ottilia could say more, Sybilla's voice sounded from within.

"Venner, is that you? You are tardy. I have been waiting for an age."

The maid vanished into the room, shutting the door with a decided snap. Ottilia headed for the stairs. She had dressed early on purpose to have time to visit Meg before her mother-in-law's schemes for the day burst upon her. At dinner, Sybilla had proposed an immediate visit to her daughter's house in an initial foray to demonstrate family support against the perceived slights to Lady Candia. A footman was despatched with a note to warn Lady Dalesford to be at home.

That Sybilla meant to enforce priority onto family affairs over the exigencies of providing for Meg's future was evident, as Francis had not hesitated to aver when they were alone in their chamber.

"She's not going to let you have a free hand, Tillie. You'll be obliged to bend your mind to Candia's concerns."

Ottilia was not alarmed. "I intend to. It is what we came for after all."

Her spouse gave her one of his sceptical looks. He was partaking of a nightcap in bed as was his wont while she sat on the dressing stool and brushed her hair, a nightly ritual which had become a precious time reserved for the privacy of marital discussion.

"Dutiful all of a sudden, wife of my heart?"

"Wretch!" But the mischief would not be suppressed. "If you must be so prescient, horrid creature, there may be a connection."

"Aha! Between who or what, may I ask?"

"Meg spoke the name of Pierre. Or I think it was that, though she would not confirm it."

"And so?"

"Candia's *émigré* pursuer has the same name."

Francis snorted. "A long shot at best, Tillie. Is that the fellow Mama spoke of at dinner?"

"Pierre de Percheval, yes."

Her husband tossed off his brandy and set down the glass on the table at the bedside. "Lord help us! We are plagued with these French refugees. First Randal with his Violette. Now Candia with this Pierre."

"Not forgetting your friend George and his new bride in Weymouth, Fan," Ottilia said, recalling the events last summer which had brought the passionate Cecile into their circle. She and Francis had returned to the seaside town in October to attend the wedding, delayed until the theatre company with which that *émigré* had been sheltering had come to the end of their tour.

"By God, yes!" Francis began rearranging the pillows he had piled at his back to support him. "All we need is for this fresh corpse of yours to turn out to be French as well."

"He's not my corpse, I thank you." Ottilia set down the brush and slipped off her dressing-gown. "And I highly doubt he will prove to be other than English."

"Why? You've no notion who he might be. Draw the curtains, Tillie. It's cold."

Francis made room for her, opening the bedclothes on her side as she pulled the curtains around the bed. As soon as she got in, he snuffed his candle and pulled them to on his side. Ottilia snuggled into him and he tucked an arm about her.

"Well?"

"Well what?"

"How do you know he isn't French? The dead man, I mean."

She blinked into the darkness, allowing her eyes to adjust. "I can't know for certain. But he had Meg in his power. He was taking her somewhere. There must be a vehicle in the vicinity of the place where they fought and he died. He must be a man of some means to be affording such a journey."

"And *émigrés* in general have little by way of means, is that it?"

"Just so. Few manage to bring more than jewels and whatever gold they can carry."

"True. I've heard it is a piece of work to have their bankers transfer funds. Indeed, it is likely well-nigh impossible since the Legislative Assembly's recent decree that the property of departed refugees belongs to the French nation."

"Did they say that? How terrible for those poor people." Ottilia sighed. "Then this Pierre may indeed be pursuing Candia's fortune."

"Undoubtedly, I should think. What is in that complicated head of yours, my dear one?"

"Only that if there is a connection — a remote possibility, I grant you — but if there is, Candia must be a better prospect than Meg."

"But why should Meg be in the case at all?"

"Because her Pierre is one to whom she looked for protection. And before you ask how in the world I can know that, Fan, figure to yourself why a woman in distress should be mentioning a man's name at all."

She had not convinced her spouse, but the niggle persisted with her nevertheless. Meg had evaded her on the name. She hoped, as she climbed the stairs to the stranger's bedchamber, that she might prove more malleable after a night's repose.

She was certainly more alert, Ottilia noted, her gaze open and moving, looking outward rather than in. It found Ottilia on the instant as she entered and there stayed, showing both wary and a trifle apprehensive.

"How do you do today, Meg? Did you manage to sleep?"

Meg gave a brief nod, but her lips remained firmly closed. Was it to be thus? Did she fear to disclose what she knew for fear of incriminating herself, or was she merely distrustful?

Ottilia saw her glance at the maid, a youthful female who had been sitting in a straight chair by the one dresser but had risen on Ottilia's entrance and dropped a curtsey. *Yes, best be rid of listening ears.* Ottilia addressed her. "Rose, is it?"

Another curtsey. "Yes, my lady."

She spoke in a shy little voice and Ottilia at once smiled, adopting a kindly note. "I am sure our guest will be the better for a cup of tea." She turned to Meg. "Or would you prefer coffee, my dear?"

A little sigh escaped the woman. "Oh, tea would be heaven!" Then she caught the back of a bandaged hand to her mouth, consternation in her eyes.

Ottilia hid her satisfaction. Meg had not meant to speak. She ignored the gesture, turning to the hovering maid. "Bring up a pot of tea, Rose. One cup only. I am going down to breakfast shortly. But be quick, if you please. We don't want to leave Miss Meg alone here."

Rose was poised on one foot in the open doorway, looking back. She set the foot down and executed another curtsey. The door closed behind her and Ottilia heard clattering steps on the wooden stairs.

She approached the bed. "Do you mind if I sit for a moment?"

Meg stared at her over the top of the hand still held at her mouth. Ottilia sat down, emitting an elaborate sigh.

"I do not blame you for not wishing to trust me. You know nothing of me after all. But you know, Meg, you may choose which questions to answer. I am not here to bully you. I only want to help."

The hand came down and a low-voiced murmur came. "So also did he."

"Who?"

A shake of the head. She would not give the name then. Ottilia eyed her for a moment, pondering her next move. How to break through? It was evident the woman had suffered reverses in the name of help. She was unlikely to be forthcoming in the matter of this Pierre either. Then what of the event itself?

"Meg, are you up to giving an account of what happened?"

Horror leapt in the woman's eyes. Evidently that was not a road she could yet travel. Ottilia leaned to pat her arm.

"Never mind. We will leave that for now. Let us concentrate only on the present moment. How are your hands?"

Meg lifted them, turning the curled palms up. "If I…" She glanced up, seemed to realise she had spoken, looked in consternation and then drew a quick breath in and out. "If I keep them so, they do not hurt."

It came out fast and low. Ottilia responded just as if she had spoken in a normal tone.

"Yes, I see. If you clench or twist in an unwary fashion, you feel the wounds. Have you been able to use them at all?"

Meg was staring at the hands, turning them this way and that. "My fingers. If I am careful. I can hold the cup by the handle, I think."

It was the longest speech she had made and Ottilia rejoiced to hear the more natural voice. It was cultured, low in pitch. She had not been wrong then, in placing Meg at the lower reaches of gentility.

"Another day will find the cuts healing as they ought, I expect." Ottilia smiled at the woman's quick frown. "You are wondering how I should know that. My brother is a doctor. Before my marriage, I lived in his house and learned a deal of medical lore from him."

For the first time, a flitter of interest showed in Meg's face, though she made no comment. Ottilia took advantage and tried a throw.

"It struck me that the man you were with may have suffered an internal injury. Oh, not at your hands," she added as the woman's cheeks blanched. "You might well have noticed if he was in any sort of physical distress. Before the — er — accident, I mean."

Had the dismay turned to question? Meg looked away from her, casting her gaze about the room instead. Was she thinking back? Had she remembered something of value? Then she turned her hand and struck at her own chest with the back of it. Once, twice, with deliberation. Ottilia seized on it.

"His chest? He had pain there?"

"Held it. Held his hand there. Sometimes." Her brows drew together and her regard became intent upon Ottilia's face. "What does it mean?"

"I believe he had an injury which may in the end have caused his death. Only a post mortem will determine the truth of it. But if I am right, you are not to blame."

For the first time a look of pure relief crossed Meg's features. Her voice became husky. "Is it possible?"

"Not only possible, but all too likely. If you can give me any account of how he was just before he died, I could be more certain."

For a moment or two Meg hesitated, but the hope must, Ottilia thought, be proving too strong. It came out staccato, but it came.

"His breath. He was labouring. More than I. He had run long. We both had. Yet I was less troubled than he. He could barely stand. He grew red, struggling. Then pale. Yes, and he clutched his throat. He staggered. At last he fell. I ran, thinking to get away. But he did not come after me… I went back." Meg gazed at Ottilia with haggard eyes. "He was unmoving. I dared not go near. I watched … waited… No sound, no motion. I thought I had done for him."

Ottilia, rejoicing at this confirmation, urged for more. "How? If you supposed him dead by your hand, how had you killed him?"

Meg shivered, her hands trembling in her lap. "I think it was his razor. I snatched it up. Attacked him. He was trying to … would have succeeded if I had not… I slashed at him. Slashed and slashed until I drove him off. And then I escaped. I ran."

"But he caught you, did he not? He held you to him?"

There was astonishment in Meg's gaze as she stared at Ottilia. "Yes. How did you know?"

"You were bloodied at the front, but you had no injury there. When did he catch you?"

"When he seized the knife. Wrested it from my hand."

"Where? Where did all this happen?"

"The room in the inn. He meant to force my consent." Meg flailed a bandaged hand, emitting a raucous laugh. "Consent! What choice had I? He had me in his power. But when he would have me submit to… I could not endure it. I fought him."

Ottilia saw Meg's distress, but the floodgates were open and she did not intend to allow them to shut again. "You defended yourself with the razor and managed to escape from the bed? Or from the room?"

"The bed, the bed." A note of hysteria was creeping in. "He caught me before I could get out. Held me fast. Captured my hand and took the weapon." Meg's features contorted. "I did not make it easy for him. I kicked, I bit, I struggled. I hurt him!" There was triumph in her tone and her eyes gleamed with hatred. "He cried out, let me go. Even then he staggered. I did not wait for his recovery. I flew. I escaped the place before he could catch me."

"But he came after you, did he not?"

Meg fell back against her pillows, spent all at once. "Like Nemesis. I know not how far I ran, nor where. I could sense no direction. In the end, it mattered little where I was. I was lost, finished. As I am. There is no future for me now."

Ottilia let this pass. It was inevitable the girl would be at her lowest ebb. In reliving the tale, she was bound to revive a sense of doom and failure.

"You are exhausted, my dear. You have been through a harrowing experience, but I am glad you confided this much."

A knock at the door was followed by the entrance of Rose with a tray. Ottilia got up, speaking on a note of deliberate cheerfulness.

"Ah, here is your tea, Meg. You will be the better for it. Tea is so refreshing, do you not think?"

A tiny smile rewarded her. "So simple, Lady Fan?"

Ottilia laughed. "Yes, let us be simple. We need not compound your difficulties with complexity." She leaned down and patted Meg's shoulder. "Come, my dear, your case is not so desperate. You will come about. There is always a way to mend things."

Meg said nothing, though her countenance reflected scepticism. She accepted the tea Ottilia poured for her, however, managing the cup, though gingerly, despite the damaged hands. Witness, Ottilia thought, to the frenzy of her defence. She likely had no notion how she was injured at the time. She probably did not even feel it, her attention engaged with the urgent need to be free of her molester. She could have cut herself about as freely as she cut him, either then or when he took the razor from her. Blades were indiscriminate.

But a message must be sent to Justice Ingham, although his patrol were likely already en route to the scene. There was a weapon to be located, and an inn too. Witnesses there must be to corroborate Meg's version of events. Yet the identity of the dead man remained a question. Along with the why and how she came to be in his power.

Chapter Six

Lady Elizabeth Fiske, at eighteen a year younger than her cousin, impressed Ottilia at once with an air of robust intelligence, unexpected in a petite girl who looked positively fragile against Lady Candia's height and bosomy figure. The latter partook of the striking Fanshawe looks, with lush brown hair, high cheekbones and dark eyes, thus resembling her aunt Harriet more than that lady's own daughter.

"You and your father are very alike," Ottilia said, taking opportunity to approach Lady Elizabeth while Sybilla was requiring her daughter to furnish an account of the latest doings of the new marchioness.

"In feature you mean?"

"If memory serves me, for I have only met Lord Dalesford once."

"Grandmama will have it I am like Papa in temperament too."

"And are you?"

"Decidedly." Lady Elizabeth gave a throaty laugh, quite out of keeping with the delicate, pointed face and its halo of curly hair of a soft brown. "At least, Mama always couples me with him when I displease her, so I suppose I must be."

Ottilia cast a glance across the room to where Lady Dalesford was holding forth on the subject of the ubiquitous Violette who evidently continued to dazzle the world. Lady Candia Fanshawe, seated beside her, did not add to the recital, rather looking a trifle embarrassed.

"I hear Candia does not resent her stepmother's popularity."

"Not in the least. She insists Lady Polbrook is kind to her, and she has grown fond of Lucille and Bastien."

Ottilia eyed the girl, but could detect no hint either of irony or disapproval. "I am not much surprised she has taken to her half-sister and brother, to say truth. Candia is a tender-hearted girl."

"Oh, she is all sensibility, my cousin. But if you ask me, this Lady Polbrook is a deal more considerate than —" Lady Elizabeth broke off, throwing a hand to her mouth, eyes dancing comically. "Oh, drat! I should not have said that."

Ottilia could not help laughing. "You need not mind your tongue before me, Lady Elizabeth. I much prefer candid speaking and, frankly, I believe you."

The girl looked guilty, but she wafted a hand in a dismissive fashion reminiscent of the dowager. "Don't encourage me, ma'am. As well Mama cannot hear me."

"Do you know, I fear you are more like your mama than I thought. Harriet is nothing if not outspoken."

The throaty laugh came again, causing the other ladies to look across at them. Lady Elizabeth dipped her head to avoid them. "She says the same of you, if you wish to know."

"My reputation goes before me, I perceive, Lady Elizabeth."

The girl twinkled. "Must we be formal? You are my aunt after all."

"Yes, I suppose I am. Lizzy then."

"Thank you — Aunt Ottilia. Or should I say Lady Fan?"

Amused, Ottilia eyed her with new interest. "You have heard of that, have you?"

"Oh, your reputation is legendary. Grandmama is forever singing your praises and telling of your skill in discovering murderers. It sounds excessively exciting."

Ottilia made a face. "Intriguing rather. It is usually more distressing and uncomfortable than anything else."

Lizzy looked unconvinced. "Well, I wish I might be clever enough to solve murders."

This chimed so well with Ottilia's purpose, she had no scruple in pursuing it. "Perhaps you may, if you care to tell me about this *émigré* fellow of Candia's. Pierre de Percheval?"

Astonishment opened the girl's grey eyes. "The Chevalier? Now why?" Her gaze lit. "Don't say you have a murder in hand at this moment? Lady Fan strikes again!"

"Hush, child!" Ottilia cast a furtive look at Sybilla and was relieved to see her engrossed. Candia was looking their way, however. "Keep your voice down, if you please. I don't wish your cousin to hear."

Lowering her voice, Lizzy begged pardon, but her tone was eager. "Tell me though, pray. Is Monsieur de Percheval involved somehow?"

"That is just what I wish to find out. What do you know of him?"

"Only what anyone else knows. He had a miraculous escape, for he left his lodging only moments before the National Guard came to arrest him."

"How does he know that?"

"He saw them beating on the door. Pierre had heard he was denounced to the Criminal Tribunal only an hour before and had to scramble to pack what he could and leave the house. It took him many days to find a way to get through the barriers."

"How did he get through them?"

Here Lizzy's tone changed in her relation of the adventure, a sceptical note entering in. "He says he hid in a wine barrel in the end. It was empty, but packed in with several full ones on a cart."

Ottilia gave her a speculative look. "You don't believe it, do you?"

Lizzy shrugged. "I have no reason not to, but a wine barrel? He's a tall man. I might fit in a wine barrel, just."

"And if that is a fantasy, the rest might also be suspect?"

"Exactly so. He is altogether too smooth to my mind. I should be glad to know him for a villain."

Ottilia was obliged to smile. "We cannot be condemning the poor man merely upon supposition, Lizzy. Or are you troubled to see your cousin imposed upon?"

Lizzy's brows drew together as she threw a worried glance at Lady Candia. "She's too trusting. I've tried to get her to question his motives, but Candy insists she's only sorry for him."

"Has she a developed a tendre, do you think?"

"She's not in love with him. At least, I don't think so. But she allows him far too much licence. Oh, she grants him no liberties, she is not so lost to propriety. But he speaks to her in a horrid caressing fashion that makes me want to slap his face for him."

"Dear me. Does he speak to any other female in that way?"

"Not that I've noticed. But of course he's made a friend of Lady Polbrook and they rattle away in French."

Ottilia considered this, feeling there might be much to be forgiven of Randal if his wife was the object of a handsome young Frenchman's flattery. Having formed a favourable estimate of Lizzy's judgement, she did not hesitate to voice her thoughts.

"Is he hoping for Violette's influence in his favour with Lord Polbrook? I doubt he will succeed."

"Of course he will not. Uncle Randal won't give him the time of day. Which, I'm afraid, makes Candia all the more determined to be kind to him."

Ottilia, with difficulty, refrained from retort. If one thing was more certain than another, Lord Polbrook could be depended upon to act in a fashion contrary to common sense. She could only pray Francis was not dragged into the business. Her spouse had suffered too much already from his elder brother's ill-judged actions. But she need waste no time on that.

"How does he live, this Pierre, do you know? He cannot look impoverished, I suppose. I presume he has a polished appearance if he has managed to enter good society."

"Heavens, yes. In appearance he is completely the gentleman. He likely has assistance from his compatriots. According to my uncle Randal's new wife, the established escapees feel it incumbent upon them to help aristocrats newly arrived from France."

"Although I gather Pierre de Percheval is not an aristocrat." Nor was Madame Violette Guizot, as Randal's bride was known before marriage, but this Ottilia kept to herself.

"No, indeed. Yet he is acquainted with those high-born *émigrés* in Society. I have heard nothing of his family connections."

"How long has he been in England?"

"A year or so, I think. He speaks of sheltering with an English family who took him in. He knew the father. Or no, his father knew the father. Some such thing, I cannot recall exactly."

This intelligence at once caught Ottilia's attention and she wondered if Lady Candia had any better information. An English family, now abandoned by this Pierre? Otherwise they would be known to be associated with him, even perhaps have provided his *entrée* into the upper echelons of society he had somehow penetrated.

She was drawn back from her speculations by Lady Elizabeth, who was regarding her keenly. "Why are you so interested in the Chevalier? Do you suspect him of a murder?"

Ottilia was surprised into laughter. "Dear me, no. I am chasing a very faint possibility of his being known to…" She faded out, unwilling to be drawn into a discussion of Meg's condition and the events of the previous day. Although if Sybilla had spoken of the matter to her daughter Harriet, Lizzy would know of it soon enough. She turned the subject. "What of you, Lady Elizabeth? Or rather, Lizzy. I must say I have felt for you in this situation."

The girl looked astonished. "Me? Gracious, why in the world, ma'am?"

"Is it not at all trying to have your debut overshadowed in this fashion?"

Lizzy's characteristic laugh came. "What, ought I to be jealous? I promise you I am not. I find it all vastly entertaining, to tell you the truth." She dropped her tone, casting a quick glance towards the coterie by the fireplace. "I dare not say so to Mama or Grandmama, but I am enjoying all the drama hugely. It was very distressing when Aunt Emily was killed, of course, and we all did what we could to comfort Candia. But the aftermath! Such a hullaballoo as there was, you cannot imagine."

"Oh, can I not indeed," retorted Ottilia, recalling all too vividly how Sybilla had become incandescent when Randal married his mistress a bare year after his first wife's death. The scandal of Violette and his illegitimate children living under his protection had been bad enough.

"Such scenes there were at home," pursued Lizzy unheeding, "with Mama vowing never again to set foot in Hanover Square, and offering Candia a home with us instead of returning to Polbrook. And then my cousin Giles must needs add to the furore — but you know all that."

To some purpose, since Ottilia had been drawn into the ramifications of a mysterious death when the Polbrook heir became infatuated with the beautiful Tamasine a year ago.

"This is tame in comparison," said Lizzy on a note of sheer amusement, "but at least I am in the thick of it this time." Her gaze became intent. "But you are solving a murder now, are you not? I wish you will allow me to partake of your investigation."

Ottilia thought nothing could be further from either Harriet or Sybilla's wishes, but she was not to be deterred from involving the child if she was likely to be useful. She regarded her with some degree of interest, tinged with doubt.

"Can you be discreet?"

Lizzy's eyes danced. "Does my mother know I am enjoying all the drama?"

Ottilia laughed. "Very well, but you must be circumspect. Don't draw suspicion upon yourself."

"From whom?"

"Pierre de Percheval. Candia too. It is vital she has no inkling there is purpose in your questions."

Lizzy primmed up her mouth and touched a hand to her breast. "I am promised. Not an undue word will cross my lips."

Ottilia had to smile. "You must be the most complete handful, Lady Elizabeth Fiske. I dare say you run rings round poor Harriet."

Her extraordinary laugh escaped the girl, but she leaned towards Ottilia with an air of suppressed excitement. "What is it you wish me to find out?"

"Ha! The old lady dragged you in, did she? Well, if she's sent you to moralise over me, my boy, I tell you now I won't stand for it."

Suppressing a strong desire to answer his brother in kind, Francis disclaimed, "Nothing of the sort. She's taken Ottilia to pay her respects to Harriet and the girls, so I seized the chance to come over."

Randal merely grunted, addressing himself to his cup. Black coffee, well sugared. Francis had found Lord Polbrook in his library at the back of the Hanover Square mansion, in morose mood and imbibing his restorative. Francis refused an offer to join him in drinking the beverage and drew up a chair.

"Where is Violette this morning?"

A sour look came over his brother's fleshy features. "Out visiting. So many of these damned Frenchies in the town, I hardly see her these days."

"I suppose it is natural she would wish for acquaintance with her own countrymen and women. She must feel isolated."

"Isolated? Got me and the children, hasn't she?" Randal set down his empty cup and pushed the tray to the edge of his large desk, setting his elbows in the vacant space and leaning in, a bleak look in his eyes. "Thought I'd done with marital discord and a wife with an eye to other men."

Both disturbed and irritated, Francis strove for patience. Randal was ever mercurial, going from buoyant optimism to raging despair in an instant. But to be harking back to the rank misery of his first marriage, which had driven him into the arms of this Frenchwoman, his erstwhile mistress, was ridiculous.

"Violette is not Emily, Randal. She cares for you. Anyone can tell that."

"Yes, but she's basking in all this adulation. I wish to God I'd never brought her to town."

So also did everyone else in the family, if his brother only knew. Francis set himself to soothe. "You are refining too much upon it, I am persuaded, Randal. You can't allow Emily's memory to haunt you."

His brother's cheeks darkened as his choler rose. "That's it, you see. She is haunting me, the witch. Here in this house, where she was killed. She's punishing me, turning Violette against me."

"Don't be ridiculous. For pity's sake, Randal, grow up!"

"Ha!" The marquis slapped a hand on the desk. "I knew it. You have come to ring a peal over me. Well, I won't have it. I won't be lectured to by my younger brother."

Francis shot up from the chair. "I'll go then, shall I? Not that I came here with any intention other than to see a brother I can't help but feel affection for, little though he warrants it."

"No, no, don't go!" Randal was on his feet, moving round the desk and Francis was pulled into a bear-like hug from the altogether larger man. "Didn't mean it, my boy. You know my temper."

Released, Francis allowed his brother to take his hands, returning the strong grip. "You're a damned fool, Randal. Don't destroy your own happiness with these idiotic suspicions."

His brother let go, nodding in a fervent fashion. "I know I'm a fool. Can't seem to help it." A wry grin dawned, along with a reluctant twinkle. "Ask Mama, she'll tell you."

"I've no wish to provoke her into going off into one of her rants, I thank you."

Randal laughed. "Driving you into a frenzy, is she? Why the deuce didn't you come and stay here?"

"Where? You must be full to the rafters."

Randal threw up his eyes. "Place is a damned circus, I'll tell you. What with Bastien racing in and out. Not to mention half a dozen girls visiting Lucille every five minutes."

"They have found playmates among the refugees, I take it?"

Randal snorted. "Might as well be back in Le Midi with French battering my ears all day long. Supposed to stick to English so they learn, but that's all gone to hell since they came to London. Candia would keep them in order if she were here, for they dote on her. Why Harriet must needs insist on her staying in Dalesford House beats me."

Fearing another bone of contention at the dissatisfaction in his brother's voice, Francis let this pass. But he seized on the change of subject, recalling Ottilia's interest.

"Who is this *émigré* fellow who is after Candia? Mama said—"

"Ha! Chevalier de Percheval he calls himself. Chevalier nothing! If he supposes he'll gain my consent, he may go to the devil. Not that he'd dare approach me. Damned flirtatious upstart! I wish Violette would hint him away, but she feels sorry for the fellow, if you please."

"You doubt his credentials? Is he not known among the refugees?"

"I can't tell that. He's been accepted, but Paris has become such a maelstrom, they tell me, any riff-raff can claim aristocratic connections and get away with it. There's not one of the family de Percheval left to say yay or nay to this so-called cousin. Not that I'd let him marry Candia if he could prove it. Hasn't a feather to fly with."

This was scarcely a surprise. Few of the refugees still pouring into England were in funds. Only the earliest arrivals had succeeded in securing some part of their former wealth.

"And that's not all," said Randal, leading the way out of the library into the little vestibule that led into the larger main hall. "The fellow runs with a set of men I could wish at Jericho. Coveney and his cronies. Bent on making his fortune one way or another, if you ask me, but he's not going to do it through my daughter."

"Who is Coveney?"

"You don't know Matthew Coveney?"

"I can't say I've heard the name."

Francis followed to the family parlour where his brother rang the bell and then threw himself into a chair by the fire. "Might as well be comfortable. Sit down, man. We'll have Cattawade bring the Madeira. Coffee hasn't done the trick."

Seating himself in a chair opposite, Francis quirked an eyebrow. "Hair of the dog, brother?"

A bark of laughter greeted this sally. "I might have imbibed a trifle deep last night." He grimaced. "Violette gave me pepper for it."

"Hence the coffee?"

Randal threw up his eyes. "She ought to be glad it's only wine with me. At least I don't waste the ready at the gaming tables. And she'd have me look kindly on this Chevalier fellow."

"What, is he a gamester?"

"Told you he runs with that set. Coveney and his ilk. Hardened gamesters, the lot of them. Redlingfield, Aldreth, Lezayre. He's another Frenchie, though he's lived here forever. Shouldn't surprise me if it was he introduced the boy into their ranks."

"Lezayre? Him I know of old. If this *émigré* of yours is in a string with that fellow, I'm not surprised he's been lured to the gaming tables. He tried his tricks on me when I was a greenhorn."

"Did he so? Damned scoundrel. Should have told me, my boy. I'd soon have sent him to the rightabout."

Francis had to smile. "No, you wouldn't. You were too busy ferreting after Violette in Le Midi."

His brother wagged a finger. "That'll do, you impertinent young hound."

"In any event, my regiment was ordered off to America before Lezayre could do any real damage. Isn't Redlingfield a viscount?"

"Yes, and bent on gambling away his inheritance. Aldreth is wealthy enough to stand the nonsense, but Coveney lives on dice and the turn of a card. Just like Lezayre."

"Not quite like Lezayre, unless he also lives by preying on fresh-faced youths and introducing them into these dens where they may be relieved of their money in the shortest possible order."

"Well, this *soi-disant* de Percheval hasn't any, so it ain't that."

"Fellow feeling then? Not that I should suppose Lezayre to feel any such thing. If he wasn't a pigeon for plucking, why befriend de Percheval?"

Before his brother could answer the door opened to admit not his butler, but his wife, a pretty blonde with a countenance sweet in repose, yet striking in animation as it now was. She evidently did not at once perceive Francis for she broke into a flood of rapid French as she crossed towards her husband, gesticulating in a wild fashion that spoke her agitation. Not quite as fluent in the language as his brother, Francis was yet able to grasp the burden of her utterances.

She had been deceived. The young man she befriended out of the kindness of her heart had proven to be unworthy. While he had been making up to Candia, he had all the time had an eye to another female altogether, for now the creature had gone off with a different man and the boy was distraught.

Randal, looking both battered and bemused, threw up his hands, responding in the same language. "Of what are you talking, *chérie*? So far I have not been privileged to understand a word of this rigmarole."

Not so Francis. If his senses did not deceive him, there was matter here more pertinent than his brother could imagine. He had risen automatically on his sister-in-law's entrance and he cut in without ceremony.

"Who is the man, Violette? Do you know?"

He had spoken in English and the marchioness turned in obvious astonishment.

"It is you, Francis? *Pardon*. I have not seen you. *Alors*, it is rude, no? Forgive, I beg. My head she goes round and round with this affair."

Francis took her proffered hand and executed a small bow. "No apology is necessary, ma'am. Only tell me if you are talking of Pierre de Percheval?"

Her eyes widened. "You know this boy?"

But Randal interrupted before Francis could answer, exploding out of his chair.

"By God, is it he you mean, Violette? Trifle with my daughter, would he? I'll break every bone in his body!"

His wife waved agitated hands in his face. "But no, *mon amour*, no! You do not understand."

"He'll understand me if I catch him going after Candia!"

"*Ma foi*, but you are of a brain small like a bird, *mon mari*! I speak not of Candia, but the other."

"What other?"

"But I have said! It is the girl from this *famille* with whom he lives."

"Which family? I thought the wretched fellow lived in lodgings."

"*Parbleu*, but you do not listen, Randal! Before, when he comes in England, he is with this *famille*, and the girl is there. But now he hears she is gone with this man — *peste*, what is the word?"

"Gone where? You mean, she's eloped?"

"Perhaps. But Pierre he does not believe. He says it is the *enlèvement*."

"Abduction? Who cares? The point is this fellow has been sniffing round my daughter —"

Francis, itching with questions, his mind leaping to Ottilia's protégée, made himself heard again, cutting into a heated rejoinder.

"Violette, give me leave a moment!"

The marchioness stopped in mid-sentence, blinking at him. "*Quoi?*"

"Do you know the name of the family? Or of this man who has taken the girl away?"

Violette gave one of those peculiarly Gallic shrugs. "Of this *famille* I know nothing. The man, it is the one evil, he that I cannot like. He makes Pierre to be foolish with the cards and the dice. Many many times have I said to him of the danger, but he is mad for this play."

Randal, who had been following this with a heavy frown, now flashed with astonishment.

"You don't mean Lezayre? Good God!"

But Francis was ahead of him. "I think she must mean this fellow Coveney."

The marchioness looked oddly pleased. "*C'est ça!* Milord Coveney. If he is gone away with the girl, it is a good thing for Pierre."

Francis did not disabuse her, but if his wife's instinct did not lead her astray, Pierre was in for a ruder shock yet.

"Will you tackle her?"

Ottilia considered, her spouse's information rattling in her mind as she sipped her favourite beverage. "On Coveney? Not yet, I think."

The hasty turn Francis took about the room spoke his disquiet. "I little thought to hear such tidings so soon."

"Well, the news was bound to leak out, if Meg is indeed the girl in question."

Francis paused in his perambulations, directing a frowning look at her. "There can't be two such abductions at once. You're the one who insisted on a connection in the first place."

Ottilia set down her cup, holding it in the saucer in her lap. "Because Pierre is not a name commonly found in England. But we can take nothing for granted. If the dead man is indeed Lord Coveney, there will be no keeping the matter quiet."

Francis threw up his hands. "Do you think I don't know, Tillie? Why do you suppose I'm restive? Why you must stumble on this passes my comprehension. If we had set out an hour earlier —"

"It is of no use to cavil at this stage, Fan. And I might point out that this was none of my doing. You absolved me at the outset, if you remember."

Her husband snorted. "I must have had windmills in my head."

Ottilia struggled to suppress a sharp retort. It was useless to argue with Francis when he was in this mood. She tried for a deprecating note.

"It need not involve the family, Fan. At least, not much. It is not as if Candia is betrothed to the fellow."

"If you suppose my revered mother won't fly into a pelter when she hears of this, you're raving, Tillie."

"A worse pelter than yours," Ottilia snapped before she could stop herself.

His dark eyes flared fire for an instant, and then a groan escaped him and he dropped into the chair opposite. Ottilia softened on the instant.

"You resemble her more than you know."

"God help me then!" He leaned forward. "Forgive me, my dear one. Again."

Mischief leapt in her bosom. "I have a very good mind to withhold it and make you grovel, you wretch."

His grin dispelled the ill-tempered look. "I would too. And you know it."

She smiled and picked up her cup again. "Sybilla may be down from her nap at any moment. Do you wish to hear my plans or not?"

"Not. But you want to tell me." She could not help the giggle that escaped and his lips twisted in the familiar wry smile. "I've not heard that in a while. Where has it been?"

A tiny shadow crossed Ottilia's mind, but she shrugged it away. "Life became a little too serious, my darling, that is all."

For a moment he did not speak, but the look in his eyes said everything. The last year had been bleak, though Ottilia was long over the worst.

"I wish it was all roses for you, Tillie."

"No, Fan, you were right. Life is an adventure. You never know what is around the next corner. The trick is to learn to weather it."

"We are, aren't we?"

She was obliged to speak over a sudden lump in her throat. "Always. Every moment."

His smile was loving. "Tell me your plans."

She took a warming gulp or two of coffee to give herself a respite. Yet her mind returned at once to the puzzle. "I think it wise to wait for Justice Ingham. I have no doubt he will come here, either today or, more likely, tomorrow. His men must discover something, assuming they find the inn Meg spoke of. We found no card to identify the dead man, but his effects must be there if he planned to stay long enough to carry through a rape."

"Then if it is found to be Coveney?"

"We will cross that bridge if we come to it."

"It would be simpler to find out from the girl, wouldn't it?"

"I suspect she is an unreliable witness."

Francis frowned. "You don't believe her version of events?"

"Her story is necessarily told as she saw it. There are always two sides. But the facts bear out in the evidence of her gown and her injuries."

"The corpse too, as I recall from what you said."

"Indeed, yes. But we cannot pre-empt the post mortem." She drank the rest of her coffee and set aside the cup, aware of her husband's frowning gaze. Was he holding back on tumbling worry to avoid distressing her? "What is in your mind, Fan?"

He cocked an eyebrow. "You can't guess? I'm waiting for you to charm me into infiltrating this coterie of gamesters."

Ottilia dissolved into hiccupping laughter. "Abominable creature, how dare you fathom me so ably?"

His lips quirked. "You are an open book, Tillie. I wish I might penetrate these infernal murderous puzzles of yours as easily as I read you."

Affection rode her, but she seized on the offering nevertheless. "I do not care to ask it of you, but will you? You need not join in the gaming — indeed, I hope you won't — but I cannot doubt they will be discussing the affair."

"Among themselves perhaps, if the surmise proves correct that Coveney is the dead man. There is no guarantee they will speak to an outsider."

"They will if you ask. I have yet to learn that gentleman gossip less than ladies."

He laughed. "There's for my sex then. I've a vague notion I may have seen both Redlingfield and Aldreth at Brooks's in the past, though I could not swear to recognising either, but I can try there. Lezayre may go hang. I have no intention of cultivating his acquaintance, I thank you."

"Did you not say he introduced this Pierre to the others?"

"It is what Randal supposed since they are both French. And it's likely, as I know from experience. The fellow's a scoundrel."

Ottilia regarded him with some degree of sympathy. He had related his own dealings with the Frenchman when he told her what his brother had revealed. Yet this was needed now. She chose her words with care.

"If he is such a scoundrel, Fan, he might be just the man we ought to probe, do you not think?"

Francis's brows snapped together. "You mean he could be the villain of the piece?"

"We need to know with whom the dead man quarrelled to receive an injury which subsequently caused his death. Without that, I fear it is Meg who will take the blame."

Chapter Seven

Her cousin's eyes willed her away, but Lady Elizabeth Fiske refused to take the hint. Determined on pursuing her part in assisting Ottilia's enquiries, Lizzy stayed close from the moment the Dalesford party arrived at Lady Harbisher's soirée.

She had every hope of encountering Pierre, since Candia's Aunt Dorothea was known to follow fashion in opening her doors to aristocratic refugees. She was equally certain the ubiquitous Violette would not be present, since Lord Harbisher, brother to the former marchioness, had entertained a violent antipathy towards Lord Polbrook since Emily's death and all the family knew he had forbidden his wife to have anything to do with her successor.

In fact the Berkeley Square mansion proved to be rather thin of company, the event clashing with several others, although Lady Harbisher, a faded wisp of a woman, contrived to pass this off.

"I so much prefer an exclusive sort of party, don't you, my dear Harriet?"

"I could not agree more, Dorothea. I cannot bear these crushes when you cannot hear yourself speak."

Lizzy heard her mother's response with amusement and looked at once to her father, who caught her eye and raised a comical eyebrow. They both knew Mama loved nothing better than to be in the thick of a busy gathering. She was as much a social butterfly as the late Lady Polbrook had been, although Lizzy counted her mother a much warmer and more generous being.

"Dearest Candia, welcome," said Lady Harbisher, clasping the much larger figure close in an excess of sympathy. Whether it was still for the loss of Candia's mother or for being supplanted by her stepmother in Society's graces, or both, Lizzy could not judge. But she was glad when the greetings were over and she could move on, catching up with her cousin as the latter was casting searching glances around the knots of chattering guests dotting the double saloon, which had been opened out for the occasion, the furniture ranged about the walls. Music filtered through from a third room, where Lizzy glimpsed a trio of musicians. A footman carrying a tray came through the open double doors and, behind him, a familiar slim-figured gentleman entered the large saloon, a glass in his hand.

"There he is."

Candia's muttered exclamation filled Lizzy with misgiving. Was her cousin more smitten than she had supposed? She followed as Candia started across, a little irritated she should show herself so eager, especially among company as sparse as this. Several eyes followed their progress as her cousin wove a path through to where the Pierre de Percheval now stood by a marbled fireplace.

It struck Lizzy at once that he was looking less than his usual suave self. His dark hair was still sleek, tied back in a queue, and the well-fitting blue velvet coat over black satin breeches gave polish to his appearance. Yet the lean cheeks seemed pale and taut, a muscle twitching as he spied Candia's approach, and his full mouth was tight, his dark eyes less than friendly.

Watchful? Disturbed? No, he looked rather to be under strain even as a slight smile appeared and he gave a bow Lizzy thought perfunctory.

"Milady Candia. I had hope I may see you this night."

"I too, Pierre. I thought my aunt must invite you." Candia's expressive eyes devoured his face. "You don't look happy. Are you well?"

Pierre appeared to pull himself together. With an effort, Lizzy thought.

"But of course." His gaze strayed to her face. "Milady Elizabeth, bon soir."

"How do you do, Chevalier?"

"As you see me, *mademoiselle. Enchanté de vous voir.*" But his eyes shifted to Candia as he said it and a softer light entered them at the touch of colour appearing in her cousin's cheek. "How is it you are in greater beauty each time we meet, *ma chère?*"

Ah, the smooth rascal was back, was he? A sliver of disgust reminded Lizzy of her mission. Had she not told Ottilia just how the Frenchman behaved? Yet she could swear the speech was mechanical. Though he spoke with the same air of gallantry, she thought she detected a brittle quality to the accented voice.

Candia took it at face value, however, laughing and tapping his arm with her fan. "Oh, Pierre, stop. Such nonsense. I am outshone by half the females in the room."

"In my eyes, not," he returned, "but I am dumb if you so wish. You have but to command, *mademoiselle.*"

"You know very well I don't look for compliments, especially from you."

She turned her eyes upon her cousin in a look that clearly invited Lizzy to move elsewhere. Lizzy met it blandly and did not budge. Candia's expression became resigned and she turned back to Pierre.

"I am anxious to know how you fare. Have you had any word from your bankers?"

He brushed this off with a gesture. "*Rien*. I believe the case is without hope. The word from Paris it is very bad."

"So I hear from Violette. Poor, poor things, it is so very sad."

Sad enough, but Lizzy had not accompanied her cousin to talk of the horrors perpetrated by the so-called Republic of France.

"I wonder you do not seek employment, Chevalier."

His brows flew up, his look haughty all at once. "I?"

"Lizzy, pray."

She ignored Candia's low-voiced admonition. "Well, if your bankers cannot resurrect your fortune, sir, it would seem a sensible course to pursue, would it not?"

"Lizzy, for heaven's sake! What would you have him do? Take the King's shilling?"

Lizzy laughed. "Nothing so desperate. Great men require secretaries, for example. Translators even, especially in these times. I am sure there must be opportunity enough, even for such as you, Chevalier."

"Such as I? What mean you, *mademoiselle*?"

The clipped tone had an effect on Candia at least, who rushed to his defence.

"Pierre is a gentleman, Elizabeth. How can you talk so? Pay no heed to her, Pierre. She is too teasing."

"I am not teasing. Nor did I mean to insult you, Chevalier. I merely suggest there are ways, perfectly genteel, to repair the situation in which you find yourself."

An ironic bow came her way. "You are too kind, Milady Elizabeth. But it does not need that you interest yourself in my affairs."

Even Candia looked taken aback at the studied rudeness of both words and tone, but Lizzy refused to be deterred.

"Oh, come now, sir. If my cousin thinks your affairs are of sufficient interest to engage her sympathies, I am only too happy to be of service."

The tautness at his cheeks became marked. "*Mademoiselle* is kindness itself."

Lizzy laughed. "No, I am not being kind. Merely helpful, I hope. After all, is it not more profitable to be thinking of ways and means to change things rather than bewailing what cannot be mended?"

Pierre's lip curled. "You would say that I sue instead for the sympathy? Believe me, *mademoiselle*, I have my ways and means in hand."

Yes, by attempting to get his hands on Candia's substantial portion. She changed tack, turning to her cousin. "Shall we tell him of Aunt Ottilia's adventure, Candia?"

Shocked surprise leapt in the other's eyes. "Lizzy! Not outside the family."

Lizzy gave a false start, throwing a hand to her mouth. "Oh, drat, I forgot!" She waved her fan at Pierre. "Don't heed me, sir. I should not have spoken. It is supposed to be a secret, though how in the world Lady Francis expects it will not leak out that this Meg woman is in Grandmama's house, I can't imagine."

While she spoke in this apparently artless fashion, she watched Pierre closely. Did he react to the name? Or was it her imagination that something flashed in his eyes? Was he a trifle paler as he looked from her to her cousin and back again.

"Of whom do you speak?"

Had his voice thickened? Lizzy was glad when Candia took the question so she could keep her attention on her quarry.

"Oh, she means Lady Francis Fanshawe. She is married to our uncle Francis. You will not have met either for they only arrived in town a couple of days ago."

"Ah, *c'est ça? Alors*, I will hope to — to make acquaintance with these uncle and aunt."

He had forgotten his English. A sure sign of agitation. Lizzy triumphed. Would he ask for more?

"You may meet them," said Candia, sounding doubtful, "although Aunt Ottilia does not much care for large parties. I dare say she will only attend those my grandmother chooses, which are few and far between."

Here Lizzy chimed in again. "But he must indeed meet Aunt Ottilia. Or Lady Fan as she likes to be called." She turned to Pierre with a merry laugh. "She is so droll and clever. Would you believe it? She is adept at solving murders." Then she wished she had held her tongue, for Candia went white, casting her a look compound of reproach and dismay. Lizzy seized her hand, remorse flooding through her. "Oh, Candia, I'm so sorry! That was maladroit. I didn't mean —"

But her cousin dropped her hand and waved her away. "I must find Aunt Harriet."

The husky note pierced Lizzy, but she made no attempt to stop Candia flitting away, instead seizing opportunity as she lowered her voice. "I should not have spoken so before her, Chevalier."

"But why? What comes to her?"

"Well, you know Candia's mother was murdered, do you not?"

He looked struck. "Ah, *oui. La marquise*, is not it? Violette spoke of it to me."

"Well, it was Aunt Ottilia who discovered the murderer. She was not married to Uncle Francis then of course. But the thing

82

is, she has since become embroiled in several other incidents of the like."

He was frowning, gazing at her in a kind of fascinated wonder, she thought.

"How is this?"

"It seems these things fall into her lap, just as they seem to have done on her journey here."

Had she gone too far? His expression changed, the dark eyes abruptly keen, searching her face. There was no trace of the gallant in him now.

"You said a name, *mademoiselle*."

Harsh was his voice. Excitement bubbled up in Lizzy. Ottilia was right. There was a connection. He must know the woman. She must tread with care.

"Name, sir?"

His glance swept the room, as if he meant to ensure they were not observed. He kept his voice low, the harshness pronounced nevertheless. "Meg. You spoke of Meg. Is it so?"

Lizzy feigned confusion. "I did? When, Chevalier?"

His eyes narrowed. "Do not play games, *mademoiselle*. I have reason to ask this. You have said she is in the house of your *grandmère*, no?"

"Who, sir?"

A flash at his eyes. Anger? Yes, she rather thought so. He was rattled. Should she capitulate?

"I will not again say it, *mademoiselle*. The name, *s'il vous plait*. Did I hear you right or no?"

"You mean Meg?"

A long sigh escaped him, and Lizzy thought she heard a tremor within it. A mutter reached her. "Safe! *Grace à dieu!*"

"I beg your pardon?"

He did not repeat it, although she was sure she had heard it correctly. Instead, he drew himself up and gave a stiff little bow.

"Excuse, I beg, *mademoiselle*."

He passed by her, threading a path through the chattering guests. Lizzy watched him approach Lady Harbisher, exchange a few words, and then he headed for the main doors and disappeared into the gallery. He was clearly leaving the party.

She had succeeded in establishing that he knew the woman Meg. And knew her well. But what did he mean when he said she was safe? Safe from what, or whom? And how had Pierre known she was in danger?

Justice Ingham, of middle years, soberly dressed and bewigged, with spectacles on his nose, looked less assured than Ottilia remembered, the gravity of his features showing both distress and impatience. Francis had set a chair for him mid-way between where she sat to one side of the fireplace, while at the other Sybilla occupied her customary cushioned easy chair with its winged high back.

"My fellows located the wayside inn where the travellers had stopped to bait. It seems the doings at The Holly Bush attracted attention enough to be of use to us."

"What doings, sir?" demanded Sybilla. "Scandalous, no doubt? Not that I wish to know. We have enough scandal on our hands as it is."

Ottilia caught her husband's eye where he stood propping up the mantelpiece in his customary fashion. He flicked a glance heavenwards but thankfully refrained from comment. She would much have preferred to see Ingham alone but there was no keeping her mother-in-law from the conference. Ottilia tried a soothing note.

"Yet it will be well to hear what Sir Thomas has discovered, do you not think?"

"Certainly, if it will induce you to send that wretched creature out of my house."

Justice Ingham coughed. "At this present, my lady, it behoves me to establish an identification and inform the dead man's family of his demise."

"His murder, you mean."

"That, my lady, is yet to be established. The body is with our appointed medical practitioner, who will carry out the necessary post-mortem."

"How long before you have the results?" Ottilia asked.

"A day or two, I expect. You know how these things go, ma'am, as I remember."

"Just so." Ottilia put her most pertinent question. "May we know if you have any inkling of the man's identity, sir? We found no card on his person, but were his effects still at the inn?"

"They were, but the landlord foolishly gathered everything up when his visitors did not reappear." Ingham pursed his lips. "One would think the fellow would have the sense to leave things as they were, especially as my runner found dried bloodstains on the carpet, the walls and the door. However, it seems the postilions, believing their fare to have absconded, went off with the hired chaise."

"Ah, we wondered about a vehicle." Francis glanced at Ottilia and back to Ingham. "You discovered where the chaise was hired, I expect."

"Grice took care to ask. I've sent him to make enquiries at The George in Southwark."

"Grice? Is that not the same fellow we dealt with before?"

"Yes, my lord, Benjamin Grice. One of my best men."

"The doings, man," came snappily from Sybilla. "What happened there?"

"I beg your pardon, my lady. I became distracted." He frowned, as if he gathered his thoughts and Ottilia was thankful Sybilla did not again interrupt. "So far as Grice was able to ascertain from various accounts, it appears there was some sort of quarrel. The woman was seen running out of a back door. According to a stable hand she was covered in blood, but one must make allowances for the exaggerations of country people."

"Not in this case," said Francis. "It's a fair description of what we saw."

"To where did she run? Not the road, I take it."

Ingham met Ottilia's eyes. "Where you found her? Apparently not. The inn is set away from the road and abuts a wooded area at the back. She ran in there. The man came out a moment or two later. Upon enquiry, the stable hand pointed him in that direction and he went after her. That was the last anyone saw of either."

There was a silence, though a myriad of questions leapt in Ottilia's head. Sybilla, her delicate brows raised, was first to react.

"This is all your doings, sir? Is there no more? It is precious little to go on."

Ingham sighed. "I am afraid that is true. However, we do have a few more details. Grice inspected the room."

Here Ottilia cut in. "They stopped to bait, you said. What room was this? A parlour?"

"No, no, a bedchamber. It was demanded by the man after they had eaten. He said his wife was in need of rest and he meant to take opportunity to wash and shave."

"Shave?" Francis's brows were flying. "In the middle of the day? Had he not done so in the morning before they set out?"

Ingham raised a hand. "Ah, now, there's a somewhat garbled story to that, but we hope to unravel it once the post boys have been questioned."

"Well?"

"According to one of the stable lads, the boys were complaining of the rough condition of their fare. He stank, either of drink or sweat and he looked as if he had not slept or had slept in his clothes. What we don't know is when he hired the chaise, whether or not the journey was premeditated. Nor where it was going."

Ottilia pursued the important issue. "What did your man Grice find in the bedchamber?"

"Very little beyond the bloodstains. The man's portmanteau had been there, and open, the landlord said. A clean shirt had been taken out but was unused. His discarded waistcoat was on the floor, along with a neck-cloth. The bed was still made, though its covers were ruffled as if it had been lain upon."

"What of his razor?" Ottilia asked, giving nothing away of her special knowledge, assuming Meg had spoken the truth. She recalled the state of the corpse. "He had shaved, had he not? His skin was smooth, I thought."

Ingham pursed his lips. "Grice found no razor."

"I dare say he remembered to look under the bed?"

"Naturally." Ingham's gaze became severe. "You are thinking it was the weapon used, Lady Francis."

She knew so, but did not wish at this juncture to tell him that. She had not mentioned it in her note. "It was not found at the scene?"

"No. A thorough search was made for any sort of weapon."

And not in the bedchamber either? If it remained lost, would that help or hinder Meg's case? Best to let it pass. To Ottilia's relief, Sybilla shifted the focus.

"What else had the landlord to say of the room? He does not seem to have known very much."

"Very little indeed, Lady Polbrook. I may say my runner only obtained the details we have by the most rigorous questioning. The landlord was voluble, it appears, but more in complaint at the mess in which his chamber had been left than in providing useful information. He was hot against his visitor for not paying him before he left."

"If he had the fellow's portmanteau there," said Francis, "I wonder he did not look for money inside it."

"He did, but the postilions, quite correctly, refused to allow any money to be taken from the purse the fellow found and insisted upon impounding the portmanteau in want of their own fare. I imagine the thing is now at The George, where I trust my runner will be able to obtain the fellow's name and take possession of the gentleman's effects."

"Did not anyone think to go in search of the truants?"

Ingham turned an exasperated gaze upon Ottilia. "No, curse the lot of them!" Then, evidently recollecting himself, he cleared his throat. "I beg your pardon, ladies. This affair is singularly irritating, not to say unsavoury."

Ottilia chased up another of the notions teeming in her head. "Was there not some case or other belonging to the woman? Or did the post boys take that too?"

"A valise. We have it safe." Perplexity showed in Ingham's frown. "Yet its contents are odd."

"How so?" asked Sybilla, intent. Was Ottilia's mother-in-law becoming intrigued after all?

"Grice went through it at the scene and I have done the same. He was right in thinking the clothing therein is all new, such as it was."

"Well, what was it?" demanded Sybilla with impatience.

Ingham coughed, his complexion taking on a ruddy hue. "Mostly undergarments, my lady, along with items of toiletry. There appeared to be only one gown."

Ottilia's mind was winging to the woman upstairs. "Also new?"

"I could not tell, ma'am, but it was of cheap muslin, bought ready made up, I imagine."

Ottilia drew a breath and slowly let it out. "Then it would appear Meg may have been abducted."

All three pairs of eyes became trained upon her: Sybilla's in shock, Francis in frowning question and Ingham in astonishment. He was the first to speak.

"Abducted? What makes you think so, ma'am?"

Ottilia counted on her fingers as she thought it through. "There was a violent altercation in the bedchamber. She ran away, bloodied. She made no mention of losing a valise. The man set out in a state of dishabille, yet he was to some extent prepared, with luggage of his own. Her belongings are new, which suggests someone else packed the valise."

"Who, the abductor?"

"Doubtful, Fan. It is far more likely he had a female accomplice. Or a servant might have done it for him."

"Done what?" Sybilla was looking bewildered.

"Purchased the necessary items and packed them."

"You are suggesting it was planned?"

"Planned and possibly connived at."

Ingham was leaning in, eager and interested. "What are you getting at, Lady Francis?"

Ottilia threw up a hand. "I fear I am getting ahead of myself. Of the facts."

"But what is in your mind?"

She met his gaze, aware that both her spouse and mother-in-law were equally intent. "I suspect there is a good deal more to this story than meets the eye. It is far from straightforward, I'm afraid, and the ramifications are likely to prove extensive."

Ingham sat back, looking decidedly dissatisfied. "That tells me nothing, ma'am."

Sybilla flung up her hands in an exasperated gesture. "This is typical. Why must you be so cryptic, Ottilia? Explain."

Ottilia glanced at her husband, who cocked an eyebrow.

"Well?"

No help there then. She set her hands in her lap, clasping them together. She raised her eyes to Ingham's again. "Forgive me for not saying this at once, Sir Thomas, but we think the victim may well be a man called Matthew Coveney. Lord Coveney, to be exact."

"A peer? You alarm me. What cause have you to think so?"

"It is a guess only, sir, based upon supposition. Meg made mention of a name: Pierre. We now know that a Frenchman, Pierre de Percheval, was distressed, having learned of the abduction or elopement of an English girl with, he evidently believes, this same Lord Coveney. It is hearsay, of course, but the coincidence cannot but lead one to make the connection."

Ingham blew out his cheeks. "Well, ma'am, as I am sure you are aware, I cannot act upon suppositions. I must pursue my enquiries in an orderly fashion." He rose. "And that, Lady Francis, is what I intend to do. May I now be permitted to talk to the female you have taken in charge?"

Her bodily ills were fading, yet those in her mind remained tortuous and unkind. Time held no meaning and Meg was hard put to it to work out how many days had passed, for the visions were all too present. Lady Fan's visits tried her fortitude, though she had succeeded in holding off further question. Easy to pretend to be worse than she was. But this invasion burst through all pretence to a hideous reality.

From the bed where she sat, dressed in a borrowed gown, she stared at the middle-aged man in dumb horror. Lady Fan had given a name but it failed to register, a corroding sense of betrayal entering in upon the instant she heard the introductory word. He was a justice? Then she was lost indeed. She glanced in reproach at the woman who had vowed to be her saviour.

"Pray don't be distressed, Meg. Justice Ingham merely wishes to ask you a few questions. He has no thought of taking you away at this time. Is that not so, Sir Thomas?"

The man gave a nod. There was no accompanying smile. But his voice, when he spoke, held no threat. "Do you mind if I sit, ma'am?"

"Take the maid's chair, sir," said Lady Fan, moving to the place where Rose had been stationed until turned out upon the entrance of the two.

Meg watched in rising trepidation as the magistrate picked up the chair and brought it closer and sat down. She shrank a little and Lady Fan came to perch beside her.

"Show him your hands, Meg."

They were freshly bandaged. Mute, she held them up to the man's gaze.

He cast a glance at Lady Fan. "I can hardly see through the gauze."

"I only meant for you to note that Meg is indeed injured herself. The cuts are healing."

"Cuts?"

Was there significance in his look? Meg's heart began to beat a little faster.

"That is why I asked about the razor, Sir Thomas."

A shiver shook Meg, drawing Lady Fan's attention. She took the hands Meg was still holding up and set them back in her lap.

"That will do, my dear. You need not be afraid, I promise you."

But she was. Deathly afraid. Retribution hovered in her sight in the person of this justice. The very word stung. Justice. Was it just, to be hounded thus? Was her fault deserving of this much punishment?

"Now then, ma'am. Or Meg, if I may?"

Her pulse pattering, she stared at the man, mumchance. What mattered it what he called her? He held her destiny in his hands.

"First things first. Can you give me the name of your companion, Meg?"

For an instant, she was bewildered. Venner? Or was it Rose? Then his meaning struck her and revulsion hit. "He was no companion of mine!" She caught her breath on the low-toned utterance. She had not meant to speak.

"His name, ma'am?"

"No." She would not soil her lips.

"You don't know it? Or you do not wish to tell me?"

"Neither."

The magistrate shot a look at Lady Fan in which Meg read exasperation. She gripped her hands together and hissed a breath at the sharp pain she caused, spreading them quickly.

"Take care, Meg!" Lady Fan captured her wrists. "Come, relax your fingers, my dear."

She curled them, aware of the quiver she could not control. Lady Fan set down her wrists and she was glad to let her hands rest in her lap where their trembling was not so obvious.

The magistrate cleared his throat and Meg looked up again. Was that a smile? It must be false. He meant to lull her before he pounced.

"Will you not help me, ma'am? You are the only witness to what happened at The Holly Bush and subsequently. Your account is needed."

Tell him all? Endure the shame and horror all over again? "I cannot."

"Or will not."

She looked away. Why did not Lady Fan speak? Had she told him what she let fall before? She had given away nothing since and Lady Fan had thankfully not asked.

"Can you tell me anything at all, Meg?"

There was gentleness in his voice now. As of instinct, Meg looked round at Lady Fan beside her, who smiled reassurance. Was it her doing? Meg's tongue loosened.

"Did you say? Did you tell?"

Her brows lifted. "I have told Sir Thomas only what I know from personal observation. Repeating what you told me will not serve. He cannot use my testimony as to the truth of what happened, you see. That would be mere hearsay. He must hear it from you directly. Do you understand at all, Meg?"

She understood that she must condemn herself out of her own mouth. Who would believe her innocent if she spoke of what she had done? Lady Fan said she had not killed him, but Lady Fan was not the justice. She gave a despairing sigh.

"What is the point? He is dead and I have no life."

"My dear young lady, you mistake," came from the magistrate. "I am not here to condemn you, but to discover the truth. I may say, you are but one avenue of the many I must explore. But you could, if you chose, make my task a deal simpler if you could bring yourself only to give me your version of events."

Meg looked him in the eye. "Is not silence the best defence?"

He actually laughed. Just as if the matter was not one of life and death.

"A fallacy, Meg. The less you say, the more you provoke an assumption of guilt."

"Guilt? Aye, you may accuse me, sir, for I am guilty." She hardly knew she spoke, the words tumbling from her writhing thoughts. "Guilty of foolishly trusting one I thought had my interests at heart. Guilty of believing in promises of fidelity only to be betrayed; believing in assurances of help, only to be beguiled into a slavery. Guilty of attempting to escape it, of fighting for my honour when my honour is already lost." She lifted her bandaged hands to hide her face, to hide the shame, her throat aching in the ensuing silence.

Presently the urge to rage her griefs subsided, the enforced habit of her miserable life returning. *Keep it down, keep it hidden. Show nothing, say less.* It was all she had left of pride and dignity, the latter eroded now almost beyond recall. Almost. If she was to die, condemned, let it be with a shred of who she was, had been once.

"Meg?"

Lady Fan's voice startled her out of her absorption. They were here still. The magistrate, silent in his chair, frowning. Meg looked from him to the woman beside her.

"You cannot save me. No one can."

A clear gaze held hers. "What of Pierre? Could not he save you?"

94

Her stomach clenched, her breath tightening. "How, when he began it? Do you think I would sue to him for succour? He has done damage enough."

"What did he do, Meg?"

She drew a sharp gasp. What had she said? She never meant to speak of it, of him. Despite all, she would bear the fruits alone.

"Nothing. I cannot say."

"Will not, you mean." The man was gruff, angry. He met her eyes, a look of sternness in his own. "My dear young lady, if you insist upon keeping your tongue in this foolish way, you will heap trouble upon yourself."

"More trouble than I am already in?"

She meant to indicate her mind's distresses, but he took it literally.

"Indubitably. At this present, I am bound to state that your prospects are poor. Figure to yourself, ma'am, how it appears to me." As if she did not know, but she kept her tongue on the hot words begging to be spilt. "Here I have a dead man on my hands, cut about across the chest, and you are the only witness. Your appearance, all over blood, has been corroborated by several people. What am I to think, Meg, if you will not speak up?"

A vision of the hangman's rope dangled in her head. Instinct threw her tongue into play and she struck at Lady Fan beside her.

"She said I did not kill him!"

She saw the lady flinch, but her gaze remained steady. The magistrate shifted forward as if he might intervene, but relaxed back as Lady Fan put out a staying hand and spoke.

"Yes, and I stand by it, Meg. I believe the qualified medical man who is examining the body will confirm it." She raised a finger as the magistrate lifted his head as if to speak and he closed his mouth again. "I know, Sir Thomas. You can take only his findings and Meg understands as much, do you not?"

The dam burst. "I understand nothing! I am dumb, debased, finished for all time. Do with me what you will, I care not." She held out her clenched hands, unheeding of the pain in her palms. "Tie me! Throw me in your cell, sir, and let me starve, if you will. What life have I left to be attempting to secure it? My life is nothing." She turned her hands, palm up in supplication. "Yet pity I must beg. Not for myself, sir, but for the life within me."

"She had not meant to speak of it," Ottilia said, as she led the way down the stairs.

Behind her, Ingham grunted. "To my mind, it came out too pat."

Halting on the landing, Ottilia turned to look at him. "You suspect a ploy? When she at once broke into hysterical weeping?"

Ingham's smile was wry. "I am bound to admit I have little faith in vapours. One of woman's wiles too often used for purpose."

Ottilia said no more, resuming her progress. Little point in argument if his experience had led him into such distrust. The revelation of the pregnancy was a shock, but there had to be something to account for the severity of Meg's self-condemnation. The implication that Pierre de Percheval was responsible for her condition was evident. Clearly there was a tale to be told, but she would not discover it from the woman while she was so distraught. Nor, she suspected, in the presence of Ingham, which had unsettled her too far to be of use. Ottilia was relieved when Meg's lamentations had brought

Venner scuttling into the room, all venom and scolding, but at least she at once took charge of the girl, crooning in between her admonitions to the visitors to be gone.

"There, there, lovey. No one will hurt you, dearie, not while I am here." And with a hateful look at Ottilia, "Leave her to me. I know how to do. Your presence only makes her worse. Go!" And then back to the weeping woman, clasping her thin arms about Meg where she had thrown herself onto the bed. "Poor thing, don't take on so. Come now, lovey, enough tears."

Ottilia had caught the justice's eye and jerked her head to the door. He moved to it with alacrity and she followed him out, a hint of mischief in her head as she saw how he took out a handkerchief and wiped his brow. But she held her tongue on the urge to tease.

Back in the parlour Sybilla became predictably infuriated at the fresh news.

"A fallen woman? It needed only that. And Gipping has just confessed to it that the servants have been talking. It will be all over town in a trice."

Which there was no denying. Ottilia sought her spouse's eye and he grimaced expressively. But he managed to turn the subject, addressing Ingham.

"Did you discover anything else of use?"

Ingham looked sour. "The woman's as close as an oyster. Except for this new turn, which conveniently obliges me to leave the subject in your custody for the present, Lady Francis."

"Custody? My house is not a gaol, sir."

"Indeed not, Lady Polbrook. Forgive me. An unfortunate slip of the tongue."

"As unfortunate as the slip on the side someone has planted in the girl," pronounced Sybilla in an acid tone, making no apology for the crudity of the utterance. "And if it is this Pierre, I will soon send him to the rightabout, daring to sniff around my granddaughter."

Ottilia thought it prudent to intervene. "My dear ma'am, there is as yet no proof of anything. We only have Meg's word for it that she is indeed enceinte, and I cannot suppose Sir Thomas will accept it without a doctor's examination."

Ingham gave a gloomy nod. "Very true. It behoves me to make certain on legal grounds, as I am sure you are aware." No one spoke the dark thought in Ottilia's mind, but she was sure it was present for all. "I shall send in our Doctor Rickward. He has a soothing way with him which, after the exhibition we have just witnessed, may well be needed."

Ottilia received a questioning glance from her husband. "Exhibition?"

Before she could answer, Ingham's dry tones sounded. "We were treated to a fit of the vapours, sir." He cleared his throat. "Your lady wife and I differ on the point."

Francis cocked an eyebrow and Ottilia had perforce to speak. "I thought it was genuine distress, but Sir Thomas has his doubts."

Sybilla snorted again and Ingham rubbed his hands together. "Well, well, ma'am, we shall see in due time which of us is right. But I have done all I can here and must take my leave."

Ottilia was grateful to her spouse for his immediate and urgent demand.

"You will keep us informed, I trust? If my mother is to continue to house this woman, we are nearly concerned."

Sybilla threw a look both surprised and gratified at her son as Ingham pursed his lips.

"I shall do so, of course, my lord, but it may be several days before I can return. However, I will despatch a note if there is anything pertinent." He made his bow to the dowager. "My lady, your servant." And then he turned to Ottilia. "I hope, Lady Francis, I may expect the same courtesy should you manage to discover more?"

She opened her eyes at him. "From Meg? But you cannot take my repetition of anything she may say."

His expression showed scepticism. "I am not so naïve as to suppose you will not be pursuing enquiries of your own, ma'am."

She laughed out. "Dear me, am I so obvious?"

"Oh, I have your measure, Lady Francis. I may say I am hopeful of, though not perhaps reliant upon, your unorthodox methods."

"Count upon it." Sybilla's black eyes snapped at Ottilia. "She will beat you to the post, man, despite my prohibition and dislike."

To Ottilia's relief, Francis hastened to usher Justice Ingham to the door and chose to escort him downstairs. She crossed to the bell-pull, avoiding Sybilla's gaze.

"Coffee! I am gasping."

"You need not try to escape me, my girl. Sit, and answer me. What do you mean to do?"

Ottilia moved to take the chair opposite and essayed a smile. "Are you going to snap my nose off if I tell you?"

She received a glare in return for a moment. And then the fire died out of Sybilla's eyes and she sighed, relaxing into her chair. "That wretched boy of mine has turned me into a crotchety old woman."

"Randal?" Ottilia eyed her mother-in-law, noticing for the first time how she had aged, the few lines she had etched more deeply into her parchment skin. "My poor Sybilla. I don't think any of us have truly understood how you have suffered."

Sybilla gave one of her dismissive gestures. "Don't start pitying me, for the Lord's sake, Ottilia! You'll send me into a fit of the dismals."

Ottilia gurgled with mirth. "What do you wish, Sybilla? Shall I say something to send you back up into the boughs? I have been telling Francis how much he resembles you in that."

This brought her mother-in-law's head up. "In temperament? Poppycock. Francis is far more even-tempered than I."

"Because he keeps his temper when you are losing yours? I assure you, he is quite as apt to go off like a rocket."

A wry smile creased Sybilla's mouth. "Is he so? He was used to as a boy, I remember, but so rarely I have forgot it. Compared to Randal's roaring temper tantrums, Francis was a saint, let me tell you. And Harriet gave her fair share to her nurses. Never with me. I nipped that in the bud at the first attempt." She sighed heavily. "She's a good girl, if a trifle empty-headed. To be truthful, it is only Randal who has caused me grief. I could forgive all, if he had ever shown the slightest remorse or pity for Emily's horrific end. But he never has, Ottilia. Not a shred. And he took instant advantage of her removal. It pains me to think any child of my loins should be so lost to all common decency and feeling."

She ceased speaking, setting a hand to her brow in the way she had when distress got the better of her. Ottilia would have spoken but for the entrance of Alice in answer to the bell.

"Coffee, Alice, if you please. Or would you prefer tea, Sybilla?" A flick of the finger was all the answer she received. Ottilia smiled at the maid. "Coffee then, thank you."

"Yes, my lady." Alice cast a worried look at her mistress and hurried to the door where she almost ran into Francis, about to enter. "Beg pardon, my lord."

"No matter, Alice." He stood aside to let her go and came into the parlour, shutting the door behind him.

Ottilia signalled with her eyes and saw his brows snap together. He lifted them in question and Ottilia gave a tiny shake of her head. "Alice is bringing coffee, dearest. Sybilla and I were just wondering what I should do next."

She saw with satisfaction that her mother-in-law opened her eyes and straightened. With an effort, Ottilia thought, and her features were still taut and paler than usual.

Francis, taking her lead, brought up a chair and placed it near his mother's. "Perhaps I may be of assistance. I was saying to Ingham that we'd had a thought of tracing Coveney's boon companions."

"An excellent notion, Fan. He has learned of a coterie of gamesters, Sybilla, which included Lord Coveney."

She was careful to leave out the source of her husband's information, not wishing to reintroduce her elder son's name into the discussion. Nor was it politic to mention Pierre de Percheval at this juncture. Sybilla's dismay was too raw.

She was visibly recovering, a tiny frown creeping in between her thin arched brows. "You hold by your view that the dead man is Coveney then?"

"We shall know soon enough, assuming Sir Thomas sees fit to inform us once he discovers the identity of the man who hired the chaise."

Sybilla slapped the arm of her chair. "Well, if you must pursue this business, I wish you will consult Jardine. I loathe the man, but he may at least advise you."

Gratified to find her mother-in-law willing to allow the pursuit of her enquiries, she agreed with alacrity to bringing in the family's man of business. "An excellent notion, Sybilla. I will write to him directly."

"Ask him to come here. At least he may clarify the legal ramifications. Which may, though I doubt it, save you going off half-cocked on some useless exploration that can only hinder your hopes."

This was said with enough acidity to cause a lift of the brows in Francis, to which Ottilia returned a faint smile. She turned the subject. "Have you any knowledge of Coveney, ma'am?"

Sybilla shrugged, clearly still affected by the earlier distress. "Only by repute. According to Harriet, who has had occasion to hint him away from Candia, she says, he is a poor prospect for a husband. He has buried one wife and is thought to be looking for a stepmother for his children. Though by my daughter's account he has precious little to leave his son. His estates are said to be grossly encumbered."

"Which tallies with our information that he is a hardened gamester," said Francis, looking to Ottilia for agreement, she thought.

"It is certainly interesting. Assuming he is our corpse, it provides in some sort a possible motive for his carrying Meg off."

Francis was wearing his sceptical look. "What, to make a wife of damaged goods?"

"And give his name to another man's child?" Sybilla's tone was rife with distaste. "This is not worthy of you, my dear. Where have your wits gone begging?"

Ottilia tutted. "I am thinking rather that he might have looked for a mother for his children. Meg did say she was sold into a sort of slavery. We know he meant to make her his mistress, and even if he knew nothing of the pregnancy at the time, that would provide an even stronger lever to keep her under his rule. If he kept her immured at his estates, he might bully her into doing whatever he wished."

Sybilla remained sceptical. "And marry her into the bargain?"

"He might, since you aver he is unlikely to find a female willing to marry him amongst his acquaintance."

"Don't you believe it. There are females so desperate to marry for the chance of having their own establishment, they will take anyone."

Francis emitted a dissatisfied grunt. "It is pointless to speculate. Until we know the dead man is indeed Coveney, there is nothing to be done."

Ottilia regarded him in a little dismay. "But you will not wait for that before seeking out these gamesters, Fan?"

He reassured her and the entrance at that moment of Alice with the welcome sight of the accoutrements for coffee on a tray put an end to the discussion. But Ottilia found her mind shifting to the urge to discover the part played in all this by Pierre de Percheval. He was acquainted both with Meg and Coveney. It could not be coincidence.

Chapter Eight

"He was definitely rattled, Aunt Ottilia, that I can vouch for," Lady Elizabeth reported.

She had come to Bruton Street on foot, accompanied, as she assured her aunt, by her maid. Excusing herself from an excursion to Hatchards on the score of not yet having finished the novel she had borrowed from the circulating library, she had set out the moment her mother and Candia left the house.

Her only worry was the question of how to see Aunt Ottilia alone, and she beguiled the walk from Dalesford House in thinking up excuses to dispense with her grandmother's company. In the event, the elder lady was out visiting and Ottilia was found to be alone in the parlour, engaged in writing at a small bureau. She left off this work at once, greeting Lizzy with an eagerness which could not but gratify her, and drawing her to the sofa set against the wall as she professed herself anxious to know how she had fared.

"Was it the fact we have Meg here in the house that rattled him?"

"No, indeed, it was my mentioning the name. I am sure he paled, and he forgot his English, which seemed to me a sure sign of agitation."

"Oh, well spotted, Lizzy." Ottilia's clear gaze showed both amusement and mischief. "We will make an investigator of you yet."

Lizzy had to laugh. "Well, I did my best, though I upset poor Candia by mentioning your having solved her mama's murder."

"Dear me, yes. The child is as sensitive upon that issue as her brother, I'm afraid. I hope you have made your peace with her?"

Lizzy waved an airy hand. "Oh, yes. Candia never holds grudges. She forgave me freely. Which, I may say, is a good thing or I might have been hard put to it to withhold our suspicions of Pierre."

Ottilia looked at her hands, seeming to examine them in an intent fashion that puzzled Lizzy. A little concerned, she ventured to probe. "Are you thinking I ought indeed to speak to Candia?"

Ottilia turned and it struck Lizzy how warm a smile she had.

"I was wondering rather if I have a right to involve you further."

Dismay invaded Lizzy's breast. "You don't mean to exclude me? Oh, Aunt Ottilia, no! Am I not a useful conspirator?"

"Very much so, but I fear Harriet will blame me, and not without reason, if this should cause you any trouble or difficulty. It can be a dangerous game, my dear."

Lizzy's heart sank. "You think I am too frivolous to take it seriously, is that it?"

Ottilia put out a hand. "No, no, my child, not at all. I am the last person to urge seriousness. My besetting sin is to be merry at the most inappropriate moments." She took Lizzy's hand in a comfortable clasp. "The truth is, murderers are desperate people. Worse, those involved around them often lose what common sense they possess in the face of such doings. We do not know how far Pierre is involved, although we have reason to suspect him to be fairly entrenched in the business, and —"

"Oh, I am certain he is," Lizzy interrupted, releasing herself and turning to face her aunt. "He pressed me on the name, you must know, and became quite harsh. Then, when I satisfied him that I had indeed said Meg, he gave such a sigh. I remember his exact words too."

"What did he say?"

"Safe. *Grace à Dieu*. And then he said farewell in a brusque fashion and left the party at once." Ottilia's attention had held upon her, much to Lizzy's satisfaction, but she did not speak. Lizzy became impatient. "Well? Do you not find it significant, ma'am?"

A tiny smile flitted across Ottilia's mouth. "Very much so. It confirms the rest."

"The rest?" Lizzy eyed the closed look that came over Ottilia's countenance. "You do not mean to tell me, do you?"

Ottilia's look became rueful. "Your grandmama will have my head if I do. Not to mention Harriet."

Disappointment gnawed in Lizzy's breast. "Must they find out?"

Ottilia emitted a snort worthy of Lizzy's grandmother herself. "If you suppose Sybilla will not discover I have involved you, Lizzy, you do not know her."

"She won't think of me at all. She is altogether concentrated on Candia, and thank heaven for it."

Ottilia laughed. "Very well, I will bring you up to date. But you must promise me not to act upon your own, nor to approach Pierre without being in company."

"I am unlikely to meet him out of it, ma'am. But why? Do you truly think him dangerous?"

"Not precisely. But he may be in a volatile state of mind, and you have said he was harsh and brusque towards you even on this little provocation. I charge you, do not run any risks."

Too eager to hear what Ottilia had to tell her, Lizzy gave the required promise without a thought to the consequence. "In any event, ma'am, it is in the highest degree unlikely I should meet him anywhere except in company."

The tale Ottilia then unfolded proved a deal more shocking than she was prepared for and Lizzy could not refrain from bursting out. "He seduced this Meg? Heavens above! Ought we not to tell Candia what sort of a man he is?"

"Don't you say a word to her, Lizzy. And pray don't run away with the idea Pierre is wholly to blame. It takes two, you know."

"Yes, but he —"

"Lizzy, you will never make a successful investigator if you are ready to condemn anyone without examining both sides to a story. Remember, such evidence as we gather may be used to send a guilty person to their death. Never take anything for granted. Always look down every possible avenue before coming to a definite conclusion, even if your instinct is begging you to do so."

Abashed, Lizzy sobered. Her mind ran over the various facts she had been told and questions began to arise. "How will you discover what really happened, if Meg will not tell you?"

"Piece by piece. And with judicious enquiry. In the first place, her claim of pregnancy has been confirmed by Bow Street's doctor, who came here to examine her earlier today."

"You thought she might have lied?"

"No, my dear. But she might have been mistaken. In any event, it was vital to know it for the truth. Further," continued Ottilia, "Francis is seeing what he may discover about this coterie of gamesters. He has gone to Brooks's for the purpose."

Intrigued, Lizzy eyed Ottilia with hope building. "What can I do? Must I sit tight? It is too dreary if I must."

"I should doubt very much if you will be permitted to sit tight, my dear. When Pierre recovers his sangfroid, I am fairly certain he will seek you out to ferret out further information, if he can."

"Do you think so indeed? But you said I should not approach him."

"In company, I said. But I doubt you will need to. He will approach you."

"How can you be sure? And what shall I say to him if he does? How much can I tell him?"

Ottilia looked amused again. "I can be sure because of what you told me of his reaction. He won't be able to resist and he won't ask Candia. You are the one who has information."

Delighted, Lizzy beamed. "Capital. Tell me just what I may reveal, if you please."

Luck favoured Lord Francis almost immediately upon his entrance into the gentlemen's club he preferred to frequent. Strolling into the drawing room he greeted a number of acquaintances and then caught sight of Emile Lezayre. The Frenchman was parked in one of the long leather sofas set in front of the two large bookcases either side of the fireplace, in apparent earnest discussion with a slim young fellow of startlingly good looks, seated beside him. Francis could not avoid the cynical thought that the sleek countenance with its womanish lips and polished hair was just the kind to appeal to young girls, assuming this was Pierre in person. Small wonder Candia was *épris*.

As for Lezayre, the man looked to be more dissipated than he had been when he tried his tricks on Francis years ago. Even in profile, the thickened jowls were florid, the chin pendulous, and a protruding belly spoke of indulgence in the flesh pots. Lezayre adhered to his old-fashioned wig and a frock more suited to an earlier style. The contrast between the two was marked, and Francis noted a suppressed air of agitation in the younger man as he moved within earshot, taking advantage of the pile of daily journals left out on the central table for the perusal of interested patrons. He picked up *The Times* and pretended to read, tuning his ears to the conversation being conducted in rapid French. He was not as fluent as Randal, but he understood enough to grasp at once that the subject under discussion was precisely the one he would have chosen.

"But are you certain it is she, *mon cher*? Moreover, if Mattheu took her, as you believe, why should she be here and in the house of such a one as the dowager marquise?"

Mattheu? Matthew Coveney? Then Violette's information was correct.

The young man shrugged. "This I cannot tell. Milady Elizabeth spoke of an adventure concerning this aunt. I forget the name. Milady Fan?"

Francis triumphed, though he bristled on hearing his wife's nickname on this brash young fellow's lips.

"I do not know the name," said Lezayre. "But if she is of the family of the marquise, you may enquire of Violette."

The other visibly shuddered. "I dare not. To speak more of Mademoiselle Pargeter to the wife of the marquis may ruin all."

Now who the deuce was Miss Pargeter? Was it the girl Meg's surname?

Lezayre was softly laughing. "You are too ambitious, Pierre. I know Lord Polbrook. Marry his mistress he might. Allow his daughter to wed an impoverished *émigré*? Never. They are proud, these English. As arrogant as our own aristocrats when it comes to lineage."

Francis was glad to think the fellow realised the hopelessness of the boy's case if he aimed for Candia's hand. But Pierre's agitation increased.

"I am not now concerned with this, Emile, but only with what can have occurred. Figure to yourself what it may mean when Milady Elizabeth speaks of this Milady Fan who, she says, falls into these things and did so en route and thus she has Meg in the house."

Lezayre looked unimpressed. "What does it mean?"

"Emile, she involves herself in murders."

A bark of a laugh escaped Lezayre. "You would say she is a murderess this female?"

"*Non*! She finds out the murderer. She it was who found the murderer of the first marquise."

This silenced Lezayre. So much so, Francis essayed a quick glance. The man seemed dazed. At length he spoke, slowly, as if he thought it through.

"Is it that you believe our friend may be dead? *C'est pas possible.*"

"You think not? Then why is Marguerite in that house?"

Lezayre spread his hands. "You jump to conclusions, *mon ami*. To me it seems the simplest explanation is that she ran away from Mattheu."

"Perhaps, yes. But more, how did he discover her? I have searched in the streets, in the inns all around since I discovered her absence from her home. But for days, and to no avail. He told you nothing more?"

"He was drunk as usual. He spoke only of Marguerite. I would not have thought more of it did I not know you call your friend by this name. That gave me to think, *tu sais*."

Pierre banged his fists on his knees. "That devil! He meant to make you think it. He sought to punish me. How could he find her?"

"This I cannot tell you. Only that he triumphed, he said, and the woman would be his within the day. As I told you, he spoke of taking her to his estate, with what purpose it is not difficult to imagine."

Francis caught a flash from the young man's eyes. Of fury? Jealousy? Either would be unsurprising if, as appeared likely, Pierre had himself had amatory dealings with Meg. His mind presented him with the inevitable consequence of such a liaison. Had the family expelled their fallen daughter? Or had she run away? In either case, it appeared her lover had searched for her in vain, while his rival somehow found her. And used her. A tool for revenge, as the boy supposed?

The pair had been silent for several minutes. A quick glance showed boredom in Lezayre's face. So much for sympathy. Pierre then gave a heavy sigh.

"What comes to her now?"

"That, *mon cher ami*, is no longer your concern. If she is in the hands of the Polbrook ménage, you will do well to keep out of it."

Typical of the man, heartless as he was, thought Francis with a surge of savagery, recalling how Lezayre operated for his own ends upon susceptible youths without compunction. That he was greased in the fist by proprietors for introducing young men into disreputable gaming houses was out of doubt. Though he could not have hoped for such from Pierre. Was it a kindly impulse to take the boy up? Or had he some other end in view?

"I cannot," came from Pierre in a tone of suppressed passion. "Until I learn what befell her."

"And then you will abandon her again?"

The young man groaned, bringing clenched fists to his head.

Lezayre uttered a mirthless laugh. "You will, if you are wise, remain aloof. Your path is set. Involve yourself no more."

Pierre shook his head with violence. "And leave her to a fate unknown? Such villainy I cannot contemplate. I must find out more. I will ask of Milady Elizabeth."

This further reference to his niece threw question into Francis's head. Was this Ottilia's doing? What the deuce was she about to be bringing Lizzy into the business?

At this point, Lezayre, happening to turn his head, uttered an exclamation. "*Parbleu*! Fanshawe?" He switched to English, rising from his seat. "Is it indeed you? *Alors*, milord, I delight in renewing our acquaintance."

He gave a ponderous bow. Francis, laying down the journal he had all the time been holding, perforce bent his body in return, reflecting that the fellow's effrontery and sangfroid were as present and polished as ever.

"How do you do, Lezayre?"

All smiles, despite a wary look in his eye, the fellow threw up a hand in an airy gesture, his attitude changed from the cynical mentor of a moment ago. "As you see me, sir, as you see me. The years take their toll, alas. And you, milord? You have yourself a wife again now, I hear."

Was this to warn the younger man? Francis could not but wonder if Lezayre suspected he had been eavesdropping.

"I do indeed. A treasure whom I cannot value too highly."

"Ah, the delights of matrimony. Never mine, alas." He turned on the word to the boy, who had risen. "I may I hope present to you my countryman and friend, le Chevalier de Percheval. Milord Francis Fanshawe, Pierre, the brother to the Marquis de Polbrook."

Reading both dismay and alarm in the young man's face as he bowed, Francis gave a nod and a faint smile. "I have heard of you, *monsieur*."

The alarm increased and Pierre's laugh was self-conscious. "Ah, indeed, milord?"

"I understand Lady Polbrook is a friend to you."

Pierre, to his credit, managed to look sincere as he clasped a hand to his bosom. "*La belle* Violette! To say truth, milord, she honours me greatly. I confess I am unworthy of her notice."

Tempted to agree in no uncertain terms, Francis merely smiled instead. If this was the sort of unctuous flattery the boy employed, he could only wonder at Candia's naivety to be unable to see past it.

Lezayre took back the mantle of the conversation. "But what do you in the capital, *m'sieur*? It has not been our pleasure to see you here for an age."

"My wife prefers a quieter milieu, sir, but on this occasion we are visiting my mother, whose interest lies with the debut and futures of her two granddaughters." He threw a glance at Pierre as he spoke and was glad to note a red tinge creep into his cheeks. He trusted the warning was implicit, but he drove it home. "The dowager's command of her family is absolute, you must know. She can be a fierce advocate on behalf of individual members."

"Ah, the dowager marquise. One cannot but have great respect for such a woman." Lezayre's lips curved in a smile that did not reach his eyes, which instead sought his youthful companion's gaze in a pointed look. He had as well have said 'I told you so'.

But the young man beside him was eyeing Francis in a manner he could only regard as both speculative and anxious.

He lifted his brows in mute question. The fellow flushed again, but his brows drew together.

"Milord, if I may ask you —"

"*Fais attention*, Pierre!"

The warning note came from Lezayre, low and urgent. The boy paid no heed.

"I have learned, milord, from Milady Elizabeth, of … of, one would say, an adventure upon your journey here, is it not so?"

Francis was moved to a touch of compassion at the underlying anxiety he detected beneath the apparent casual approach. He quashed it, mindful of Ottilia's reading of the fellow's callous conduct towards the woman Meg. But the opportunity was not to be dismissed.

"You've heard that, have you? My niece is a deal too loose tongued, I fear. It is not a tale lightly to be touted around the town. Especially in such a place as this, where listening ears may be expected."

He hoped his message was understood and noted Lezayre at least had taken it in the brief widening of his eyes. But Pierre appeared too intent.

"Pray do not blame Milady Elizabeth, milord. She was in a way to praise your good lady wife. It is that Milady Francis has given succour to an unfortunate, is it not?"

Debating for a moment, Francis wondered how to tackle this. Tillie would take it head on, would she not? He chose caution. "In some sort. I may say there was little choice. The woman was standing in the middle of the road. My coachman was obliged to stop."

The look of enquiry in Pierre's eyes was almost painful. "She was … she was lost perhaps?"

Francis glanced from him to Lezayre, who was frowning now, but rather at the boy than at himself. He fired his cannon. "She was in a stupor, sir, and covered in blood."

Horror leapt in the boy's eyes and his cheeks, before red, now blanched. "*Sacré*! Injured! *Espèce de diable*! He has hurt her, this devil."

"Pierre, hold your tongue!"

But the boy waved a hand with some violence, his gaze trained on Francis. "Speak, *m'sieur, je vous en prie*. It is bad? And where is he? I swear this time there will be no mercy."

Lezayre seized him by the shoulder, hustling him to one side and speaking in French, rapid and urgent. Francis held his ground, unable to decide whether to mention the dead man or not. It would seem there had indeed been a fight. But how much was it politic to reveal? Until they had a positive identification, it was still conjecture that the body was Coveney.

Pierre's voice rose a trifle, enough to attract attention from a couple of other patrons of Brooks's standing a little way off, who both turned their heads. Francis debated the wisdom of remaining, since an altercation must ensure the matter became public property. On balance, it mattered less than discovering what he could. And then the boy shook off Lezayre's restraining hand and strode swiftly back to Francis.

"*M'sieur*, relieve me, I beg, of an agony too great to be borne." He spoke low, his tone earnest with an edge of hostility. No trace now of the earlier polish. "The woman, she is hurt? How? It is bad, no?"

Francis cast a quick glance behind. The interested men appeared to have resumed their interrupted conversation. He kept his own voice at a level to remain unheard beyond the immediate circle as Lezayre moved back to join them, looking resigned.

"She has cuts on her hands and a few bruises only." He heard the breath sigh out of Pierre and saw the tautness lessen at his jaw. *Relief? Not so easily, my fine young friend.* "I cannot, however, say as much for her state of mind."

He was conscious of satisfaction as consternation crept into the Frenchman's eyes. "*Alors*, you would say she is … how, milord?"

Francis glanced at Lezayre, who appeared thoroughly discontented, and back to Pierre. "You will have to give me reason to confide in you, sir. What is your interest in this woman?"

Lezayre threw up his hands. "Ah, *c'est ça!* Have I not said so, *mon cher?*" He pushed past to confront Francis. "Heed him not, I beg, milord. He has an idea in his head that the woman you have there is the same as one he knows. Who can tell if this is so?"

"It is so! Who else, Emile? This Meg is Marguerite, I know it. This devil Coveney shall answer to me, *je jure devant dieu!*"

Francis hesitated no longer. "If Coveney is the man Meg was with, sir, he will answer only to his Maker. He is dead."

This time not only Pierre whitened, his eyes registering shock. Lezayre's jowly features paled too, dismay entering his face. It was he who first found his tongue.

"Dead how?"

"Killed, sir. Murdered. And this Meg of yours is the only witness."

Pierre de Percheval fell back, a groan of despair escaping his lips.

"Pierre! Pierre, *écoutes!*"

116

Pierre looked up into Francis's face. "Milord, do you permit that I visit the unfortunate you have in your care?"

"Pierre, are you mad?" Lezayre burst in.

"For what reason, sir?" Francis asked, unsure.

"If this Meg is indeed Marguerite…"

"You wish to verify the fact?"

"It is, I believe, *sans doute, m'sieur.*"

Francis looked to Lezayre and then returned his gaze to Pierre, who squirmed at the condemnation he read there. "I cannot sanction such a visit without consulting with my wife. Nor, I may add, without first asking Meg if she wishes to see you."

"Ah, no, she will see me first in hell!"

"*Mon ami*, if you go this road," Lezayre added, "I wash my hands of you."

"I fear you will find that impossible, Lezayre," said Francis. "If our corpse proves to be Coveney, and if a supposition of my wife's as to the cause of his death proves accurate, you will both of you be required to give an account of yourselves to Justice Ingham of Bow Street."

Pierre stared at him. Lezayre cut in, savagery in his tone. "To what end, milord Francis? *Quoi*, is it that you accuse me? That man is nothing to me."

"He is your gaming companion, sir. Or one of them."

"*Alors*, is one to answer to Bow Street merely on account of playing cards with a fellow? You can say this of *tout le monde, m'sieur*! In this case, a procession veritable goes to make answer to such question."

"I think not, Lezayre. You, Aldreth, Redlingfield and young de Percheval here will, I trust, suffice. You are all known to be gambling cronies together. Unless you can add to that particular list?"

Lezayre appeared infuriated. "Do you say you have passed our names to this justice of whom you speak?"

"Not so far, sir. Until we know for certain the dead man is indeed Matthew Coveney, there was no necessity to bring your names into the equation."

Lezayre visibly relaxed, letting out a relieved sigh. "You have alarmed me without need, Milord Francis."

Francis cocked an eyebrow. "Indeed? And here I had thought you might be willing to go along with me to see the body."

"See the body," repeated Lezayre in horrified accents, recoiling. "*Ma foi*, what next will you say?"

"You would not then care to assist the authorities? You know the man well after all."

"I to go to Bow Street? Not in this world, *m'sieur*, not in this world." He then turned from them and marched away, thrusting through a group of men that had gathered a little way off. Pierre rose to confront Lord Francis.

"I will go with you, milord."

Francis had also been watching the exit, but he turned his dark gaze on Pierre. "To Bow Street?"

"First, yes. Then, if it please you, to the house of the dowager marquise."

"If, I presume, you are able to make a positive identification."

"*C'est exacte.* If Coveney it is, then I know she is Marguerite and I must see her, whether she will or no."

The bustle in the Bow Street office was a deal more disorientating than the other evening when Francis came to report the body. A ragged looking man was standing in the dock, in process of being interrogated by a magistrate in the open court on the dais, while in the public area below the iron railings that closed it off, several loungers waiting to be seen rubbed shoulders with clerks, vociferous complainers and officials of the court.

Francis pushed through to a fellow at a desk, who was writing in a ledger, and asked for Justice Ingham.

"Wait," was all the reply he got, the clerkly official not even troubling to raise his head.

Bristling, Francis rapped the table to get his attention. The man looked up and his face changed as he took in the condition of the visitor. Francis repeated his request, taking a lofty tone.

"Kindly inform Justice Ingham that Lord Francis Fanshawe is here to see him."

The man rose with alacrity. "Beg pardon, sir. It's busy as bedamned in here. The boy will show you the way." He called over to one of the loungers, a lad who was leaning by an inner door. "Here, Joe!"

The boy straightened and came across, touching his forelock. "Yessir."

"Take his lordship up to Sir Thomas."

Francis nodded to Pierre to stay close and followed the boy Joe through a rabbit warren of corridors, up a narrow staircase to the first floor where their guide knocked on the first of three doors and entered at a call from within.

"Come."

The boy opened the door and Francis walked into an office crowded with bookcases, two desks and piled boxes of beribboned files. At a desk at the side a clerk was seated, head bent over papers, and at the other Sir Thomas Ingham sat, engaged in conversation with a burly individual of stolid aspect who stood in front of the desk.

Ingham rose. "Lord Francis! What brings you here? Do you have news for me?" He came out from behind the desk as he spoke, glancing curiously at Francis's companion.

"This is the Chevalier de Percheval, Sir Thomas. It is possible he can identify the body."

Ingham's keen glance examined Pierre from under a frowning brow. "Indeed? How so?"

Pierre executed a small bow. "I have acquaintance with Lord Coveney, *m'sieur.*"

Ingham's frown intensified. "You do, do you? What makes you suppose he may be the dead man, sir?"

Francis would have answered for him, but the words held an undertone of menace and he caught a glance from Ingham that gave him pause. Was it meant for a warning? Had Ingham uncovered the information he hoped for from the postilions?

Pierre's poise deserted him. "*Alors*, why is it you ask of me in such a fashion? I have come in willingness, *m'sieur*, at the desire of Milord Francis."

Ingham's features cleared into his customary look of urbanity. "Ah, indeed. Very public spirited of you, Chevalier. Nevertheless, I would appreciate an answer. Have you any reason to suppose the dead man to be your friend Coveney?"

Pierre curled his lip. "He is no friend of mine, *m'sieur.*"

"Acquaintance then. Come, sir, it will be best for you to be direct with me."

So far from complying, the Frenchman gripped his lips together, his dark eyes fairly glaring. He cast a look at Francis in which reproach mingled with suspicion. Recalling his wife's methods, Francis essayed a soft approach. "My dear de Percheval, there is no necessity to be reticent. Sir Thomas is a fair man. He will not jump to conclusions."

Ingham harrumphed. "Quite right, sir. I must gather what evidence I may."

Pierre looked decidedly dissatisfied. He glanced at the other occupants of the room. "Before these? You wish me to speak of these things in so public a fashion?"

Ingham gave a resigned sigh and signed dismissal to the burly man and his clerk, who set down his pen, rose and followed the other out of the room. Ingham set a couple of chairs before the desk.

"Pray be seated, Chevalier. And you, my lord, if you will."

But the Frenchman stood his ground. "Do you not desire that I look at this man? It is not your wish to find if he is my acquaintance? It is for this I came, *m'sieur*."

"Presently." As he again invited the visitors, with a gesture, to be seated, Justice Ingham managed a smile which looked spurious to Francis. Something was up, but what?

Pierre hesitated, and then moved to take the indicated chair. Francis sat down on the other, which had been set at an angle that afforded him a view of his companion's profile. Was it intentional? He watched Ingham walk around the desk and retake his own seat, setting his elbows on the desk and leaning a little toward the Frenchman.

"Now, Chevalier, let us be frank. I have reason to believe the corpse I have on my hands is indeed that of Lord Coveney. Yet how came you to think it was he?"

Still the young man held back. Francis regarded him covertly. His pose was rigid, his jawline tight. Was this reticence a form of outrage? Or just plain fear? Francis recalled his earlier warning. Had the fellow taken fright because of it?

"I am waiting, Chevalier." Ingham, at his blandest.

In one violent movement, Pierre sprang up. "*Alors*, you wait in vain, *m'sieur*!" Before either man could act, he flung over to the door, wrenched it open and was gone.

Francis was already up and after him when Ingham called out.

"Let him go, my lord!"

In the doorway, Francis watched the Frenchman disappear into the well of the staircase. The deuce. He had lost his advantage. One could scarcely chase the man down without raising a stir. He turned back into the room.

"My apologies, Sir Thomas. I had hoped to resolve this quickly."

Ingham had also risen and came to join him at the door. "No matter, my lord." He raised his voice. "Benjamin!"

A clatter of feet on the stairs produced the burly fellow who had been with Ingham at the start of the interview. "Blow me, sir," he said to his superior, "he went orf like a bat out of hell. Nearly knocked me orf my feet he did."

He spoke with a flat stolidity that poked at a long-buried memory. Francis stared at the fellow's square features and a hasty exclamation escaped him.

"Benjamin Grice! Now I remember you."

A grim smile creased the man's lips, his peculiarly fixed stare settling on Francis. "I'll be bound you do, me lord. A fair business was that. All of two years gone, I'd say."

"More." The reminder of the investigation into the late marchioness's murder, in which the Bow Street runner played some part, could not but rattle him for a moment. The only aspect of that hideous time he could view with complacency was its delivery into his arms of his darling wife.

He was snapped back to the present by Ingham, inviting him to be seated. "For I have much to tell you, my lord."

"Ah, have you? I thought as much. You've discovered the dead man is indeed Matthew Coveney?"

Ingham beckoned Grice over. "Tell his lordship what you found out."

The runner came to the desk as Francis and Ingham sat down. He was again wearing his official face, one that gave nothing away.

"It's them post boys, me lord."

"You found them?"

"Aye, and the landlord at The George were able ter tell me as it were Lord Coveney who hired the chaise. He done it the day before seemingly, and the boys picked him up, along with the female party, at…" Here he hesitated, glancing for guidance to the magistrate.

Ingham looked across, distaste in his features. "Coveney was at a Covent Garden bawdy house."

Francis stared. "A brothel? The girl too?"

"Apparently. She was waiting with him there. We know the place of old. Starkey's they call it. Situated in Maiden Lane. A woman called Gussie Stark runs it. One of these sometime high flyers who ended her career by setting up as a madam. You know the type, I dare say. Our fellows have been obliged to pay official visits there on more than one occasion, though Starkey doesn't take kindly to it when the law comes calling. Grice, you'd best go back there and see what you can discover about this affair."

Francis, a trifle dazed by this new turn, caught at a fleeting memory from the recent conversation at Brooks's. "One moment." He again turned to the runner. "Do you imply the girl was residing in this bawdy house?"

Grice gave a shrug of his bear-like shoulders. "Can't say as she was, me lord. She were collected from there along with this

Coveney character. To say truth, I were more wishful of getting them post boys to give an account of all the argy-bargy at that there Holly Bush, once I'd heard all they could tell me of the alleged condition of the deceased, who were so much the worse fer his load of liquor seemingly as he snored in the carriage all the way."

Francis was less interested in this history than the implication contained in Meg having been in this brothel. Ottilia would fasten upon that point without doubt. Ingham recalled his attention.

"This Frenchman you brought here, my lord. What is his connection to Coveney?"

"At that, are you? I am not surprised he would not speak of it, to be frank with you, Sir Thomas. It appears there was some sort of rivalry between them over the girl. De Percheval had no notion where she was and had been searching for her. He was furious to know Coveney had found her, which you may verify to be the case from one Emile Lezayre, another of his cronies."

Ingham drew a sheaf of paper towards him, picked up a pen from a silver standish and dipped it into the inkwell. "Once again, if you please. Emile —?"

"Lezayre. The other two we know of from my brother's account are Lord Redlingfield and Aldreth. Henry Aldreth, I think it is." Ingham wrote steadily, jotting the names. "The three, along with de Percheval, formed a coterie of gamesters with Coveney."

Ingham looked up, his gaze keen. "Gamesters? Small wonder the fellow didn't care to open his budget to me. Not that we waste resources chasing down every establishment in the town to check if they're playing faro, bassett or any other illegal game. Know where they were wont to play?"

"I don't. At one or other of their houses, I imagine. Possibly at Brooks's, which is where I found both Lezayre and de Percheval today."

"Or at Starkey's perhaps," suggested Ingham, setting down his pen. "It is not unknown for that female to accommodate parties of gamesters, especially if they wish for female company as they play."

Francis, having learned from Ottilia to be alert to detail, saw fit to question this. "If that were so, de Percheval would surely have thought to look there for his innamorata."

This brought him under a suddenly piercing stare from Ingham. "You believe he's the fellow who got her with child?"

"From what I overheard and what he said later, it seems likely. He was anxious to see how she did and there appeared to be matter for guilt. And what with him running off like that…"

He faded out, reflecting that the Frenchman's famous polish had been severely tested. The veneer he had cultivated clearly covered up a disposition quite as passionate as Ottilia believed Meg's to be. His interest deepened.

Ingham cut into his thoughts. "By the by, my lord, pray inform your lady wife that the post-mortem indicates a pierced lung from a broken rib." A wry twist curved his lip. "No doubt she knew that."

Francis could not forbear a laugh. "She surmised as much, sir."

"Yes. Well, I'm afraid the mitigation is minimal. My fellow is adamant the knifing brought it on, although the break was older and must have occurred before the attack."

Chapter Nine

The house in Maiden Lane was in the ordinary style, a large building set a little back from the road and enclosed by railings. The façade was at one with others in the rest of the street, grey and unimposing, rising several stories with sash windows and a pillared portal. Ottilia had anticipated a rough and seedy environment, but the immediate area she could see, as she took her husband's hand to step down from the hackney, looked respectable. A couple of urchins were employed in sweeping the roadway clean of dung and debris, and the lane was free of loungers beyond a couple of men in mufflers, hats pulled down low, who might have been lookouts posted to watch for the law since it was plain they were taking stock of the newcomers. She urged Francis to tip the road sweepers as Hemp, who had been riding on the box with the jarvey, stepped up to the door and rang the bell.

"It does not look like the sort of place we were led to expect," she observed, once more looking over the front of the house.

Francis cocked an eyebrow. "What did you expect?"

"Something a little more…"

"Disreputable? Obvious? Wait until you get inside. Likely the place will be opulent, gilded and overdone."

She raised her brows at him. "You would know, of course."

"By repute."

"Oh."

"Don't be naïve, Tillie. Did you think me a saint?"

She gave a little sigh. "Yes, Fan."

He eyed her with a look both tender and amused. "My precious idealist, I would I could match up to your image of me." [+]

The door had opened and Ottilia heard her steward announcing their names and asking for Mrs Stark. She touched a hand to her spouse's chest.

"You do, little though you realise it."

He smiled and shook his head, but said no more. That he had agreed to escort her to this bawdy house proved the truth of Ottilia's assertion. He was indeed a saint, especially to do so in the face of her mother-in-law's expressed disapproval when she had ventured to suggest it after Francis had related his meeting with Lezayre and Pierre, in addition to all he had learned at Bow Street.

"What can you be thinking of, Ottilia? Do you mean to enter such a house? Francis, you cannot allow her to do so."

Her husband had turned a wry face upon Ottilia. "I had rather escort her than find she has gone off there with only Hemp to protect her."

"He would protect me very well," Ottilia returned, breaking in upon Sybilla's heated protests without ceremony, "but I should infinitely prefer your company."

"I ought to have known it was asking for trouble inviting you both here," grumbled Sybilla. "I declare, I almost feel myself back in Weymouth with all this going on. As if I did not guess this affair would prove to be seedy in the extreme." She threw up a hand. "Very well, do as you please. But no secrets, do you understand me?"

Ottilia had pledged herself to keep nothing back, although she might well expurgate more sordid details. She took Francis's arm and he led her through the open door and into a spacious hall which was decidedly overdone. Under a hanging chandelier, that lit up the blue-papered walls and sent light reflecting from mirrors on either side, lay a colourful oriental carpet. Marble-topped sideboard tables stood against each wall, beyond which were stands with pegs for coats and hats, and a wicker chair by the door which must house the rather beefy footman who had let them in.

This was nothing, however, to the magnificence of the parlour into which the footman ushered them, which was a welter of deep red, gold and white marble. Daylight was excluded by heavy velvet drapes at the windows but a plethora of candles made the gilded sofas shimmer and two chandeliers fit for a ballroom twinkled above.

Taken aback, Ottilia stood blinking, her nostrils offended by convoluted aromas of stale tobacco and alcohol overlaid with a heavy perfume, as she took in the huge mirrored mantelpiece and the brightly patterned carpet with its red ground.

"Did I not prophesy as much?"

Her spouse's amused tone made her turn. "You did, but heavens above, Fan! Candles at this hour?"

"These places operate at all hours, Tillie. Besides, it is after noon. I dare say the room has only just been prepared. The fire looks fresh."

Moving into the centre of the room, Ottilia was able to verify this as the coals in the grate were still smoking with a few small flames licking through here and there. The candles in the wall-sconces were also new, standing tall with no drips. She turned where she stood, puzzlement wreathing her mind. This was a world of which she knew little.

"Is it meant to invoke the right mood? What is the purpose of all this grandeur?"

Francis came to join her, wearing his wry look. "It is to reassure the patrons that the wares here are of a higher class than they may expect elsewhere. Also to inform them they will have to pay through the nose for its privileges."

Ottilia balked. "Wares! How demeaning. And is this sisterhood made up of such women as Meg? Disgraced through no fault of their own? Or at least, guilty only of succumbing to a seducer's wiles. It is pitiful, Fan."

"We are not here to engage in a debate about the rights and wrongs of prostitution, Ottilia. It serves a purpose, remember. And better a place of this kind than the open streets."

Undeniable. Yet the plight of the unfortunate women incarcerated in this house could not but draw Ottilia's ire. However, when Francis spoke in that tone, she knew better than to provoke him further.

She was relieved from the necessity to hold her tongue as the door opened at that moment, producing a woman of middle years, as unlikely in this setting as she could be. Dressed in a modest ensemble more suited to a housekeeper than a madam, the woman known as Starkey, if this was she, was reed thin, tall and willowy, with as sour an expression as Ottilia had ever seen on a countenance in which a former beauty was traceable in the high cheekbones, the symmetrical oval shape of her face and the large, slanted eyes. The lips, perhaps once full, were wrinkled and flat. Ottilia at once suspected the set of good teeth she exposed as she opened her mouth to speak were false.

"I know who you are," the woman said, addressing herself to Francis. "I've had that runner nosing around already, and he said. But you've no call bringing your lady wife here. I don't hold with ladies in my domain. This ain't the place for 'em."

Ottilia wasted no words. "Are you Mrs Stark?"

Her sharp eyes turned in Ottilia's direction. "I am. They call me Starkey, but that's familiar and I won't have no stranger using it."

It was no surprise to Ottilia to see Francis bristle. "You will address my wife with courtesy, Mrs Stark."

"Ho, will I, my fine lord? And you bringing her where she's no business to be."

Her spouse became haughty. "We'll have none of your insolence, I thank you. My wife is here for a sufficient purpose and you will be good enough to answer anything she asks you with due deference."

"Or what, my lord? You'll lay violent hands on me? I've a stout fellow ready for you, if that's your temper."

Ottilia thought it prudent to intervene before Francis indeed lost his. She moved towards the woman, forcing a smile. "Come, Mrs Stark, we have not come to quarrel with you. Perhaps you do not realise the case in which Meg stands. She is in grave danger, you must know."

She was glad to note her spouse opted to keep quiet and leave her to manage, although she noted he was yet smouldering. Her words had a visible effect on Mrs Stark, for her fine arched brows snapped together.

"How so?"

"Unless we can prove otherwise, I am afraid Meg will take the blame for the murder of Lord Coveney."

Mrs Stark fell back, throwing a hand to a scrawny bosom, flattened by age, her gaze wide. "Murder? That robin redbreast never said nothing about murder!"

Seizing her advantage, Ottilia did not hesitate to drive in the message. "Coveney was severely cut about. I know, for I saw the body." No need to mitigate the business with the now confirmed pierced lung. "And Meg had blood all over her person, and her hands were cut. She says she used a razor."

The madam was staring at her, her eyes dilating, and she grabbed at the back of a sofa which happened to be the nearest support. "She killed him then."

"That is not certain."

"You said he was cut about."

With reluctance, Ottilia yielded. "But that may not have been the cause of death."

Mrs Stark's eyes began to lose the shock, a measure of evidence of thought creeping in. Was she weighing the implications?

"There's one regular customer gone. A good thing I made him pay down his dust before he went. Not that it won't be a loss to the house, for that it will, no question."

Francis predictably exploded. "Is that all you can say, woman? The fellow is dead and by all accounts, you helped him to his doom. Did not you foist this woman onto him?"

Ottilia gave an inward sigh as the woman's eyes sparked.

"Foist? Foist? It was he brought the wench here, I'll have you know. Not that I wanted her, but he paid handsome for me to keep her safe for him. I've no use for a female in the family way. What, months without a penny coming in? No use to me is that. Not to mention the midwife and the lying in and all. Bad enough when one of my girls makes a pig's ear and gets herself with child. I won't keep 'em here, that's sure. Send 'em off to the country 'til it's over."

Despite her innate disgust, Ottilia was intrigued at this evidence of compassion. Or was it merely expedience? "Where in the country?"

"Ottilia!"

But Mrs Stark was nothing loath. "My sister married a farmer. He don't like it, but he swallows it because I pay up. She looks after them well enough and the bastards have a home of sorts. They help around the farm. Ezra ought to be glad of the free labour, but not he. Grumbles every time I send one down."

An unprecedented warmth towards the woman rose up in Ottilia. "You have a good heart, Mrs Stark."

The woman flushed and blew out a dismissive noise. "Pshaw! Suits me to keep a girl while she's got her looks, that's all. When she loses 'em, out she goes."

"All this," Francis cut in with impatience, "is hardly germane. What can you tell us of Coveney's dealings with this girl Meg?"

Mrs Stark's eye flew fire. "Do you suppose I keep a journal? How should I know how he dealt with her?"

Knowing her spouse, Ottilia cut in swiftly, "My dear Mrs Spark, pray don't fly up into the boughs. My husband is merely anxious." She threw a deprecating look at her irate husband, who answered it with a tightening of his lip and narrowed eyes. She moved to the woman, producing a smile. "Do you think you and I might remove to another room, ma'am? This atmosphere is a little uncomfortable for us all, I fear, and I have no wish to distress you any further."

The woman hesitated, throwing a darkling glance at Francis before returning her gaze to Ottilia's face. Her tone was grudging.

"If you care to come to my private sitting-room, my lady, we can talk there."

It was the first time she had used the title, and Ottilia hoped it might mollify Francis sufficiently to allow her to withdraw with Mrs Stark without further interference.

"Thank you, that would be most helpful." And to her husband, "Will you wait here or in the carriage?"

His temper looked to be cooling, but his tone was clipped. "I'll wait outside the door."

She might have known he would refuse to leave her altogether out of his reach. Mrs Stark's expression was contemptuous, but she thankfully said nothing.

"Lead on, if you please, ma'am."

The appellation elicited a grim smile, but the woman turned for the door. Hemp was discovered in the hall, stalwart by the front door in company with the burly footman, who looked, now Ottilia had leisure to notice, a trifle battered about the nose and jawline.

Her ear was assailed by a murmur from Francis who had kept close as they left the overpowering parlour. "She has a pugilist for a guard. A good thing we brought Hemp."

Not that Hemp was himself an exponent of the art of boxing, but Ottilia knew her steward, who was half a head taller than Starkey's man if not as beefy, could give a good account of himself at need.

Mrs Stark led them down the hall, through a back door, along a short corridor and into a little parlour which, in another establishment, might have been given over to a housekeeper. It was furnished simply but with comfort and none of the brash strappings of the front room they had just left. A small sofa and a comfortable chair were set either side of the fireplace, and a little bureau graced the far wall. Under the single window stood a cupboard with a bank of ledgers dumped on top. Mrs Stark might not keep a journal, but she evidently kept accounts, as a successful businesswoman must.

Francis was in the doorway, glancing about with a degree of approval. Ottilia guessed he was thinking she could come to no harm in here. She signalled to him to close the door and sat, at Starkey's grudging invitation, on the sofa while her hostess took the chair.

"I can send for tea or coffee, if you wish for it, Lady Francis."

"Thank you, but I will not trouble you. I doubt I will detain you for long. And Lady Fan will do, Mrs Stark. Is it simpler."

"Lady Fan it is then." Mrs Stark gave a decisive nod. "I'll tell what I can, my lady, for you've treated me decent from the first and I'm one to give credit where it's due."

Ottilia smiled her thanks, ignoring the implication against her outspoken husband. "You are very good. It will probably make things easier if I tell you that we know a valise was packed for Meg, with new clothing and accoutrements." She watched the touch of wariness come into the woman's eyes and gave her a straight look. "It was rather obvious a female must have seen to it, and as obviously it was not Meg."

Mrs Stark's eyes snapped a little but she gave another of those nods. "Yes, I did it for him. Sent my assistant out to buy what was needed. Wouldn't be the first time, you understand, as I've had to kit out a female who come with nothing."

No doubt. A frisson of the betraying disgust attacked Ottilia, but she fought it down. "Yes, I see. You packed it yourself?"

A snort greeted this. "Have to do everything myself if I want it done right. She's useful, but scatty, that Merry. Never was no use to me the other way. Too old and hadn't no nous for it. Nor no feller in his right mind would want her. I felt sorry for her though. What can you do?"

Ottilia's feelings veered. "I said you had a good heart, did I not?"

"Pshaw! Nothing to that. Do what I can for 'em. I know what it is to be destitute, Lady Fan, so I do. It ain't given to every woman to rise above it and make good. I had my time, I can tell you, and when it were over, I didn't waste my blunt on fripperies and I were able to buy this place and set myself up for life. It ain't like that for most and you don't forget the bad times, and I hope I'm a Christian woman for all them as despise my calling."

"I begin to believe Meg was lucky to be brought to you, Mrs Stark. It might have been so much worse for her."

Mrs Starkey snorted. "Well, if she's up for murdering Matthew Coveney, I don't see how it could well be any worse now."

"Very true, but that was not your doing."

Unexpectedly, the woman's face puckered. "Well, it was, in a way. I didn't treat her right. Matt made me fume, he did, the way he just plonked her on my hands, just as if I'd nothing more to wish for. I didn't make her welcome. Nor I didn't warn her to beware of Coveney, for I know what he is — was." She drew a breath Ottilia thought to be unsteady. "Can't believe he's gone. Been a fixture here for years has Matt. Not that he's a good 'un, for he ain't, him and his cronies making merry in my house for all the world as if they own it."

"About that, Mrs Stark," Ottilia broke in, stemming the flow. "Is it true that he and his friends were used to gamble here?"

"That they did. I've a couple of rooms set up for the purpose. Worth it to me, as they pay for the privilege and for the girls on top, as you might say."

Ignoring the last, which could not but kick at Ottilia's prudery, she hastened to check for the personnel involved. "Who were his cronies, ma'am?"

"The usual lot. Ted, Lord Redlingfield that is, Harry Aldreth and that Frenchie."

"Which Frenchie?"

"The old oily one. Don't like him. Never have. He's a cheapskate and shark on his own account. Nor he's no use for a girl." She then threw a hand to her mouth, flushing. "Beg pardon, my lady. I didn't mean to speak so free."

"It makes no matter. I understand you, I believe. You mean Lezayre?"

"That's it. Though t'other one, the young feller, came now and again. Didn't look to me like he enjoyed it above half. He weren't one for laughing his head off with the others. Nor he never got himself in liquor like the rest, nor took no advantage of the girls." She threw up a hand. "I don't mean to say he's like that old Frenchie. Couldn't afford my price, that's all. Couldn't afford to gamble either, I think."

This was all valuable information and Ottilia did not hesitate to dig for the matter in which she had most interest. "This young Frenchman was de Percheval, I take it?"

"Something outlandish. Pierre they called him."

"Did you ever hear of any bad blood between him and Coveney?"

"Ha! Bad blood? Matt couldn't abide him. Was used to grumble as this Pierre were an upstart boojoy who hadn't ought to have no place with the likes of your kind, my lady."

"Bourgeois, you mean? Why did Coveney think that?"

"Because he come to England to batten on his countrymen and hadn't no better shelter than a plaguy parson which was known to his father long ago, he said. Reverend Pargeter, and he don't move in your circles, though he's a gentleman born."

"Heavens, Mrs Stark, you have uncovered a mystery for me, I think. If Pierre was staying with this Reverend Pargeter, then Meg must be his daughter, for we think Pierre spoke of her by that name."

Mrs Stark stared, her mouth dropping open. "Are you telling me Matt deflowered a clergyman's daughter? And one, by all accounts, too religious for his own good."

"No, I am not saying so at all. How Coveney found her I don't yet know, but it was not he who was responsible for her condition."

A shrewd look entered the other's eyes. "It'll be the Frenchy then, will it? That accounts for Matt's doings then, that does."

"How so?"

She sniffed. "You asked if there were bad blood. Well, it went deeper nor that. This Pierre, seemingly, snatched a girl, a lady I mean, from under Matt's nose." *Candia? Yes, it must be for had not Sybilla said Harriet had to hint him away?* "He's looking to marry again, see, and he were hunting among the girls what them mothers parade around to get a husband every season. He were making progress with one of 'em, and in comes Master Pierre, all French accent, young and as handsome as the day, and takes her fancy straight off. Matt's nose is well out of joint and he don't like it. They come to blows. Well, it were one of them meetings, and Pierre gave Matt a bloody stroke with his sword. A flesh wound, he said, but he smarted in his pride for it."

But that would not account for a blow to the chest. Then Pierre had not done the damage on that occasion. "Was there any other fight between them? They came to blows, you said. Was there a physical fight, before the meeting perhaps?"

"Not as I know of." Mrs Stark shifted her shoulders. "Not with this Pierre in any event. But he were quarrelsome, were Matt. There were a pretty set-to more than once upstairs and I had to send my lad in to break it up."

"Recently?"

The woman pursed her lips. "Might have been. You have to understand, Lady Fan, as I'm a busy woman nights. There's all sorts to arrange and I'm here, there and everywhere. I can't be pandering to the whims of a set of brawling gamesters every five minutes."

She spoke with the sharpness that seemed to be habitual to her. No doubt endemic to the life since she apparently had many difficulties to contend with. Ottilia got up.

"I must thank you, Mrs Stark. You have helped me a great deal."

Her hostess rose also. "I'd ask why it's you as is doing all the work, my lady, if I were one of them daft males who think a woman has the brains of a flea. But it puzzles me nonetheless."

Ottilia laughed. "Quite outrageous, is it not? I try my poor husband's temper unduly by involving myself in these investigations. I am incurably inquisitive, I'm afraid."

"Don't tell me. It's more than that, or I'm a dunce. Must be affecting you or your family to have you bestirring yourself to come to my establishment, for you ought not to be here and that's a fact."

"True enough, which is why my husband would not allow me to come alone."

"Ah, he's your protection, is he? Well, I can't blame him for that, but he'd do well to mind his tongue better."

Ottilia thought it prudent to refrain from answering this, instead expressing her thanks again and making good her escape. Although she had reason to be glad of Starkey's garrulous tongue. She had gleaned vital information.

"Heaven knows what we should tackle next, my dearest," she said, having relayed the pertinent points to Francis in the carriage on the way back to Bruton Street, "for this has raised more questions than it answers."

"What have you in mind?"

"I must tackle Meg about this Reverend Pargeter. I have hopes she may crumble and confess the truth when I tell her I know he is her father."

Francis, whose temper had thankfully subsided as he waited, found her hand and squeezed it. "You are indefatigable, my only love. I wish I could emulate your manner with such people as that dreadful harpy."

"She is more warm-hearted than you would guess, Fan. But let us not dwell upon that. Do you suppose you might find out more about these brawls from Redlingfield or Aldreth?"

"Ha! It's to be my task to tackle them, is it? I thank you. I foresee a thoroughly enjoyable couple of meetings."

Mischief bubbled up in Ottilia and she set her free hand on his chest, though she could see his face only dimly in the dark interior of the ancient coach serving as the hackney Hemp had whistled up.

"Be thankful I don't send you to beard this over-religious parson."

"Is that a promise?"

"Milady Elizabeth!"

Lizzy turned at the low-voiced call, her gaze at once encountering Pierre de Percheval standing a little way off. There had been a note of urgency in his voice and a flutter of anticipation went through her. Had not Ottilia warned her Pierre would approach her?

She glanced at the coterie of young people with whom she was engaged. Her cousin Giles was regaling the company with an anecdote of his travels through Italy, which Lizzy had heard before. She would not be missed. Slipping unobtrusively out of the circle, she looked quickly around the saloon in search of

Candia and spotted her at the far end in earnest discussion with her stepmother Violette.

Pierre was shifting into a corner, moving behind the concealing bulk of two talkative and buxom matrons. Lizzy followed, both amused and intrigued by his havey-cavey manner. There could be no doubt he wished to question her about this Meg woman's presence in grandmama's house. As she joined him, he smiled with that unctuous charm she so much deprecated and Lizzy felt a rush of disgust. Had he used it to seduce the unfortunate Meg? Not, she reminded herself, that it was proven he was the culprit.

"I must at once thank you, milady, that you answer my need."

"What do you want with me, sir?"

The smile faded. "*Pardon.* Is it that I have offended you?"

Lizzy regrouped. She was not being a good conspirator. She infused a touch of warmth into her voice. "How should you, Chevalier?" A muscle twitched in his cheek as he hesitated, eyeing her with, she thought, a good deal of question. Lizzy took the bull by the horns. "You want to know about Meg, is that it?" His eyes flared. She had shocked him. She did not wait for his response. "When I gave you her name the other night, you were discomposed."

He pursed his lips and blew out a slow breath. Then seemed to capitulate. "*Alors,* is it to be thus? You make it more easy, *mademoiselle.*" His dark gaze held hers. "You have seen her perhaps?"

"Not I, sir."

"Know you then if she is yet well? These wounds, do they heal?"

Lizzy began to feel a little less hostile. He cared then, did he? A trifle of confusion arose as she reflected that he knew more than she had supposed.

"I'm afraid I cannot tell you that either."

"Ah, *bon dieu*! Then you know nothing more than I."

"Are you worried about her?"

"Of a surety I am worried. What would you? The villain is dead and Marguerite … if she has killed him, *c'est a faute de moi* that she dies for it."

He had muttered it all low and vibrant, and it struck Lizzy how accurate was Ottilia's reasoning that those around a murder became distrait and perhaps therefore dangerous. She itched to know more. But Aunt Ottilia had given her specific instructions and it behoved her to try to adhere to them.

"I know Justice Ingham went to see her. Also that he intends to have a doctor visit her." She did not add for what purpose.

He was frowning now. "This magistrate. Yes, I have met him also. I did not think he has compassion enough to send to Marguerite a doctor."

Lizzy hesitated. She was not authorised to say it, but ought she? How might he react to her special knowledge? The temptation proved too great.

"He is not sending a doctor to tend her wounds, Chevalier, but to verify if she is indeed *enceinte*."

A horrified look came over his face. He had not known then. It was swiftly veiled, though his colour was still heightened as he looked away, biting his lip. A fillip of fury loosened her tongue.

"Why do you look so, Chevalier? You said it was your fault if she dies. Is this to your account?"

His head shot up. Eyes blazing, he faced her. "You accuse me?"

141

"I am asking you, Chevalier. I cannot help you if I don't know the truth."

His face changed. "You seek to help?" He became eager. "You will intercede for me with Milady Francis? You will ask that she allows me to visit Marguerite? I would speak with her, *voyez-vous*. I must see her. You will arrange?"

Lizzy hesitated. She had a certain advantage now. Should she not use it? "If I am to help you, sir, it behoves you to trust me, does it not?"

He looked wary. "How, mademoiselle?"

"With pertinent information. Meg will give no details of her circumstances. She is close-mouthed to a fault, sir. We cannot help her if we do not know her background."

"We, you say?"

She ignored the deep suspicion in his tone. "What or who is her family, Chevalier?"

A closed look came over his features. "This I cannot say."

"Cannot? Do you mean to imply you do not know? I tell you now I don't believe you." He glanced quickly about, frowning, and Lizzy realised her voice had risen. She lowered it again, softening her tone. "Come, Chevalier. You sought me out. If you are so concerned for Meg's welfare, will you not help her so far?"

She saw Pierre draw breath and he jerked his head, shifting further from the concealing pair and checking, as she immediately did too, that they were not observed.

Lizzy caught him up. "Well, sir?"

He lowered his head towards her, speaking almost in a whisper. "You think to bring *la pauvre* Marguerite to her family, *n'est-ce pas*? It is not so easy. Monsieur Pargeter, the father you understand, he is — how shall I say? — a man not forgiving."

Scarcely surprising, if his daughter had fallen from grace. "Did he disown Meg?"

Pierre wafted an impatient hand. "This I know not. I heard only how Marguerite is gone from the house, none knows where. This only from a maid, who spoke of things most terrible. I dared not approach Pargeter."

Lizzy's growing sympathy for him died. "Why not? Why not do the honourable thing, Chevalier?"

His lip curled in the old way. "You would say it is for me to offer to wed her? To confess all to such a man? Pargeter will first see me dead!"

"Is he so implacable? Would he not have forgiven Meg if you were to marry?"

"He forgives nothing. *Rien.* He is a man of God, strict like these fathers Puritan. He speaks only of sins, of the evil he seeks to eradicate, of damnation. He prays and all must pray with him. A house intolerable. Endure it I could not. And he damned me for an ingrate and said he would never see me more. I could not go back, even did I wish to."

Somewhat appalled, Lizzy had yet the wit to realise she was not being told all the truth. He looked a trifle shifty as he spoke. If this Pargeter was an enemy, could he have known Pierre for his daughter's seducer? She was struck by a fresh thought.

"What of Mrs Pargeter? Is she quite as bad?"

Pierre's features softened. "Ah, the good Helen? *Non, par exemple.* A woman of great heart she is, Madame Pargeter. She deserves not to be tied to a man she fears. She is — how do you say? — under his feet?"

"Under his thumb." An idea surfaced. "If she has such a heart, she must wish to know what has befallen Meg. Is there no way you could approach her without encountering her husband?"

He eyed her for a moment. "I may not. But you, Milady Elizabeth, you could do this."

"But I don't know the woman."

"This we can remedy."

"How, pray?"

There was calculation in his face now, she was sure of it. She waited, half repelled, but guiltily intrigued at the notion of participating so far.

"She goes, this Helen, with a basket. He believes she goes to give to the poor, but Marguerite tells me it is to visit the market, that she may buy what Nathaniel he does not approve. Trinkets, *vous voyez*. Such things as he considers too much of luxury, like scented soap. And tea." He must have seen something in her face, for he added, "Yes, *mademoiselle*, he is such a man. The food it is plain. Water at table. Coffee, yes, black and without sugar. The tea it is forbidden. And he at least makes to wash in cold water. Madame Pargeter arranges that the servants bring hot in secret, for Marguerite, and for me. I do not know if she herself follows this custom of her husband."

His disgust was patent. Lizzy could not forbear a shudder at the thought of a life of such austerity. Small wonder Meg snatched at the proffered warmth of physical love, disastrous though the consequence proved. But here was a plan to be made.

"What then do you propose, Chevalier?"

Chapter Ten

Eyeing her rescuer in silence, Meg struggled with her conscience. Dared she admit to that identity? Could she trust Lady Fan so far? She must be itching to be rid of her. No one wanted her now, least of all the one whose retribution she feared even more than the fate that threatened her.

She had graduated from the bed to a comfortable chair brought in by the woman Venner. She would not leave the chamber, though clad in the borrowed gown she looked presentable enough. Too conscious of her position in this household, and privy, through the superior maid, to the dislike of her presence expressed by the dowager marchioness, Meg was torn between the convenience of such a hiding place and the debt of gratitude she was piling up. She had repaid it with contumely and a refusal to open her lips. And here was Lady Fan again, armed with knowledge she had no right to possess.

She had taken a seat on the straight chair normally used by Venner, who had been summarily ejected. She was unsmiling, that penetrating clear gaze fixed upon Meg as she waited for her response. Something had to be said.

"How did you find out?"

Lady Fan's features relaxed. "I have been to see Mrs Stark. She was most forthcoming."

"She cannot have told you what she does not know."

"But you can tell me, Meg. Come, do you still mistrust me?"

The breath caught in her throat. "I mistrust everyone."

"Have I betrayed you?"

"You brought that magistrate here." It came out in a tone more venomous than she intended.

Lady Fan's gaze did not waver. "Yet I did not allow him to hale you off to gaol."

Meg took refuge in silence. What could she say? She read determination in Lady Fan's face. She meant to have it all and then she would go to him and he would come for her and nothing could save her. The memories rose and she was unable to keep the sob from her throat. The words tore out, a desperate plea.

"He will use me so harshly. You do not know him. I had rather die than go back."

"Of whom are you talking, Meg? Your reverend father?"

"Reverend!" She spat the word. "Do you know what it means? Deserving reverence. I could not revere him. Fear him, yes. Anything were preferable than to incur his displeasure. But it is not cruelty, you see, no. It is the hand of God's justice, forced upon him because it is his duty to uphold God's law. He is not doing it. God is doing it through him."

Aware how vicious she sounded, Meg subsided into silence, fighting the urge to scream. She had learned the hard way to keep her feelings within, to hold her tongue on utterances that could only bring more pain.

Lady Fan did not speak for a moment. When they came, her words were unexpected. "Poor girl. He sounds a very tyrant."

Unused to have it so readily accepted, Meg felt warmed. "You believe me?"

"I have no reason to doubt you. Indeed, your bodily ills bear witness. I gather Mr Pargeter is a religious zealot. I am sorry. It must have been very hard to live under the dominion of such a man. Is that why you ran away? Did he find out you are with child?"

The memory leapt and Meg shuddered. "Not that." She sucked in an unsteady breath as the images crept back. "He caught us."

"You and Pierre?"

"He should not have been home. We dared only when he was officiating at church. I feigned illness that Sunday and Pierre sneaked out of the service and came to me." She spoke jerkily, twisting her hands as the contorted visage filled her inner eye. "We were unlucky. It was raining hard. The church roof leaked. He cut his sermon short. He … he came to my room to see how I did." She swallowed on the rising lump in her throat. "Not from fatherly concern, but only to ensure I spoke truly, that I was indeed laid down upon my bed. Which I was, God help me!"

She could not go on. The words that came with spittle from his mouth were etched in her mind. *Evil incarnate. Whore. Jezebel.* For in his view she, not her lover, was the worse culprit. Like Eve, she must have been the temptress, luring Adam with her wiles.

"What did he do, your father?"

Hardly aware of the other woman, Meg spoke in a voice deathly with the hideous aftermath. "He ordered Pierre to be gone from his house. Then he fetched his cane." Meg hardly knew she was relating her thoughts as they came. "I was incarcerated for a week or more. I lost count. Gruel and water. Hours of kneeling prayer. Bible passages to read. I dared not disobey. Helen managed to get bread and soup to me on occasion. I know not how. She had her ways. When I was permitted to re-join the family, I had a penance of silence upon me. None might speak to me and I could not leave the house. When I knew…" Her voice died, the terrible discovery reviving all the dread that accompanied it.

"When you realised your condition? Go on, Meg."

The urging from Lady Fan was gentle. Meg looked across and found kindness and warmth in those eyes. Her resistance dissipated.

"I escaped. I had to. If he found out…"

"Where did you go?"

She drew a painful breath. "I wanted to find Pierre. I went to that man because I knew of their acquaintance. It was a mistake. Pierre had spoken of him. Not as a friend. They quarrelled, I think. But he was the only clue I had. He promised to help me." Her fingers clenched into fists. "He lied. He deceived me. I went with him because I had no other choice."

Meg half expected more questions on her dealings with the man Coveney, but instead Lady Fan surprised her again.

"Who is Helen?"

"My stepmother. My own mother died in childbirth, the babe with her. I was three or four, I think. He married Helen to fill the void. Not for love, but for necessity. I doubt she knew what she had taken on. She told me once it was her last hope. She had been on the shelf for years. She learned somehow a way to do his bidding but to find means also to mitigate the austerity of our existence. I was sorry to leave her without a word, but I could not put her at risk."

"By confiding your secret? Yes, I see."

Lady Fan looked thoughtful and Meg was glad of the respite. She knew not whether she was relieved or regretful to have broken silence. Yet she could not have held back for dread of being returned to the bosom of her family. Bosom? The place for cherishing, for giving life and nourishment. The Pargeter bosom was wanting in these attributes. A greater mercy to be delivered to the hangman.

"Well, we must keep you then, Meg. Will that content you a little?"

"I am an imposition."

Lady Fan smiled. "True, but it does not therefore follow that you must be ejected."

A hollow laugh escaped Meg. "You are a strange woman, ma'am."

"An oddity? I am content to be so." Lady Fan's gaze became speculative. "Will you tell me more of your dealings with Coveney?"

"Dealings? I had no desire to deal with him in any way, but my situation was desperate. He left me with the woman Starkey, for safety he said, while he went to find Pierre." Meg's fingers curled with the echoing distress. "She was not … kind. I feared her sharp tongue. Then, when I realised what sort of a place it was, I feared she might force me to share the shameful life those girls endured. It was all I was fit for after…" She could not say it. How could she couple her sin, born of affection, with the vile words her father had used?

"But Coveney came back for you?"

"He told me Pierre denied it all, that he would have nothing to do with me, that I must not hope for rescue from him."

"He lied, my dear."

Meg drew an unsteady breath. "I do not know. I dreamed every day, when I was pacing my chamber, locked in, that he would find a way to come for me. To send a message. He never did."

Lady Fan set a hand on hers. "My poor child. I expect he feared your father's wrath. I understand, however, that he did search for you when he found out you were missing. And that he was distressed to discover you had gone away with Coveney."

149

"He discovered it? Why then did he not come after me? Why did he wait to know I was absent?" The acid burning in Meg's gut began to spill. "No, Lady Fan, you will not make me believe he cares. I was to him a toy for his present pleasure. I know it amused him to defy my father, for he delighted in the trickery we were obliged to practice. Until it went awry. He did not lift a finger to save me from retribution."

Lady Fan appeared to accept this, yet Meg half wished she might find excuses for Pierre's defection, mitigate the offence.

"What then did Coveney offer to make you consent to go away with him?"

A half-sob escaped Meg. "Sanctuary. He promised me a place on his estates. He spoke of a cottage, that he might care for me until the babe was born."

"You believed in this generosity?"

"Am I quite a fool?" Meg spat the words. "I guessed there would be payment in kind. I was naïve enough to think he would wait. He was impatient. But after Pierre…" Her breath caught. "I could not endure it." She drew breath once, twice, struggling against the rising horrors yet again. "God help me, I wanted him to die!"

Jardine's features, customarily severe, were overlaid with an expression of ill-concealed impatience as he listened to Ottilia's account.

"You say this woman is upstairs now, my lady?"

"Yes. So far I have managed to keep her here. At least while Justice Ingham conducts his enquiries. Will you see her?"

"To what purpose?"

The lawyer's tone was dry and Ottilia bridled. "To hear her account. I had not thought that far ahead, but if you were to act for her you must needs listen to what she has to say."

Jardine pursed his lips. "It is not my custom to undertake actions of this nature, my lady. Moreover, I am not a barrister. I thought you requested my attendance for the purpose of seeking advice."

Beginning to understand Sybilla's dislike of the man, Ottilia strove for calm. "I did, Mr Jardine. Can you advise me?" Was there a faint look of satisfaction in the man's eyes? He seemed to Ottilia to soften slightly.

"What in particular do you wish to know, my lady?"

Breathing more easily, Ottilia took a seat and bade him do likewise. He bowed and chose a straight-backed chair, looking nevertheless as if he did not mean to remain for long.

"I am in hopes I may discover the person who administered the blow which—" She broke off as Jardine held up a hand.

"Insufficient. A jury will have scant interest in anything but the woman's attack."

"Surely if it is relevant, this must be taken into account."

"Relevant, but not lurid, nor immediate. The prosecutor will take care to dwell upon the recent attack, without which no death would have occurred."

True enough, and Ottilia had suspected as much. "You are saying I am wasting my time?"

The corners of the lawyer's pallid lips shifted into something almost a smile. "I do not say so. You are wise to hunt for any mitigation which is open to you. Counsel for the defence may do as much in the opposite direction."

Ottilia's animosity was overtaken by eagerness. "Then it may be worth pursuing Pierre de Percheval perhaps? He is the man responsible for Meg's condition, you must know."

At once a sceptical look overlaid Jardine's features. "Dwelling on the woman's immorality cannot be expected to engage a jury's sympathies."

"But a tale of what poor Meg endured at her father's hands might, do you not think?" She gave a brief account of the aftermath Meg had related.

He remained cynical. "Some might consider the punishment just. Others might be moved to pity. Juries can be manipulated by skilled rhetoric. They are human after all."

Unlike Jardine himself. Ottilia suppressed the thought. No doubt his detachment had come about through exposure to the prevalence of criminality. She stuck to her guns. "Then they may be so moved. And this Frenchman lived there. He must know what it was like in that house. Whatever ammunition I can garner could be of use."

Another purse of the lips. "Your best hope, my lady, is for a diminution of the charge. On the face of it, I cannot think any jury would be induced to find the woman innocent if the charge is murder."

"Manslaughter, then? Could not a jury recommend such a reduction?"

"Not to the charge, no. Whatever it is, the judge will ask the jury whether they find her guilty or not guilty. A jury may, however, put in a plea for clemency if its members believe there was no intent to kill." The cynical look became pronounced. "Or if, indeed, the woman or her counsel manages to engage their heartfelt sympathies. The versatile tongue of Mr William Garrow has proven successful in that line."

Ottilia jumped on the name. "I believe I have heard of him. Are you acquainted with Mr Garrow?"

"I have met him."

"If you will not act for Meg, will you provide me instead with an introduction to the gentleman?"

"I did not say I would not act. Merely that it is not my custom so to do."

Hope burgeoned. "Then you will?"

"Perhaps."

Ottilia drew a breath. "Then it behoves me to produce as much evidence in Meg's favour as I can."

The lawyer nodded and rose. "There will be a number of procedures to be undertaken by the courts before the case comes to trial in any event. You have a little time."

"Thank you for that comfort at least." Ottilia got up too, urgent now. "I trust you are willing to give me the benefit of your opinion, should I need to consult you again? Once I have found anything relevant, I mean."

He bowed. "By all means, my lady."

"And if there is sufficient to sway a jury to her side, you will take Meg's case to Garrow? Or another with a gift for rhetoric?"

"Produce your mitigation, my lady, and I may consider it. I do not deal in lost causes." With which, he made his adieux and left Ottilia half in hope and half seething.

It proved worthwhile to Francis to enlist his brother's aid. On walking round to Hanover Square, Francis found Randal on the point of setting out for Tattersall's to find a quiet filly for his daughter Lucille.

Randal, already coated for the outside, took his hat from the waiting valet.

"Come with me, Fan. Haven't seen hide nor hair of you for days."

Francis hesitated but a moment. He could as well accomplish his mission in his brother's phaeton as out of it.

"A very good notion. I need a private word."

Randal gave him an odd look, but the butler had the front door open and Francis followed out to the equipage waiting in the road outside, its harnessed pair of chestnuts looking restive as the groom held them by the bridles to keep them steady. Randal swung himself up and shifted along the seat to give Francis room, taking the reins into his gloved hands.

"Let them go, Stibbs."

The groom moved out of the way, the horses started off and Stibbs leapt for his perch behind as the phaeton passed him.

Randal began at once talking of his purpose in going to the sale at Tattersall's, moving on by degrees to his son's riding prowess. "Fearless that boy is," he disclosed on a note of pride. "Would you believe he tried to mount Alexander?"

"Do you mean that brutish great stallion of yours? Good God, was he thrown?"

"Beast of a horse wouldn't let him get on, thank the Lord, or I'd have been for it. She worships that boy."

"Violette? No doubt."

It struck him how completely his brother had become a family man now he was married to the woman he loved. Dared he speak of it to Mama? Would it appease her at all? He suppressed a sigh. Nothing was likely to soothe Sybilla's volatile temper until this business of Ottilia's was settled. Which reminded him of his mission. He broke into his brother's panegyric about Bastien's horsemanship without ceremony.

"Randal, I need your help."

His brother cast him a disbelieving glance. "Here's a new come-out, my boy. What's to do?"

Francis lowered his voice. "I need an introduction to both Redlingfield and Aldreth."

"And you come to me for it? I've turned a card or two with Redlingfield. He's more of my generation. The other is years younger and I scarce know him." A frown preceded the inevitable question. "This to do with the business of this female you've got tucked up in Bruton Street?"

Surprised, Francis stared at him. "How the deuce do you know about it?" Then he let out a resigned laugh. "Oh, the servants, I must suppose."

"Of course. Gipping tells Cattawade everything that goes on at my mother's house. How else am I to keep one step ahead of the woman?"

"Randal, for pity's sake! Do you tell me you have Gipping in your pay? Spying upon Mama? She'll tear you limb from limb!"

Randal gave a self-conscious laugh. "Nothing of the kind. Know the old lady wouldn't like it, but she must know Gipping and Cattawade are old cronies. Too fly not to guess how I get my information, I'll warrant. And don't think it don't work vice versa because it does. Can't call my soul my own, what with my mother on the one side and Violette on the other." He swivelled his head to glare at his valet on the box. "And you keep your mouth shut about this, Stibbs, if you know what's good for you."

"You don't need to worrit your head over me, my lord," came the laconic reply. "Know how to keep my tongue." He coughed. "But if his lordship wants Lord Redlingfield, I'm thinking he'll be at Tattersalls."

Francis swivelled. "That's providential. Why, Stibbs?"

"His man told me he's after a new team for his curricle."

"Ha! Good man, Stibbs. See, my boy? Servants know everything." Then Randal surprised him. "Was it Coveney, Fan? The dead man, I mean."

Francis cursed. "How the devil did you know that?"

155

A snort very like their mother's escaped his brother's lips. "D'you take me for a flat? You come asking about Coveney and his cronies, Violette's in my ear about this plaguy Chevalier and some female he's mislaid and you've had Ingham on your doorstep. Two and two make four, Fan, last time I counted."

Francis had to laugh. "I didn't think you had it in you."

"Don't need to tell me," said Randal on a gloomy note. "Quite aware the old lady and you think me half a head emptier than a regular noddy."

Heat rose to Francis's face and he was relieved his brother was obliged to give attention to his horses to negotiate a passage between a heavy dray at a halt by an alehouse, with a couple of burly fellows unloading barrels, and an oncoming coach and four. They were not far from Hyde Park Corner, near to where the horse dealer's premises were situated.

Stibbs proved to have gauged the matter correctly within a very few minutes of the gentlemen entering the sale courtyard and leaving the phaeton in the groom's charge, along with other vehicles belonging to Tattersall's numerous patrons. Randal, having greeted a number of acquaintances on their way through, at once drew Francis's attention to a dissolute looking fellow standing a little back from a group watching the horse currently being paraded back and forth for the benefit of the patrons under the colonnaded corridor.

"There's Redlingfield."

Vague recognition came as Francis examined the man with a critical eye. He was tall and rather thin, with a look of dissipation in indrawn cheeks and puffy bags under the eyes seen, even at this little distance, to be bloodshot. Was it habitual? Or had the news of his friend's death caused a sleepless night? If he knew from Lezayre that Bow Street was involved, his rest might well be disturbed.

"Present me, brother."

Randal lifted his eyebrows but sauntered in the man's direction. Redlingfield looked round as the marquis moved in beside him. He nodded. "Polbrook."

"How de do? Have you met my brother Fanshawe?"

Francis gave an inward curse at his elder's direct approach, but it had an instant effect. Redlingfield stared under brows that snapped together.

"Lord Francis, I presume?"

Clearly, he must have spoken with Lezayre. Was there suspicion in his eyes?

Randal indicated the quarry as he looked back at Francis. "Viscount Redlingfield, Fan." He grinned and winked. "Leave you to it." Without further ado, he moved off, hailing an acquaintance.

Francis was left confronting the other man. He wasted no time. "I take it you've heard the news about your friend?"

Redlingfield's thin lips twisted. "To some purpose." He glanced about and Francis heard a barker asking for bids on the horse. The sale was beginning. Redlingfield lowered his voice. "Let us withdraw a little."

This ready acquiescence augured well. Francis followed as the taller man wove a path through the patrons concentrated on the rising bids to a spot near the entrance to the interior rooms. The viscount turned there, checking they were unobserved and too far away from the crowd to be overheard.

"Why the excessive caution, sir?"

Redlingfield's mobile mouth sneered. "You are acting for Bow Street, I understand."

Francis gave a short laugh. "Nothing of the kind. I am merely attempting to unravel a mystery which fell into my path on my way to the capital."

The sneer became pronounced. "Pure disinterest? It won't do, Fanshawe. Your wife's fame goes before her."

Damnation. Did the whole world and his wife know about Ottilia's preoccupation? It could not be helped. "The plain fact is, Redlingfield, we are stuck with this woman until the mystery is solved. What do you know of her?"

A shrug came. "Little more than any other, I presume."

"Come, sir, you were one of Coveney's cronies. You cannot be entirely ignorant of his interest in the girl."

The man turned his eyes away, looking towards the sale area. "I don't believe he had an interest. Except to score off that young fool de Percheval. I dare say you know all about that."

"I know there was bad blood between them. What happened?"

Redlingfield's rather keen gaze returned to his face. "Why the excessive interest? Didn't the girl wield a weapon of some kind? Why look further?"

Francis gave it to him straight. "Coveney did not die from her attack. It's likely an old wound caused his death."

The stare became piercing. "And you want to know who inflicted it, is that it?"

"That is it in a nutshell. Can you help?"

"You want to pin this on de Percheval, do you?"

Francis sighed his exasperation. "I have no desire to pin it on anyone. I am merely seeking information to determine the truth." It struck him as he said it how completely he had absorbed Tillie's thinking. In the past, he might have reacted just as Redlingfield was doing, picking on the easy solution.

The viscount appeared to relax a little, rocking back on his heels. He hesitated, pursing up his lips a little, his look becoming wary. "I am not sure I can help you."

"If it troubles you that the quarrel we are talking about concerned my niece Lady Candia Fanshawe, I already know it."

"Then why do you need my help?"

"Detail, sir. Facts. What precisely happened?"

The viscount gave a sudden smile which transformed his face, giving Francis an inkling of why he had a reputation as a rake.

"Matt wanted a wife, silly fellow. He didn't know how to value his freedom. Thinking of his children, he said. Faugh! As if a ripe plum off the marriage mart would be content to settle to mothering. Women are trouble, I told him. They have their uses, but they're a damned nuisance if you let them into your life."

An unsatisfactory marriage? Although was not the man a widower? Francis let it pass. "Very well, and what happened?"

Redlingfield made a derisive sound. "He went after your brother's girl. I could have told him Polbrook wouldn't countenance such an alliance, but why bother? It was amusing to watch him make an ass of himself. Until de Percheval came into the picture and made a beeline for Lady Candia. He had the entrée through Polbrook's wife, of course, and one can't blame the girl for preferring the fellow to Matt. Which female wouldn't?"

"But Coveney thought he had been cut out?"

"With a vengeance. It made our play deucedly uncomfortable, with the two of them glowering at each other. Lezayre tried to keep the peace, but Matt's a foul-tempered brute when he's crossed. He went for de Percheval's throat and we had to haul him off. The boy challenged him. Coveney shouldn't have accepted since the fellow is years his junior, but Matt has ever flouted such rules. He has no honour." Redlingfield stopped suddenly, a sudden frown catching at his brows. "Had no honour, I should say. I'm not yet used to the notion he's dead."

Irritated at losing the thread just at the relevant moment, Francis pushed for more. "You'll adjust fast enough. They met then?"

The sneer returned. "If you can call it a meeting. A tame fight. De Percheval pinked him in the shoulder. It wasn't a deep wound but Matt was infuriated. Could barely stand the sight of the boy and swore revenge." A sour smile came. "He took it and it cost him his life. He won't be missed by many."

"By you?"

Redlingfield's cheeks darkened a trifle. "He was a fine card player. Disgusting in his cups, but sober he was almost unbeatable. He fleeced us all time and again. It drove me mad but I admired him for it." A wry grin curved his lip. "And I couldn't withstand the urge to try and beat him. It'll be a bore to play with the others now. Lezayre is a cautious gamester and Aldreth can hardly tell a spade from a club. Ought not to play at all, silly clunch. But he's addicted."

Interesting as these details were, they yet failed to build much on the emerging picture. Francis switched attention. "What of Aldreth? Was he a friend to Coveney or was it merely the gaming?"

A short laugh escaped Redlingfield. "A friend? Harry couldn't stand Matt. He's another fool in his cups. They came to blows any time either one was three sheets to the wind."

Chapter Eleven

Lizzy watched her quarry picking through a collection of old clothes on a stall, wondering how to approach her. She had never been as far north as Bloomsbury and the mean streets round about the little square had both surprised and repelled her. Dirty, ill-kept and narrow, they suffered from lack of light and a profusion of muck and debris in the roadway. Even the market, though bustling, demonstrated the poverty of the area with hawkers selling pies from trays, tradesman bargaining directly from the back of wagons and a profusion of covered stalls like the one where Helen Pargeter occupied herself.

Pierre had made himself scarce, waiting with the hackney around a corner of the square. Lizzy suspected he would be watching from a concealed vantage point and was not entirely sorry for it. His anxiety had infected her. Her heart pumped uncomfortably in her bosom and she was conscious of a rise of guilt that she had not consulted Aunt Ottilia before she ventured upon this excursion. Not that she anticipated any danger from this woman, but her conscience would not acquit her of succumbing to Pierre's insistence.

"It is of an urgency, Milady Elizabeth. Wait it cannot. It must be tomorrow. Can you escape Milady Dalesford? And Candia, she will allow you to go alone?"

Lizzy was surprised. He had gauged the situation perfectly. It was easy enough to fool Mama, but Candia was another matter. She had not failed to note her cousin going apart with Pierre and Lizzy read jealousy under the pose of sisterly concern.

161

"It made you look most particular, Lizzy. I hope you were not badgering poor Pierre about seeking employment again."

Lizzy had seized on this. "He ought to seek employment. It's ridiculous for him to continue battening upon his fellow Frenchmen."

Candia was diverted into argument, but she became suspicious the following morning when Lizzy said she would not accompany her cousin upon a visit to Hanover Square.

"Why won't you come? Where are you going?"

"Nowhere. I had rather carry on reading *The Romance of the Forest* than listen to you lecturing Lucille."

"Aunt Harriet doesn't like you reading those gothic novels. Besides, I don't lecture. And Lucille needs me. She's my sister, Lizzy, and if I don't advise her, who will? Violette has no time for the poor child."

Aware Candia had been neglected by her own mother, Lizzy understood her cousin's concern, but she used the situation with a ruthlessness she had not known she possessed. "Well, you don't need me there. Besides, my French isn't nearly as good as yours and Lucille chatters so fast I can barely follow her."

A rare frown creased Candia's brows. "Why are you being like this? You know very well Lucille enjoys your wit and liveliness. Elizabeth, what are you up to?"

A faint warmth crept into Lizzy's cheeks but she tossed her head. "You don't have to play elder sister with me, Candia."

Her cousin sighed, drooping a little. "Why does everyone suppose me to be blind? It was just the same over that dreadful time with Mama. I saw how Aunt Ottilia singled you out and I know what's going on over in Bruton Street just as well as you do. Last night you went apart with Pierre and now you refuse to come with me to Hanover Square. What is going on, Lizzy?

Aunt Harriet will have a fit if…" She faded out, clearly unwilling to make an outright accusation.

"If you must have it, I'm rather tired, that's all."

Candia had eyed her with a mixture of hurt and suspicion in those lustrous dark eyes of hers. "Very well. But pray remember Grandmama before you engage in secret assignations."

Lizzy managed a disbelieving laugh. "You've got windmills in your head, Candy. And I'm not afraid of Grandmama. She doesn't ring peals over me. Though I concede it must be uncomfortable for you when she goes for your papa."

This proved a fortunate remark, for Candia had befriended her half-siblings in despite of Sybilla's antipathy and she hurried off on her promised visit to Lucille with but a passing admonition to Lizzy to be careful if she was doing what she ought not.

The result of all this was to invest the scheme with a spirit of adventure which only began to dissipate when Lizzy found herself on her own and confronting the task of accosting Mrs Helen Pargeter.

She was a slight female, dressed in a sober brown pelisse and a plain bonnet that hid her face. Lizzy waited until Helen turned in her direction as she moved to examine a garment on the end of the stall. Her countenance was thin, her complexion sallow and worn, making her look older than Lizzy had anticipated. With a fleeting thought of Ottilia's possible reaction, she gathered her courage and stepped up to the stall.

"Mrs Pargeter?"

The woman looked up, question and a hint of apprehension in eyes of a surprisingly bright colour somewhere between blue and green. "Yes?"

Lizzy hastened to explain herself. "You do not know me, ma'am, but I am charged with a message for you."

The eyes showed astonishment, consternation and then hope, in quick succession. "From—?"

"One who dare not approach you directly."

The bright eyes flared with eagerness. "Meg? Is it Meg?"

A pang smote Lizzy and she did not hesitate. "Yes. At least, I am not her deputy, but I know where she is."

She heard Helen's swift intake of breath and watched her cast a quick, fearful glance about. Apparently satisfied, she set down the garment in her hand, shifted the basket on her arm and moved away from the stall, motioning Lizzy to accompany her. Her tone sank. "Tell me, pray."

At once the unauthorised nature of her dealings thrust into Lizzy's mind. What would Ottilia advise her to say? Not that she could now conceal the truth, having ventured thus far. Yet she prevaricated. "She is in a great deal of trouble, Mrs Pargeter. Worse than you might think."

The other's cheeks paled. A gloved hand seized Lizzy's wrist in a painful grip. "Do not try to spare me."

It was Lizzy's turn to look about her, to ensure they were not overheard. The bustle of the market proved useful, for none had eyes or ears for anything but their immediate interest, either in idling over purchases or encouraging custom.

"Meg was picked up in the road by my aunt on her journey here." In a few swift sentences she put Helen in possession of the bare facts. "I am indebted to Pierre de Percheval for a means to find you."

Helen's intent gaze had not wavered from Lizzy's face as she spoke, though it reflected her changing thoughts. But at mention of this name, it flared again, this time with anger and she released Lizzy's wrist abruptly. Her tone was low but harsh. "Is he here?"

"He brought me." It was out before she could weigh the wisdom of saying so.

Helen was already hunting the crowd, a blaze at her eyes as she directed them at faces near and far. A mutter reached Lizzy. "He dared not approach me, well for him. I'd know how to do if he did."

"But he suggested a way for me to find you, Mrs Pargeter, and he brought me here."

The eyes returned to her face, doubt clouding them. "How am I to help her? I would if I could."

Lizzy did not know either but she tried. "Could you come to her?"

Helen shrank a little. "No. I haven't the means."

"I can take you there."

The woman looked scared now. "I don't know who you are."

"I am Elizabeth Fiske. My father is Lord Dalesford."

It was plain the name meant nothing, and the title evidently did not help. "What have I to do with lords? Or Meg, for the matter of that?"

"I told you she had fallen into my aunt's hands. Aunt Ottilia is Lady Francis Fanshawe. She is a woman of great compassion and very clever. She is seeking to prove Meg's innocence."

Helen stared. "Why?"

"Because that is what she does. She is known for her success in that line."

"I don't understand."

"There is no time to explain. Pray take my word on it that Meg is in safe hands. Will you not find a way to come to her?"

"Now?" A fearful look replaced the confusion. "No, no, I am expected. It will not do to be late."

Lizzy began to feel desperate. Having come so far without permission, she had best not fail or it would be wasted. "There must be a way, ma'am. If not now, perhaps later or tomorrow? I can fetch you if I command use of my carriage. Will you not trust me?"

"It is not a matter of trust. You do not know. I cannot…" The woman faded out, her gaze suddenly intent upon the basket which, in her agitation, had bumped against her slender waist.

"Mrs Pargeter?"

The woman held up a hand. "Wait!" Silent, Lizzy watched the concentrated pose, fascinated by the light of hope and anticipation that crept into the worn features. A decisive nod finished it. "It will work. It should, if we are careful." Her gaze returned to Lizzy's face. "Tomorrow. But you must promise to follow my instructions to the letter."

"How can you locate Aldreth, Fan? He sounds to be exactly the fellow we are looking for if he and Coveney indulged in fisticuffs."

Ottilia tried not to sound impatient as Francis set down his glass and took up his fork again. She ought not to have broached the matter until he had taken the edge off his hunger, but time was pressing. He could have gone after Aldreth today had he not become distracted with Randal at Tattersall's sale rooms. She could have screamed when he told her, arriving back at Bruton Street only in time to change his dress for dinner.

"A pity Aldreth wasn't there, but at least I was able to prevent Randal wasting his blunt on a team he doesn't need and incurring Violette's wrath. I told him he would undo all the good of her gratitude at his procuring the filly for Lucille."

Ottilia could not quite curb her irritation, but she targeted it otherwise. "I see my dear brother-in-law must needs rely upon you for marital advice as well as everything else."

Francis had cocked an eyebrow. "A trifle cynical, Tillie. It's not like you. What is the matter?"

She had shrugged it off. "I think you've had enough to bear from that quarter."

"He is my brother, Tillie. As a boy I used to worship him. Randal guided me and looked out for me when I was a raw youth. He drives me crazy on occasion, but he still has my heart."

Ottilia's melted at the words and she smiled, setting a hand to his chest. "Yes, of course he has. Forgive me. You are a loyal brother, Fan."

He had kissed her and she let the subject drop, leaving him to his ablutions. He joined her and Sybilla in the parlour just as Gipping announced that dinner awaited them and Miss Mellis, also late, hurried in as they were sitting down.

"I slipped up to ensure Miss Pargeter had been served, Lady Francis. Her appetite is better, I think."

Ottilia agreed and thanked her. Teresa Mellis was necessarily to some degree in their confidence, but had offered no opinion beyond overseeing Meg's welfare, although she left it largely to Venner, saying it was better so since she would not be there much longer. Ottilia's question to Francis, however, brought her head up from her plate.

"I beg your pardon, but is it Mr Henry Aldreth you mean?"

Ottilia looked across the table. The words were diffident as always, but clearly larded with import. "Yes. Is it possible you know him?"

167

Both Francis and Sybilla paused in eating, staring at the companion in surprise. Clearly embarrassed at the unwonted attention, Teresa's thin cheeks flew colour.

"I knew Harry well at one time. In his youth, I mean. I was his dear mother's companion before I came to her ladyship."

"Good heavens, Teresa, why could you not have said so before?"

Miss Mellis coloured again, giving her employer a deprecating look. "I did not know Lady Francis was wishful of speaking to him."

"Very much so," said Ottilia, intervening before Sybilla could annihilate the poor woman. "What is best to be done? Will he come here if you request it?"

Teresa gave one of her rare smiles. "Oh, yes. Harry was disposed to be fond of me for I indulged him in playing at battles with his toy soldiers and reading to him too. He had no patience to do so for himself. He was very naughty and would not mind his tutor. He had no father, you see, and poor Mrs Aldreth had not strength to insist upon it. She was very sickly."

Francis had resumed eating, but his interest was evidently aroused. "Had he no guardian? Surely someone must have been in charge of his affairs. By all accounts, he is extremely wealthy."

"Oh, the trustees saw to his fortune, but there was no one set over his conduct. At least, I believe the lawyer was joined in guardianship with Mrs Aldreth, but he had no hand in day to day control. I fear poor Harry grew up rather wild."

Which no doubt accounted for his reckless habit of gaming, Ottilia decided. But that was beside the point. "Will you send to him, if you please? It is becoming a trifle urgent."

Sybilla clinched the matter. "Do it tonight, Teresa, and I will have Gipping send it. We cannot afford to wait since you are off to your sister's the day after tomorrow."

"Let Tyler or Hemp take it," Francis said. "There is no need to trouble your overworked servants, ma'am."

Ottilia sent him a grateful look. Their own men could be relied upon. "Will you ask him to wait upon you in the morning, Miss Mellis?"

Francis snorted. "By all accounts, he is unlikely to be sober in the morning."

"You had best make it noon, Teresa," said Sybilla.

Teresa Mellis was looking flustered, but she acquiesced without argument. "As you wish, ma'am."

"But will he come at all?"

"Why should he not, Fan?"

"Because Lezayre gave Redlingfield the impression I am working with Bow Street. If Aldreth thinks so, chances are he will take fright and refuse to come anywhere near the place."

Ottilia looked to Miss Mellis. "What do you think? Ought we to go to him instead?"

A hint of amusement entered the companion's eyes. "Harry has no concept of danger. He was ever fearless. Or perhaps I should rather say reckless. As a boy at least. His tutor was used to say he would walk blindly into anything."

"Well, you are not walking blindly into his orbit, Tillie. The fellow sounds altogether unsuitable to be visited. Let him come here."

Sybilla applauded her spouse's dictum and Ottilia felt obliged to accept it. She followed Sybilla to the parlour, leaving Francis to his solitary port, what time Miss Mellis hurried away to write the required letter. Her mother-in-law settled into her accustomed chair and fixed Ottilia with her penetrating black gaze.

"Where do we stand?"

Ottilia could not forbear a mischievous smile. "We?"

"I'll have no impertinence, I thank you, my lady Fan, if you must call yourself by that foolish appellation."

"Would I dare?"

Sybilla snorted. "You would dare anything, dreadful child."

"I only use Lady Fan because it simplifies things, Sybilla."

Her mother-in-law rapped on the arm of her chair. "How much longer must I put up with all this disruption?"

"I wish I knew. We are further forward now that Meg has at last told me her story. If I could think it would be of use to us, I would tackle her pastor father, but I am loath to introduce him back into her life, poor girl."

"Why? He ought to be informed. What if she were hung and he knew nothing of it?"

Ottilia could not withstand a shiver of distress, but that at least was not imminent. "She won't be. Not immediately. Though I consider it the height of inhumanity to allow a female to endure all the tribulations of childbirth only to put her to death when the babe is born."

"A barbarous practice, I agree. We must certainly save her from that if we can."

Thankful to have won even this little approbation from her acerbic mother-in-law, Ottilia began to wonder how she might proceed if they failed to learn anything useful from Aldreth.

The parsonage was set back from the road in grounds adjoining the far edge of a cemetery, within sight of the squat church tower with its tall spire. Lizzy was relieved to find the environs a trifle more prepossessing than the area around the market, bounded as it was by green fields to one side with the village spreading into the town on the other. Helen had spoken of the place as being in Marylebone, although it seemed to be very much on the border with the less salubrious Bloomsbury.

As the carriage turned into the short drive, Lizzy's pulse accelerated. She rehearsed in her head the phrases she had invented to accommodate Helen's ruse. They had given place to her own when she had earlier contrived to escape Candia's suspicious eye and order the town carriage the moment her mother and cousin had driven off in the landaulet.

Lady Dalesford had been unsuspecting but concerned. "You are not sickening for something, are you, my love?"

"I am perfectly well, Mama. Only we have been racketing about so much I am positively exhausted. Besides, I am closing on the end of my book and am desperate to finish it."

"Very well, dearest. Perhaps it is well if you rest before the ball. Lady Wooborough was a close friend of Emily's and we must support Candia, must we not, my love?" She turned to her niece on the words with a sympathetic look.

"I am growing more used to talk of her, Aunt Harriet." But her cousin's eyes were upon Lizzy, brimful of suspicion.

She hastened to acquiesce. "I shall be ready to attend, Mama, never fear."

"Good girl. Come, Candia, or we shall be late."

Lady Dalesford thankfully swept her other charge off before Candia had an opportunity to throw her more than a speaking glance of enquiry. She met it blandly, but with a knot of trepidation in her stomach. She ought to have sought Aunt Ottilia's guidance, or at least have warned her in a note. But the plan was made and it might not come off. In which case, she need not confess the whole.

She had no qualms in setting off alone, since she was driven by one of their own coachmen with both a groom and footman in attendance. The butler had insisted upon sending Charles.

"You will not set forth without a footman, my lady. His lordship would not approve."

Doubtless Papa would disapprove of the whole expedition, but Lizzy was relieved not to be further questioned once she had stated she was visiting the wife of a parson. Snade had not agreed to order the carriage until he knew her destination. He could not gainsay her, of course, but it had taken a little cajolery on her part before he consented to do her bidding.

Yet at this moment, with the carriage stopping at the entrance to a two-storied building of dull red brick with a plain white portal, unadorned beyond a simple cornice and half pillars set into the surround, she felt all the force of daring to act alone. Pierre's account of the Reverend Pargeter, coupled with Helen Pargeter's evident apprehension, rendered Lizzy distinctly nervous of meeting him.

"It is of no use to try to charm such a man," Pierre had warned. "He is of this kind who says a female must be modest, to take the back chair."

"Seat," corrected Lizzy automatically. "What if I come the earl's daughter? Will that impress him?"

Pierre had let out a derisive laugh. "He cares not for rank. You must be serious. Do not make the jest."

Lizzy had never felt less like jesting. The whole enterprise had taken on the aspect of an ordeal rather than an adventure. Only the hope that her intervention might be helpful to Ottilia kept her from turning tail and running away.

Charles opened the carriage door and let down the steps. Her heart beat fast as the footman helped her out and then went to ring the bell while she waited, casting a glance across the façade of the dour building. The windows were tall and narrow, the brickwork worn and covered over at the foot with moss, the whole giving off an air of coldness.

A maid opened the door and Charles enquired for the mistress of the house, giving Lizzy's name. The girl's eyes widened, but she curtsied and invited Lizzy to enter.

The hall, dark-panelled with little access of light, felt stifling, but the maid led the guest directly to a front parlour which was even more unwelcoming. The wall panelling was plain and dark, the one window failing to improve the sense of gloom. A carved mount over the fireplace, empty of coals even on this cold March day, lent little beauty to the scene, and the darkness of the furniture only added to the look of supreme discomfort.

"I'll tell the mistress, my lady."

Lizzy walked to the window to catch a reassuring glimpse of the coach and the servants waiting for her outside. She felt rather as if she had entered the lion's den and began to hope the parson did not put in an appearance. If fortune favoured her, he might be about his duties. Except that Helen Pargeter's scheme included his participation since she needed permission to leave the house.

This reflection caused a flutter in her bosom and she was abruptly sorry for the girl Meg, despite never having met her. How dreadful to live without the freedom to do as you wished, subject to the authority of a despot. She could barely repress a shudder. She really must take care to marry a man of lenient persuasions.

"Lady Elizabeth, I understand?"

The voice was male, and cold. Fright froze Lizzy's tongue as she turned, encountering a bleak gaze in a countenance severe beyond expression.

This scarecrow of a man must be the Reverend Pargeter. He was suited in black from head to foot except for a pristine white neck-cloth and had the look of a starved ascetic. A black wig, wholly unadorned and tightly queued, served to emphasise the pallor of a long, thin face, lacking animation and with a pair of bloodless lips. Lizzy had as well confront a corpse.

Fighting down revulsion, she produced a spurious smile. "Why, yes. And you must be Mr Pargeter. How do you do?"

He looked at her proffered hand, moved a step in her direction as he extended his own and merely touched the tips of his fingers to hers. Then he transferred the cold gaze to her face. "You wished to speak to my wife?"

"Indeed I did, sir. I have heard of her charitable works from an acquaintance and I hoped — I thought perhaps I might assist. Only in a small way, you understand, but so much better a use for those garments too worn for wear — instead of making them into rags, I mean." Aware she was gushing, Lizzy stopped short and took a breath. Mr Pargeter's expression did not change. Nor did he speak. Lizzy felt compelled to continue. "I hoped Mrs Pargeter would consent to come to my house and — and choose which articles might be of use to her."

The reverend gentleman's eyes narrowed a trifle. "You did not bring them with you?"

A nervous laugh escaped Lizzy. "Good heavens, no! I should have had to bring a trunk. There are so many, you see. My mama — Lady Dalesford, you know — will never throw anything away."

She could have blushed at the bare-faced lie. In fact her mother was over-generous with old clothes, passing them on to the servants the moment they became too old-fashioned to wear, except for those made up in expensive material that could be re-used. But the Reverend Pargeter did not take up the point. He crossed to the twisted rope that served for a bell-pull.

"My wife is no doubt about her duties, but she may spare you a moment or two."

This did not augur well for the scheme. Lizzy pressed on with assumed brightness. "I am told Mrs Pargeter's patchworks are exquisite. Such a boon they must be to the recipients. I hear she actually turns them into down coverlets. I wonder how she finds all those feathers."

Mr Pargeter turned and a dry note entered his voice. "Chickens."

Blank for a moment, Lizzy could only stare at him. "Chickens?"

"Feathers, ma'am. My wife has the cook keep chicken feathers. My parishioners likewise will provide her with the same."

"Oh. How — how enterprising."

"Waste not, want not, Lady Elizabeth."

"Of course, yes. So sensible." What in the world would he say if he could see how much was wasted in the Dalesford household?

As if he heard her thought, he cast her a look of decided contempt. "It is not, alas, a proverb much taken to heart by our aristocracy. In this house, we practise as we preach."

"Very commendable, I am sure, sir."

Mr Pargeter bowed, evidently impervious to any possible ironic interpretation. "We do our poor best to follow the dictates of Our Lord."

Unable to think of anything to say in response, Lizzy merely smiled, wishing Helen Pargeter might not be long delayed. At least her formidable husband appeared to accept the concocted excuse. She sought her mind for some innocuous subject, but consciousness of her duplicity rendered the exercise fruitless under the eye of Meg's father. He did not initiate any subject himself, seeming content to wait for the appearance of his helpmeet in silence. Lizzy tried not to fidget, wishing he might invite her at least to sit down. Not that any of the hard wooden chairs or the settle, too much like a pew for comfort, looked to be bearable, for there was not a cushion in sight.

"In this house we do not pamper the body."

Lizzy's heart bumped uncomfortably. Had the wretch an uncanny ability to read minds? Her mouth went dry and she could think of nothing whatsoever to say. A fervent wish that she had not embarked upon this enterprise possessed her and she cast an agonised glance about the panelled parlour. Her eye fell upon a patch of carved shelving set into the wall and loaded with leather tomes. She spoke at random. "Have you many bibles, sir?"

The reverend glanced at the books and brought his gaze to bear upon her face. "I certainly have no novels. These are tracts and learned treatises or sermons."

Lizzy could be in no doubt that he held her and her ilk in contempt. A bubble of hostility grew within her, superseding the apprehension. "Each to his own, Mr Pargeter. I confess myself much entertained by novels."

He continued to regard her, mockery in his eyes. "No doubt. The curse of your circle, ma'am. Or one of them. Abominations all."

"You are very frank, sir."

"I speak as I find, Lady Elizabeth."

Burning resentment possessed Lizzy, but she tamped it down. It would not aid her cause to be quarrelling with Helen's husband. As it was, she had grave doubts of permission being granted for an excursion in her company. The man clearly considered her tainted by the devil merely on account of her rank.

She was relieved when the door opened to admit Helen Pargeter. She was just as Lizzy remembered although, without a bonnet and framed with sandy hair mostly confined under a cap, her features were comelier and she looked less worn. She glanced at Lizzy but did not acknowledge her in any way, merely looking enquiringly at her spouse.

"This is Lady Elizabeth Fiske, my dear. She wishes to donate old clothing for your patchwork."

Lizzy moved forward, holding out a hand and smiling. "How do you do, Mrs Pargeter? I have heard such praise of your efforts from a friend and I would very much like to help you with them, if I may."

The slight dame looked so bewildered, Lizzy could almost have believed her ignorant of the whole scheme.

"Help me? You sew, my lady?"

Lizzy managed a spurious laugh. "No, indeed, ma'am. I am most unhandy with a needle. But I have a positive trunkful of old garments and I would very much like you to come to my house and choose what might be of use to you."

The bewildered look deepened and Helen Pargeter looked from Lizzy to her husband. "Go to your house? I don't know…"

"Do say you will. I have my carriage here, ma'am. We may go directly and I will have my coachman bring you back again in a trice."

"In your carriage? Oh dear, I don't think… I am in need of more patterns, it is true, but… Ought I to go, Nathaniel?"

The diffident manner was so changed from the assured woman of yesterday that Lizzy found it hard to maintain her own role. But she must appear eager. "I do hope you will not object to it, sir. I promise to take the greatest care of Mrs Pargeter's welfare and bring her safely back."

The reverend's lip curled again. "My wife is capable of taking care of herself." He turned to Helen. "Go and put on your bonnet and pelisse, my dear."

She looked doubtful. "You think I should go?"

"You need patterns, you say. I would not have your chosen charitable works halted for want of material to pursue them. And we must consider the benefit to Lady Elizabeth's soul." He turned his mocking eye on Lizzy. "A good deed may serve to undo a tithe of the harm done by vice."

Lizzy gave him a smile of false sweetness. "I thank you for the opportunity, Mr Pargeter."

He merely bowed his head. "Go, Helen. Lady Elizabeth will await you in the carriage."

Helen Pargeter hurried out and her husband held open the door, a command in his eye as he looked at Lizzy. She was tempted to flounce out, but she had gained her point. There was little future in alienating the horrid creature. Instead she curtsied and walked past him with lowered head and a modest mien.

Helen joined her within a few moments, hurrying out of the house and glancing back as if she was fearful of being prevented at the last moment. She clambered up the steps and almost fell into the seat beside Lizzy, speaking with breathless haste. "Let us go, quickly! Nathaniel is angry."

Lizzy's fright returned and she leaned across to speak to the footman who was folding the steps. "Tell Beoley to go at once, Charles."

"As you wish, my lady."

The door shut. The footman's voice was heard and the coach moved off as Charles swung up behind. Lizzy did not speak until they were out of the short driveway and bowling down the road.

"What happened? Did he seek to forbid you?" In the dim light she saw Helen was trembling and set a hand upon those tightly clasped in the woman's lap. "I am so sorry. I hope you will not suffer for this."

Helen Pargeter's bright eyes turned on her, brimful of agitation. "It is not that. I am fearful rather of seeing Meg. I don't know what to say to her."

"You will know when the time comes, I am sure." Lizzy had no notion where the soothing words came from, but she had to say something. "I have prepared a valise containing some old clothes which I hope will serve to convince your husband."

Helen waved this away. "He will not enquire into it. He does not interfere in domestic matters, provided we adhere to his decrees. But it was well thought of, my lady, thank you."

Lizzy wanted to ask what had made the reverend angry, but she was afraid of being betrayed into showing her ill opinion of him. "I hope I did not say anything to annoy Mr Pargeter."

To her surprise, Helen Pargeter gave a hoarse laugh. "You might have remained silent throughout, yet he would still have been infuriated. Nathaniel despises the aristocracy, I am afraid."

"I rather got that impression, yes."

"Do not be insulted, pray. It is just his way. He holds certain views that … that others might consider rigid."

Lizzy could not withhold a burning curiosity. "How do you bear it, Mrs Pargeter?" A flare of something showed in the woman's eyes and Lizzy hastily retracted. "Forgive me. I have no right to ask."

"Pierre has spoken to you, I think."

"Shrewd of you, Mrs Pargeter. He did say a little about the deprivations of your life."

Helen gave a little sigh. "One grows accustomed. I have learned how to manage."

How to manage *him*, she might have said. Lizzy felt a wave of sympathy, but held her tongue on the words hovering there which must be unwelcome, if not resented.

"Well, I am glad we pulled off the scheme. I cannot think Meg will be other than delighted to see you."

Helen made no answer. She fidgeted awhile, pulling the edges of her pelisse together over her plain petticoats. At length, she cast Lizzy a frowning look.

"Have you permitted Pierre to see her?"

There was censure in the tone and Lizzy hastened to disclaim. "It is not up to me, ma'am. That decision rests with Aunt Ottilia. I admit I have not asked." She hesitated, but there was no use withholding the truth. "I have to confess, ma'am, that I have not told Lady Francis of this visit."

Shock widened the woman's eyes. "She does not know I am coming?"

"She does not even know I sought you out. But I am persuaded she will be glad of it. I know she is anxious to make contact with Meg's family or I would not have—"

"Lady Elizabeth, this is not right. I believed you were acting with your aunt's authority."

"I am, in a way. She charged me to discover what I could from Pierre de Percheval. I can vouch for it she will be greatly relieved to see you. As will Meg, I am sure," she added, hoping to turn Helen's mind to the point of the exercise. She appeared to succeed for the worthy dame fell silent, her gaze seeking the view beyond the window. Whether she saw the increasing traffic and the busy London streets was doubtful. Lizzy sought for a less tricky subject. "Have you been doing your patchworks for many years?"

"Yes. I was used to do them before my marriage, for pleasure. I began in earnest for a way to emulate my husband's devotions." Her bright gaze met Lizzy's. "Now and then I dispose of a patchwork for profit. A female trader at the market acts for me. I have brought a little money from my nest egg for Meg. I imagine she is destitute?"

"She had nothing but the clothes in which she stood, ma'am. Though the dead man had made provision, my aunt said."

"It was not for him to do so." A vicious note entered her voice. "Not that I suppose for an instant her vile seducer might provide for her. Pierre de Percheval's honour is wanting."

Contrary to Ottilia's expectation, Henry Aldreth gave her an immediate impression of an overgrown puppy rather than a hardened and cynical gamester. Large in every respect, he bounced into the parlour and, ignoring everyone else, roared a greeting and enveloped Teresa Mellis in a comprehensive hug, lifting her quite off her feet.

"Melly, Melly, you old darling! How the devil are you?"

Without giving the blushing companion an opportunity to respond, he set her down and planted a noisy kiss upon either cheek, to which she uttered a giggling protest.

"Harry, Harry, stop! Oh, dear, you have not changed a bit!"

"Course I haven't. Why should I? But look at you! Where have you been all these years? Why haven't you summoned me before? Do you mean to give me pepper for my sins? I'm a very naughty boy, Melly, worse than I ever was!" He gave a raucous laugh at his own words and released her, glancing around the room. Ottilia watched him take in the dowager, delicate brows raised, and then pass over her own countenance and fasten upon Francis, standing in his accustomed place by the mantel. "Ah, Lord Francis Fanshawe, is it? Ha-ha, I am before you, sir. Lezayre has told me all."

Francis stepped forward. "May I present my—"

"Now I know why you sent for me, Melly, you old rogue, you," interrupted the other, rounding on Teresa Mellis again. "What, d'you think to have me clapped up at last?" He threw back his head and roared again, what time Ottilia received an exasperated glance from her spouse. She cast him a mischievous look, unable to help a bubble of amusement. It was going to prove a piece of work to pin this volatile creature down. But Miss Mellis, no doubt aware of her employer's ironic eye, was hastening to perform the introductions. Ottilia watched the portly Aldreth bow over Sybilla's hand.

"M'lady. Wish you weren't here, have to say, ma'am. Word is you terrify the stoutest heart." Not that he sounded in the least afraid. On the contrary, he was altogether hearty and the words were clearly insouciant. He shook hands with Francis and then his pudgy features turned at last to Ottilia, unexpectedly lighting up. "The mystery woman! Heard all about you, ma'am." He coughed behind his hand in a manner Ottilia assumed intended delicacy. "Certain acquaintance of mine was pretty voluble on the subject."

Ottilia batted it out in the open. "Mrs Stark? Oh, you need not colour up, sir. We are not mealy-mouthed in this house. Besides, I would much prefer you to be frank."

Aldreth grinned like a sheepish schoolboy and Ottilia had no difficulty in understanding why Teresa Mellis had been attached to the younger version.

"Suits with me, ma'am. Never was one to remember to mind my tongue, eh, Melly?" He threw an enveloping arm about the companion's shoulders, looking down at her with affection. "Many's the scold old Melly has given me. Without effect, I may say. A hopeless case, ain't I, Melly?"

"Harry, pray… You will give Lady Polbrook a false impression." Teresa slipped out of his grasp, her colour heightened. "Don't listen to him, Sybilla, I beg."

"Why not?" Sybilla's black gaze raked the man. "I find him refreshingly honest. I can't bear these duplicitous sycophants. Sit down, Aldreth, before you break something."

It took some time to settle the fellow. Francis moved to pull forward a chair with Teresa's doubtful assistance. She bustled the visitor into it and then perched on the sofa opposite, gazing at him with eyes that seemed to drink him in, setting up an inevitable speculation in Ottilia's head. Was this Harry a substitute for the son she never had? It was to be hoped he'd had no hand in helping Matthew Coveney to an early grave.

"Now then," said Sybilla, once she was able to command the man's attention, "tell us about Coveney, if you please."

An explosive sound issued from Aldreth's lips. "Old Matt? Faugh! Fellow's dead, ain't he? Wish to know what I thought of him, do you? I'll wager you already have word of our dealings." His gaze turned on Ottilia. "Starkey told you it all, did she? How we came to blows, eh? The feller drove me to it, I'll tell you. Had a nasty tongue on him and he despised me. Only played with me because I've got more ready than I know what to do with and he won more from me than anyone else."

Francis took the words out of Ottilia's mind. "And that infuriated you?"

"Lord, no, Fanshawe. Never worries me to lose and I win as much as I drop. No, it was Coveney's insults I couldn't stomach. Belittled me."

Ottilia did not trouble to infuse sympathy into her tone. This man, she judged, was honest to a fault. "Belittled you how?"

His puffy lips curled in discontent. "Paraded his superior education. Never much heeded my tutors, did I, Melly? My own fault. Didn't see the need for all that Greek and Latin. But Coveney — he'd trot out those Latin quips of his and give me that stinking leer to show it was something to my discredit. Wouldn't have cared if the others hadn't laughed."

"Even Pierre?"

Aldreth gave a snort. "Not he. Came in for his share of Coveney's sarcasm often enough, the young Frenchie. But he chose dignity." A rueful grin came. "Dignified I ain't, ma'am. Only have to look at me."

"You fought him?"

The already familiar belly laugh sounded. "When the others couldn't stop me, I did. I confess it freely, I'm a devil when I'm drunk. Could've happily killed Matt a score of times, if you want the truth. Can't be sorry he's dead, so if you want me to weep for him, you're out of luck, my Lady Fan."

Startled, Ottilia blinked at him. "You know me as that?"

The schoolboy mischief showed again. "Told it to Starkey, didn't you? Has a soft spot for me, old Starkey. Like Melly here, eh, Melly? Do you love me still?"

"Harry, behave!"

He leaned across and made as if to slap her, playfully beating his hand back and forth in the air. "Ah, you do, you roguish old dame, you know you do!"

The companion's girlish giggle lent colour to his assertion. Ottilia intervened, partly to save her blushes, but also in a bid to return the erratic Aldreth to the point of his being there.

"When was the last time you got into an altercation with Coveney? Do you remember precisely, Mr Aldreth?"

He rolled his eyes. "Lord, I don't know. Not lately, for I'm not one to strike a man when he's down and Matt was devilish sore after he'd been set upon."

Ottilia's mind jumped and she caught a glance of similar surmise from Francis, who cut in at once.

"Set upon? When? Was it mohawks? How was he hurt?"

Aldreth pursed his lips. "Bludgeoned, by his account. He and the young Frenchie fell in together when they were walking home. Feller jumped them, Matt said. Came out of nowhere seemingly. Caught Matt a heavy blow across the chest."

The subsequent account Aldreth gave, though brief, leant colour to Ottilia's conviction.

"Matt staggered and cried out. The young Frenchie grapples with the feller, but he got away, Matt said, and made off as fast as he could."

Francis put the pertinent question. "Did either of them chase after him?"

"Frenchie ran for half a street, but came back to see after Matt."

"Despite being enemies? I had not thought de Percheval capable of it."

Aldreth grunted. "Ah, he's a good lad at bottom. Misguided, if you ask me, but aren't we all? Matt took the worst of it. Silly clunch wouldn't go to a physician, though we all told him he ought. Had trouble breathing, see."

Ottilia exchanged a glance with her spouse. There could be no doubt this was the origin of the broken rib. She said nothing of it, however, pursuing the most important point.

"Did either of the men see this robber's face? Was he masked, or—?"

"Too dark, ma'am. It was after two in the morning. There are few street lamps round Starkey's way. Footpad chose his spot well too. 'Sides, it was all over in minutes. Shouldn't think either of 'em had half a chance to take note of the feller's phiz. Much one like another these footpads. Dare say Bow Street might know them as individuals."

"Did Coveney think to report the attack?" asked Francis.

"Not he. Told you. Wouldn't even see the sawbones. No use thinking the Frenchie would set foot in Bow Street either."

Francis bent an enquiring look on the man and Ottilia remembered his report of Pierre's jumpiness when he had accompanied him with the intention of identifying Coveney.

"Scared of the authorities, is he? Now why, Aldreth?"

A wry grin appeared on the other man's face. "You're asking a gambler, Fanshawe? Who isn't shy of Bow Street? These Frenchies are scared silly of the law, by all accounts. Can't say I blame 'em, with what passes for justice over there. Who knows what the feller might have done to put his head in jeopardy?"

"This begins to be interesting," Francis said in a low tone, his eye on the couple visible through the doorway. Although it was unlikely Aldreth would hear anything other than his own voice as he stood bantering Teresa Mellis in the upstairs corridor. "What did de Percheval do to get himself denounced if, as it is rumoured, he is not of the aristocracy?"

"What are you thinking, Fan?"

He shrugged. "I'm not, that's the difficulty, Tillie. It could be anything unlawful."

"Or merely political."

His mother snorted. "That tells us nothing. It is all political."

"But if it is not merely on account of his birth, Mama, it must be something specific."

"Just so. He could have backed the wrong horse and found himself out of favour. Did he work for the government and make some error?"

Francis ran over various possibilities in his mind and came up with one. "A spy?"

"Not if he's afraid of the authorities."

Sybilla let out an explosive breath. "Of what use to speculate? Once you inform Ingham about this attack, he will pursue de Percheval and take his statement."

Francis caught Ottilia's expression and at once knew she had made one of those leaps he was never able to emulate. But he answered his mother instead of making enquiry in her presence. "That won't tell us why this Pierre was obliged to fly the country."

"What matters it?"

"It may matter," said Ottilia, a faint frown in her gaze. "There is an oddity in this attack business. I cannot quite put my finger on it. But I have a feeling Pierre's account will prove pertinent."

Francis knew her well enough to be sure she already had some notion in her mind. Before he could pursue it, Teresa came back into the room, looking pink and flustered, and addressed herself to the dowager as she shut the parlour door and approached the company.

"I do beg your pardon, Sybilla. Harry is still rather a trial."

Sybilla waved this away. "As it chances, I liked him. A scapegrace, I don't doubt, but I can see why you grew fond of him, Teresa."

Teresa's colour fluctuated. "I cannot help it, I confess. But he is very naughty and his manners have not improved." Francis noted with interest an unaccustomed softening in her features as she sank back down to the sofa. "It was a joy to me to see him again. I am so glad you needed to speak to him, Lady Francis. Was he of use, do you think?"

Ottilia gave her warm smile. "Very much so, Teresa. I am most grateful to you for arranging his visit."

A ring at the front door brought Teresa to her feet again. "Oh, dear, I do hope that is not Harry back again." She glanced worriedly about the room. "Did he drop something? He was used to leave things everywhere, I remember. So untidy."

"Stop fretting, Teresa," snapped Sybilla, also rising. "If it is he, you may see to it yourself. But if it is some other, tell Gipping to deny me. And then attend me in my sitting-room." She added, as the companion hurried out, "For my part, I am done with visitors for the morning. I shall retire and leave you two to determine how you may contrive to talk to the wretched Pierre. Just don't bring him here, that's all I ask." With which, she swept from the room, leaving Francis relieved. He wanted nothing more than the opportunity to find out whatever it was his wife had in her head about the footpad's attack upon the dead man. This was denied him as Gipping entered the room.

"Lady Elizabeth Fiske, my lord."

Lizzy tripped in, glanced at Francis in a manner he found oddly furtive and, locating his wife, came quickly across the room.

"Aunt Ottilia, thank heavens! I was afraid you might be out."

Ottilia was already rising, catching the hands held out to her. "My dear child, what in the world is amiss?"

"Oh, not amiss. The contrary. Only—" To his astonishment, Francis found himself the recipient of a look part impish but somewhat apprehensive withal. "I had hoped to find you alone, but it can't be helped."

"What has occurred, Lizzy?" His wife's tone was calming and authoritative.

Lizzy emitted a small, tight breath. "You will scold me, I dare say, for acting on my own and I know I deserve it, but—" A hideous presentiment shot through Francis. Before he could voice it, Lizzy's eyes lit with excitement. "—it has paid off, really it has. I have brought Meg's stepmother to see her. She is waiting in the hall."

Shock was almost instantly superseded by rage and Francis heard the ensuing words only in the periphery of his mind.

"Mrs Pargeter? You found her?"

"I found her and I persuaded her to come. We had to engage in a subterfuge to fool her husband — such a horrid man, Aunt Ottilia! — but she was so anxious for Meg she found a way."

"Oh, well done, Lizzy! Bring her in at once!"

The girl sped forth and Francis found his tongue, speaking rapidly and in a low tone. "You involved Lizzy in this business? Ottilia, how could you? How dared you?"

She looked startled as she turned to him, but also contrite. "I should not have, I know. I never meant for her to—"

"To act on her own? You don't know that girl! Hot at hand she is, but that is neither here nor there. You had no right to—" He was obliged to break off as Lizzy re-entered the parlour accompanied by a drab little woman in an outmoded bonnet and pelisse. She looked nervous as Lizzy drew her to meet Ottilia.

"This is Lady Francis Fanshawe, Mrs Pargeter, who has Meg in charge. Oh, and this is my uncle, Lord Francis."

The woman bobbed a curtsey and Francis gave her a nod. "Ma'am." He felt choked with the things he wanted to say to his wife, who, to his chagrin appeared as cool and collected as ever.

"Mrs Pargeter, how do you do?"

"I do very well, my lady, but I've to apologise at once. I thought Lady Elizabeth had your permission for this visit, but—"

"Say no more, Mrs Pargeter. No apology is necessary. I had been wondering how to get word to you of Meg's plight. I could not be more pleased that you are here, I assure you. Meg will be so happy to see you, I think."

The woman was visibly relieved by Ottilia's warmth as she shook the hand held out to her but her brows drew together. "Will she, ma'am? I fear she'll be too ashamed to speak to me. That, or in one of her dark moods. Though there's reason enough for it now, I hear."

"Lady Elizabeth has told you all?"

"As much as she knows."

"I told her I hadn't seen Meg myself, Aunt Ottilia. But I explained everything you told me."

Francis could not prevent himself from throwing a deeply reproachful glance at his wife. She caught it and a faint grimace crossed her face, but she kept her attention on Helen.

"Is Meg prone to these dark moods? I must tell you that exactly describes her. She does not wholly trust me, I'm afraid."

Helen's fingers worked aimlessly and she gave a hopeless sort of sigh. "She's never been one to trust easily. It took me an age to befriend her, such a scared little mite as she was."

Francis found his fury dissipating into interest. He was still highly displeased with Ottilia's machinations, but there was much to learn here. He cut into the sympathetic silence. "Since you are here, Mrs Pargeter, you had best see Meg at once." His wife jerked a little and Francis was conscious of a trifle of regret for his harsh tone. Not that he was any the less angry with her. Ottilia spoke, however, with all her usual calm.

"Yes, indeed. I will take you up. Come, ma'am." She slipped ahead a little and Helen Pargeter followed, leaving Francis confronting his niece.

"Well, Elizabeth?"

She looked at him, seemingly wavering between triumph and apprehension. "Oh, dear. You do look cross, Uncle Francis."

"I am cross, Lizzy. What were you about, going off on your own to find Mrs Pargeter? This is not a game."

"I know. Of course I know that. Only my task was to—"

"Your task? Do you mean to tell me your aunt actually asked you to involve yourself in this—"

"Heavens, no! Well, yes, but only with the greatest reluctance. I wanted to help. I begged her to let me help, if you must know."

"Yes, I dare say you did. But that is no reason for—"

"Oh, heavens, you are cross with Aunt Ottilia! And it's my fault. Pray don't be, sir. She warned me not to do anything by myself. She told me it could be dangerous and I wasn't to act alone. She can't be blamed, really she can't."

Incensed, Francis was betrayed into indiscretion. "She can be blamed for telling you anything about it. If she knew you better, I doubt she would have done."

To his further annoyance, a peal of laughter escaped the girl. "Too true, indeed. Oh, dear, I fear Mama has told tales of me."

He threw up his eyes. "If you must know, it is your father who speaks of you as a little minx, and he's not wrong." The suppressed anger rose again. "But this is the outside of enough. You have no notion how risky these situations can be. I have very nearly lost your aunt Ottilia more than once and she's been in far more danger than I can bear. And she's a grown woman, Lizzy, more than capable of holding her own and highly observant too. You — you're a slip of a thing and barely more than a child. If you were threatened, what could you possibly do to save yourself?"

Rather to his reluctant admiration, Lizzy did not buckle. She lifted her chin, defiance in her eyes. "I may be young, sir, but I'm not a fool. And I would give a good account of myself if I had to, so there!"

He gave a wry smile and softened his tone. "I'm sure you would try. But I must ask you not to run your head into danger again."

"But I didn't! I only—"

"Listen to me!" She subsided and he gave a faint laugh. "Obedient girl!" He moved to her and took her hand, giving it a squeeze between both his own. "I do understand. It is exciting, is it not? Intriguing too."

"Oh, so much! And my life is so dull, if it was not for all the drama with my uncle Randal's wife."

Francis released her. "You're enjoying that, are you? I suppose I might have guessed."

The deep-throated laugh that was so incongruous in her sounded and he had to smile. "So you might, Uncle, if you have taken Papa's words to heart."

He winced. "Don't let your grandmother guess at it, for pity's sake."

"Oh, I can wheedle Grandmama out of her twittiness, never fear."

He became serious again. "That is as may be, but will you promise me not to go blindly into anything again?"

"Well—"

"If you won't, Lizzie, I shall have no choice but to forbid Ottilia to tell you anything more of the business. Nor to allow you to participate in any way whatsoever."

She looked crestfallen and Francis decided he had got through to her at last. She gave the required promise, although he had every intention of curtailing her involvement in no uncertain terms, once he had Ottilia alone.

Meg had given up the attempt to calm her troubled thoughts with reading. Besides, the volume of poetry Venner brought was filled with too many lovelorn expressions to be of comfort. Instead she stood at the window and watched the comings and goings of those who serviced the Bruton Street house: maids shaking out cloths and mats; tradesmen's delivery boys coming through the long garden burdened with full baskets; a footman off with a message; now and then the black man she had seen at the start, slipping out with a crony to drink from a tankard. She could hear the desultory sound of deep voices talking, and occasional laughter. An ordinary world, comforting against the barren desert of her future.

When the door opened, Meg did not turn at once, assuming it was the girl Rose with a tray of refreshments. Lady Fan's voice startled her.

"Meg? You have a visitor."

Her stomach swooped as she turned, half expecting Pierre, but the figure in the doorway was female, as well known to her as her parent. Almost as unwelcome.

"Helen?" Fear gripped her. "Is he here?"

Her stepmother moved into the room, her gaze holding Meg's. "You think I would betray you?"

A shaft went through Meg. "Why not? Everyone else has."

Helen halted. Meg shot a look at Lady Fan, author of this unwanted intrusion.

"Why did you tell her? You promised!"

Her saviour did not flinch. "Mrs Pargeter is not here by my agency, but I don't mean to excuse myself on that account, Meg. I had every intention of informing your family when I could locate them. It would not be right to withhold your predicament from those whose business it is to protect you."

Meg felt the tremble start up. "Protect! Did I not tell you? Did I not show you what my fate would be if you sent me home?"

"Hush, my dear!" Helen was before her, catching at her unquiet hands. "Hush now, girlie … softly… There. Soft now, soft."

The murmuring took Meg back and her tears spilled. She fell into her stepmother's arms, taking comfort as she had long years ago, a small child smarting from a beating or one of his terrible scolds. Somewhere in the background she heard the click of a latch, but the much-needed release was too strong to make sense of it. When she emerged from that embrace she had not enjoyed for an eon, she was shaking and found herself drawn to sink down upon the bed, Helen at her side, supporting her with one arm while she proffered one of her always pristine pocket handkerchiefs.

Meg took it and wiped the ravages away. Then she fiddled with the embroidered edge. "You should have made me learn your skills, Mama Helen."

Helen took her fingers and stilled them. "You never had the patience."

Sorrow cut at Meg's heart. "Too late now. I am doomed, Helen."

"Lady Francis does not believe so, she tells me."

Meg looked round and then remembered the latch. "Has she gone?"

"Yes. You may talk freely."

Meg fetched a long sigh. "I will never be free again."

Helen pulled away a little. "Must you take such a gloomy view? It looks bad, I grant you, but there is always hope. You make your own future, you know, my dear."

A faint laugh escaped Meg. "You always say that."

"Because it's true. What good would it have done me to rail against fate when I found out Nathaniel's foibles?"

"Foibles! He is a monster!" Meg sprang up, fear rising again. "If he finds me now, I am lost. I had rather face the hangman!"

"Now you are being ridiculous." Helen did not move from the bed, but her gaze followed Meg. The question came abruptly. "How far gone are you?"

"I don't know. Three or four months? They will spare me until the babe is born, I know that. He won't."

"Lady Francis appears to think you will not be found guilty at all. Or at worst, it will be manslaughter."

Irritation claimed Meg. What did it matter what the law did to her? To be kept from the other power was more urgent. "You never answer me when I speak of him thus. Why, Helen? You know what he is."

Helen looked away. "He is my husband, Meg. When you marry, you will understand."

"When I marry?" Meg emitted a harsh laugh. "Have you run mad? Do you see Pierre here? Do you see his ring upon my finger?" She held her hand up, fingers spread. "He has done all he intended already."

Helen's gaze found hers. "He arranged for Lady Elizabeth to find me, however."

A lift of faint hope. "Pierre? It was his doing?"

"So I understand."

"Who is this Lady Elizabeth?"

"She is niece to Lady Francis. She knows Pierre socially, it seems." Helen's tone became dry. "He appears to have established himself in that milieu."

"He already had before he left us. He is ambitious, you see. A mere parson's daughter is not good enough for Pierre de Percheval. Oh, I made a convenient toy for his pleasure. But a wife?"

"Then why did you go seeking him, Meg, if you knew he would not do the honourable thing?"

Meg's bravado collapsed. "I could not bear the thought of what my father would do if he found out. Anything was preferable to that fate."

Helen stared her out. "You would have lived with Pierre as his mistress?"

"Yes." Defiant, Meg tossed her head. "Why not? I was ruined in any event."

"And when he married some high-born female? What then?"

Meg had never considered beyond the necessity to escape, but she knew the answer without having to think about it. "I would have joined the ranks of women like Starkey. What other choice had I, if he abandoned me?"

"You could have come home, Meg. Nathaniel may be harsh, but he would not leave you destitute upon the streets. He would never commit so unchristian an act."

Meg's hands clenched. "But he would impose his penances upon me. He would tear the babe from my arms and give it into the hands of strangers. He would all but kill me with unkindness until I might as well be dead."

Helen said nothing and Meg dropped into the chair brought in for her use.

"Will you tell him?"

Helen's brows snapped together. "That you are here? No! And if he should discover it, I will not own to having known."

Meg found a smile from somewhere. "You were always adept at wearing your two faces, Helen. I would I had your skill."

"You are too impulsive, my dear. If you had learned to be still, to bide your moment, to be dutiful in his sight…"

"As you are? I always pitied you, Helen."

"Then don't," came the tart response. "I contrive to live life much in the way I choose to do. I am my own mistress, my dear, for all it may not look so on the surface. I am careful, Meg, that is all."

Meg shuddered. "Were you never afraid of him?"

"At first, yes. Nathaniel only raised a hand to me once. I took care never again to give him reason. It was a valuable lesson, if not in the way he intended."

Meg's resentments flew into her heart. "Oh, his lessons! Don't talk to me of his lessons. I hate him, I tell you, hate him! I wish him dead that he may go to his precious Lord — if the Devil does not take him instead as he deserves." She covered her face with her hands, overcome by the memories. She heard movement and felt her fingers taken, dragged down. She looked up into her stepmother's worn features, the eyes reflecting sadness.

"I wish I knew how to help you, child."

Meg thrust down the anguish and tried to smile. "You cannot, Helen. It is too dangerous. That is why I did not tell you what I meant to do."

"I would have tried to stop you, though I expect you knew that."

Meg shook the hands that held hers. "Not that. I did not want you to be obliged to hold a secret from him. I could not bear his wrath to fall upon you."

Helen released her. "Do you wish to know what he said when he found you were gone?"

"No. I wish to know nothing of him."

"I will tell you regardless. He said, 'Poor child. She little knows how the Almighty weeps for her.'"

"Did he? Did he indeed? Must I thank him?"

"You don't understand, Meg. Nathaniel pitied you. He did so even as he punished you."

Meg laughed, a hollow sound. "And that makes it better? Are you trying to make me care? Don't waste your breath, Helen."

"I am trying to help you to understand your father, but I see it is useless. Or perhaps too late."

"Much too late."

Helen sighed. "In some ways you are just like him."

"Never!"

"But you are, if you will only realise that he is driven as much by passion as are you. His passion is for the word of God, for his beliefs. Yours, Meg, is a passion of rebellion. Did you not succumb to Pierre out of some notion of punishing your father?"

Meg stared at her, struck by the possibility of a truth she had never looked at. "If I did, he may rest easy. I succeeded only in punishing myself."

"Oh, Meg… Can you not try to rise above these base feelings, even a little? For once?"

"I did, once. I snatched at happiness when it offered, Helen. It eluded me. It eludes me still. Pierre…" Meg could not go on.

"You love him? Truly?"

"He does not love me. He used me." She made an attempt at a smile which went awry. "He never spoke of love. I assumed it, believed it, because I wanted to. He used endearments, you see. I made more of them than he meant. That became all too clear when…" Her voice became suspended again.

"I must go, I fear. I cannot be long absent or the excuse will not hold." Meg rose automatically and received a breathless embrace. "Here, take this. It's not much, but it is something." Helen thrust a knitted purse into her fingers. "I will try to help you somehow. I will find a way. Fare well, my child. Keep faith." And then she was moving, hurrying to the door with the remembered gait. Impelled, Meg called after her, "Thank you, Helen. It was boon to have you come to me."

Helen turned at the door. "We will contrive, you'll see. Keep faith."

Meg clutched the purse, unable even to think of opening it, bereft and forlorn as she felt. She was once more alone among strangers.

Chapter Twelve

Ottilia was not insensitive to her husband's unusual silence as they were dressing for dinner. The presence of Diplock and Joanie might preclude a discussion of private matters, but Ottilia was accustomed to desultory chat even while the servants were in the room.

Had she made a mistake to wait for Helen Pargeter outside Meg's room? If she was truthful, she had not wanted to confront the brewing storm. She had told herself it was politic to wait, while the unexpected visitor and Lizzy were in the house, but now the unspoken condemnation was oppressive. There had been no opportunity to air it, Sybilla having heard from Venner of Helen's presence. She had come down from her sitting-room just as the front door shut behind the visitors and wasted no time.

"Was that Meg's mother? How did she find out the girl was here?"

Ottilia had personally seen them out and she turned, ushering Sybilla into the parlour. "Mrs Pargeter is her stepmother." She adroitly avoided the latter question. "It seems she came in secret, without informing the Reverend Pargeter, which I must admit is a relief. I cannot think his intervention would make our task any easier."

Sybilla was successfully diverted. "She did not tell him the girl is here? What a nuisance. He might have removed her, and welcome. What did this female have to say?"

"She was much shocked, and she is not sure her visit did Meg a great deal of good."

"Then you have gained nothing by it."

Ottilia thought otherwise, but it was plain her mother-in-law was in one of her twitty moods, complaining of having agreed to go to a party that evening and declaring she had half a mind to cry off. Her presence kept at bay the subject clearly uppermost in Francis's mind, as indeed it was in Ottilia's. He barely glanced at her, his jaw set, and such remarks as he contributed to the conversation were clipped and to the point. If Sybilla noticed it, she made no comment, but Ottilia's sense of impending thunder increased.

By the time she was ready to go downstairs, she knew she could not endure a dinner laced with tension. Then this party must intervene to keep them in this unsatisfactory state all evening? Unbearable. Dismissing the maid, who retired with the basin of water she had brought, Ottilia waited for her husband's valet to help him into his evening coat.

She caught Francis's gaze in the mirror and he turned.

"Don't wait for me, Ottilia."

She met his eyes. "I am in no hurry."

His brows drew together and his regard was measuring, she thought. The use of her full name told its own tale. He turned away.

"That will do, Diplock. Leave us, if you please."

The valet bowed and withdrew. Ottilia waited only until the door closed behind him before taking a couple of steps towards Francis.

"You are angry with me about Lizzy. I have no excuses, Fan. I should not have involved her. I knew it at the time, I confess."

A muscle worked in his cheek and she guessed he was holding his temper in with an effort. "Then why did you?"

She made a helpless gesture. "Will it make any difference if I burble a plethora of reasons? I judged badly."

The frown intensified. "That's all? That is to be the end of it?"

"What do you want me to say? If you are looking for regret, I have none. I could wish Lizzy had not acted without consulting me, but the outcome has been happy. I cannot be sorry for that."

"Yet you admit it was ill-judged to involve her at all."

"I have said so. It began without intent. I wanted to quiz her about Pierre, that was all. But she leapt in at once, wanting to help. She found it exciting."

"Of course she did." A derisive note entered his voice. "She's eighteen, Tillie. It's not like you to be obtuse. Couldn't you see what sort of a girl she is? Couldn't you guess she would jump in with both feet? You should hear Dalesford on the subject of his daughter. She's an impulsive, mischievous little minx."

"I found her, on the contrary, both discerning and thoughtful. Oh, she has an excitable manner, but her grasp of essentials—"

"In other words, she's a girl after your own heart." Francis threw up his hands. "It's immaterial, Tillie. You had no business to be giving her any task at all. Who knows what sort of imbroglio she might get into? Just the fact she went off seeking this Pargeter woman on her own is enough to tell you she is not to be trusted." He had paced away as he spoke, but turned back on the words. "I made her promise not to go blindly into anything again, on pain of being totally excluded, but I don't want you to use her in any way again, do you understand?"

Ottilia hesitated. She ought to acquiesce at once, but she was plagued by a sense of injustice. Had she done so very wrong?

An inkling of a deeper truth lurked in her mind. "Is this because of Sybilla? Are you thinking she would—"

"She would create merry hell and you know it." His dark eyes were sombre. "But if you are thinking I'm merely afraid of raising my mother's ire — or my sister's and Dalesford's for the matter of that — you are wide of the mark." He came to her then, gripping her shoulders, a flare of violence in his gaze. "Do you ever think what it does to me when you put yourself under these threats of potential danger? How the deuce could I face any of them if Lizzy were to be hurt when I know what it is to suffer that gut-wrenching dread of losing you?"

Her mind drained of thought, her bosom flooding with agonizing guilt, Ottilia gazed at the fierceness in his face. Her vision blurred. Francis uttered a groan and she was dragged into his embrace. His lips crushed hers in a convulsive kiss and then her face was buried in his coat.

"Tillie, Tillie, my darling heart … you know not what you do to me." The hoarse words whispered into her ear and she wept.

Presently, his hold loosened and he leaned back to look into her face. Ottilia tried to smile, her voice husky. "I won't ask forgiveness, Fan. You know my heart. I wish I did not fret you so, but if I swear to change, I will be forsworn in no time. I am what I am."

A wry smile curved his mouth. "Yes, and it's what I love about you." He kissed her, lightly this time. "Will you keep Lizzy out of this?"

She set a hand to his chest. "As far as I can, Fan, I promise. I won't encourage her. But you know as well as I do that these things impinge upon you once you are in them. I may not be able to prevent her involvement. Nor may Lizzy either," she added in haste.

Francis let out a sighing breath. "Then I must warn Dalesford. He may have better success in keeping his daughter out of harm's way."

Pierre had responded eagerly to Lizzy's signal at the Wooborough ball, anxious to hear the outcome of her approach to Helen.

"She wants to speak to you, Pierre."

"Marguerite? She will see me?"

"Not Meg." Lizzy clicked an impatient tongue. "Mrs Pargeter."

"Helen? It is that she will curse me, no?"

"I doubt it. She is not pleased with you, but she wants to see you nevertheless. She charged me to tell you to meet her in the Bloomsbury market where you took me to find her. Tomorrow at ten. Will you be there?"

"She acts for this Pargeter? She seeks to make me show myself that he may punish me, that is seen."

Lizzie emitted a short laugh. "I don't know her very well, but I should think that is the last thing Helen Pargeter would do."

"Ah, you do not know, milady. He is cunning like the fox that one. In her way, she contrives, yet he has the mastery of her; as he commands so she obeys."

"If you ask me, she is an accomplished actress. All I can tell you is that she made this request after she had seen Meg. And it is of no use to ask me what passed between them because Mrs Pargeter did not confide in me."

Pierre scanned the crowd, hunting for Helen's familiar brown bonnet and pelisse among a plethora of similar garments worn by the poorer element obliged to eke out a living as he had done in those weeks of terror, as he dodged the agents of

Lafayette and Vergniaud's spies. Along with servants, these people formed the bulk of the market clientele. He spotted Helen at last, hovering between a stall selling old clothes and one offering, along with other toiletries, those scented soaps she would secretly purchase. Remembrance of her little kindnesses to Pierre flickered in his mind and he hesitated no longer, pushing through the crowd to reach her.

"Madame! Helene!"

She turned on him a gaze in which a trace of alarm showed and was swiftly borne away as recognition flared. "You came. I thought you might be too much a coward to approach me."

Her voice clicked with suppressed feeling and he knew he was unforgiven. He opted for truth.

"Such I was, madame, but Milady Elizabeth has said you wish to see me. Also that you have seen Marguerite."

A grim look entered her face as she stared up at him under the concealing bonnet. "That brought you, did it? I guessed as much. Not that Meg has any such faith."

"She hates me? She has reason."

"In justice she ought, but she went to find you in preference to facing her father when she found out she was with child."

"I know it."

"Then I wonder you let her run off with that fellow and did nothing to stop it."

"Coveney! I knew not of this until it was too late. But what did he do to her? How has he hurt her? She did right to kill him!"

Helen emitted an exasperated sound. "I might have expected you'd make as much of a song and dance as Meg herself. The point, Monsieur de Percheval, is not that he's dead, but that Meg is like to hang for it."

"They cannot. A woman with a child within? It is of a cruelty unimaginable."

"More cruel than the deaths mounting up under your countrymen? Man, woman, child, it doesn't matter, does it?"

"For this you accuse me? Am I in Paris? Is it I who suffer these to die?"

"Not them, no. But you condemned Meg, sir, as sure as I'm standing here, when you seduced her in my house."

"*Sapristi*, do you think I do not know? Do you think I do not regret? It is for this I begged Milady Elizabeth to speak with you. It is my desire most ardent to speak with Marguerite, to own my fault, to beg of her forgiveness."

"And that's all? Have you no scheme for her relief? Can't you think beyond your own torments? You disgust me, sir."

He flinched, but what could he say? He deserved it all.

Helen met his gaze steadily for a moment, and then turned away. Galvanised, Pierre seized her arm.

"Wait! Do not go, madame. Your words are just. Yes, it is that such thoughts are selfish, but this is not all. I wish above all things to make amends. Yet how? I am barred from that house. The Dowager Marchioness does not approve me, I know. Milady Polbrook, who is my friend and countrywoman, she tells me this."

Helen's expression was guarded, but she did not move. She looked at his hand gripping her arm and he at once let go.

"Forgive, I beg, madame. I hope I have not hurt you."

She shook her head. "You hurt my Meg, not me. I had hoped you were a better man, Pierre. I thought if I approached you, I could do Meg a kindness. You're a witness, you are. Or you could be. You ought to be willing to find a way to act for her relief. An honourable man, a gentleman, would not hesitate. He would let nothing stand between him and the woman he had wronged. Nothing, Pierre." Of a sudden, she came close, looking up at him with a fierce intensity that echoed in her voice. "Meg has lost all hope. You can give her that. If you so choose. You can give her life." She nodded. "Life. Remember that."

Then she turned from him and was threading so swiftly through the press of people, he could not have stopped her if he tried. As it was, he stood like a statue, the word ringing in his mind: life.

The drawing room at Brooks's appeared to be full of acquaintances Francis had not seen for an age, to a man bent upon delaying him with anecdotal histories in which he had not the smallest interest. While he made polite noises, he scanned the place for any sign of the young Frenchman, or one of his gaming associates. He groaned at the necessity, but having forbidden his wife to involve Lizzy any further, he could scarcely object to it when she requested him to find out Pierre de Percheval and arrange a meeting. He had entered a caveat however.

"Where, if you please? Mama won't tolerate his coming here."

An echo of Ottilia's mischief sneaked into her gaze. "I shall leave that to your ingenuity, dearest. Unless you care to question him yourself?"

He cocked an eyebrow. "Do you care to enlighten me as to your suspicions of this encounter with a footpad?"

Her warm smile appeared. "Wretch of a creature, you know me too well."

The night's intimacy had eroded all trace of the quarrel between them and he drew her into his embrace, cradling her as he looked into her face.

"So well, my dear one, I will not rob you of your pleasure. You are dying to meet the boy, are you not?"

She gurgled even as she delivered a light tap to his chest. "Fiend."

He laughed, kissed her and let her go. "Breakfast. I am going nowhere without sustenance."

"I swear you have two stomachs, Fan," she said, preceding him from the bedchamber.

"I have a perfectly normal appetite for a grown man, I thank you, my lady Fan. Gipping understands as much."

His mother's butler, accustomed to providing a morning meal fit only for a bird in Francis's opinion, had responded suitably to a quiet word in his ear, after which a selection of viands appeared each day, substantial enough to satisfy the most ardent trencherman. Francis, armoured by beef and bacon, set forth on his mission with less reluctance than he might otherwise have felt.

For some time, it looked as if his efforts would prove abortive. But then Redlingfield strolled in. With a word of excuse, Francis deserted the fellow currently boring him and hailed the older man.

"Well met, sir. Just the man I want."

Redlingfield let out a weary sigh. "Again? What more do you want of me, Fanshawe? I told you everything I knew."

Forgetting his main aim, Francis pounced on this. "You did not mention the attack upon Coveney and de Percheval."

The other's brows shot up. "That flurry? What is that to the purpose? Apart from Matt's incessant complaints of his injuries."

"It is very much to the purpose since the blow he received accounts neatly for the broken rib that killed him."

"Is it so indeed?" Redlingfield's gaze widened but held. "Then you have your answer and need trouble us no more."

Ignoring this, Francis pressed for anything further he might glean of the matter, recalling Ottilia's interest. "He complained of pain to his chest? Aldreth says he refused to consult a surgeon."

He came under narrowed scrutiny from the fellow's shrewd eyes. "You've seen Harry then. Ah, of course. He was your informant."

An odd note in his voice struck Francis. Was there more to the business? He lowered his tone to a conspiratorial murmur. "What do you know, Redlingfield?"

The other man's brows drew together and he glanced about as if he checked for listening ears. Then he jerked his head towards a far window and sauntered away. Francis followed, senses on the alert and joined the viscount, who stood looking out into the street below. He spoke without turning his head.

"Matt was convinced the attack was deliberate. He swore some enemy meant to wound him. Even kill him. He was ready to accuse us all of hiring an assassin."

"Aldreth said nothing of this."

A mocking glance came Francis's way. "Harry was never sober enough to notice much beyond Matt's grumbling of his hurts. Besides, Matt never seriously supposed it could be Aldreth. Myself or Lezayre were alleged to be jealous of our losses to him."

"What said the Frenchman to it?"

"He tried to make a joke of it but made a poor showing. Lezayre supported de Percheval, who pooh-poohed the notion. In fact he became decidedly obstreperous over it. He had tackled the man, do you see, and claimed it was a random attempt at a robbery."

"Claimed?"

Redlingfield's gaze came around, an odd light within it. "Did I say claimed?"

Francis met the look squarely. "Why claimed, Redlingfield?"

The other man shifted his shoulders, glancing away and back again. "It is vague at best, but it struck me at the time."

"Well?"

Redlingfield sighed. "If you must have it, I found de Percheval's refutation overly emphatic. Why so vehement? I recall his words: No one seeks to kill *you*, milord Coveney. *You*. He emphasised that. I noted it particularly."

Francis digested this, a stir of possibility in his head. "He believed he was the intended victim rather than Coveney?"

"It rather looks that way, does it not?"

Remembering the discussion after Aldreth's visit, Francis pursued this. "An agent from Paris perhaps? It seems likely he fell foul of the French authorities."

Redlingfield's lip curved into a sneer. "I should not be at all surprised. His credentials were ever in doubt, though Lezayre vouches for him."

"You've no knowledge of what he may have done to be obliged to flee the country?"

The sneer became more pronounced. "Well, it wasn't to escape the vengeance of the mob on account of his origins."

"How can you be sure?"

"Because he's a black leg."

"A gambling cheat?"

"Difficult to tell. But his fingers are too practised for an amateur. He can shuffle and deal like lightning when he forgets to pretend. He snaps the cards as if they are part of his fingers. It's the one giveaway he has not managed to conceal. Lezayre knows too, for I've seen him nudge or frown the boy down when he does it."

This was the last thing Francis had expected. "You spoke of Coveney's skill as I remember."

"Ah, but this is of a different order. I'd wager the boy recalls every card played and can predict every hand, even if he doesn't fuzz the cards to his advantage."

"You believe he is so skilled?"

Redlingfield pursed his lips. "He scans his hand in a flash, though he affects to hesitate over his discards. If you watch his eyes when he is not attending, you can see the calculation as he overlooks the play. I suspect he knows exactly which cards every player holds, at least when it is his deal."

"Ah, then he does fuzz the cards?"

"I think he rather shuffles the pack to his advantage. He uses his discards to force others to play to whatever strength he holds."

"How can you know that?"

"Because when he allows himself to win with us — and makes a song and dance of his success as if it is rare — he does it with panache. He makes it look an accident that the cards fall his way, but to my belief it's no such thing. If you wish to know what I truly think, he could have taken any one of us to the tune of thousands any time he chose."

This put a whole different complexion on the matter. "A *chevalier d'industrie*, you think, fleecing the rich?"

Redlingfield's laugh was derisory. "Or the not so rich. There are few men of property left in France to be relieved of their gold. Though I doubt the new regime have eradicated gaming."

"And if he played off his tricks on members of the Legislature…"

"He would no doubt be wise to make himself scarce." Redlingfield flung up a hand. "But that part is pure supposition. You had best tackle Lezayre or the boy himself, if it interests you."

It interested Francis exceedingly, but he could not imagine the elder Frenchman would be induced to confide the truth, if indeed he could be found.

"Have you seen Lezayre lately?"

"He's lying low, like the rest of us until this business is settled. Try Starkey's of an evening. If he's not there, she may have word of him."

He gave a nod and moved away with deliberation, giving Francis no chance even to thank him. In a moment, he had left the drawing room.

Francis returned his gaze to the street below, pondering. No sign of either Frenchman. If he wanted Pierre's direction, it looked as if he would be obliged to consult Violette, assuming Randal's wife knew where the boy lived. He was about to turn away to leave Brooks's with the intention of repairing to Hanover Square when he caught sight of Lizzy's father on the other side of St James's Street. Dalesford would be aiming for White's.

Without thought, Francis threaded quickly through the chatterers to the door, heading for the stairs. In a moment, he was cramming his beaver on his head and, collecting his topcoat without bothering to put it on, sped out into the street and hurried after the earl. Dalesford was about to enter the portal of White's when Francis hailed him. He smiled in recognition.

"Fanshawe, is it you indeed? I had hoped to find you at the Harbisher do some days since, but Harriet said you and Ottilia would not come on account of your mother's prejudice."

Francis laughed as they shook hands. "The repercussions would be more than my life is worth, I fear."

Dalesford grinned. "Devilish woman is my mother-in-law. Always terrified me. My poor Harriet lives in dread of being called to account. 'Would Mama approve?' is her criterion for everything."

"I'm glad I caught you," said Francis, aware how much his sister stood in awe of Sybilla. "I was going to seek you out, Gil. Need a word in your ear. It's about Lizzy."

His brother-in-law let out a mock groan. "What has that little minx of mine done now?"

Gilbert Fiske, Earl of Dalesford, was a man of slight proportions, though of a good height, who had bequeathed his features to his eldest daughter. In him, the chin was stronger and the nose more prominent, but the overall look was unmistakeable. Especially now, his expression resigned but withal showing a glimmer of amusement.

"I'm afraid it's no laughing matter, though not serious as yet. It might become so, however, if Lizzy is drawn any further into the business."

Dalesford's brows drew together. "What business?" Then they flew up. "You are not talking of the female your wife is harbouring? The one who arrived all over blood and is said to have done away with Coveney?"

Francis let out an exasperated expletive. "Is it all over town? Or did you have it from Harriet?"

"I had it from Randal. He was haranguing me about Candia and that young Frenchman who's been hanging about her. What has Lizzy to do with the matter?"

Francis told him in a few succinct words, playing down Ottilia's part out of loyalty. "I've told Ottilia not to involve Lizzy further, but as she pointed out, there is no saying but what young Pierre may drag her in as she has been his conduit to the Pargeter woman."

Gilbert whistled. "What a rigmarole, Fan! Typical of my Lizzy to go ferreting about where she's no business to be."

"That's why I'm telling you, Gil. You are far better placed to keep her safe. I've warned her of the dangers, and told her she must not act on her own again, but—"

"No sense in that, old fellow. The minx would only plead it was in some sort forced on her. 'But I had to, Papa,'" he said in fair imitation of Lizzy's voice, "'or I would have died of starvation.' That, if you will believe me, is what she said after she climbed out of the window and escaped when Harriet locked her in her bedchamber."

Francis had to laugh. "She's certainly enterprising. And she has courage."

"Too much." Though the note of pride in her father's voice did not escape Francis's ear. "I'll keep an eye on her."

"Will you have a fatherly word? You can tell her I was your informant, if you wish. She'll think the worse of me for ratting on her, I dare say, but that is preferable to her running foul of some villain, if there is one in the case."

Dalesford clapped a hand to his shoulder. "Don't vex yourself over it, Fan. You've enough on your hands, by the sound of it. You may leave Lizzy to me."

The undercurrent of sympathy did not sit well with Francis. He might find Ottilia's machinations frustrating, but the faintest suggestion of criticism, whether real or implied, was intolerable to him. He did not take Dalesford up on it. After all, he might simply be referring to the tasks he had in hand since the advent of Meg Pargeter into the Fanshawe entourage. No less than his mother did he long for the day they might be rid of the woman.

He bid Gilbert farewell, slipped on his topcoat and set off in the direction of Hanover Square, hoping the new marchioness was at home for once.

The resumption of normal life proved inordinately dull to Lizzy. She was relieved when the morning visit was over, especially in Candia's company. She was in bad odour with her cousin, from whom she had been obliged to endure a passionate catechism.

Where had she gone on those two mornings? And Lizzy need not think her activities were secret for Candia had questioned the footman. Was she meeting with Pierre? She was involving herself in this business of the female Aunt Ottilia had taken to Bruton Street, was she not? She need not deny it. She would get into trouble, and cause trouble for Pierre too. Had he not suffered enough?

Lizzy parried these questions as best she could, while reflecting that she had grossly underestimated Candia's feelings for the Frenchman. Was she smitten to the heart? In the end, Lizzy was provoked into revealing more than she ought.

"Candy, for heaven's sake! Suffered? He has not suffered nearly as much as poor Meg. And it's his fault!"

Candia's lustrous eyes had grown enormous, filling with moisture. Her voice became hushed. "What do you mean?"

Struck at once with remorse, Lizzy tried to backtrack. "Nothing. I'm sorry I said anything."

"It is too late now. Of what do you accuse him?"

Desperate, Lizzy blurted out the truth. "He really isn't what you think him, Candy. He's duplicitous and ambitious. Although I hope he may redeem himself a little now. At least he has shown remorse for his misdeeds."

"What misdeeds? What has he done?"

"I can't tell you that."

"Why not? Surely I have a right to judge for myself? I know Pierre has made mistakes. He admitted as much."

"Mistakes! He ruined that girl!"

Which sent Candia into a frenzy of weeping as she rushed from the den to hide in her bedchamber. She refused to discuss the matter again with her cousin and an uneasy truce prevailed. Lizzy could only hope the knowledge of the truth might make a dent in Candia's partiality.

The walk home from Grosvenor Street, where the pair had been spending the morning with Lady Phoebe Graveney, the betrothed of Candia's brother, was short and attended by Lizzy's maid, leaving no opportunity for private discussion, to Lizzy's relief. Her mind reverted at once to her preoccupation with Meg's plight and she could not help wondering how Pierre was faring with Helen Pargeter.

They had just turned into George Street when Lizzy spied a vaguely familiar figure loitering near the entrance of Dalesford House. Pierre? No, too thin and too darkly clad to be him. His hat, with its rounded top and wide brim, typical of a particular class of person, struck with familiarity.

"Who in the world is that?"

Candia's question came just as the man's identity shrieked into Lizzy's consciousness. She froze, seizing her cousin's arm in a vice-like grip. Candia's yelp brought the stranger's head round and Lizzy found herself staring into the austere and pallid features of the Reverend Pargeter.

He stepped forward, blocking the steps up to the porch. "As I thought, Lady Elizabeth. You have deceived me."

Lizzy's pulse thrummed but she stood her ground, trying to sound haughty. "How so, sir?"

That faint sneer curved his mouth and disdain was in his tone. "You need not dissemble, my lady. Nor look down your nose at me. You have consorted with de Percheval and drawn my wife into your machinations."

A gasp from Candia drew Lizzy's head round and she threw her cousin a warning look before turning back to Pargeter. "Where had you your information, sir?"

"I had it, madam, via the evidence of my eyes and a knowledge of the deceitfulness of your kind."

The insult conquered Lizzy's fear and shot her into fury. "Stand aside, Mr Pargeter. You have no right to prevent my entering my own house." She signalled to the maid. "Nancy, ring the bell."

Pargeter made no attempt to stop the maid, who slipped past him at a run, fairly tripped up the stairs and set a peal echoing within.

"Let us go inside, indeed, my lady," said Pargeter with apparently unimpaired calm. "I have a great desire to speak with de Percheval, who is at this moment within."

"Pierre is here?" came in a squeak from Candia. She brushed past Reverend Pargeter and hastened up the steps to join the maid.

Lizzy, leaping to a rapid conclusion, stared at the gaunt figure before her. "You followed him!"

"I did. My wife's demeanour since she returned from her expedition with you disturbed me."

"Good heavens, sir, do you say you spied upon your own wife? How despicable."

His lip curled. "You would say so, of course. Duty is a concept little understood by your kind."

"That is what you call it?"

"Speak as you choose, Lady Elizabeth, you will make no impression upon me. I am armoured by the Lord's will and testament." He turned as the door opened, leaving Lizzy flat to approach the butler who had allowed Candia access and was waiting in the aperture. "I am Reverend Pargeter. You have Monsieur de Percheval within. I wish to speak with him."

Snade's bland expression did not alter. He looked towards Lizzy in mute question. She followed Pargeter up the steps, gave an infinitesimal shake of the head and passed within as the butler stood aside.

How it happened she was unable to fathom, but even as Snade turned back to bar Pargeter's entrance as she thought, Lizzy heard Pargeter speak right behind her.

"You will produce de Percheval at once, if you please."

She turned on the man. "I shall do nothing of the kind. How dare you barge into my house? You are not welcome here, sir."

He did not flinch. "Lady Elizabeth, I take that tone from no one but my God. Nor is it for a mere mortal to say where I may or may not enter."

Lizzy fairly gaped. "Sir, your arrogance is unbelievable." She looked to where the equally imperturbable butler yet stood by the open door. "Snade, show Mr Pargeter out."

The reverend threw up a hand. "He touches me at peril of his soul. I am an instrument of the Lord."

Before Lizzy could think of a suitable response, a new voice spoke from the rear of the wide hall. "*Alors*, it is myself you seek, *m'sieur*. Do not, I beg, trouble Milady Elizabeth."

A glance showed her Pierre, standing just outside the open bookroom door. There was time for no more than a brief glimpse of Candia within as hell erupted.

With a roar, Pargeter streaked past her, raising his cane. Pierre took the full impact of his flying body, crashing to the floor, Pargeter on top of him. For a frozen moment, Lizzy watched in horror as his assailant seized Pierre's head and banged it down once, twice. Then the reverend was up, his cane flailing about the fallen Frenchman, whose groans were barely audible under Candia's screams.

Instinct sent Lizzy tumbling to the rescue, yelling for assistance. "Snade, seize him! Candia, get out of the way!" She grabbed with both hands at the arm wielding the cane, striving to bring it away. "Stop! Leave him alone!"

Showing surprising strength for so slight a man, Pargeter threw her off so violently that she went spinning, almost losing her balance. By the time she had righted herself, she saw the butler was grappling the reverend from behind, attempting to drag him away by main force. Yet the strokes continued to find their mark, Pierre evidently too dazed to be able to do more to protect himself than cover his head with his arms, which took the brunt of the attack.

Appalled, Lizzy charged back into the fray, calling for more help as she did so. "Charles! Someone! Help!" Again, she tried to halt the attack, clinging to the reverend's arm for dear life. With Snade on his shoulders he could not so readily be rid of her, she hoped.

He roared again, rearing up and shaking himself free. Snade fell back. Lizzy held on, but Pargeter turned on her with a snarl, seizing her fingers and prying them loose.

As she made to grab him again, from the corner of her eye she saw the cane rise and fall, towards her this time. The hit came backhand, catching her across the legs. Lizzy yelped and sprang back.

"Lizzy! He hurt you! Oh, why does not anyone come?"

Over Candia's tearful protests, she heard the welcome sound of feet thumping down the stairs and male voices calling out.

"Devil take it, what is going on?"

But there was no time to answer or look, nor tend to the stinging somewhere beneath her petticoats. Pargeter had returned to the attack, belaying Pierre about the body without mercy.

Lizzy did not stop to think. She flew at the reverend, leaping onto his back and seizing him about the shoulders, much as she had done to her father in play as a small child. She held on as he thrashed. Then a male hand pulled the cane from Pargeter's grasp as he struggled to be rid of the incubus and sent it spinning across the hall.

"Let go, Lizzy!"

Papa! She released her hold and almost fell as she slid off Pargeter's back. Staggering, she saw her father and the footman Charles struggling with the reverend while Candia was on her knees beside the groaning Pierre. At least he was still alive! A quick glance showed that the butler had fared ill. He was sitting in an attitude of collapse upon the porter's chair.

Grunts and curses came from the three struggling men as her father and the footman fought to subdue the violent intruder. Just as Lizzy's mind was going this way and that in a bid to think how she might help, Pargeter broke free. In a moment, he was out of the still open door, pursued by Charles. She could hear them running, but her father was bent forward with hands on his knees, panting.

"Papa, are you hurt?"

He let go a whoosh of breath and pushed upright, gasping out, "What the deuce was all that about?"

There was no concealing her activities now. "That was Mr Pargeter. He is Meg's father. The girl who Aunt Ottilia—"

"Befriended," he finished. "Yes, I know all about that. Fanshawe told me what you've been up to, you impossible minx. But what the devil was the fellow doing here?" He swung his gaze upon the victim. "And why is de Percheval here, I should like to know? What have you been about now, Lizzy?"

The resigned tone drew a wry laugh from her. "It's not my doing, Papa. Not this at least. But I think I know why Pierre is here."

"Well, don't tell me now. We'd best get the fellow onto a sofa in the parlour and send for Ellington. I only hope that lunatic hasn't broken any bones."

At this, Lizzy shot to the back of the hall where Pierre still lay, a tearful Candia beside him. She dropped down on the other side of the man, shushing at her cousin.

"Do be quiet, Candia, you are not helping. Pierre, can you talk? Where does it hurt?"

"It hurts him all over, I should think," Candia snapped, brushing her hands across her cheeks and sniffing. "That horrid creature beat him to pieces. We must help him up."

"Not yet. Wait for Papa." Lizzy heard her father talking with the footman, who had evidently returned. She turned her head, calling out. "You lost him, Charles?"

The fellow was out of breath. "Chased him all down the street, my lady — but he's fleet. Dived down a side street and vanished."

"Never mind it now, Charles," said her father. "Get to Doctor Ellington's as fast as you can and bid him come here instanter." He added as the footman went off on his errand, carefully closing the door behind him, "Snade, help me get this gentleman into the parlour. Cushions, Nancy. Pile them up on the sofa. Hurry, girl."

Lizzy saw the maid run. "Gracious, is she still here?"

"Cowering behind the stairs, I shouldn't wonder. And who shall blame the poor girl?" Her father joined them, looking down at the fallen man. "Is he conscious?"

Lizzy looked round at Pierre just as Candia cried out. "He's fainted!"

"Give place there, Candy. Let me check his limbs before we move him."

"Pargeter followed him from the market," said Lizzy, watching her father run his hands along the Frenchman's arms and legs.

"Which market?"

"One near the parsonage. Pierre went there to meet Helen Pargeter. It's where I met her."

"I knew it!" Candia threw her a furious look. "I said you were involved. Now see what has come of it."

Lizzy ignored her. "I am anxious for poor Mrs Pargeter. He will likely exact revenge upon her for our deception. He is a terrible man."

"Then you had no business to be encouraging him to come here."

Exasperated, Lizzy looked up. "For heaven's sake, Candy! I won't be held responsible for the wretched man's actions. I was trying to help Aunt Ottilia save Meg from the gallows."

Candia's mouth dropped open and Dalesford ceased his labours and glanced up with a warm look. "That's my girl. I've been waiting to hear your excuses, but that one I can't fault."

A lump rose to Lizzy's throat. "I did not mean for it to come to this, Papa, I promise you."

A faint smile creased his mouth as he rose. "One never does. Well, I think this young man has escaped the worst. It's mostly bruises."

"How can you say so, Uncle Gilbert? That man banged his head on the floor. He may have a concussion, or worse."

"I doubt he's cracked his skull, if that's what you mean, child. I dare say his head may ache for a day or two."

"But he's unconscious!"

"He's in a good deal of pain. Shocked too. Snade, fetch brandy to the parlour. If he does not wake in a moment, we'll carry him into the parlour between us."

Lizzy itched to be doing. "I think I will walk round to Grandmama's and tell Aunt Ottilia what has happened."

Her father threw up an admonitory finger. "No! I don't want you running foul of Francis again. He'll be incandescent. You stay here and help Candy minister to the fallen. I'll do the honours once the doctor has been."

The atmosphere in the Bruton Street parlour was growing icy. Ottilia struggled to keep her temper as Sir Thomas Ingham remained adamant. She had given him as much information as she had gleaned from the various interviews, dwelling on the clear intimation that the death blow Coveney received had been administered by someone other than Meg, but she signally failed to convince Justice Ingham. He had come for his prisoner and nothing appeared likely to move him from his purpose.

"These histories are all very well, Lady Francis, but you have naught by way of proof. I can delay no longer."

Ottilia had taken a stance at a point between Ingham and the parlour door, as if she might thus keep him from the path that would lead him to Meg. She tried another tack.

"Yet what will it profit you, sir, to remove the poor woman to a draughty cell where her condition must necessarily deteriorate?"

"I cannot help that, ma'am." There was an edge to Ingham's voice. "She is a felon, guilty of a vicious attack which killed a man."

"Innocent until proven guilty, sir," Sybilla pointed out. She was standing near the fireplace, looking perfectly fierce as she backed Ottilia up, despite her oft expressed desire to be rid of Meg Pargeter.

Ingham visibly bridled. "I believe I know the law, Lady Polbrook. I also know my duty."

"To incarcerate a pregnant girl in one of your dungeons?"

"We do not have dungeons, my lady."

Glad of her mother-in-law's support though she was, Ottilia could not feel these acerbic remarks were helpful. Justice Ingham's tone was becoming steely. She tried for a softer note.

"I have no wish to interfere with your duty, Sir Thomas, but if you are afraid Meg may abscond from here, could you not post a guard in the house?"

"I cannot spare a man indefinitely, Lady Francis. You must understand there are imperatives I can no longer withstand."

"Ha! Your superiors are on your back, is that it? Then why not say so, man?"

Ottilia saw a muscle working in Ingham's jaw and intervened again before he could answer Sybilla. "I dare say you are under pressures of which we know nothing, sir. I can appreciate that. My concern is for Meg's health. She was in a debilitated state even when Lord Coveney took her in, never mind the aftermath of the events leading up to his death. You propose to remove her to Bridewell, I presume, where she will have no access to good food, to washing and general personal care and it may be weeks before she comes to trial. I am afraid she may not survive."

Ingham sighed. "I will see she is housed as well as possible, ma'am, but I can make no promises."

"Is it money?" demanded Sybilla. "Has she to pay her gaolers to receive decent treatment? I will stand the nonsense, if that is so."

"A good thought, Sybilla, but I would still prefer Meg to remain here." Ottilia moved further into the room, approaching Ingham. "I can set my steward Hemp to guard the door. Not that I suppose for an instant that Meg will attempt to escape from here. Where would she go? She is terrified of her father's wrath and she has abandoned all faith in Pierre de Percheval's possible help. Sir Thomas, there really is no danger of her vanishing from this house."

"Nevertheless, ma'am, I must insist on removing her to a more suitable location."

"But—"

Ingham held up a hand. "It is useless to argue the matter, ma'am. I make every allowance for your partiality and I have given you as much leeway as I can."

Was there no moving him? Ottilia brought out what she hoped were her big guns. "If you must have it, sir, I am almost certain of the identity of the man who delivered the blow that broke Lord Coveney's rib. I told you of the attack upon him and the young Frenchman, did I not?"

"By some footpad or other? I don't see—"

"It was not a common footpad. I cannot yet give you a name, but if I am right there is every reason to hope he may be persuaded to come forward."

"How so?"

"He is nearly connected." Ottilia hesitated, but why withhold it now? It was all she had left. "I am talking of Meg's father."

"Her father?" Ingham stared in evident disbelief. "How is that possible? I thought you said he was a parson."

"Indeed. But a religious zealot who tyrannises his family and forces them to live his own ascetic style of life."

Sybilla looked to be no less taken aback, blinking at Ottilia. "When did you take that idea into your head?"

Ottilia brushed this off with a gesture, warming to her theme. "Sir Thomas, he is just the man to exact vengeance. He meant to hurt de Percheval, but Lord Coveney unfortunately took the hit. At least, that is what I believe. I have not yet had an opportunity to question Pierre, and—"

"Be that as it may, Lady Francis, it is clearly supposition. I can act, as you know, only on facts. You oblige me to reiterate those I know. Meg Pargeter perpetrated a vicious knife attack upon Lord Coveney and he died of his wounds."

"But he did not, as you know well. Your doctor's post mortem—"

"Painted a possible alternative picture, yes. Try if you can convince a jury, ma'am. You will no doubt continue your investigations. Bring me proof and I will reconsider. Meanwhile, however, I mean to take Meg Pargeter prisoner, like it or not."

"Well, she does not like it, and nor do I, sir. High-handed nonsense. What, if you please, are these imperatives of which you speak?"

Justice Ingham turned on Sybilla. "Since you insist, Lady Polbrook, I have been plagued by the dead man's relatives. Not to mention the new Lord Coveney's guardian and trustee. All of whom are, naturally enough, clamouring for justice."

"In other words, you are bowing to outside pressure. I had not thought it of you, Ingham."

Ingham reddened. "I regret to be obliged to disappoint you, my lady, but that is not an imperative likely to weigh with me."

Ottilia leapt in before her mother-in-law could wither him for this impertinence. "We do understand your difficulty, Sir Thomas, and I am only sorry I have not yet been able to satisfy your requirements." She threw the fulminating dowager a warning look and drew a breath. "I see there is no moving you, sir, so I must acquiesce."

His relief was patent. "I thank you, ma'am. If you will lead the way, we will proceed. My fellow is waiting in the hall. He will accompany us."

He turned for the door, but Ottilia, an idea burgeoning, stepped in swiftly. "One moment, sir. Would you object to it if I sent a female attendant along with Meg?"

Ingham pursed his lips. "What, to remain with her?"

"If possible. She cannot remain in the prison, but I can have her housed at an inn nearby if you will permit her to visit Meg and do what she may to make her comfortable."

He stood frowning, evidently turning it over in his mind. To Ottilia's chagrin, Sybilla put her oar in.

"Heavens above, man, why do you hesitate? Have you no compassion at all?"

"Hush, Sybilla," Ottilia begged as Ingham pokered up again. "Sir Thomas has been very patient. What do you say, sir? Would it be too much of an imposition?"

She had struck the right note. Ingham gave her a slight smile. "I see no reason why it should cause a difficulty. I will instruct Mrs Lount accordingly."

"Thank you. And may I visit Meg?"

"Certainly. She is merely being held. We are not monsters, ma'am." This with a darkling look towards Sybilla, who met it with a toss of the head but thankfully chose not to comment.

Resigned to the inevitable, Ottilia moved to the door. "I will have Venner pack a valise for Meg, but we will try not to delay you unduly. If you will follow me, sir."

Meg knew not if the blanket of calm that fell over her was numbness or relief. At least she had not broken into hysterical sobs like the woman Venner. Her throat felt too thick for speech, but she croaked her acquiescence for the benefit of Lady Fan, who looked to be dismayed despite the cool tone.

"I did what I could, Meg. I am sorry."

"You need not repine, ma'am. I am ready."

She glimpsed Ingham just outside the door, and another stolid fellow beside him. Her gaoler? But Lady Fan was speaking again and she tried to listen, although her mind was beginning to feel as if it were filled with cotton.

"Rose, if she is willing, will go with you. My man Hemp will arrange for her accommodation close by. She will come to you daily and attend to your needs."

At which, Venner entered a tearful protest. "Nay, my lady. None but I will attend her."

"No, Venner. I cannot deprive her ladyship of your services. But Rose may be spared. I have sent for her."

"Rose? Pray what use will she be in a place of such misery?"

Lady Fan became sharp. "That will do, Venner. If you wish to be useful, you may set about packing a valise for Miss Pargeter." She put up a finger as the elderly maid began a protest. "Now, if you please."

Meg found her knees weak and sat down abruptly on the bed. She could hear Venner muttering in the background as she moved about, but the sense of being divorced from the proceedings increased even as the bustle continued about her. She was vaguely aware when Rose appeared, heard her gentle acceptance of her new duty and was glad, somewhere in the periphery of that welcome blankness, to think she would not be quite alone.

His name whispered across her heart, giving rise to a faint thread of yearning. Meg quashed it. Pierre was lost to her. Even had he wished, he could do nothing for her now. It was over. Helen's words came back to her. Keep faith? No, she need not struggle to do so any longer. She could accept her fate and be still.

She rose at Lady Fan's urging, but the thick woollen shawl draped about her had no effect upon the ice creeping through her veins. Vaguely, she took in the face of the justice, her nemesis now, and the broader one of the other, expressionless as he took hold of her arm. She was glad of his guidance as she negotiated the stairs, glad to think she need not act for herself, that some other would direct her steps, her life, her future.

The thought that she had none flitted across her brain, and she was glad of that too. There was no need to think. She would do as they directed, speak as they wished. They would end this purgatory and she need never again fear the monster's wrath.

Chapter Thirteen

Ottilia sipped at the cup of coffee hastily sent for by Sybilla, but found it hard to swallow through the ache at her throat. Aware of Sybilla's anxious regard, she looked across and tried to smile.

"I will be well again presently."

Her mother-in-law produced a fierce glare, wafting an impatient hand. "Don't tell me. I know what you are doing, wretched girl. Where is Francis when he is needed? He would soon check this nonsensical tendency of yours to blame yourself."

An involuntary sob attacked Ottilia. "How can I help it? I failed her."

Sybilla leaned towards her, the familiar snap at those black eyes. "Stop it at once, girl! You did not fail her. There was nothing you could do and you know it. Ingham has his rights. Even I could not gainsay him."

Ottilia gave a watery chuckle. "Yes, your disapproval was patent. Thank you for standing with me, especially when you have been wishing Meg away."

"Oh, pish! If you don't know by now I don't mean the half of what I say in my testier moods…" Sybilla sighed. "Not but what I did wish her away. But not to a horrid prison. Those places are perfectly vile."

Ottilia sipped again, the urge to weep receding. The coffee warmed and comforted as it always did. "I don't think he means to incarcerate her in Newgate or some other like establishment. She is awaiting trial, not proven guilty. Although at Bridewell she will be in company with prostitutes and vagrants, poor girl. Unless he means to give her a private cell, which is my hope."

"Wherever he keeps her, it cannot compare with her accommodation here and for that I must pity the woman."

Ottilia was less exercised by Meg's present situation than the potential of her future incarceration, which would indeed be a great deal more uncomfortable if Ottilia did not succeed in mitigating her culpability.

"I thank heaven for her being with child. At least it gives me time."

"Time to do what, Ottilia? You have pursued every avenue to no effect."

"I have not yet tackled Meg's father. But I must first speak to Pierre. I only hope Francis has succeeded in setting up a meeting."

Sybilla set down her own cup. "Yes, whence came this notion of Pargeter being the boy's attacker?"

Ottilia took a fortifying draught of coffee. "It struck me that the attack was an odd sort of thing for a common footpad to do. One man to tackle two? These fellows normally work in pairs or gangs. Moreover, would it not be more productive to attack from behind and take your victim unaware? A blow to the back of the head would bring him down and give you an advantage. By the time he could gather himself, you would have his purse and be off. To attack two at once is madness, for one at least is bound to retaliate."

Sybilla's lips twitched. "One might almost suppose you to be an expert. Had you a secret career as a pickpocket before you came to me?"

"You are forgetting my nephews," said Ottilia, laughing. "Neither Tom nor Ben would dream of setting upon one of their friends without the other's support, imps as they are. The rest is pure logic."

"So far I follow you, but why would Pargeter not equally wait for his victim to be alone?"

Ottilia finished the last of the liquid in her cup and set it down. "That I cannot tell you for I don't know the man. But supposing the attacker was not a footpad, and assuming Pierre and not Coveney was the intended victim, who else is there to suspect?"

"Yes, but why choose the dead of night and hide in an alley? It is hardly conduct to be expected from a parson."

"By Meg's account, he is an unusual sort of parson, to say the least." She almost added Lizzy's name but recalled in time that Sybilla remained ignorant of her granddaughter's involvement. The front doorbell sounded at this moment, and Sybilla gave vent to the thought that leapt into Ottilia's mind.

"This will be Francis at last, thank heaven."

But the voice that answered Gipping's enquiry was loud enough to hear from above, and was not Francis's. Ottilia could not make out the words, but the tone was both authoritative and bombastic, raised in evident argument. She glanced at her mother-in-law. "It is not Fan. Whoever it is, he sounds decidedly out of temper."

Footsteps stamped up the stairs and approached the parlour door, which opened to reveal a harassed-looking Gipping, blocking the doorway. A figure stood behind him, but Ottilia could not properly see the man.

"Begging your pardon, my lady, but this gentleman insists upon having speech with you. May I admit him?"

Sybilla eyed him with raised brows. "Who is it, Gipping?"

"He says he's the father of the young lady who was residing upstairs, my lady. But…" The butler was clearly reluctant to commit himself further. Was there some doubt?

Ottilia could see her mother-in-law was no less startled than she as an amazed glance came her way. "Speak of the devil," she murmured.

A crack of crude laughter escaped Sybilla and she nodded to her butler. "Admit the gentleman, Gipping."

The butler came into the room and stood to one side to make his announcement, affording Ottilia a clear view of a black-clad man of skeletal aspect, hatless and looking a trifle dishevelled, his cravat askew and a tie at the knee of his breeches hanging loose. Small wonder Gipping was doubtful of his reception.

"The Reverend Pargeter."

Pargeter walked into the room, cast a glance across the dowager Ottilia could not but deem disdainful, and turned a cold fish-like gaze upon her.

"You must be this Lady Francis, I surmise. I have come for my daughter."

For a moment Ottilia did not speak, weighing her options as she took in the fellow's unlikely condition. She had hardly expected to be confronted with a scarecrow of a man in a state almost of dishabille. What in the world had happened to bring him here, somewhat out of breath if she was any judge by the quick rise and fall of his breast, and clearly shaky on his own legs?

If she gave him immediate notice of Meg's departure, would he vacate the place before she had a chance to question him? Hoping Sybilla would not pre-empt her, she rose and took a step towards the man.

"I am Lady Francis Fanshawe, yes, sir. I have been wishing very much to have speech with you." An instant frown gave notice of Pargeter's surprise. Ottilia caught a questioning glance from Sybilla and gestured. "May I present the Dowager Marchioness of Polbrook? She has been hostess to your daughter these many days. No doubt you will wish to thank her."

Her intent to rattle the man failed of its effect. A faintly sneering look crossed his face as he threw a glance over Sybilla and returned his cold gaze to Ottilia. "I am not here to bandy words with your aristocratic connections, madam. Nor do I approve of my daughter's sojourn in such a house."

An outraged gasp from Sybilla sent urgency through Ottilia. She was thankful her spouse was not present to hear this impertinence. Francis would throw the fellow bodily from the premises. She stepped quickly forward, putting out a hand towards her mother-in-law. "Pray don't take the bait, ma'am!"

Predictably, Sybilla's black eyes snapped and she rose to confront Pargeter. "I will not stay to be insulted in my own house. How dare you, sir?"

Pargeter did not flinch. He met the attack head on. "I am armoured by my Maker, madam. I dare anything. No man, nor woman, may claim rights above the instrument of the Lord, be they lowly peasant or ranked as high as the King."

Sybilla turned a baffled face upon Ottilia. "The man is mad. I wish you joy of gaining any point with him."

Pargeter ignored this, looking again to Ottilia. "Produce my daughter, madam. Or must I search the place for myself?"

This proved too much for Sybilla, who stepped up to him before Ottilia could intervene. "You do so at your peril, sir!"

The sneer became pronounced. "I do not fear your threats, madam. The Lord is my protector."

"Well, he has done a poor job of protecting your daughter, sir. From you, as I understand it."

"Sybilla!"

But Pargeter remained unruffled. "My dealings with my daughter are not your concern, madam. I act according to the dictates of the Almighty, whose laws I am on this earth to uphold. Fornication outside the sanctity of marriage is a sin. Sinners must be punished for the good of their own soul."

Sybilla flung back towards Ottilia. "If the fellow means to preach at me, I have done."

Relieved, Ottilia moved to her. "Give me leave, ma'am." She lowered her voice to a murmur. "You need not converse with him. Let me try."

Sybilla gave a curt nod and made for her chair. Ottilia raised her head to Pargeter and essayed a smile.

"Let us begin again, Mr Pargeter. May I ask how you came to know your daughter was here?"

His eyes had been following the dowager, a faintly smug look in them, she thought. But he shifted his gaze to meet Ottilia's. "The machinations of the devil and his instruments on earth can never be long concealed, madam. How the matter came to my ears is irrelevant. What is more to the point is how my daughter came to be in this house after she left the protection of mine. This I mean to establish once I have her back in my care."

"Unfortunately, sir, you come too late. Your daughter is no longer here."

Pargeter's brows snapped together. "You lie, madam. My wife saw her here not two days since."

"True, she did. But Justice Ingham from Bow Street removed Meg this very day. Had you come an hour earlier, you might have spared her being haled off to gaol."

Pargeter eyed her in silence, as if he sought to fathom whether she spoke the truth. Ottilia raised her brows.

"You may verify this for yourself, Mr Pargeter, if you choose. But I must warn you Sir Thomas will refuse to release his prisoner, even at her father's instigation."

He reared up his head, eyes flashing. "If the Law has taken her, I will not seek to gainsay their right."

"Oh, indeed? Pardon me, but did I not understand you to say that you abided only by God's law?"

Her sarcasm failed to pierce him. "The Lord's will is shown in this. He would not suffer an innocent to be taken."

"Ah, but she is innocent, Mr Pargeter. Lord Coveney did not die by her hand." Ottilia struck hard. "Indeed, it may well have been by your hand, Mr Pargeter."

His eyes flared. "Mine? Impossible!"

"Oh, but it is eminently possible. Coveney died from a pierced lung due to a broken rib. That break was inflicted by a violent blow in an earlier altercation. An attack, Mr Pargeter, by an unknown man who meant, I am persuaded, to hurt Pierre de Percheval."

The man's pallid features tightened. "He I have suitably dealt with. What or who is this Coveney?"

So he did not know the whole. Ottilia gathered her forces. "You failed to obtain the full story from your wife, I take it?"

His brows drew together and she read a degree of puzzlement in his eyes. "It was enough to know she had deceived me, along with that female, an instrument of yours, no doubt. This Lady Elizabeth with her story of old clothes and patterns, lying to my face."

Ottilia could not forbear a quick glance at her mother-in-law, who had indeed caught the reference and was staring in shocked surprise.

"Lady Elizabeth, you say?"

Pargeter did not even acknowledge her interruption. "Taxed with a charge of deception, my wife broke down and confessed her visit to this place. I heard no more for I had an urgency upon me at that moment."

"To come here?"

"To carry out my duty, madam, as regards the betrayer of my charity. It is done and I am here. You may relate your history."

"Oh, she may, may she?" Sybilla had risen again and she came forward. "Sir, I take leave to tell you your callous attitude disgusts me. If you were truly an instrument of the Lord, as you claim, you would take care to know the truth before you acted."

"Madam, all truth is known to the Almighty. He sees everything."

"So he may, but you, sir, are not God."

Leaning close, Ottilia intervened in a lowered tone. "Do not argue with him, ma'am. It is useless."

"I shall be arguing with you 'ere long," returned Sybilla on a warning note. "Lady Elizabeth?"

"That I will explain presently. Let us concentrate on the matter at hand, if you please."

Sybilla gave her a narrow look that boded ill, but fell back a little nevertheless. Ottilia turned to Pargeter, who appeared to be wholly uninterested in the exchange. His mind evidently ran on one track alone.

"Mr Pargeter, I do not believe I am willing to relate your daughter's full history. Suffice to say my husband and I found her in the road upon our journey here. She was in a terrible state of stupor and she was covered in blood. The body of a man was found in the nearby wood. We took Meg in and informed the authorities. But the wounds she inflicted upon the dead man were superficial. I have told you how he died. Unfortunately, the authorities still consider her attack to be the catalyst of Coveney's death. My object is to have the charge reduced from murder to manslaughter, if, that is, I cannot persuade you, Mr Pargeter, to tell Sir Thomas Ingham your part."

He had listened, she thought, with scant attention, as his immediate words confirmed. "It is as I thought. She is at heart a whore."

"Good heavens, sir, is that all you can say? Your daughter is in danger of her life!"

"She is in His hands. Too sunk in sin to be reclaimable upon this earth. Yet He is all forgiving. After He has punished, He will take her to His bosom."

Frustration and fury attacked Ottilia in equal measure. There was no making an impression upon such a mind. Yet she could not help the protest. "You have not listened to a word I have said, sir. Meg's attack upon this man occurred in a bid to prevent his taking advantage of her. She does not deserve that harsh word. From you, of all people. Have you no compassion? The God I know is merciful."

There was no change in his expression, no slightest evidence of softening. Yet he nodded. "Indeed He is. His will be done."

Ottilia turned to her mother-in-law, throwing up her hands. "This is hopeless."

Sybilla snorted. "I could have told you that from the first instant." But she charged back into the fray, wagging a forefinger in Pargeter's face. "You prate of your duty, sir. Do you not have a duty to right and justice? This daughter of yours has been cruelly wronged. She is a victim of circumstance. The Almighty knows it, if you do not. Take care His retribution falls not upon you instead."

Pargeter bowed his head. "If He deems me unworthy, He will do with me as He wills. I will pray for guidance." The head came up again, fire in the eyes. "In the meanwhile, I must not neglect my flock. Their needs supersede those of a condemned sinner."

With no word of farewell, no bow of acknowledgement, he drew his scarecrow body to its full height, turned and strode from the parlour, leaving the door open. Ottilia heard his steps flying down the stairs and the slam of the front door thereafter and was abruptly overtaken with a ridiculous desire to burst into fits of laughter.

She controlled it, moving to close the parlour door. Turning, she met her mother-in-law's gimlet stare and sighed. "Oh, Sybilla, must you ring a peal over me now? Have we not borne enough this day?"

For a moment the issue hung in the balance. Then the fire died out of Sybilla's eyes and she wafted a hand towards Ottilia's chair.

"Sit, girl." She took her own seat, settling into it with a grunt. "I've said it once and I will say it again. The man is mad."

"If to be blind to everything beyond one's own outlook is insanity, then I agree. I am sorry for Mrs Pargeter."

"Be more sorry for yourself at this moment. Not that I suppose for a moment you dragged young Elizabeth into this business. An impertinent little madam is that girl and I would guess she badgered you, is that it?"

Gratified, Ottilia could not but confess the truth. "She did, but I need not have succumbed. I have already endured Fan's severest scold upon the matter, Sybilla, in particular because he knew you would be furious if you heard of it."

Her mother-in-law snorted. "Because he has no daughters. Give him one, child, and you will soon see how readily he succumbs to female wiles. She will twist him as easily as Elizabeth's fingers twist Dalesford, that I can promise you. The man is besotted with that girl and always has been."

"It is not inevitable. I am persuaded you cannot say the same of Randal with Candia."

"Don't talk to me of Randal! He has but one obsession. And if that Violette of his is not mixed up in this business, you may call me a Dutchwoman."

"Yes, but I don't think she is, except as Pierre's passport to the *bon ton*. Francis heard her talk of Meg's elopement, as it was first thought to be, but I doubt Violette knew how far his association with Meg had gone." Ottilia hastened to deflect the conversation into a less controversial channel. "Be that as it may, I'm sorry to say it is true that Lizzy and Mrs Pargeter deceived the parson. Not that I blame either for that, but—"

"Why send her into that house, Ottilia? Of what were you thinking?"

Ottilia sighed. "I did not do so. Lizzy acted on her own when she accepted a commission from Pierre to approach Helen Pargeter. I was wholly ignorant of that scheme until Mrs Pargeter arrived here with Lizzy. But I do not mean to mitigate my own part. I should not have confided as much to her."

Sybilla wafted a dismissive hand. "I have no doubt you warned her not to do anything untoward. Harriet has done so a score of times, to no avail. The girl is perfectly unmanageable and Dalesford is to blame, for he was never strict enough with her. Mark my words, it will be just the same with any daughter of yours. Francis is in the same mould as Dalesford when it comes to his affections."

Ottilia smiled as a pointed look came her way. "You mean to imply that he indulges me disgracefully. He does and I adore him for it. And this, I hope," she added, as yet another ring at the front door sounded, "is the man himself at last."

"I trust it may be found to be Francis. It has better not be the parson's unfortunate wife this time. I warn you I will not endure another Pargeter within these walls."

But the voice that answered Gipping produced a leap at Ottilia's heart and in a moment her husband walked into the parlour. She rose to greet him.

"How have you fared, Fan? I must tell you, as Sybilla will bear out, that we have been subjected to a visit from the appalling Pargeter."

He had taken the hands she held out and leaned in to plant a kiss upon her cheek, but at this he drew back, frowning. "What, Meg's father? He came here?"

"With a vengeance," said Sybilla and launched into a recital of the invasion. "I could wish you had arrived but ten minutes ago," she finished, "for you might have hastened his departure with a well-aimed kick to the posterior."

"It sounds as if he deserved it," said Francis, who had urged Ottilia back to her chair and brought forward a seat beside her for himself. He was still lightly holding her hand and he squeezed it now as he turned to her. "My poor love, did he pour the vials of his wrath upon your head?"

"Oh, he was not so much angry as filled with righteous justifications. His beliefs, I think, are sincere, but his mind runs on one track and it is impossible to make an impression upon him. He does not listen and he hears only what he wishes to hear."

"The man is out of his senses," stated Sybilla for the umpteenth time. "Say what you like to him, he comes back at you with the will of the Lord and that is all he understands."

"I think he is rather cunning than mad. He wields his religion as a weapon and uses it unmercifully." Ottilia returned the pressure of her spouse's hand and smiled at him. "But what of you? Did you find Pierre?"

"I did not. But I met Redlingfield at Brooks's and what he said of the attack upon Coveney and the Frenchman supports your notion that something was out of true there."

"How so?"

"It appears Coveney was convinced he was attacked by some enemy, but de Percheval seemed rather to suppose he was the intended victim."

Sybilla jumped in before Ottilia could respond. "What, he thought Pargeter had attacked him? Ottilia taxed the man with that, but he denied it."

"He avoided the question rather," Ottilia amended. "But did Pierre think it was Pargeter?"

"Redlingfield didn't know. We discussed why it might be a French agent, and he made a most interesting disclosure."

"About Pierre's background?"

"Not that. But he believes the boy is an accomplished *chevalier d'industrie*. He thinks he may have lived by crooked gaming."

Sybilla pounced. "I knew there was something havey-cavey about that fellow."

Ottilia paid no heed, her attention still on Francis. "He is a cheat?"

"Or merely an expert player. But you may find out for yourself. I have arranged for you to meet him tomorrow." He threw an apologetic glance at his mother. "At Grosvenor Square. I enlisted Violette's aid, since you don't want him here, ma'am. She will send a note of the time as soon as she hears back from him."

Before Ottilia could respond with her gratitude, the front doorbell pealed yet again, several times, as if some urgent hand were tugging at it, sending Sybilla into a frenzy.

"Oh, for heaven's sake! Who in the name of all the gods is that now? Are we never to have a moment's peace? One might be living in the middle of Bartholomew Fair!"

Ottilia was not less exercised herself, half fearing the return of Pargeter. "It is certainly someone with a pressing desire to be admitted."

Francis was on his feet and heading for the parlour door. "I'll go and see. If it's Pargeter, I will head him off, Mama." He vanished through the door and, in the listening hush in the parlour, his voice was presently heard intermingling with another.

"It does not sound like Pargeter," Ottilia offered.

"Well, who is it? I declare, if I am obliged to endure much more—"

"Ma'am, here is Dalesford," Francis interrupted, walking back in, and Ottilia spotted the earl at his heels.

She had met him only once before, but knowing Lady Elizabeth better now, she was at once struck by his resemblance to his daughter. His aspect at this moment, however, drove the thought from her head. He looked to be highly preoccupied and his clothing, rather like that of Pargeter, was a trifle disordered as he moved towards his mother-in-law.

"I beg your pardon for barging in like this, ma'am, but I thought it right to bring this news to Francis and his lady."

"What news?" Sybilla's obvious apprehension mirrored Ottilia's. "What has happened? Is someone dead? Injured?"

Dalesford threw up a hand. "Nothing so dreadful, ma'am. At least, Lizzy was a trifle hurt because she tried to stop him, but—"

"Stop who?" cut in Ottilia, a swift presentiment rushing into her brain. "Was it Pargeter?"

He blinked. "How did you know?"

Francis lifted an eyebrow at her, though he spoke to the earl. "She always knows. What was it, Tillie?"

"He was dishevelled and out of breath when he came here." She ran an eye over Dalesford. "I take it you were obliged to intervene yourself?"

He glanced down at his person and gave a mirthless laugh. "It took both myself and the footman to haul him off the boy. I've not had time to re-arrange my clothes."

"The boy?" interrupted Sybilla. "What boy? I thought your sons were safe at Dalesford."

Francis answered, although Ottilia had already guessed it. "He means de Percheval."

For a moment Sybilla stared, speechless. Then she turned her black gaze upon Ottilia. "I told you he is insane. What, he attacked the boy in your house, Dalesford? What in the world was he doing there?"

"De Percheval? He was waiting for Lizzy. It appears Pargeter followed him from the market where he had gone to meet the wife."

Ottilia, recalling how Pargeter had said he had dealt with the betrayer of his charity, went for the most pertinent question in all this. "Did he hurt Pierre badly?"

"He beat the poor boy almost senseless until I managed to get his cane off him. We have de Percheval on the sofa in the parlour. I waited for Ellington to get there before I left, but the girls are taking care of him."

"Is he conscious? Can he talk?"

"He's conscious, but dazed. He is a good deal bruised and battered. I imagine the doctor will prescribe him something to make him sleep."

Ottilia looked at her husband. "We had best give him a few hours then. Do you mean to keep him in your house, sir?"

"I can hardly throw him out in that state. Harriet does not care for his being there because of Candia, but what would you? I left her on the point of sending to Violette, but I can't imagine Randal will sanction his being moved to Grosvenor Square."

"I should think not indeed," Sybilla interjected in irritated tones.

Ottilia ignored this. "Then we will come tomorrow, if you don't object to it. After what has transpired today, it becomes more imperative than ever that I speak with Pierre."

Chapter Fourteen

Despite the aches, the jabs that accompanied every motion he made, Pierre felt justly chastened. His conscience craved the pain. Too long had he gone unpunished for his misdeeds. Too long endured the greater agony of running from the threat of retribution. Salutary, to receive his deserts from one who deemed himself the Lord's emissary. It cleansed him enough that he could take heart to make amends. Marguerite must be his road to salvation.

He was grateful for the care he had received, but it must end today. It was no longer fitting to be one with a world he meant to abandon, along with those ambitions, blasted now, which had taken him too far from the path of right.

Hissing against the protest from his many bruises, he dragged his body from between sheets, pulled the curtains aside and sat on the edge of the four-poster, pausing to catch his breath.

A knock at the door produced a footman, armed with a jug and towels. "Your hot water, sir."

Pierre looked up and recognition slid through his discomfort. "Ah, you, I think, are my saviour, no? Along with *m'sieur le comte*?"

The footman reddened. "It was nothing, sir. I was glad to be of help."

"But it was more, much more, than nothing, *mon ami*. Without you, Milady Candia has said this Pargeter will have beaten me to death. How are you called?"

"Charles, sir," the man told him, moving to set the jug down in the basin on a washing stand. "I'll help you, shall I?" He came back to the bed, looking down at Pierre with an expression of frowning concern. "You look none too ready to be shifting for yourself yet."

Pierre threw up a hand, and then winced at the pain this caused him. "It is enough, *mon ami*. I must trespass no longer upon such hospitality."

He struggled to push himself to his feet and Charles set a hand to help him. "I'd say you need a day or two yet, sir."

Accepting his help, Pierre came to his feet. "I may recover as well in my lodging, Charles. But yes, this aid of yours is welcome *en ce moment*."

With the footman's assistance he managed his ablutions, cursing at sight of the many patches of purple that had manifested across his chest and down his legs and arms.

"Your back is relatively clear, sir," said Charles in a consoling tone.

Pierre could have wished his back had taken the brunt rather than his limbs and torso. He was afraid it would be many days before he could move again with ease, and the effort to dress, in clothes newly pressed as he discovered, proved too much for his feeble state. He was obliged to call a halt and sat down on the bed in his breeches and shirtsleeves, rueful.

"I am weak, *enfin*."

"That's what I thought, sir. I'll manage the neck-cloth for you. It's washed and pressed, though it could do with a trifle of starch. There now, sir." Talking gently all the time, Charles slid the waistcoat onto him and did up the buttons. Pierre allowed the man to ease him into his coat, cursing again at the stiffness in his arms and the general discomfort across his bruised ribs. Even using a hairbrush, which the footman handed to him at first, was too difficult.

"*Alors*, I am like an invalid! I cannot manage."

"Allow me, sir." Charles took the brush out of his hand and set about dressing his hair for him. "If I may, sir, I'd say you'd do better to remain here for a space where you have support. Nor I don't think the young ladies will be suited with you leaving before you're able."

"These milady, Charles, they are generous. I do not think milor' will be content."

"I don't know that, sir. Mr Snade told me his lordship is wishful for the sawbones to come again today."

"Then I will wait for this. An ingrate I am not, Charles."

The footman assisted him with his boots and helped him to his feet. "There, sir. How does it feel now?"

"It is well. The head clouds a little, but the body moves, even if with difficulty."

"I'll come down with you, sir, in case you need a hand. You'll find his lordship in the breakfast parlour, but I don't know if the ladies have yet risen."

Pierre entered upon a domestic scene, with a number of persons engaged in breaking their fast, seated around a table which was larded in an informal way with silver dishes and a scattering of china pots and bread baskets. To his embarrassment, his entry into the room provoked a chorus of feminine exclamation and protest.

"Pierre! What are you doing up?"

"Gracious, are you better?"

"Of course he is not, Mama. He is leaning on Charles, can't you see?"

"Bring him here, Charles! Sit here, Pierre. You ought to have remained in bed."

Ushered to a place beside Lady Candia, he sank into the seat. Negotiating the stairs had tired him and he was unable for the moment either to respond to the continuing discussion about the wisdom of his having risen, or do more than smile as he recovered his breath.

Presently, he took in the presence, along with both young ladies and Lord and Lady Dalesford, of a woman he did not know who was eyeing him with an interested gaze from across the table. She was sipping at a cup, but not partaking as the others were of the dishes now being offered to him.

"Take some ham, Pierre. Or beef, if you prefer."

"He ought to stick to eggs," suggested Lady Dalesford. "Meat will be hard for him to swallow."

"He must build up his strength, Aunt Harriet."

"Why don't you ask him what he wants, Candia?" This from the Lady Elizabeth, who was sitting next to the stranger. "I dare say the Chevalier knows best what will suit him."

A crack of male laughter drew Pierre's attention and he glanced to the head of the table. His host was seated there, but Pierre's eyes met those of another man lounging to his left. Recognition hit and he spoke for the first time.

"Milord Francis?"

His lordship inclined his head. "Indeed. I was sorry to hear of your misfortune, sir."

But Pierre had no answer as realisation struck. He looked back to the unknown woman, a beat beginning in his breast. "Ah, madame, then it is you who has rescued Marguerite! For this, I thank you, from the bottom of my heart."

A hush fell over the company and Pierre, confusion seeping in, glanced about the silent faces. Lady Elizabeth looked dismayed, the rest uncertain but for Candia, whose eyes were misty, her aspect almost tragic as she met his glance.

"But I have said what? Is it wrong to speak thus?"

From across the table, the wife of Lord Francis spoke for the first time, in a voice both warm and apologetic. "I had not meant for you to hear this so soon, Chevalier, but I am afraid Meg is no longer under my care."

A hideous possibility made his guts wrench. "It is not he? This Pargeter? He has taken her? *Ma foi*, but he will kill her!"

"Oh, Pierre…"

He had no room for Candia's distress, wholly concentrated upon the Lady Francis, who spoke again.

"No, no, it is not that. Though Mr Pargeter did come for her. But he was too late. There is no way I can soften this for you, sir. Meg is in prison."

Spots danced in Pierre's vision and his senses swam.

Ottilia watched as the footman lowered the young Frenchman to the sofa and piled cushions at his back. The boy, who was still alarmingly pale, sank his head back and closed his eyes.

"Brandy, Charles," commanded Lord Dalesford, who had thankfully fended off both his daughter and young Candia.

The latter was in a tearful state which Ottilia could not feel was helpful even as she sympathised with the cause of it. The girl was evidently smitten and was in for a good deal of heartache. Inevitable, since she would never have been permitted to marry Pierre. But youth, Ottilia knew, gave rise to impossible hopes.

Lizzy plainly had no amatory interest, thank heaven, but a murmured conversation at the breakfast table while the rest of the company's attention was concentrated on Pierre's shocked response to her news, had provided Ottilia with a very good reason for her fussing over the fellow almost as much as her cousin.

"I feel very much to blame, Lady Fan. If that horrid man did this to Pierre, I dread to think what he may have done to poor Helen Pargeter. And I'm the one who dragged her into this."

"You are not responsible for Pargeter's actions, Lizzy."

"Yet he would not have come here at all but for my interference."

"He would have found Pierre out one way or another, my dear child. I suspect he tried before."

But at this point she had lost Lizzy's attention as the girl's father took charge, his calm tones cutting in under the cacophony. "If everyone will be so good as to be quiet for a moment, we may get somewhere. Candia, enough! Sit down, Harriet, if you please. Charles!"

"My lord?" A footman came forward at the call.

"Monsieur de Percheval will be more comfortable on the sofa in the small parlour. Help him, if you please. Snade will make up a tray and he may eat there."

The Frenchman, sitting in a slight stupor and white to the lips, made no objection to the move. He had been frozen thus for several moments after Ottilia's announcement, deaf to all efforts to rouse him.

Lord Dalesford had frustrated any design of the young ladies to accompany the boy and instead looked at Francis, who had remained aloof while the women twittered about the sufferer.

"Take your wife along, Fan. She may use this opportunity to put her questions."

It appeared, however, that it would be some moments before Pierre was ready to answer anything at all. Ottilia could not but suspect his temperament was as volatile as Meg's, with a tendency to take a pessimistic view. She took the opportunity to study him freely while he was recovering. His face, undeniably handsome, had escaped injury, although the backs of his hands as they rested upon his chest were seen to be bruised. He had likely used them for protection. One could scarcely blame Meg, starved of affection and subject to

251

Pargeter's puritanical regime, for succumbing to the charms of this youth, however much one deprecated his part in robbing the girl of her innocence. Nor indeed was Candia's partiality surprising.

The thoughts faded as the footman re-entered with a tray containing a decanter and a glass, the butler on his heels burdened with another on which reposed a covered plate and the makings for coffee. In the bustle as Dalesford urged a tot of brandy on the boy and ordered the disposition of the tray, Ottilia found her spouse at her elbow.

"What do you think of him?" he asked, sotto voce.

"I was just thinking how well he and Meg must agree," she returned in the same tone. "He seems quite as volatile and just as prone to act the Tragedy Jack."

A stifled snort of laughter brought her gaze round to Francis and one eyebrow quirked. "I don't say you're wrong, but he has endured a severe beating."

"Dear me, yes. I don't mean to suggest either has not reason enough to be despondent."

"But you think they both react poorly to misfortune?"

"Just so. Meg is apt to despair and Mrs Pargeter says it is in her nature."

"From what I've seen of de Percheval, you may well be right. Not that it is of use to either now."

He moved to join Dalesford, who was signalling by the door, leaving Ottilia prey to a trifle of despondency herself. At this moment, she was equally unhopeful of a happy outcome. She stiffened her spine against the creeping negative feeling. She would not give up.

Dalesford left the room, accompanied by the servants and Ottilia saw that Pierre had roused himself sufficiently to be able to start upon his meal. His colour was improving, though he looked preoccupied and did not seem to be aware of the presence of herself and Francis in the room.

She took a chair opposite the sofa and waited until he had swallowed a few mouthfuls of the dish of scrambled eggs before she spoke.

"Do you feel equal to a discussion, sir?"

He looked up from the plate, his eyes haggard. "Of what use to discuss, madame? It is finished and this fate of Marguerite I will have in my heart all my life."

"Dear me, sir, are you in the habit of giving up so readily?"

He threw up a hand and the fork waved. "What more is there to do, madame? One is at the mercy of those in power, no? Once a person is imprisoned, it is over."

"My dear de Percheval," said Francis, coming across from the door, "you are confusing our English justices with the current Parisian Legislature. In this country we do not treat our accused in the callous fashion of your unfortunate compatriots. Meg is innocent until proven guilty by a proper jury."

Pierre's cheeks pinked a trifle and he looked abashed. "*Pardon, m'sieur.* Yet she has attacked this Coveney, no? And he is dead."

"But not by her hand," put in Ottilia, seizing opportunity. "And you may well be in a position to help her."

"How, madame?" He indicated his person. "As I am I can do nothing for some days."

Ottilia regarded him for a moment. Was he bent upon abandoning Meg and pursuing Candia again? "I am sure you will be welcome here until you are fully recovered, Chevalier."

His eye sparked at that. "You believe me altogether despicable? How should I remain? Milord Dalesford he is generous, yes, but impossible I may make advantage of this. I go at once, madame."

As well, Ottilia reflected. What would Randal's reaction be should he find his daughter cheek by jowl with a fellow he had rated an upstart? But if Pierre meant to leave here, time became precious. It behoved her to use it well.

"You asked how you can help Meg and I have a way. It requires only a feat of memory from you, Pierre — if I may?" He shrugged permission, eyeing her with puzzlement. She gestured. "This is not the first attempt upon you, I surmise."

Surprise flickered in his gaze. "*Non, bien sûr,* madame. But how is it you know this?"

"From one of your gambling coterie," said Francis. "You and Coveney were attacked, were you not? In the early hours."

"It is so, *m'sieur.* But this attack it did not succeed. Milord Coveney took a hit, but I had luck to frighten the fellow and he ran away."

Ottilia played her hand. "That hit was the inadvertent cause of Coveney's death, sir."

"But, no. Bruised he was, yes. He complained of it a great deal."

"The blow broke a rib, Pierre. When he grappled with Meg, or perhaps due to his exertions, a shard from the rib pierced his lung, which collapsed. That is what killed him."

A horrified look crept into Pierre's face. "But this assuredly makes it that Marguerite is to blame. They will say so."

"True, but I have hopes the verdict may be manslaughter and not murder."

His horror did not abate. "This is better how? She is yet doomed by this."

"To prison perhaps. There is also the hope of mitigation in light of her attempt to defend herself from his assault. There is every possibility a jury may be led to be sympathetic."

Pierre gave a mirthless laugh in which scorn was paramount. It was plain his experience of the law, as operating in France at the present time, was unhappy. Ottilia chose to ignore it.

"To succeed in this, however, I need your testimony, Pierre. Do you have any notion who your attacker was?"

A wary look came into his gaze. "It was dark, madame. The hat it was pulled down close and thus his face it was concealed."

"But you must have some idea of his height and size." Ottilia slipped in a clue. "Tall and thin perhaps?"

There was no mistaking his instant dismissal. "*Au contraire,* madame. Small he was this man, shorter than I by far. And thin, no, I do not say so. It was a thick body that I held. Without his stick, he was nothing. Thus he ran from me."

As of instinct, Ottilia looked to her husband, exchanging with him a glance of mutual confusion. If Pierre was speaking the truth, her supposition was blasted. Francis gave it voice first.

"Then it cannot have been Pargeter."

Pierre dropped his fork. "Pargeter? Ah, no. He I would know at once."

"Are you certain, Pierre?" Ottilia gestured at his person again. "After we heard how he came at you here, I was certain I had guessed aright."

A vehement shake of the head came. "But, no, Milady Francis. It is of all things what this Pargeter detests, this way of deceit, of hiding his intent like an ambush. No, this is not his character."

Ottilia caught her spouse's quirking eyebrow and gave him a questioning glance. He smiled.

"For once, my love, it would appear you have judged awry."

She gave a tiny laugh, though troubled withal. "It would seem so indeed." She turned back to Pierre. "I have only encountered the Reverend Pargeter once, but I grant you Meg is terrified of him. More so than she is of facing the rope."

"Ah, do not!" Pierre shuddered. "But yes, I believe this. He has been to Marguerite most cruel. All her life, madame. She told me of her suffering at his hand. It is all in the name of *le bon dieu*, you understand. He believes that he is just, that all he does is right. Thus he came at me in sight of all, here in this house, to serve me my punishment. Never would he skulk in an alley to wait and come upon me unaware. This is not his way."

Thinking rapidly, Ottilia readjusted her ideas. "But you did not think it was a common footpad, did you?"

The wary look reappeared. Pierre set aside his tray, the food largely uneaten. "Why do you say this?"

Francis took the question. "Redlingfield told me so."

"How can he know? I said no word to him of this."

"He's a shrewder man than you give him credit for, my young friend. He noted how you told Coveney no one was out to kill him." The emphasis caused Pierre to close his lips in a thin line. "Redlingfield also spotted your skill with cards. There is too the haste with which you left Bow Street when Justice Ingham sought to question you. You are playing a deep game, are you not?"

Her spouse's tone was bland, with nothing of accusation in it, but Ottilia noted how the boy drew into himself, tightening up. She tried her soft approach.

"Keep your own counsel, Chevalier. We need not pry into your personal concerns, except as they impinge upon your willingness to serve as a witness for Meg."

"A witness? But I saw nothing. Since this Pargeter forbade me the house, I have not seen Marguerite."

"Ah, but the damage, my dear Pierre, was already done."

He flinched, but his eyes flared. "I know my fault, madame." He gestured at his body. "For this I have taken my punishment. It needs not that you tell me my duty, Milady Francis. Already I had the plan that Milady Elizabeth will bring me to the house where you stay that I may pledge my life to Marguerite."

"That is why you were waiting here? Pargeter followed you, I surmise?"

"I think he has seen me with Helen in the market where I have spoken to her. She I believe will also suffer." He drew a sighing breath. "My account grows."

"But you may yet come down upon the credit side, sir."

"How, when Marguerite is out of my reach?"

"Yes, how?" demanded Francis, entering the lists. "You have lost me, my love."

She threw him a smile. "I am thinking of mitigation. If Pierre will come forward and speak to Justice Ingham, his testimony cannot but assist with a plea of self-defence." She turned back to Pierre. "You are not only witness to the cruelties inflicted upon Meg by her father, which go some way to explaining her state of mind. You are the author of her condition and the father of her child. You, more than anyone, may speak in her defence. She was trying to find you when she fell into Coveney's hands, Pierre."

He appeared to ruminate, looking down at the bruised backs of his own hands. Ottilia began to think there was more to the Frenchman than she had foreseen. Despite his avowals, he was, she felt certain, weighing the disadvantages to himself.

Was he truly penitent, or did Meg's incarceration conveniently absolve him from taking any further action?

At length he looked up. "Madame, I must first recover my strength. Will you see Marguerite?"

"Assuredly. Do you wish me to convey a message to her?"

He wafted a negative hand. "If I speak, it is to Marguerite alone. I do not use the lips of another."

If? Then his expressions of regret were empty. Ottilia began to feel defeated.

"Will you perhaps tell Milady Elizabeth how Marguerite is placed, madame?"

Francis started, his gaze flying to Ottilia's. She all but rolled her eyes, turning back to Pierre.

"No, Chevalier, I will not. I cannot have Lady Elizabeth involved further. Her part is ended. If you wish to know Meg's condition, you will have to discover it for yourself."

He looked chagrined, and Ottilia was glad to note she had pricked him. She was exercised by his refusal to discuss the possible identity of his earlier attacker. In the back of her mind she began casting about for another way to elicit the necessary information. How much did Violette know of Pierre's origins?

After a brisk walk to Hanover Square, Ottilia found they had arrived opportunely when Cattawade informed them Lady Polbrook was closeted in the Blue Salon with a gentleman caller.

"A countryman of her ladyship's," added the butler in a tone redolent with disapproval.

Ottilia looked a message to her spouse who cocked an eyebrow, but obliged at once. "Which Frenchman, Cattawade? Speak freely, man. We are on a mission."

"It is that Monsoor Lezayre, my lord, the same who introduced a certain foreign gentleman to her ladyship," disclosed the austere butler, betraying his intimate knowledge of Polbrook family affairs.

"Is it, by God?" Amusement was in his face as Francis turned to Ottilia. "Shall we interrupt?"

She could not withstand a mischievous smile. "Oh, we must barge in at once, without doubt."

Cattawade gave a tiny sigh. "I will announce you, my lady."

But Francis was already at the door to the Blue Salon. "No need. Have you forgot we are usually inmates here? Or we would be if there was any room." With which, he opened the door and gestured for Ottilia to enter.

She walked into a scene of peculiar intimacy in a setting utterly unsuited to a tête-à-tête. The Blue Salon was as elegant as she remembered, with the wallpaper and upholstery to the chairs that indicated its name. But a subtle change in the atmosphere was visible in the cushions dotted across the sofas, the repositioned chairs grouped about a walnut folding card table, and a couple of frivolous and colourful French figures on the mantel along with an ormolu clock, above which the portrait of the first marchioness had been replaced with a charming painting of the new one, its style reminiscent of Gainsborough. Violette's handiwork had rendered the place a good deal more cheerful. She was sitting on a sofa placed to catch the heat from the fire, a florid gentleman of middle years close beside her.

The pair had clearly had their heads together, but upon the entrance of the Fanshawes, Violette's exquisite features under the prinked and curled blonde locks were turned towards the newcomers, surprise etched there. The gentleman, after one startled look, immediately rose and executed a courtly bow.

The marchioness was first to recover, rising gracefully. "*C'est vous, Ottilie. Quelle surprise.*"

"How do you do, Violette? You must forgive the intrusion, but this cannot wait."

The gentleman made to efface himself, but Francis thankfully stepped in.

"Don't go, Lezayre. You are the very man we need. Allow me to present you to my wife."

"*Enchanté*, Lady Francis." The Frenchman bowed.

Violette cut through the introductions. "But what is this, Ottilie? Why do you come to me? Francis, speak!"

"We have just come from Dalesford House where Ottilia has been talking to your friend, Pierre de Percheval." Francis looked at Lezayre as he spoke but it was the marchioness who answered.

"Ah, *le pauvre* Pierre! It is for this I have sent to Emile. He knew not of this beating so terrible which I have myself heard from Harriet. *En verité*, it is a miracle this priest he has not killed *ce garçon.*"

Ottilia leapt straight in. "I am less concerned with this attack than the earlier one." She cast her eyes on Lezayre. "You are familiar with what happened on that occasion, are you not, sir?"

Violette opened her eyes wide. "But of what do you speak, Ottilie? Another? Pierre has said nothing of this to me."

Lezayre flourished a hand. "Footpads in the night, madame. It was nothing."

"In fact it became highly significant, Lezayre," said Francis, "since Coveney died of the blow he received then."

Lezayre's astonishment was evident. "But I thought you said it was this girl of Pierre's who killed him."

Ottilia took this, setting aside Violette's obvious confusion for the moment and explaining the discoveries. "That is why I am anxious to discover the person who attacked the two that night. Pierre is convinced it cannot have been Pargeter, as I suspected. I am hoping you, Violette — and more likely perhaps you, Mr Lezayre — may be able to help me."

"I? But I have not known of this at all," protested Violette.

"Nor was I present at the time," Lezayre added. "I cannot assist you, Lady Francis."

"Ah, but you can, sir. You, more than any other, know Pierre's background." She noted instant withdrawal in Lezayre's face and prepared to do battle, but Violette forestalled her, a trifle of apprehension visible in her gaze.

"What is it you mean, Ottilie? Why do you ask such a thing as this?"

"Because she believes this Pierre of yours is not who he says he is," said Francis before Ottilia could respond. He threw an accusatory look at the older man. "Is that not so, Lezayre?"

He received a glare from Lezayre who, like Pierre before him, firmly closed his lips. But Violette's gaze went from him to Francis and back again. Had she an inkling or suspicion already? Ottilia set a hand on her spouse's arm in a bid to keep him from saying any more and stepped in herself.

"My dear sir, we are not acting on a mere whim. A girl's whole life is at stake."

"Ah, you would say this Marguerite?"

"Just so, Violette. Pierre admits his responsibility for her situation, but he will not help me to find the person who attacked him."

Lezayre let out a scoffing noise. "A footpad? How can he find such, madame?"

"Yet he has himself suggested it was not a footpad. Lord Redlingfield distinctly heard him say he thought the man was trying to kill him."

"You must have heard that too, Lezayre," cut in Francis. "For my money, I should suppose the two of you have discussed the possibility in detail."

Violette struck her hands together. "But why? I do not understand at all. Who is it that could wish to kill Pierre?"

Ottilia went across to her, catching her unquiet hands. "That is just what we are trying to find out. Violette, if you know anything of Pierre's true past, I must beg you to tell me."

"But me I know naught, Ottilie. He is like me, the exile. He escapes these terrible *canaille* who have made themselves *gouvernante*, who kill and kill and kill. *Naturellement* Pierre is afraid."

Ottilia released her hands. It was clear Violette had been as much taken in as any other. She gave her a tiny smile. "I am afraid it is not quite as you suggest, my dear."

Violette threw up agitated hands. "Then it is how, Ottilie?"

Ottilia turned her gaze upon Lezayre as she answered. "We suspect Pierre is something of an adventurer. He may or may not be related to the family of de Percheval. His flight from France was not on account of his origins, was it, Monsieur Lezayre? He came rather to escape retribution, possibly just."

Lezayre was beginning to look a trifle shifty as Violette regarded him in frowning puzzlement. He did not speak and Ottilia found her husband's gaze upon her in a questioning look. She changed tack, going for the jugular.

"I do trust you will not have cause to regret having perpetrated a fraud upon society, sir, when it becomes publicly known that Pierre is not what he claims to be."

Lezayre's jaw dropped, his fleshy jowls trembling, fear in his eyes. "A threat? You would fright me with this?"

Ottilia smiled. "I hardly think it needs my intervention. Truth will out."

Violette pounced. "*Alors, Emile, c'est vrai?* Speak, you!"

Reddening, Lezayre spread his hands. "I tried only to help the boy. A headstrong boy he is. He chose his victim ill, *c'est tout.*"

"*C'est tout?* This is all you say to me?" With which, Violette broke into impassioned French, accompanied by much Gallic gesticulation.

Ottilia's command of the language was poor, but she knew her spouse had fair fluency and drew him to one side, lowering her voice. "What is she saying, do you know?"

"She's a little fast for me to follow all, but she's giving him pepper."

"I can see that for myself, Fan."

"Hush!" Francis was watching the pair, listening to the swift give and take. "She is saying he has endangered her position ... 'is it not precarious enough?'. Lord, I did not think she realised."

"But he? Is he giving any hint of what we want to know?"

Francis grinned. "She is not giving him a chance to get a word in."

Ottilia let it go a moment or two, but Violette's tone became increasingly shrill and impatience claimed her. "We will have to intervene." Without thinking she hit a pitch calculated in the past to bring her nephews up short. "Violette! Violette, be silent, if you please!"

Violette halted mid-sentence, her startled gaze flying to Ottilia, who took instant advantage, moving in.

"That is better. My dear, you have every right to be upset, but this is getting us nowhere."

"*Oui, mais je suis desolé, Ottilie, absolument desolé.*"

"I understand, but let that be for the moment. Monsieur Lezayre here is my last hope of finding means to mitigate Meg's fate."

At this, Violette turned once more upon her elderly countryman, fierce in both face and voice. "*Alors*, he will do as you wish, *n'est-ce pas, mon vieux*? This you owe to me."

Ottilia felt a passing pang of pity for her brother-in-law, and the fleeting thought the precipitate marriage might not have been entirely Randal's doing could not but obtrude. However, she had no time to indulge the notion now.

"Monsieur Lezayre, it is imperative you keep nothing back."

"It is useless to do so now, in any event," cut in her spouse. "Pierre is a black leg, is he not? He uses his skills to fleece his victims. Or does he fuzz the cards to cheat them?"

The elder man's cheeks suffused with colour. "He does not cheat! *Ma foi*, but do you think I would introduce a villain to the world? To cheat at cards it is of all things dishonourable to gentlemen of your milieu, no?"

The truth of this was evident in the look Francis gave him, but he let it pass. "In which case, he's a skilled enough player to make a living by gambling, is that it?"

Lezayre let out a defeated noise. "*Eh bien*, if you must have it, the boy is unequalled. He can recall every discard, thus he knows which cards are still to play."

"And as dealer? Redlingfield said he can shuffle and deal like lightning. Do you tell me he does not shuffle the pack to his benefit?"

To Ottilia's intense satisfaction, the fellow began to fidget under the combined gazes of his auditors. Her spouse had hit the mark. She took a hand.

"Come, sir, it is useless to prevaricate. Whether or not you deem such to be a skill or a cheat is irrelevant now. That was his undoing in Paris, was it not?"

Against all etiquette while the women stood, Lezayre sank into the sofa, setting his elbows on his knees and staring at the floor. He spoke low, with weariness.

"Pierre was a fool. He took Vergniaud for many thousands of francs. This was in the Gironde, you understand, where Vergniaud was of the Council. A fool Pierre was to deal thus with such a man, a lawyer of renown. Pierre went by another name then but Vergniaud knew him for a connection to the de Percheval — a cousin, you understand, distant and born to a common man, but yet of the family."

"Ah, *le scélérat!* He has denounced Pierre?"

Lezayre looked up. "Pierre believes Vergniaud gave him up to Lafayette of the National Guard, in revenge. Lafayette denounced him. Pierre heard of it in time to make his escape. But this Vergniaud, he is not satisfied, so Pierre believes, and thus he sends an assassin to accomplish his death."

"And you believe that?" Ottilia could not help the sceptical note, ignoring the little cries of distress emanating from Violette.

Lezayre shifted his shoulders in a discontented fashion. "I think Vergniaud has more to trouble him, for he is of the Legislature in Paris now. Pierre is obsessed. He dare not show his skill in these circles for fear it may expose him to Lafayette's spies. Thus he chose instead to fly at higher game."

He avoided Violette's eye as he spoke and she blew out an exasperated breath. "Randal he will never permit. This I have told to Pierre many times."

Francis cocked an eyebrow. "Candia?"

Lezayre spread his hands. "What would you? The boy is sure he may win in the end, if the girl is enough in his spell."

"Conceit or arrogance?"

"Oh, he is remarkably good-looking, Fan, and he clearly has a deal of address. I believe poor Candia is indeed under his spell, as you put it, sir." But Ottilia brought him ruthlessly back to the point. "You have no faith in this spy business then? You think it could not have been Vergniaud's assassin who attacked Pierre and Coveney that night?"

To her surprise, it was Violette who took this. "But no, Ottilie, it cannot be so."

"Why not?"

"If it is that one comes for him, Pierre he is already dead. My friends who come more, each week more come, they tell to me how it is danger even to speak a word. The shadows they have spies, and many die, even that they are not denounced."

"I did think it a trifle far-fetched, my love," said Francis. "Any tool of a member of the French government would surely go about the business in a more efficient manner. A dagger in the back perhaps."

Violette threw out a hand towards him. "*Mais oui*, Francis. This is what I think."

Ottilia, her last hope fading, looked from one to the other. "Must I accept then that it was a common footpad after all?"

"I fear so, Tillie." He glanced at Lezayre. "But we have at least got at the truth of Pierre's background."

Violette seized his arm. "Francis, *mon cher frère*, speak no word of this to my Randal, *je vous en prie*! It is trouble enough for that

Pierre is at Dalesford house *en ce moment*. Already he swears he will bring at once Candia home. But me I know she desires to remain with Harriet."

Francis covered her hand with his own, a wry smile appearing. "Have no fear, Violette. I will not breathe a word to my brother." But Ottilia was not surprised when he added, sotto voce for her ears alone, "I have no desire to set Randal off on one of his rampages."

"No indeed." Her gaze remained on Violette, who had reverted to French, once more engaged in close discussion with Lezayre. "I wonder if she will drop Pierre now."

"I imagine she will keep her distance. She's safe enough for the moment, since he won't be showing himself in public in his condition. Pargeter did his work well."

The name wrought powerfully upon Ottilia and she turned to Francis, both eager and anguished. "Helen!"

His brows flew up. "I beg your pardon?"

"Helen Pargeter. He may have served her similarly, but that is beside the bridge."

"What are you talking about, woman?"

"Could she have been the one to set upon Pierre?"

"Have you run mad, Tillie? What in the world made you think of such a thing?"

They were walking back to Bruton Street, Ottilia's hand tucked in her husband's supporting arm, having left Violette and Lezayre to fight it out. It was plain Violette would be airing her grievance for some time, and Ottilia had thought it prudent to retreat. Besides, the new notion had rapidly taken possession of her mind and she had no hesitation in speaking out.

"Do you recall what Pierre said of the attacker? He was small and was nothing without his stick. He ran away."

"Very well, but how could that lead you to suppose it might have been this Pargeter woman?"

"Well, it was not her husband. Nor, if Violette and Lezayre are to be believed, could it have been a French assassin."

"Highly unlikely. Why would he run off?"

"Just so, Fan. That is what makes it so suspicious. He, or she if it was Helen, had delivered a hit to put Coveney out of count. But then Pierre grappled him and deprived him of his weapon. Any spy, or even a footpad, would at that point have brought out a knife or dagger, do you not think?"

"Possibly, but I still don't see—"

"Figure to yourself, just for a moment, that it was a woman. She took a chance, but aimed poorly and got the wrong man. She knows she cannot fight hand to hand with a man of Pierre's stature. What other recourse is open to her but to free herself and take to her heels?"

She eyed her husband's profile as he digested this. She needed his reassurance, fearful she was grasping at straws. But the conviction was growing upon Ottilia that she had it right this time. She was scarcely aware she spoke her thoughts aloud.

"She was distressed and angry at Pierre for defiling Meg. By Meg's account, Pierre at that time appeared to have come out of it without a scratch. He was banished from the house and Pargeter's brand of justice fell upon poor Meg, who endured the severest punishment. What is Helen's part in all this?"

Francis spoke at last. "You think she did it for Meg? To avenge her?"

"I suspect she meant to punish Pierre for what Meg had suffered."

Her spouse let out a snort. "But how, Tillie? Would you have me believe she donned men's clothing and crept out of the parson's house at dead of night? And how would she know where to find him?"

Ottilia fluttered her free hand in a despairing way. "I don't know, Fan. She is a woman of ingenuity. She had her ways, Meg said. She's had years of circumventing Pargeter's stark regime. Lizzy says she purchased old clothes at the market for her patchworks."

"Which explains how she acquired men's garments, I dare say. But creeping out at night?"

"Why not? If she was dressed as a common man, with her hat pulled down over her ears. That is how Pierre described it."

"And Pargeter had canes enough, you will tell me."

Ottilia let out a laugh. "Clearly I have no need to tell you. Well?"

He set his hand over hers and squeezed. "You make it sound plausible, but then you always do, my dear one. I admit it still looks thin to me. And if you are right, why did she not confess it at once when Lizzy told her about the broken rib, as I suppose she must have done."

"One can only guess at it, but I dare say she was too afraid to come out into the open for fear of Pargeter discovering it. If you had heard him, Fan, you would not be surprised at anyone concealing their peccadilloes from the wretched man."

"A peccadillo? To masquerade as a man in the middle of the night for the purpose of attacking de Percheval? In any event, Pargeter might well be glad of it since he beat Pierre himself."

"Most certainly he would not. He is the instrument of the Lord, not his wife. He would consider it his duty to punish her for taking on his role, I dare say, never mind the rest."

Her spouse's tone became teasing. "A despot, is he? I ought to take a lesson from him and find means to keep my darling wife in better order."

"And find your darling wife on the other side of the door within the day, running to her brother for protection."

His laugh rang into the empty street. "Patrick would parcel you up and send you back instanter. He's no match for his sister, as he's told me a dozen times."

"Fiend!" Ottilia delivered a light slap to the arm she held. "I wish you will be serious."

He sighed. "What do you wish, my persistent one? We can't go ferreting out this Pargeter woman now. Mama will be fretting herself to flinders by this."

"No, and I need to think this out. My brain is reeling and I am gasping for coffee."

Chapter Fifteen

It was strange for Meg to feel safer behind a locked door than she had for weeks past. The room was stark, the makeshift bed narrow, the straw that served for a mattress little protection from the cold stone floor and Meg, huddling in the shawl, had found the single blanket inadequate last night to keep out the pervasive chill. She'd slept ill, and been glad of Rose's early arrival, cherishing the jug with both hands to warm them until the numbness gave place to the prickle of her wounds, not yet fully healed.

"Let me pour some in the basin, miss, so you can wash."

The maid's wrinkled nose revived the memory and stink of stale bodies penetrating the building. Meg's sense of smell had dulled after hours of incarceration in the airless room, the high barred window remaining shut. At least she was set apart from other female prisoners, private in this end cell instead of the large room next door from which shouts and groans had issued throughout the night.

She did not linger over her ablutions, shivering in her shift while Rose abstracted a clean one from the valise. She was glad of the girl's help, relieved to be quickly dressed in the same petticoats and gown, wrapped once more in the thick shawl.

"I'll take this away and fetch your breakfast to you, miss. The landlady where I'm staying is making up a tray. I won't be above a moment."

Rose knocked on the door and the female gaoler, a formidable dame who looked with scant approval upon the privileged prisoner, let her out. Meg shrank at the sour glance she received before the metal door clanged shut again. She knew not why she was despised, unless her penurious state was to blame. Ought she to proffer a tip? She had the few coins Helen had given her, the purse tucked deep into her stays, but she dared not use them for such a slim purpose. Had she been provident when she left the parsonage rather than distraught, she might have broken into her father's strongbox. Not that she would have dared so far, even had she been in her wits. Of what use to repine? Her life was over. She would rot in this or some other gaol until Pierre's child was born, and then...

But the unnamed future fate had become all too real in this place. Meg shied away from that inevitable end, taking consolation only in the knowledge the monster could not get at her within these walls.

The food Rose presently brought to her was plentiful. Meg ate ravenously at first, stuffing several slices of the crisp bacon into her mouth and washing them down with hot, sweet coffee, laced with cream. She ate more sparingly of the baked eggs, instead partaking of the warmed rolls with a thick layer of honey, the cloying sweetness welcome balm, momentarily pleasurable. She smiled at the maid.

"Thank you, that was good."

The girl bloomed. "I'm glad, miss. Is there aught you need before I go?"

"No, Rose, I am content." But as the maid was gathering the debris onto the tray, she bethought her of the freezing night. "Stay! Do you think you might procure me another blanket, Rose?"

Consternation leapt into the girl's features. "Oh, miss! I don't know as I can. Were you cold?" She went to the bed, little more than a wooden box open at the foot, and felt the rough blanket, lifting it to expose the dirty straw beneath. "Goodness, I didn't think last evening, miss, worrited as I was to get you fed and all. Terrible that is. I'll do something to better it, see if I don't."

Touched by the fierce tone, Meg seized her hand as she passed the little stool which, along with a disgusting bucket, was the only other furniture the room boasted.

"You are kind, Rose. I am so relieved Lady Fan sent you with me. I should have been wretched all alone here."

Rose patted her hand. "Now, don't you trouble none, miss. Hemp said he'd come today — her ladyship's steward he is — and I'll ask him. He's a fellow as get things done is Hemp, for all he's from foreign parts."

A vague image stirred in Meg's mind. "Ah, I remember. He was there when they found me."

"Yes, and he arranged all in the room after, though you might not recall it, miss, as ill as you were. You wouldn't think it, but that Hemp is as well-spoken as a gent. Had an education, he says, and was brought up decent. He'll see as you get proper bedding, miss, no question."

Relief and gratitude swept through Meg as the maid retired. At least she would enjoy a degree of comfort until the trial. A shiver shook her at the thought and she could not help a faint lift of hope that Lady Fan might yet save her.

The day passed slowly. Rose slipped in to bring her a sandwich and more hot coffee, armed with the welcome tidings that Hemp had been and was gone off to see what he could achieve. The maid had been gone with the tray for only a short time when the key sounded in the lock, the door opened and Lady Fan walked in.

Ottilia swept a glance about the sparse surroundings and suffered a momentary regret she had not made more effort to keep Meg in Bruton Street. She essayed a smile as she crossed to the stool where the forlorn figure sat.

"Poor Meg, I am sorry you are so poorly housed."

Meg dropped her gaze, fidgeting with her petticoats. "It serves." She looked up again. "Rose has asked your man to arrange more bedding. I was cold last night."

One look was enough to inform Ottilia why. "Heavens, I should think you must have been frozen. I am so sorry. I ought to have seen to it myself."

Meg shifted her shoulders. "It makes no matter, ma'am. You have other things to do."

"True, yesterday was eventful." Ottilia dropped to her haunches, the better to address the girl and see her face. "I have much to tell you, Meg." She noted how apprehension crept into the girl's countenance. Was there hope too? A wave of dismay swept through her. She was failing dismally. But she must fulfil her purpose here. "My dear, I have no good tidings to report, I am afraid. I will not attempt to flummery you, for I have so far failed to locate the person who might help your case."

The girl's lips quivered, but her voice was steady. "I did not suppose you would."

"Well, I have one more avenue to attempt, but let that be for now. Meg, your father came seeking you within an hour of your departure."

That drew a horrified gasp. "He came? Oh, why will he not let me alone?"

Ottilia put out a hand. "Be of good cheer. When he heard you had been taken to prison, he more or less washed his hands of you. He spoke much of God's mercy, but I think he will not lift a finger to help you."

"Then I thank God for it." Fierce now, her fingers curled like claws, Meg spat the words. "He would see me hang and praise the Lord for serving me as I deserved. Oh, did I not know it? Better the rope than his brand of justice."

"Yes, I rather got that impression, my dear. Unfortunately, it appears he was not the man who attacked Pierre and Coveney the night he received the fatal blow. Pierre was adamant it could not have been Reverend Pargeter."

At this, Meg's gaze became intent, painful enquiry within the expressive orbs. "You have seen him?"

The moment had come. For all her harsh words of the young Frenchman, Ottilia felt positive her news would be distressing to Meg. She leaned forward, setting a hand on Meg's tense fingers.

"Your father came directly to us from Dalesford House as we later learned."

"Dalesford House? I don't understand."

"It is where my sister-in-law resides. Mr Pargeter followed your friend from the market where Pierre met with your stepmother Helen. He gained access to the house and I'm afraid he set about Pierre with a cane before he could be stopped."

Meg stared, dazed incomprehension in her face. "He beat Pierre?"

"Severely, yes. The boy was badly bruised. Indeed, when I saw him this morning, he could barely move."

Meg released her hand, throwing it to her bosom. To Ottilia's mingled consternation and astonishment, she began to laugh, a raucous sound, mirthless and causing catches at the girl's breath. Ottilia rose as Meg began to rock back and forth, tears squeezing from her eyes. The vapours? She summoned her most authoritative tone.

"Stop, Meg! That will do. Come now, look at me!" But the laughter was already turning to sobs, Meg's hands clutching about her body. Ottilia set a hand to her shoulder and gentled her tone. "Enough now, my dear. You will make yourself ill."

Meg paid her no heed whatsoever, seemingly utterly lost in the bursting hysteria. Ottilia could sympathise. She had experienced the dam bursting for herself after a prolonged period of burying all emotion. But it would not do. At any moment, her cries would bring the stern gaoler. Drastic measures were called for. She moved in front of Meg and, with deliberation, dealt her a sharp slap on the cheek. The shock of it had an effect. Meg ceased her lamentations and the rocking stopped.

Ottilia caught her by the shoulders. "That is better."

Meg stared at her for a moment, and then dissolved into a much more normal fit of crying, and real tears seeped from her eyes. Ottilia let her weep without restraint for several minutes, patting her and muttering soothing noises. The bout had clearly been a long time coming. A pity the wretched Pierre had not compassion enough to be here when he was needed to administer the sort of comfort Ottilia knew from her spouse. Only Pierre did not love Meg as she was loved. Or at all. Compassion overcame her. Willingly could she have slapped the Frenchman instead, vile seducer that he was. But Meg, it was soon apparent, had nothing but pity for the author of her ills.

She drew a sobbing breath. "Poor Pierre. He little understood the monster's method. I could have warned him had I found him." Anxiety entered her voice and she looked at

Ottilia, wiping her tears with her sleeve. "He was where, you said? Did they help him?"

"At Dalesford House." Ottilia shook her pocket handkerchief out of a sleeve and gave it to the woman. "Use this, Meg."

"Thank you." She blew her nose, her breath still ragged as she spoke again. "Who are they? Is he there still?"

Ottilia took the pertinent question. "Pierre went there to find my niece Lizzy, I believe. She it was who found Helen and brought her to you."

"But is he there? What did they do for him?"

It was plain Pierre's fate outweighed everything else. Meg's affections at least were fixed, it would seem.

"A doctor was called and Pierre was put to bed there. He was able to get up this morning, but only with help, I understand. He was insistent he would not remain there."

Meg appeared to derive scant satisfaction from this intelligence. She rose and began to pace about the confines of her cell. "He will never manage alone. The monster has no mercy. He would have broken Pierre's bones if he could." Horror leapt in her eyes and she turned sharp about to face Ottilia. "Did he break any bones?"

"Thankfully, no. And Pierre managed to save his face from injury, to the detriment of his hands, but he remains as handsome as ever."

A tremulous smile hovered on Meg's lips and her gaze softened. "He is beautiful, is he not? Yet his mind, his soul, are more so."

Ottilia could readily have disputed this encomium, but she held her tongue. There was more matter to be thrashed out here.

"Meg, I wish to ask you something."

"What is it?"

Apprehension again? Ottilia sighed as she too rose to her feet, flexing cramped muscles. Really, it was a piece of work dealing with this female. She was as cagey as the Frenchman. One could not help the reiterating thought they were well suited, if only matters had turned out otherwise. She took the plunge.

"It is in my mind that perhaps it was after all Helen who dealt that blow to Lord Coveney."

Meg blanched, her fingers coming up to twist at her lips. Her voice was hushed. "Helen? But … but how?"

Ottilia spread her hands. "Try to think of it without prejudice, Meg. Helen has access to old clothes. She could have purchased men's garments. You have yourself said she has her ways. Could she get out of the house at night, do you think?"

Meg was trembling. "Helen … yes, she had her ways, but … I don't know, I don't know."

"Let us suppose she could. Had she means to discover where Pierre went and what he did? Might she have followed him?"

Dismay crept into Meg's face. "But if she knew … if she found him…"

"Why did she not tell you, is that it?"

Meg nodded and Ottilia read misery in her eyes. Did she think it a betrayal? "But you did not confide in Helen, did you? She had no notion you were with child until Lizzy told her. She supposed you safe. If she did try to hurt Pierre, it was for you, Meg. She will have been distressed that you suffered the consequences and Pierre was merely banished. Perhaps she meant only to waylay him, to take him to task. Or to tell him what your father did to you."

"No! No, it cannot be. Helen would never…" Meg faded out, fidgeting, her eyes darting here and there as if she would escape whatever thoughts were turning in her mind. Ottilia waited. At last Meg spoke again, fearfully. "I asked her how she bore it. She said she learned long ago not to draw his fire. She had her ways, but I don't know them. I don't know how she managed, only that she succoured me upon many occasions. She comforted me with sweetmeats I was not allowed, and she anointed my bruises in secret. She gave me a rag doll to keep under my pillow. But openly to defy him? She dared not."

Ottilia broke into these reminiscences. "But this was not open, Meg. It was secret, under cover of darkness and disguise. Is that not just what you are saying? Is it not precisely how Helen might set about it, if she wished to succour you."

"But to hurt Pierre?"

"Perhaps she did not mean to. Perhaps she took the cane for protection, or merely to threaten."

"You said she struck at Coveney."

"Yes, and I thought it a mistake. But suppose it was deliberate. To have him out of the way so she might accost Pierre since she could not get him alone."

Meg was silent, eyeing Ottilia as if she confronted a snake, unknowing which way it might jump. Then a long sigh escaped her. "She will never say. If she did, she won't say."

"Even if it might save you?"

A spasm crossed Meg's face. "She could have told me then, when she came. Or you. Have faith, she said. But she did not tell me what she meant to do."

Ottilia caught at the unquiet fingers for a moment. "To tell it would be to open herself to your father's censure. Helen would know such a confession must become public property in a trial. I dare say she hoped there might be another way."

"What way?"

"That I do not know."

"You said he spied upon her?"

"Your father? Yes."

"Oh, he will punish her cruelly," Meg cried, striking her hands together. She winced and curled them up.

"Your palms are still painful?"

"Only when I forget. Oh, Helen, Helen…" She covered her face with her hands.

Ottilia could not judge how useful it had been to discuss the matter with Meg. On the one hand, the confirmation of secret doings bore out her suspicion. On the other, Meg had nothing concrete to add to break the dilemma. She would have to tackle Helen direct.

"I must go, Meg. Is there anything you need? A book to read perhaps?"

The hands came down, but Meg did not respond to the question. "What do you mean to do, Lady Fan?"

Ottilia gave her a reassuring smile. "I have not given up the fight, Meg. I must contrive to speak to your stepmother. Do you suppose your father would incarcerate her as he did you?"

"Oh, no." No hesitation there. "He would not serve Helen so. She will be obliged to pray and read lessons upon deceit. Recite them too. But a wife has privileges granted by the Lord, you see. He would not be as harsh as…"

"As he was with you? Then there is hope I may be able to converse with her. If I am right, I promise I will do my utmost to persuade her to come forward."

Meg became suddenly breathless. "But he! Don't let him come here. Tell them, Lady Fan. Tell that justice to keep him away from me."

"You mean your father?"

"Of course." Meg drew a rough breath. "Not the other. Pierre will not come."

Having heard the Frenchman for herself, Ottilia could not bring herself to contradict this sentiment. She had no faith in Pierre's conscience pricking him into action. Besides, what could he do? His intervention would likely only serve to distress Meg the more.

The church was cold and dark, the service poorly attended. A pity the Reverend Pargeter's parishioners appeared reluctant, for Ottilia felt decidedly conspicuous even in the row somewhat removed from the altar and pulpit. As strangers, she and Francis must always have been noticed, but she had hoped not to draw Pargeter's attention too early. No sooner had the service begun, however, than she caught the cold eyes raking her even as the fellow recited the first prayer.

"He's spotted you," muttered her spouse.

"Yes, I realise it," she murmured back.

"Scrawny specimen, isn't he?"

"It is hardly surprising in one who lives like an ascetic. But hush, Fan."

His tone dropped to a whisper. "Don't fret. I can't imagine he'll hear us with the echo in this ghastly place."

The discontent in her husband's voice was not lost on Ottilia. He had tried to argue her out of the excursion, insisting that Monday would do as well if she wished to try and accost Helen Pargeter.

"Better even, Tillie. For all you know she may attend this blasted market on a daily basis."

"Perhaps, although I don't know where it is. But more to the point, I cannot be sure she is permitted out of doors at this present. She is in disgrace, remember."

"Then she likely won't be allowed to go to church either."

But Ottilia could not believe a man as zealous as Pargeter would not feel it incumbent upon his unfortunate wife to partake of every opportunity to cleanse her soul in the sight of the Lord. It appeared now, however, that Francis might have been in the right of it for Ottilia could not identify Helen Pargeter among the few figures in the front pews. There were two behatted females, heads bent over hymn books and she could not swear to it that either was Helen. The most likely was a lone figure seated more or less in line with the crucifix above the altar. Ottilia would rather have expected her to be in front of the raised pulpit before the nave, under her husband's eye. But that place was clear.

As the organ started up and a hymn began, Francis spoke close to her ear. "I thought you meant to sneak up on the wife and avoid this plaguy Pargeter fellow."

"I'm afraid there is no hope of that now."

"Well, he had better not harangue you or I shall know what to do about it."

Ottilia drew an exasperated breath. "No brawling, Fan, I beseech you."

"Don't be ridiculous, Tillie. I merely meant I shall take the wretch to task if he dares to speak to you amiss."

Not for the first time, Ottilia wished he might have been persuaded to allow her to come with only Hemp for escort, but Francis was adamant.

"If you think for one instant I will allow you to go off without me into the vicinity of a fellow who thinks nothing of thrashing a man in a stranger's house, you may think again. By your own account as well as Lizzy's, he has no respect for rank."

She was obliged to concede as much, adding, "Nor for women neither, I fear."

"Ha! And you expect me to let you career off alone? And don't prate of Hemp. He's a good enough fellow, but I entrust my wife's protection to no other man, I thank you."

Ottilia craned her neck as Pargeter began his sermon. Surely Helen, if that female was she, must set her gaze upon the priest as he spoke of the wrath of God and quoted from the Bible on the nature of repentance. But for the remainder of the service, the woman kept her eyes firmly ahead and only bent her head to pray. There was nothing for it but to wait for the final Amen.

"At last," came in a hiss from her spouse as the few attendees began to shuffle out of the pews, to the accompaniment of the organ's last notes dying away. Ottilia rose with alacrity.

"We must hasten, Fan."

He exited the pew and stood aside to give her room, his gaze upon Pargeter. "I think the fellow is bent upon accosting you, Tillie. He is looking this way."

But Ottilia had eyes only for the woman in the front pew. She had risen with the rest, but remained where she stood, looking neither to right nor left as Pargeter came down from his pulpit. He paused by the woman for a moment, said something inaudible, and she at once resumed her seat.

It was enough for Ottilia. "It is Helen. I am going forward."

She hastened down the aisle, passing those on the way out, intent upon making it to Helen Pargeter before the woman's terrible husband could prevent it. But as she neared her goal, she saw he had parked himself directly in her path, waiting. He spoke when she was within a few feet of him.

"What brings you to my church, madam?"

Before she could respond, Francis, bristling as she had known he would, thrust in beside her.

"You, sir, will address my wife with courtesy."

He had no visible effect upon Pargeter except to turn the man's glance upon him.

"Wife?"

"I am Lord Francis Fanshawe, Mr Pargeter, and I take leave to tell you your manners leave a good deal to be desired."

Fascinated, Ottilia watched the disdain grow in Pargeter's face. "I answer only to God, sir, for my manners as well as everything else." His cold gaze swept Ottilia again. "I repeat, what do you here in God's house?"

Ottilia opted for truth, responding before her incensed spouse could retort. "I am here to speak to Mrs Pargeter, sir, and not to you."

This brought the female's head round and Ottilia spied a look of fright in the features that indeed belonged to Helen Pargeter. Both her tone and the rider, however, failed to pierce Pargeter's armour.

"My wife has no desire to speak to you, madam. You have wasted your time."

"I think not," cut in Francis. In one swift movement, he pushed in between Pargeter and the pew, elbowing the fellow out of the way. "Go on, Ottilia. I will hold him."

She took instant advantage, catching at the startled Helen's hand and dragging her up from the pew and away to the side aisle. She spoke low, with urgency.

"My husband will not let him follow. I must talk to you alone. How may we manage it, Helen? Are you permitted to roam abroad?"

Helen looked agitated. She cast a quick glance back to where the inevitable altercation had broken out between Francis and Pargeter. Ottilia trusted it would not come to blows, but she had little time.

"Come, Helen. My husband will not be able to hold him for long. Answer!"

Helen's gaze came back to her. Even in the dull light afforded by the rose window above the altar, her eyes were seen to be dilated. She spoke in a subdued fashion, but on a fierce note withal.

"He thinks I am obedient, but I have a method to escape. Not today."

"Tomorrow?"

"Longer. I need a day or two to lull him."

"Tuesday then?"

"Wednesday. It is market day. Legitimate for me to be abroad if he should discover it."

Ottilia contained her impatience. "Very well, so be it. Where do I find you in the market? Oh, and which market?"

"Lady Elizabeth knows it. There is a stall where I purchase old clothes. She may tell you." Ottilia would have spoken then, to refuse Lizzy's further involvement, but a warning hand crept about her arm and gripped. "No word, ma'am. Only listen! We cannot be seen together there. When you come, do not speak or look at me, but follow where I go." With which, she stepped away from Ottilia and raised her voice to a pitch evidently designed to penetrate the nearby hubbub created by the continuing argument between their spouses. "I have no wish to converse with you, madam. Margaret has chosen her path and that is all. Pray leave me be."

Pargeter must have heard, for he turned short about and crossed to join his wife, who set a possessive hand within his arm and leaned close to him as if she sought protection. Pargeter lifted his chin at Ottilia.

"You are not welcome in my church, madam. Neither you, nor your husband. Seek not to come here again."

"Have no fear," came on a snap from Francis as he joined the party. "Nothing would induce me to set foot in your church a second time. Good day to you, Sir Parson."

The sight of her spouse almost emulating the wretched creature's manner threw Ottilia all too close to a fit of merriment. She was glad to be turned about by Francis and fairly marched down the side aisle towards the church door. He had evidently divined her condition, for he broke into scolding the instant they stepped out into the welcome daylight.

"Don't you dare start giggling, you terrible woman! It was not in the least funny."

She bubbled over. "Oh, Fan, if you could but have seen your own face when you said that last. How could I help it?"

A reluctant grin dawned. "Wretch! I meant it too. What an appalling man he is. I believe Mama is in the right of it to say he's mad."

She tucked her hand in his arm as he signalled to Ryde, waiting with the carriage a little way off. "Well, it was worth it, my dearest, for I have an assignation with Helen."

He turned a frowning gaze upon her. "Not in this damned draughty church, I sincerely trust?"

"No, in the market. And Fan, I am sorry for it, but I will have to ask Lizzy for the direction of the market and the stall Helen spoke of. She gave me no chance to ask questions."

"I'm not surprised if she must answer to that lunatic."

"Just so. But you won't object to it, will you?"

He did not answer directly as Williams, driving the coach, drew it up before them. Ryde had walked up beside it and now opened the door and let down the steps. Ottilia allowed Francis to hand her in without comment, waiting in some little trepidation as he sprang up into his place and the groom shut the door upon them. She waited only for the carriage to set off homewards.

"Fan?"

He looked round and gave an impatient sigh. "Are you waiting for my permission to approach Lizzy? For pity's sake, Tillie, you know well you'll do it in any event."

She set a hand to his chest. "Yes, but I don't by any means wish to do so without your agreement."

"Do I have a choice?"

She was obliged to concede he had a point, but chose the part of prudence and remained silent. Her docility was presently rewarded for his arm came about her and he rested his head against hers for a moment.

"Forgive me, sweetheart. That blasted parson put me out of temper."

She could not withhold a gurgle. "I noticed. I had anticipated he would, to be frank."

"That's why you tried to stop me accompanying you, I dare say."

She saw no reason to belabour the point, but reverted to her arrangement with Helen, explaining what had been said.

"It sounds a trifle hugger-mugger, Tillie, more suited to the stage."

"Indeed. Rather like something dreamed up by The Grand Ferdinando."

"Ha! Our Weymouth impresario."

"Just so. At least we have not had to contend with play-actors as we did last summer."

"Well, that plaguy parson is quite as bad, if not worse." Francis drew her closer. "Do as you must, my love. No doubt Lizzy will be only too delighted to be called upon again, even if it is only in so small a capacity."

"Will it content you if I take Hemp?"

He turned his head, eyeing her in the dimness. "Trying to be rid of me?"

"Of course not. I am only too relieved you were with me today. But I fear you may be a trifle de trop in my discussion with Helen."

"We'll see come Wednesday," was all the assurance her spouse vouchsafed, with which Ottilia tried to be content.

Chapter Sixteen

His wounds had kept Pierre confined to his lodging for several days, obliged to consume the poor offerings made by his landlady and to rely upon her young son for aid at need. He was able to manage most things for himself now, but dressing his hair and tying his neck-cloth still defeated him. He had not had occasion to pull on his boots as yet, but he was beginning to think of venturing abroad when Lezayre at last paid him a visit.

His friend was welcome, the tidings he brought, though not entirely unexpected, less so.

"The marquise is infuriated. I do not believe she will forgive me."

A pang of regret smote Pierre, despite the determination that had consolidated while he languished, recovering from the beating. "How much have you told her?"

Lezayre let out a disgusted noise. "I had said nothing but that my tongue was forced by this Fanshawe woman."

"Milady Francis?"

"She is like a fox, that one. Too cunning, and sniffing in places where she has no business to be."

Pierre sipped at the wine his friend had brought. "Yet she has helped Marguerite."

"To the detriment of others, yourself included. You may have secured a match with a price on her head but for this Lady Francis."

Pierre shrugged, and winced at the spasm this brought. "It was not your desire for me, Emile, that I should marry for money. You wished for me to use my skill upon boys to lure

289

them in for you." He watched the red tide rise up Lezayre's cheeks and was momentarily sorry. He held up a hand. "I judge you not. I desire only you will believe this life is not a life for me."

"Your skills are known now, Pierre."

There was venom in the tone and Pierre reflected, not for the first time, that Emile was perhaps less a friend than he pretended. Useless now to say so, nor to protest.

"It means nothing, Emile. I am no more a part of this milieu. It is finished."

"Yes, because of this Lady Fan."

Pierre set down his glass with a snap. "No, Emile. It is for Marguerite. I have wronged her and for her sake, I can no longer live this way."

Emile's gesture encompassed Pierre's person. "For that you have suffered enough. Was it not her father who gave you this thrashing?"

"Violette has told you? It is so."

Lezayre pursed his lips. "You fear this story will become known to the world? You are a fool, Pierre. The marquise will say nothing."

Pierre resumed his drink. "I do not fear the marquise. I think only of how I may find a way to help Marguerite."

"This again? Pierre, you are stubborn! What is she to you? Yes, you enjoyed yourself, but the girl is nothing. Why does it matter what becomes of her?"

Rage enveloped Pierre but he controlled it, speaking with deliberation. "A cheat I am perhaps, but a villain I am not, Emile. I am not noble, but I come of noble stock."

"Here is a conceit." The jeer in Lezayre's voice set his teeth on edge. "You aspire to nobility now? It suited you well enough to pretend when you thought to snare an heiress. But pretence is not enough for you. What high-minded deed do you contemplate, my fine young friend?"

At that Pierre sighed. "This I have not yet determined. But there is one to whom I may sue for help." He set down his empty glass and leaned in, putting out a hand. "From you I desire one last favour. Will you take a message for me?"

Lezayre looked anything but willing and his tone was grudging. "To whom? The lady Candia perhaps?"

"No, Emile. To her cousin, Milady Elizabeth."

"Oho! Flying high again, Pierre?"

"No. It is Marguerite alone who occupies me. But Milady Elizabeth knows all and she will help me. I have no other go-between."

"You are planning something again, aren't you, Lizzy?"

Lady Elizabeth groaned aloud, stabbing her needle into the unsteady pattern emerging within her embroidery frame. "For heaven's sake, Candia, how could I be? You know well Papa has forbidden me to involve myself further in the business."

"Since when has that stopped you doing whatever you wish?" Her cousin's dark gaze became fierce, her fingers motionless upon the white work on which she was engaged. "Grandmama is perfectly right. You are spoiled, Lizzy."

"I thank you. Are there any more aspersions you care to cast?"

Candia's glare held for a moment and then the pose collapsed as her eyes filled and she sighed. "I didn't mean it … oh, Lizzy, I miss him so!"

Setting aside her work, Lizzy leaned across and patted her cousin in a soothing fashion. Having no engagement this morning, the two girls were seated in the old nursery on the upper floor of Dalesford House, a room currently given over for their use as a den or sitting room since the younger children were absent from town.

"I do understand, Candia. But you know Uncle Randal would have been furious if Pierre had remained in the house."

Candia brushed the wet from her cheeks and caught Lizzy's hand before she could remove it. "If you mean to meet him, take me with you, Lizzy."

"What makes you think I have any such intention?"

The hand was dropped. "Do you think me blind? I saw that old Frenchman come up to you last night."

Lizzy gave an inward curse. She might have known her cousin's eagle eye would be upon her. She had been somewhat astonished herself to be singled out by Monsieur Lezayre and, if she was honest, a trifle dismayed by the request he brought. Not that she was averse to the potential meeting, although how she could help Pierre remained a question. But Lizzy could by no means shake off the reminder given to her by Ottilia when she asked for the location of the market where she could meet with Helen Pargeter.

The Fanshawes had paid a morning visit upon the previous day and Aunt Ottilia drew her aside for the purpose.

"I obtained Francis's permission to ask you, Lizzy, but I must beg you won't attempt to engage with this business again."

Lizzy had laughed then, having no expectation of becoming further involved. "There is no hope of that, Aunt. Both parents have forbidden me to have anything more to do with it."

The warm smile she so much liked had appeared in Ottilia's face. "Such a bind to be obliged to practice obedience, do you not think?"

Lizzy had burst out laughing. "Oh, you are so refreshing, Aunt Ottilia. Anyone else would have expressed their satisfaction."

"Well, I understand how restrictive it is to be female and single. Marriage — if you manage to fall for the right man — will make your life a good deal easier."

The affection in Ottilia's eyes as she looked across to where Lord Francis stood in conversation with Papa had struck a pang of guilt into Lizzy's breast. She had been the cause of creating a rift between them. Of brief duration perhaps, but Aunt Ottilia had been scolded because of her actions. She knew not how to express this without appearing to pry and so held her tongue. But the memory could not but sneak into her mind when Pierre's friend approached her with his proposition.

"Pierre does not wish to embarrass you, Lady Elizabeth, with anything improper. He suggests therefore that you walk in the park and he will rendezvous with you there."

Lizzy spoke her first thought. "He is recovered enough for that?"

"Yes, indeed, my lady. He is stiff a little, but he is able to walk abroad. May I carry a message to say you will oblige him?"

"Why does he wish to see me, do you know?"

Lezayre gave a shrug. "This I cannot say. He tells me you have before assisted him. What say you, *mademoiselle*? Tomorrow? Or the day following perhaps?"

Lizzy hesitated, her aunt's words leaping in her head. She ought to refuse. But the core of curiosity and thirst for adventure that characterised her would not be quieted.

"At what time?"

"Pierre leaves this to your convenience. He will be at the assigned place at whatever time you may appoint."

A rapid review of her engagements yielded result. She could slip away while Mama was taking her afternoon rest tomorrow night. Papa would be at his club. Candia? Well, she must escape her cousin's eye.

"Tomorrow then, at two." The usual saunterers and those in carriages taking the air would not be abroad until a later hour.

But Lizzy had failed to take into account Candia's jealous vigilance. What to say? How to deflect her cousin? She prevaricated.

"Do you mean Lezayre?" She gave an artistic shudder. "Horrid creature. I can't think how your Pierre comes to have such a friend."

Candia's steady gaze did not waver. "He spoke to you of Pierre, didn't he?"

Lizzy raised her brows. "Were you listening?"

"I wasn't close enough."

The regretful note almost provoked a laugh from Lizzy, but she managed to suppress it. "Well, you may be easy. All he said was that the Chevalier is in a way to be recovered from his ordeal."

Candia eyed her. "I don't believe you."

"Why should you not?"

"Because I know you, Lizzy. Besides, if that was all, he would have told me too. He knows Pierre and I are friends."

"Yes, and he said I should be sure to tell you," Lizzy offered, improvising rapidly. "Apparently Pierre is almost ready to walk abroad."

"Oh, Lizzy, stop it! You are wearing that look of yours."

"Which look?"

"The one you always wear when you are up to mischief. Such an innocent face, just as if you weren't the naughtiest child imaginable."

For the life of her, Lizzy could not prevent a mischievous laugh. "You had that from Papa, I dare say."

"I had no need to hear it from him. I've seen it for myself countless times. Do you forget how much we were together as children?" A misty sort of smile hovered on Candia's lips. "You have no idea how I cherished those moments, Lizzy. It was as if I had a sister, even though you got me into trouble more times than I care to count."

Guilt swamped Lizzy and she was moved to cross to sit by her cousin on the sofa, seizing her into a hug. Feeling tremulous herself, she gave in to impulse.

"I am going to meet Pierre. But are you sure you want to see him, Candy? Won't it just make it worse for you?"

Her cousin was drying her eyes, but she looked round at this. "No! It's horrid not seeing him at all."

"But I've no notion what he wants. And I've pledged not to get involved again."

"Then why did you agree to meet him?"

"Because he needs my help. How could I refuse?" She took one of Candia's hands and gripped it. "You do realise he has his whole mind upon this Meg, don't you? I do him the justice to own that he feels his wrong and is sorry for it, and for her plight."

Candia released herself, a hard note entering her voice. "But he doesn't love her."

Lizzy was convinced he did not love Candia either, but she refrained from saying so. "Well, that may be so, but there is no denying he set in motion the events that led to her being in prison."

"Pierre didn't kill that man!"

"No, but Meg was looking for Pierre when she fell into the man's hands. She is carrying his child, Candia."

This brutal truth caused her cousin to throw her hands over her face, hiccupping sobs emanating from behind them. Lizzy waited for them to abate.

"Candia, I really don't think you should come. It will only distress you. And it may well inhibit Pierre from speaking as he wishes. He can be perfectly frank with me."

The hands came down. "I am coming. I won't interfere. I won't even listen, if that's what you want. I'll stand off while he talks to you, but see him I must."

Nothing would move her from this standpoint and Lizzy was obliged to acquiesce. She could only hope Pierre had nothing too discomfiting in mind.

"This is no fit place for you, milady. I wonder milord permitted you to come here."

There was some justification for Hemp's candour, Ottilia could not but admit. Before her marriage, such a market as this would have held no terrors for her, used as she then was to the jostling, the pungent aroma of unwashed flesh mingling with the stink from kennels and the occasional whiff from a passing lavender seller. The ceaseless chatter and loud cries of vendors assaulted her ears, a ragged urchin scrabbling for scraps almost cannoned into her but for her steward's quick action in heading him off, and she was plagued by a persistent seller of pies and sweetmeats proffered on a tray until Hemp showed him a raised fist.

"I have turned soft since becoming a ladyship," she told him with a forced smile. It was not entirely true. Last year's fateful pregnancy, with its attendant disaster and the weakness that followed had left her too debilitated even now readily to endure such a crowded venue. She could wish Helen Pargeter had appointed a less stressful rendezvous. Glad of the formidable stature of her escort, Ottilia shifted closer and took his arm.

"Can you see this stall selling old clothes, Hemp?"

"No, milady. Let me guide you out of this crush. It is thinner on the periphery."

Within a very few minutes, he had threaded through the press of bodies within the square to a paved area in front of a row of dilapidated buildings. Relieved, Ottilia took a moment to catch her breath, trusting her steward would not report back to Francis with an account of the ill condition of the area. Hemp was scanning the market.

"Milady?"

"Yes?"

"There is a woman with a basket looking at you."

Ottilia flashed a glance back at the market and caught sight of Helen Pargeter. She did not look again, lowering her voice to an urgent whisper.

"Don't look at her, Hemp. Follow where she leads."

"Without looking, milady?"

"Oh, you know what I mean. Don't be obvious."

One of his rare deep laughs emanated from the steward. "I cannot be other than obvious, milady."

True enough. Hemp was unusual in these parts, and tall to boot. He was scarcely likely to go unnoticed. Although he had drawn eyes as they passed through the market, Ottilia thought most attendees were too occupied with their own concerns to pay much attention. A couple of idlers had stared for a while, but no more.

"She is moving, milady."

In a moment, the figure in a drab coat and hat Ottilia recognised from Sunday's encounter slipped into sight along the street, walking with a quick step, head bent just as it had been in church.

As Ottilia fell in behind with Hemp, she could not but reflect how Helen had perfected the art of being unobtrusive. Who would pay attention to a woman dressed so plain, scurrying about like a brown mouse, the basket indicating her errand? Was this her shield against her reverend husband's punitive regime?

She made a circuit of this end of the market and then vanished down a side street. Ottilia increased her pace, tugging at the steward's arm.

"Quick, Hemp! We must not lose her."

"I think she will wait for you, milady. Did not you say she instructed you to follow?"

He was found to be right. As they turned the corner, the figure was seen to have stopped, bending down to tie a lace on her shoe. A flare of admiration rose in Ottilia. Ingenious. The woman was adept, it would seem.

Without a glance back, Helen straightened and walked on. The street was thinly populated. At one door, a woman was shaking out a rug; a fellow with a heavy sack on his back trudged towards the market; and two females stood in conversation in front of a pawnbroker's window. Both looked up with some awe at Hemp as he negotiated Ottilia past them and turned down another street where Helen had already gone. It was perhaps fortunate that interest in Hemp overshadowed her appearance in this locality. Without him, Ottilia felt she would have drawn attention merely by the quality of her garments.

After another two turns, the way began to seem tortuous. "It is to be hoped we can find our way back to civilisation," she remarked.

"As well you opted to pay off the hack, milady. We will find another easily enough."

Reassured, she was again glad of his support, half wishing she had not persuaded Francis to let her go without him. It was a lesson to realise how well he shielded her and she vowed not to find it irksome for the future.

They had just passed a quiet little tavern with a weathered sign, appropriately depicting a crescent moon under the words "The Silver Moon", when Helen checked, glanced back as if to assure herself she was followed, and then opened a door and entered.

"An inn? That can't be right."

"Let us find out, milady."

In a moment it became clear that the door through which Helen had vanished was not a public entrance, lacking any sort of signage, although the building appeared to be part of the tavern. Hemp thrust the door open, revealing a dingy interior hallway, ill-lit but for a thin shaft emanating from an open door at the other end.

The steward went in first, cast a glance around and held the door wide. "It looks safe enough, milady. Come."

Not without a slight rise both of distaste and trepidation, Ottilia ventured into the hall. The rhythm of her pulse increased as Hemp closed the door behind her, enveloping them both in muffling dark with a musty odour. On instinct, Ottilia headed for the light at the rear and paused in the doorway.

Helen Pargeter was in the act of lighting a wall-sconce with a spill, adding brightness to a small room inadequately equipped for a parlour. A two-pronged candelabrum, with candles alight, stood upon a centre table to which a couple of straight-backed wooden chairs were set. A fireplace at the far end, presently empty of flames but with wood ready laid, gave promise of potential warmth. Its surround was simple, the mantel bare of any ornament beyond a heavy clock, and the only other piece of furniture was a wooden settle set against the near wall, its seat thankfully cushioned. Ottilia moved to the small latticed window in the back wall and looked out upon a paved yard given over, it appeared, to waste from the tavern kitchen.

"What is this place, Helen?"

The woman had not yet spoken, still busy at a second wall-sconce. Not that the provision of more light rendered the parlour any more habitable.

"I am sorry the fire is not lit, ma'am." Helen turned on the words, blowing out her spill and setting it down on the table. "This is not my day or Josh would have seen to it."

"Josh?"

Helen glanced from Ottilia to the steward, stalwart by the door, and back again. "Joshua is by way of being my champion, Lady Fan, just as you have yours."

Astonishment held Ottilia silent for a space. Champion? A secret life? Was the fellow a lover? Her mind leapt. An alternative that had not entered into her calculations. Could this Josh be the key?

"How much of a champion, Helen? How far might he go for you?"

Helen's slight figure stilled, her gloved fingers stiff upon the wooden surface of the table as she met Ottilia's gaze across its barrier.

"You have that, have you? How did you guess it?"

Ottilia gave a long sigh. "You were my last hope. It did not occur to me you might have employed another."

A nod confirmed the suspicion. Helen indicated the chair set into the table next to where Ottilia was standing. "You had better sit down, ma'am. I will fetch him." Hemp gave way as she went to the door, but she paused there and turned back. "Hope for nothing, Lady Fan. I will not give Josh up to the authorities."

She disappeared on the words and Ottilia was glad to see Hemp watching her exit. She lowered her voice.

"Where has she gone?"

He slipped into the room. "Through a door opposite, milady." A disparaging glance about the room made him grunt. "Not the most salubrious place for clandestine assignations."

"I suspect it is conveniently out of the way for her purposes." Pargeter could know nothing of this other life. Meg must be similarly ignorant. "A surprising woman, Helen Pargeter."

"There is no end to the cunning of your sex, milady."

Ottilia eyed him. "A trifle cynical, Hemp."

"Not without reason."

He closed his lips in a thin line, a shadow Ottilia had seen before entering the dark eyes. She had long suspected there was a female in his Barbadian past who had soured him. She would not pry and Hemp was ever close-tongued. Besides, she had more urgent matters on hand.

"I fear my errand may prove empty, Hemp."

"This Joshua is of no use to you, milady?"

"Not if Helen will not permit him to come forward."

"How is he involved?"

She sighed. "It would seem he is the fellow who delivered the fatal blow to the victim Coveney."

"The one that broke his rib?"

"Just so."

Footsteps in the corridor put an end to the discussion. Hemp retreated to the door, standing to one side to allow Helen Pargeter to enter. She was followed by a man very little taller than herself, dressed in homespuns and with an apron over all. A thickened waistline threw the memory of Pierre's voice into Ottilia's head: "It was a thick body that I held."

The fellow Joshua exhibited an obsequious manner, bobbing two or three bows as Helen gave Ottilia's name. She was both touched and amused to note the bald patch on the top of his head, though he wore his sparse and greying hair tied in the nape of his neck. He looked to be well into his middle years, with features unremarkable but for a somewhat bulbous nose and fleshy jowls. The thought could not but obtrude that here was hardly material for a lover, never mind a champion.

His voice was gravelly. "An honour, my lady."

"Sit down, Josh," instructed Helen, setting a chair for him.

He looked alarmed. "Before her ladyship?"

"She is sitting, don't you see? Sit you down, man." Thus badgered, the fellow took the chair, what time Helen fetched another from a dark corner and set it next to his, settling into it and folding her hands on the table. "Now, tell her ladyship about that night."

The alarm in his face increased. "You promised it would not come to light."

"It won't go outside these four walls."

The fellow Josh threw a panicked glance at Hemp standing just beyond the door, his bulk filling the aperture. Ottilia set herself to soothe.

"You need not fear my steward, Josh — if I may? He is discreet and utterly trustworthy. Nothing you tell me will be repeated by Hemp." She could not make the same assurance for herself, but best not to mention that.

Josh hesitated, and then out it came in a rush, the rough voice low. "I'm not a man of violence. I did it for Helen. So she'd rest easy. Only I chose my time ill. I'd followed him for days — the lad, I mean. Nights mainly. He was in the habit of going to a…" He faded out, casting an anguished look at Helen, who set a hand on his arm and squeezed.

"Say it, Josh. Whatever she is, this ladyship is not squeamish." Her gaze returned to Ottilia. "A house of ill repute is what he means, ma'am."

"Mrs Stark's bawdy house. Yes, I know it," Ottilia said, with the hope of putting the fellow at his ease. "You may speak freely, sir. Young Pierre de Percheval and his cronies gambled there."

Josh's brows lowered. "That was the trouble. I never expected the other man to be with him. I waited in the alley, listening for his step. I was to stop him and give him Helen's message."

"You did not intend to use your weapon?"

Josh sniffed and rubbed a fist across his nose. "Only if he proved obdurate. Helen wanted him to offer marriage to Meg."

"It's what he ought to have done at the start." Helen's fierce gaze was matched by her tone. "When Nathaniel found them even. But, no. He upped and ran from the house like a coward. Next thing, Josh reports he's living like a lord among the gentry. Never mind poor Meg left behind to suffer. He needed telling. He needed to know what he'd unleashed on her. And to rescue her." Her hand once again gripped the arm of the man beside her. "Only it went awry. It wasn't Josh's fault. I should never have forced him to it."

Her champion — if one could call him that — shook his head at her. "You didn't force me, love. I botched it up is all." He turned his gaze back to Ottilia. "I ran out, you see, meaning to stop the lad. That's why I had the cudgel up. Only then did I see the other one with him. Big fellow he was." He wiped at his nose again. A gesture of agitation? "I didn't think, my lady. It was instinct. I struck at him. Then, before I could do more or speak, the lad grabbed me. Much stronger than I'd have guessed he was. I'd no chance to say my piece. All I could do to get away from him and run. I'm sorry for it all, my lady, but I can't change it." He drew a shuddering breath. "And now Helen tells me as that fellow died of the blow."

Moved by his evident distress, Ottilia hastened to correct this. "Not directly, Josh. It was unfortunate, but you did not kill him."

"Might as well have done."

"No, indeed. Had he rested, the rib you broke would have mended in time. As it was, he chose to use Meg's situation to his advantage. There was a struggle and she ran away. Somewhere in that situation a shard from the broken rib pierced his lung. That is what killed him."

Helen spoke up, urgent now. "But they won't have it that way. Bow Street. A jury. They'll say it was Josh's blame. You said it yourself. Without that blow, the fellow wouldn't be dead. And I won't have him arrested. It's not his fault."

Yet she would let Meg hang for murder? But Ottilia did not say it aloud. Tact and patience were needed here. Whether her persuasions would carry weight remained a question. She began on a doubtful note.

"To be honest with you, Josh, I cannot be certain your testimony would make a deal of difference. Justice Ingham is plagued by Coveney's family, as I understand it, baying for blood."

This intelligence appeared to afford Helen's champion a flood of agitation, for he rubbed his nose with a vigorous hand and clenched and unclenched the other where it rested on the table. A glare came Ottilia's way from Helen.

"Is that to fright him more? They don't get Josh's blood, that I will swear to."

"No, indeed. It is Meg who will pay the price. Her defence of her own honour will be taken as an attack. I fear it is too much to hope that a jury composed entirely of males, no matter how good and true, will see the matter in a sympathetic light. There can be no doubt Meg did cause Coveney injury with his own razor and her blood mingled with his upon her hands and body. She was a pitiful sight when we found her."

The graphic account, deliberate on Ottilia's part, had a clear effect upon Josh, whose red-mottled features visibly paled. But Helen Pargeter proved immune to the tactic, a fierce note entering her voice.

"I'll not have you play upon his sympathies, ma'am. You've no need to paint that picture for he knows the whole already. I'll not hesitate to say he's my confidant, for you've guessed that much."

Ottilia became tart. "Then why did you bring me here to meet him? I supposed you had Meg's interests at heart, Helen."

"I do, but Josh comes first."

The finality in her tone was telling. Ottilia was conscious of a corroding sense of defeat. She tried another tack. "You sent for Pierre, did you not? What did you hope for from him?"

"To prick his conscience. What else? Let him go to this justice of yours and tell his part. Let him take the consequence upon himself. It's his blame from the start, all this."

"But he cannot testify to the fateful blow Coveney received."

"Why can't he? He was there. He tackled poor Josh, who's no match for him. He can say what happened as well as Josh. Let them think it was a footpad. It's what Pierre supposed, isn't it?"

"No. He thought it was a paid assassin from France, come to visit retribution upon his head."

It was evident this came as news to Helen, for she stared in a blank fashion. Josh, for a wonder, took it up.

"But they don't send after these *émigrés*. Not to England. We've one or two drink in the tavern. Not aristos as the Frogs call 'em. Ordinary folk. They say it's a free for all and anyone can be denounced now. But if they get out, they're safe enough. Too much chaos for them Frogs to be chasing after 'em once they've crossed the channel. 'Sides, any French spy would get short shrift over here."

Josh spoke with animation and gestures that gave Ottilia an inkling of his attraction for Helen. After the parson, his lively interest must come as a refreshing change. She was frowning, her gaze still on Ottilia.

"Pierre must have known that."

"Ah, but you don't perhaps know him as well as you think, Helen. He is in fact a gamester of some expertise. Apparently he was denounced because he took a considerable sum from a notable French official and he fears the man's vengeance."

"He's a liar then, as well as a heartless seducer?"

The hard note gave away Helen's determination on vengeance of her own. She would sacrifice Pierre over Josh, even if the latter's evidence could do more to mitigate Meg's sentence. Ottilia sighed aloud. "You wanted me to know so that I will stop searching, is that it? Yet you nevertheless expect me to keep my tongue, to refrain from passing this information to Justice Ingham."

A sly smile crept onto Helen Pargeter's lips. "You won't do that. I've taken your measure, Lady Fan."

"Have you indeed?"

"Oh, yes. You won't speak if you can't produce the witness. No point. And you won't send this Ingham of yours, or his runners, hunting down poor Josh neither."

"Why would I not?"

"Because he's not your murderer. You've no call to set the dogs on him."

Stymied, Ottilia glanced towards her steward, who acknowledged the look with a flick of his brows upwards. His deep voice cut into the thickened atmosphere.

"I will go and hunt up a hack, milady, while you stay safe here."

She nodded and Hemp slipped out of sight. What to do? Could she bypass Helen? Appeal to the man instead? One could not but admire Helen's sagacity. No matter for wonder she had so well survived her unsatisfactory marriage. Ottilia opted for truth.

"You have me at a stand, Helen." She turned her gaze upon Josh, who was looking decidedly hangdog. Was there a conscience here to be pricked? "You are a worthy man, Josh. I can see you care for Helen's welfare and that is admirable in you. My mission is to save the life of an innocent. Meg is a victim of circumstance."

Helen was on her feet. "That'll do! Josh, you've heard enough." She tugged at the man and he came to his feet, but his eyes were on Ottilia.

"My lady…"

307

But Helen pushed him towards the door. "Back to your duties now. I'll see you on our day."

Ottilia called out to him as he went. "If you change your mind, Josh, you will find me at Lady Polbrook's house in Bruton Street."

He stopped in the doorway and turned his head. Ottilia saw an uncertain look in his face before Helen thrust him out of the room and a faint thread of hope ran through her. And then Helen turned on her, spitting fury.

"How dared you do that? I told you not to play upon him, Lady Fan."

Ottilia rose to face her. "Because you know he feels it?"

"Feels it? Of course he feels it. He's a caring man. Wish to God I'd said it was me now. I thought it was safe to bring you here, but now…"

"Have no fear, Helen. You have ample time to wield your power over the man."

"Power, is it? The only power I have is his affection and I won't use that. He's a good man. He doesn't deserve to be dragged through the mire."

Ottilia became tart. "Oh, come, Helen, do you take me for a ninny? You are afraid if he speaks up your secret must be blown. I don't blame you for not wishing to face Pargeter's vengeance."

Helen's flush and the way she avoided Ottilia's gaze told her she had hit the mark. The woman's tone became gruff.

"You don't know him." Her eyes came up again, a species of anguish in them. "If I didn't have Josh, I couldn't endure it."

Moved despite herself, Ottilia stepped up and took Helen's hands, squeezing them hard. "I do understand."

"Milady?"

Her steward appeared in the doorway. "I am coming, Hemp." Ottilia released Helen's hands. "You are a brave woman, Helen. You will weather it."

There was no leaving the house without the company of at least one servant. Lizzy opted for the footman. Not only had Charles assisted with the rescue, he had more or less valeted Pierre while the Frenchman was staying at Dalesford House.

"It is to meet the Chevalier de Percheval, Charles, to discover how he does."

"Indeed, my lady?"

The footman regarded her with a modicum of suspicion, but Lizzy preserved an innocent front. He could not prevent her actions, but she did not doubt he was perfectly aware of the prohibitions laid upon her. The servants always knew everything. She set herself to cajole.

"It really is only a meeting, Charles. Lady Candia is coming with me, you know. She will be down in a moment."

His frown cleared. "Very well, my lady."

Lizzy turned away to the hall mirror to hide a smile, pretending to adjust her bonnet. Her cousin's conformity and kindness had long since won approval from the Dalesford domestic staff. To a man, like Candia herself, they pointed the finger at Lizzy at the slightest hint of mischief.

On this occasion, however, Candia's nervous excitement was unlikely to pass unnoticed. Her colour was heightened and there was expectation in her eyes as they flicked about the greensward the moment they entered Hyde Park by the Grosvenor Gate. A sharp intake of breath told Lizzy she had spotted the Frenchman.

"You've seen him? Where is he?"

Candia pointed to one side of the double row of walnut trees. "There, over by that tree."

Her voice was tremulous and Lizzy was obliged to conceal an inward groan. Was this going to prove complicated? She hailed Pierre as their steps brought them within hearing distance.

"Chevalier?"

He turned his head and waved. Then Lizzy saw his face change as he took in the presence of her cousin at her side. Consternation? It was quickly veiled as they came up and the Frenchman made a deep bow.

"Milady Elizabeth, I thank you for coming." Then the smooth tone she loathed was in his tongue. "And Milady Candia also. Ah, *ma chère*, to see you is a boon I had not expected."

Lizzy watched in some irritation as he took her cousin's gloved hand to his lips, the quick rise and fall of Candia's bosom and the shine at her eyes betraying her state of mind. Her voice became fluttery.

"Are you better, Pierre? Such a beating as that horrid man gave you! I dreaded you would be laid up for weeks."

He released her hand, producing a smile which Lizzy thought mechanical. "*Mais non, ma chère.* I am stiff a little, and there are yet bruises, but it is a bagatelle."

"A bagatelle! No, indeed." Candia's smile was blinding. "But I am glad you are better. Will you be well enough to attend the Askern party tomorrow? Or no, perhaps that is too much to expect."

Pierre's face closed like a door and his tone became clipped. "No parties, Candia, *ma chérie*. I shall attend no more these pleasures of the Ton. It is finished."

All the anticipation in her cousin's face collapsed. "Finished? Oh, no, Pierre, why?"

By the changes in his features, Lizzy thought he struggled with himself. A sacrifice too far? Did he truly mean to abjure fashionable life?

Pierre glanced at the footman standing at a discreet distance and brought his gaze back to Lizzy. "A moment, Milady Elizabeth, if you will permit?"

"As you wish."

He drew Candia aside a little and lowered his voice, but his words were still audible. "There was never hope for us, *ma chère* Candia. You are too far above me, unworthy as I am."

Her cousin's breathy response was tearful. "Not to me. Never to me, Pierre."

"You do me too much honour, *chérie*. It is a fraud that I am. Also, I have done a great wrong — you know it, I think — and this I must right."

A sob escaped Candia. "I know and I d-don't care. Are you g-going away?"

"This I do not yet know, but it is possible. *En tout cas*, I do not again show myself in the world you inhabit."

"Oh, Pierre."

With a gesture Lizzy could not but find poignant, he reached to wipe the wet from Candia's cheeks.

"Do not weep for me, *chérie*. You make me to feel more a villain."

Well, and he was one, Lizzy reminded herself, pained for her cousin's distress. But Candia's plight was nothing as compared to that of the girl he had ruined. She did him the justice to own that he knew it, felt it, and seemed determined to act upon it.

Time to end this farce before Candia disgraced herself. She stepped in.

"Remember your promise, Candy."

Her cousin's large eyes turned in her direction, misty yet. She caught a hiccupping breath. "I remember. Give me one moment."

To Lizzy's combined astonishment and disapproval, she then flung her arms about Pierre's unwilling neck and pressed herself close against him. His arms flailed, then closed about her for a brief instant, before he took hold of her shoulders and put her from him.

"*Adieu, ma pauvre* Candia."

Her cousin, clearly unable to utter a word, gave a nod and turned, walking rapidly away down the path. Concerned, Lizzy signed to the footman.

"Go after her, Charles!"

He went at once in pursuit, catching up with Candia fast and keeping pace behind her. Lizzy breathed again and turned on the culprit, fuming.

"Well, that was pretty!"

His countenance, no longer wearing the gentle air he had cultivated for her cousin's benefit, showed a like anger. "Why have you brought her? Is it not enough that I must renounce the life I made?"

"She insisted. She saw Monsieur Lezayre come up to me and guessed I was coming to meet you. Not that I know why I agreed, if this is your attitude, sir."

He was at once contrite. "Ah, no, forgive me, I beg. This was hard for me, Milady Elizabeth. I do not like that I have hurt her."

"That is past praying for, Chevalier."

He flung up a hand. "Ah, do not! You know, I think, that to this title I have no right."

"So I understand. What do you want of me, sir?"

Trouble returned in his features. "I must see Marguerite. Know you where they hold her? This prison. Is it a place where one may visit?"

Lizzy sighed. "I have no notion at all. However, I cannot think it would be difficult to find out. Why don't you go to Bow Street and ask?"

She was treated to a horrified glance. "Bow Street? To see again this justice who asks of me the questions? *C'est pas possible!*"

"Well then, I don't see—"

He cut her off, leaning in, his gaze intense. "But you, Milady Elizabeth, you may discover, no? You have the ear for this Madame Fan and she may tell you. She knows all."

An impatient exclamation escaped Lizzy. "I cannot ask my aunt. I am expressly forbidden to involve myself in this affair, Pierre."

"But you are here, *mademoiselle.*"

Lizzy detected both cunning and triumph in his face, though his tone remained perfectly respectful. Really, if it was not for the plight of this Marguerite of his she would turn about and leave him flat. She prevaricated.

"And if I were able to help you in this, Pierre, what do you intend? What is your purpose in finding means to see the poor girl?"

"This I cannot tell, but see her I must."

"And distress her for naught? What if she has no desire to see the author of her misfortunes?" He looked as if she had struck him and Lizzy was a little sorry. She threw out a hand. "That was unkind."

"No, it was just." Low and vibrant now. "I feel it as you desire I should." His head came up. "You ask me what I may do. I know not. Yet my heart commands me in this. I know, *mademoiselle*, as you do not, what it is to be condemned, to have the stomach heat with fear when it comes to me that a man will have my life. And this I may permit Marguerite to face alone? *À cause de moi?* No, *mademoiselle*. A thousand times I say to you, no!"

Moved, Lizzy set a hand on his arm. "I believe you."

He drew a breath, audibly ragged. "If it were in my power to vanish her from that place, as I vanished myself, this I would do." His shoulders sagged. "*Mais c'est impossible.*"

"Yes, I suppose so," Lizzy agreed. But a startling notion was forming in her head. Altogether too daring. Yet its simplicity beckoned, tantalising the little devil that dwelled deep inside. She banished it back to its cave.

"Let me see what I can do."

Pierre's gaze lit. "You will help me?"

"I can promise nothing, but I will try."

Chapter Seventeen

From his position at the mantel, Francis watched his wife where she stood at the parlour window, one hand twitching at the fall of velvet drape in a way that could not but trouble him. Ottilia had never before looked so defeated. He had nothing to offer beyond a platitude, but use it he must.

"You did everything you could, Tillie."

She turned her head, the clear eyes dull. "Did I, Fan? Everything?"

"What more is there? You have tracked down the culprit. If he won't come forward—"

"He would have to, if I forced the issue."

Francis eyed her. "Do you want me to tell Ingham?"

A smile flickered and died. "To spare me? It would be just as much a betrayal."

"And if I had done it behind your back you would never speak to me again."

She came to him then. "Don't raise spectres, Fan. I can't go through that again."

"Nor I." Even the memory of the hideous estrangement between them last year, though brief, was painful to him. He covered the hand she had touched to his breast and brought it to his lips. "What would you have me do? Shall I see this Josh fellow for myself and try if I can persuade him?"

Her fingers clung to his for a moment and then released them. "I appreciate the offer, but no. If it is to be, it must be voluntary. A witness coerced will not serve."

"Why not, Tillie? If he is under oath, he must tell the truth."

She gave a little sigh, and went to the bureau from where she extracted a missive and gave it to him. "I wrote to Jardine." As Francis made himself master of the letter, she went on, "As he says, the truth of itself is not enough. If a jury is to be swayed to sympathise with Meg, the whole background is needed: of why he did it, for Helen's sake, and why, for Meg's sake, she asked it of him. And that strikes at the root of both their fears, for this secret liaison will become public property. In truth, I cannot blame either for wishing to conceal the matter."

"Yes, I see. But Jardine thinks Pierre's testimony may be useful."

"Not of itself." She retrieved the letter and slipped it back into the bureau drawer. "We need Josh's testimony too."

"An impasse then."

She threw him a glance in which a faint echo of her mischief hovered. "That is what I said."

"You didn't. You put the blame squarely on yourself as you always do."

"Oh, don't, Fan." She put her hands to her face and rubbed at her cheeks. "How can I help it? I pledged myself to save Meg and I have failed. That is the long and short of it."

Distress threw Francis into sharpness and he crossed to intercept her, seizing her by the shoulders. "I won't let you do this to yourself, Tillie. You've beaten the odds before. It is not over. There is time. Who knows but the fellow may find the courage after all?"

A trifle of light crept into her eyes. "Do you think so?"

"It's possible, isn't it?" He smiled down at her. "Come, my dear one. I won't have my intrepid wonder woman admit defeat."

To his relief, this drew from Ottilia her characteristic gurgle. He drew her close and kissed her, gratified by her convulsive response before he let her go.

"I do love you, Fan. You are the best of husbands, did you know?"

He cocked an eyebrow. "Naturally. I've been schooled by the best of wives."

He received a light hit in the chest.

"I am no such thing and you know it."

"Well, you try very hard. I'll give you credit for that."

"Fiend!"

He rejoiced at her lighter mood. Whether it would hold remained a question. His mother's return from a visit to Dalesford House threatened to destroy it at a stroke. She entered in a tempestuous fashion, breaking into speech at once.

"All the devils of hell are come upon us and it is your fault, Ottilia!"

Seeing the dismay leap into his wife's features, Francis at once sprang to her defence. "That is the outside of enough, ma'am. I won't have Tillie harangued. Whatever has occurred, she can scarcely be held accountable for everything."

His mother snorted. "You need not jump down my throat, boy. Ottilia knows I don't mean it, though Harriet may justly complain of her dragging Elizabeth into the business. Do you know what that wretched child did?"

Francis groaned. "No, and we don't want to, I thank you."

Unheeding, his mother swept on. "Harriet is convinced her daughter is hankering after that French boy as well as Candia." She flapped a hand at Ottilia as she spoke. "You need not be uneasy. I did not betray the child to her mother. Harriet does not know all she has done on your behalf."

Ottilia sank into a chair, looking perfectly white. "But what did Lizzy do, Sybilla?"

Sybilla brought it out with a ring. "She went to meet de Percheval in the park, in a most clandestine fashion. And, if you please, she took Candia with her. What have you to say to that?"

It was evident Ottilia had nothing to say to it, but the consternation in her face was enough to throw Francis into speech. "Tell the tale without all these accusations, Mama, for pity's sake! Tillie is distressed enough."

Sybilla's sharp eyes focused on Ottilia and her brows drew together. "Why? What has occurred? As if I did not have enough on my plate."

"We will tell you presently, ma'am. What happened with de Percheval? And how did Harriet come to know of this meeting?"

Sybilla plonked into her chair. "She found out because Candia came back from it in floods. Harriet had the greatest piece of work to drag it out of her for she would do nothing but weep and protest her heart is broken. When Harriet taxed Elizabeth with her part, she pretended she had done it for Candia's sake. Well, she may have fooled Harriet, but it is as plain as the nose on your face that she has thrust herself into this Meg business again."

"Oh, good Lord, I thought Gil had scotched that."

"So also did he, but no. But will Elizabeth say what she meant by it? She will not. Sticks to it buckle and thong she went only to chaperone Candia. Which, if it were true, shows less than common sense."

Ottilia spoke at last, her voice surprisingly eager. "She does not lack sense. She is merely impulsive. Though what in the world Lizzy thought she could accomplish by meeting the boy I have no notion."

"Is that all you have to say, Ottilia?"

"Mama!"

"Oh, stop glowering, Francis. I am not going to harangue the girl." Sybilla eyed Ottilia in a frowning way, despite his attempt to catch her eye. "What is it, my dear?"

Ottilia rose. "Tell her, if you please, Fan. I am going to our bedchamber for a space before we must dress for dinner."

Francis was on his feet. "Shall I come with you? Do you need anything?"

She waved away his solicitude, her smile a trifle tremulous. "Nothing, Fan. I just need to think."

He watched her go, debating whether to ignore his mother's questions and go after her. The matter was settled for him.

"Well, boy? Are you going to enlighten me?"

The hackney deposited Ottilia on the doorstep of Dalesford House. She had gone to the room she shared with Francis only to don her cloak and hat and fetch a pair of gloves. Francis would be grieved at her duplicity, but it could not be helped. Her purpose was sufficient. In hope of appeasing him, she took Hemp, who had eyed her with suspicion as they rode.

"Does milord know you are gone out, milady?"

Ottilia was betrayed into a conscious laugh. "It makes no matter, Hemp. I am only going to be gone a short while."

Hemp rang the bell and Ottilia was relieved when the footman rather than the butler answered the door.

"Ah, Charles, is it not? Pray tell Lady Elizabeth I wish to see her. I will wait in the small parlour." So saying, she bade Hemp await her in the hall and swept across to the room where Pierre had been accommodated upon the day she came to see him after he was attacked. A cheerful fire burned in the grate and the candles were alight, giving a warm glow to the room.

Ottilia had paced back and forth across the carpet only two or three times in an agitated way before the door opened and Lizzy tripped into the room. She was looking less than her usual bright self. Not precisely apprehensive, but it was evident she was wary.

"Aunt Ottilia? You wished to see me?"

"I did, Lizzy. Shall we sit?"

She took a seat upon the sofa Pierre had used and patted the place beside her. Lizzy approached with obvious caution.

"Have you come to ring a peal over me? I suppose I deserve it."

"Do you?"

The girl fidgeted, looking away. Then a tiny echo of her erstwhile mischief showed as she turned back. "You would have done the same, Aunt. Pierre sent a message by Monsieur Lezayre. He needed my help. I couldn't refuse."

Ottilia had to smile at the pleading note. "Especially when you did not wish to."

The girl's characteristic laugh rang out and she sat down at last. "Oh, I knew you would understand."

"Yes, but why Candia?"

"She badgered me so. She saw Monsieur Lezayre approach me and guessed. Not much escapes Candy, you know. She is a deal sharper than most of you realise."

"I believe you are right." Ottilia plunged directly to the heart of the matter. "What did Pierre want of you?"

Lizzy became animated. "That is just it. I was wondering what excuse I might contrive to visit you at Bruton Street, only—"

"Only you were afraid of running foul of your grandmama?"

The characteristic laugh came. "That is it exactly."

"She is not pleased with you, I fear."

Lizzy disregarded this, sounding earnest. "But I meant to tell you, indeed I did. Pierre wants to see Meg, but I don't know just where she is held. Pierre asked me to find out."

Ottilia strove with her itching conscience, but her need was too urgent. "It is providential he contacted you. I want to see him myself. Is it too much to hope he gave you his direction?"

"Indeed he did. I am to send a note to his lodging."

A long sigh escaped Ottilia. "Excellent."

She found Lizzy's questioning gaze upon her, although she was clearly hesitant. Ottilia could not withstand a smile.

"You are dying to ask, I dare say."

A giggle escaped the girl. "Guilty as charged."

Ottilia hesitated. She had conceived this plan upon hearing Lizzy had made contact with Pierre. But had she the right, in the face of Sybilla's disapproval, to draw the girl back in? Meg's desperate predicament won out.

"I am hoping, now that he is so penitent, I might after all persuade Pierre to testify in court on Meg's behalf."

Lizzy's gaze held hers. "Why? Has something happened?"

It was Ottilia's turn to fidget. Frustrating for the girl to be left out. What harm would it do to tell her? She was speaking almost on the thought.

"I have discovered who administered the blow that broke Coveney's rib. Only Helen won't let him come forward."

"But Meg is her stepdaughter."

The shocked note drove Ottilia to explain. "The circumstances are such that one can appreciate her reluctance. Yet it leaves me with no other avenue to save poor Meg, although the hope of swaying a jury with Pierre's story is feeble at best. If I am honest, it is a last-ditch attempt."

Lizzy set a hand on her arm and squeezed, her tone sympathetic. "I am so sorry, Aunt Ottilia. I wish there was something I could do."

The utterance at once brought home the indiscretion of speaking so freely. "And now I have done precisely what I should not. After all the uproar too. For heaven's sake, Lizzy, don't try to do anything! On my honour, there is nothing you can do."

"But I promised Pierre I would find out where he can find Meg."

Ottilia looked her full in the face. "If I tell you where Meg is held, will you promise only to pass on the information and act no further in the business?"

There was hesitation now. Ottilia thought she detected a guilty look flit across the girl's face, but it was quickly hidden. She pressed the point.

"Lizzy? You have not some scheme in your head?"

The girl dipped her eyes. "I am always scheming, Aunt. But what do you suppose I could do that you can't?"

Ottilia gave a half-shrug, feeling distinctly uneasy. "I have no notion, but you are filling me with foreboding. You are not thinking of tackling Helen yourself, I hope? If so, I beg you won't. You may put her in grave difficulty even by attempting to see her."

Lizzy looked up at last with a smile. "I can safely promise you I won't do that."

Less than satisfied, Ottilia eyed her. "You will send a note to Pierre as he asked?"

"Of course."

"Where is his lodging?"

"It is in Lower John Street, off Golden Square. Number Five."

The ready response was reassuring, as far as it went. But Ottilia could not shake off a conviction Lizzy was keeping something back.

"You won't visit him there, I trust."

"Certainly not. It would be most improper."

"That would stop you, would it?"

This elicited a naughty twinkle. "In this instance, yes, Aunt Ottilia. I have no mind to compromise myself with Pierre."

Her qualms by no means allayed, Ottilia told her where in Bridewell to find Meg. Compelled, she added a warning. "If you do have some scheme in your head, Lizzy, I trust you will look at the possible consequences before you act. As I have had occasion to say before, this is not a game."

"Oh, I know that, Aunt Ottilia." Lizzy spoke with both impatience and irritation. "Lives are at stake. It ceased to be amusing when Pierre got beaten. But you can't lose, Aunt. Meg will be saved, I'm sure of it."

Having no great faith herself, Ottilia chose not to answer this. But having Pierre's direction gave a lift, albeit slight, to her spirits. She left in a happier frame of mind, and had the good luck to slip back into the house before either Francis or Sybilla had an inkling of her absence. Only at night as she was dropping into sleep did it occur to her to question the confident ring of Lizzy's assertion.

The visitor was a stranger to Meg. A slight cloaked figure, she stood upon the threshold, glancing at the bare walls, the barred high window and then, almost an afterthought, at the room's occupant.

"Forgive me, Miss Pargeter."

A mellow voice and an engaging smile as she moved towards the makeshift bed where Meg huddled against the wall, the

323

quilt Hemp had supplied clutched about her against the seeping cold. She stared at the woman. No, a girl. Young.

"I thought it was Rose. Who are you?"

A smile, warming and kind. "I am Lizzy Fiske. Lady Fan is my aunt." A gloved hand was held down to her. "You don't know me, but I know all about you. It was I brought Helen to see you, you know."

A catch in her heart. If there was affection for her somewhere in this world, it reposed in Helen. Had not Lady Fan meant to ask her... The memory snaked out of sight. She found it hard now to recall what had been said. It seemed an aeon ago. But the hope burgeoned nonetheless.

"Is she here? Has Helen come?"

A shade of dismay crossed the other's face. "Not Helen, no. But I have brought you a visitor. He is waiting without."

He? Her breath faded. The banished image leapt from its secret cache and flew into her head.

"He would not come in until I had your permission for it. He is afraid you may not wish to meet him."

The name whispered on her breath, mirrored the trembling at her bosom.

"Pierre?"

"Shall I tell him to enter?"

"No!" An involuntary cry. But if he was here...

Lizzy sat on the stool and reached out to tug at the quilt. "Come, Meg. You must not receive him like this."

Resisting, Meg pulled the quilt protectively closer. "Why has he come? Is it to pity me? Crow at my fall?"

Desisting, Lizzy sat back, regarding her with a frown. "Meg, he is truly repentant. He is determined to help you."

"How? There is nothing he can do."

"We don't know that." Lizzy rose. "I will call him."

Panic took Meg. She threw aside the quilt, thrust forward and seized at Lizzy's cloak. "Not yet! I look a very scarecrow. My hair! My face!" She pushed out of the wooden frame of her cot and flung over to the valise, hunting among the meagre toiletries for the brush Rose used upon her. Lizzy's hands brought her gently away.

"Sit, Meg, sit. Your hair is well enough and you need no adornment. You are a little pale perhaps, but that is all."

Pressed, Meg sat on the stool, glad of its support, for her legs seemed like to buckle under her with the weight of sudden oppression. She did not want to see him, to rake up the embers of the sleeping fire, but the yearning deep within surfaced in tremors she could not control.

Lizzy was at the door. Opening, speaking in a low tone, stepping aside. And then he was there. Pierre, as comely as the visions, yet different, his expression grave. Sorrowful?

"Marguerite?"

That name, a caress on his lips, too well remembered. Her heart softened into tenderness and all her ills, for an endless moment, vanished into nothing.

"I know not how to speak to you, Marguerite, so much at fault am I for all you suffer."

And the world returned at a stroke. The four bare walls, the barred window, the endless doom. She ought to reproach him, scream and tear his face with her nails like the harpy who dwelled in her depths. The words wrenched out through no will of her own.

"I looked for you."

"I know, *ma pauvre*. I did not know it then."

He did not move from where he stood. A vision of her restless mind? Was he there indeed? "He said you wanted

325

nothing to do with me. He said he told you and you laughed. Like a devil."

His tone changed. "Who said it? Coveney? He has lied, Marguerite. He said nothing to me. The first I have known that you are in trouble is when I hear Coveney has gone with a girl, boasting he has my Marguerite. And then Milady Elizabeth here, she speaks of Meg. From this moment, Marguerite, I am in hell, even until now."

A note of passion in his voice called to an answering need. Meg lifted a hand, almost put it out towards him. Yet the core of disbelief and despair tapped remindingly on her brain. This is a dream, conjured. He is not here.

A hissing breath sounded. "*Ma foi*! Your hand, Marguerite!"

She turned it, found again the criss-cross scars, healed but unfaded, raised, red and raw. Like a child, she opened the other, held both palm up towards the apparition.

"They are better now."

But the wraith, if it was one, uttered a cry and came to her, fast and furious, throwing itself down upon its knees, seizing the hands, burying its face in them, setting its lips on the scars and … weeping?

"Pierre … Pierre…"

She spoke it softly, hardly able even now to believe in the reality of his presence. But the grip was fierce, hurting even. The lips were soft and hard and hot upon her hands.

Abruptly, he released them and sat up, a look of anguish in his eyes. "Marguerite … *mon ange, ma belle, mon amour*…"

Such words! Thus had he spoken in the very throes of love. Words which dragged the heart from her bosom and wound it irrevocably about his image, which took her deeper into sin and led her to this cold and empty place. She found her hands still open before her, looked at the wetness there in wonder and then back at his beloved face.

"It is he indeed. He came."

His eyes spilled tears as he gazed upon her. Meg stretched out to touch them, her fingers trembling against his cheek. He caught them, kissed them, fierce and urgent.

All her deadened senses began to hum, her pulse pumping with life as it had not pumped in an age. Words spilled out of her, unthought, unregarded, as if they had been waiting for this moment.

"You made my life a star. If he had not found us, I would have been happy forever. You gave me a reason to live, to hope, to dare defiance of him. My Pierre. Mine. That he could not take away from me."

He threw up his head. "Ah, do not! Marguerite, I did you a great wrong and see what has come of this." His glance swept the room and came back to her. "It is *affreux*! What will I say to you? What may I do? Tell me, *ma chère* Marguerite. Curse me if you will, but do not say I gave you happiness."

She could not look away from him, mesmerised by the sight of him kneeling there, unwilling to lose the magic of his presence. That, only that, please God. Not the other. Not the gloom and horror of this place. Her hand was resting in his. It was enough.

"You are here. That is everything to me."

His face twisted. "Marguerite, you rive my heart in pieces. This contentment I cannot endure. Rather I will have you revile me for the villain that I am."

Meg drew in a ragged breath and sighed it out. "I cannot. I love you. There, it is said."

He winced. "This I do not deserve."

Meg squeezed his hand. "Will it make it better if I tell you that I have heaped curses upon your absent head? I was glad when I heard that he beat you. Glad and sorry both, Pierre. I don't want you to suffer."

"It is well that I suffer. Your situation it is to my account, Marguerite. You know this. Why do you forgive? It is not right."

She smiled. "God teaches us forgiveness, does he not?" She moved a little closer. "Hold me, Pierre. One last time."

His gaze darkened, luminous again. The embrace was convulsive, but the arms encircling her gave strength and vigour to her, filling the dead spaces with life.

A feminine cough drew Meg's attention and the embrace slackened. She looked round as Pierre did and saw Lizzy had moved from the door. She had forgotten the woman was there.

"Loath as I am to interrupt you, I must remind you, Pierre, that we have not much time."

"Ottilia, will you cease this pointless roaming? You are wearing out my carpet."

The tetchy tone had no effect. Ottilia barely heard it, buried as she was in flittering thoughts as she sought this way and that for what action to take.

Her mother-in-law spoke again. "Francis, say or do something, for heaven's sake!"

That penetrated. Ottilia halted in her perambulations and turned to look at her spouse, who regarded her gravely from where he stood in his customary stance at the mantel.

"I have said it all already." A wry look came into his face. "You may try again at Pierre's lodging, Tillie. What did the landlady say precisely?"

Ottilia waved a hand to brush this aside. "It is of no consequence. Something is niggling at me and I cannot shake it."

"Concerning the boy?"

She did not answer. Best not said before Sybilla. She was all too apt to go off like a rocket if Lizzy was again mentioned. Ottilia had been obliged to endure a tirade of complaint about the girl's activities, harder to endure when she was by no means certain Lizzy was not scheming again.

"I did try to keep her out of it, Sybilla, but your granddaughter has a mind of her own."

"Too independent for words, that girl. And the worst of it is, Harriet tells me she admires you and may take you for her model. God help you then, I told her."

"I thank you, ma'am."

She had received one of the dowager's black looks. "None of your sauce, Ottilia. You know perfectly well why I say so."

Guiltily aware of having embroiled Lizzy in the first place, Ottilia could not deny it and the absence of Pierre from his lodging had put her on the fidgets. Accompanied by Hemp, she had taken the first opportunity that offered to escape on her errand, chafing when she drew blank and recalled her clandestine visit with Lizzy at Dalesford House two nights since. The landlady said Pierre had gone out early and was not yet returned. Was he visiting Meg? Ottilia could not rid herself of the fear Lizzy might have taken it into her head to go with him.

Francis came up to her. "Be still, Tillie. Come, sit. I'll send for coffee."

She allowed herself to be shepherded into a chair by the fire, but the sense of restlessness remained. Worse even, under the sharp gaze of her mother-in-law.

Sybilla's tone softened. "What is troubling you?"

How to answer such a direct question? She saw her husband's eyes were on her even as he tugged on the bell-pull. Ottilia shifted with discomfort and parried as best she could. "To have the means to help Meg and not be able to use them. If I can at least persuade Pierre to testify, we are halfway, even though Jardine stresses the need for Josh to do so as well."

Sybilla snorted. "Don't talk to me of Jardine. Hateful man."

"But he knows his business, ma'am," cut in Francis. He settled in a chair beside Ottilia. "From his last note, I did not think him sanguine of a happy outcome."

"Far from it, Fan. But it's all I have."

He set a hand on hers. "I won't take it away from you, my love, but don't get your hopes up too high."

She sighed. "Hardly, since there is no sign of Josh relenting and I failed to find Pierre."

He said no more, but turned the subject. "Mama, when do you expect Teresa back?"

Sybilla raised her brows. "Are you itching to be gone, boy? I will still need you."

"For what, ma'am? As far as I can tell, there is little to be gained by our presence. Especially now Pierre is no longer a danger to Candia."

"If you think I am content to be left here to manage the family under these circumstances, Francis, you may think again. It is your wife who has stirred all these coals."

Ottilia felt her spouse bristle beside her and set a warning hand on his arm. To no avail.

"That is unfair and untrue. I won't have you blame Ottilia, ma'am. It is none of her doing that my brother chose to bring Violette to town. Nor is she in any way responsible for the vagaries of the members of our family. Do you forget what we owe her?"

"Fan, enough, if you please."

He turned violent eyes upon her. "No, it's not enough. I am sick and tired of this constant nagging. You are who you are and I love you for it. I won't have you vilified."

Ottilia tightened her grasp on his arm. "She does not mean it, Fan. You know well Sybilla cares for me. She is fretted by—"

"So am I fretted. So also are you. My mother does not have a monopoly on fretting."

Releasing him, Ottilia looked across at her mother-in-law and found her with black eyes twinkling. She flung up a hand. "Spare your breath, Ottilia. Let him get it out if he needs to." Her gaze shifted to Francis, who was wearing a heavy frown. "Passing over your impertinence, Francis, I am altogether of your mind. You are a good son and a better husband."

He rolled his eyes, looking, to Ottilia's relief, a trifle less enraged. "Praising me to the skies, Mama?"

A rasping laugh escaped Sybilla. "What, and puff you up in your own esteem? Ottilia said you were apt to take on a head of steam without warning. Don't you know better than to ape your mother, foolish boy?"

He broke into laughter at that and Ottilia breathed more freely. But then Francis found her hand and lifted it to his lips. His tone was rueful. "She's right, my love. I heaped my coals on her head because I don't want to heap them on yours."

Ottilia clutched his hand. "I've rubbed you raw, have I not?"

He grimaced. "Yes, but no matter."

"It does matter." She kissed his hand in her turn. "When this is over, I will make it up to you, I promise."

He released himself and caressed her face. "I'll hold you to that."

"That'll do, that'll do," came in testy fashion from Sybilla. "No more billing and cooing, for the love of God!" The distant doorbell interrupted them. "Oh, who in heaven is this? I hope Gipping has the sense to deny me."

A voice in the hall below penetrated to the parlour, interspersed with an indistinguishable murmur in response, presumably from the butler. Then the voice came again, clear and fully to be heard.

"Is Lord Francis within? In the parlour? I'll go up."

Francis was already crossing to the door. "That is Dalesford, if I'm not mistaken."

Sybilla uttered a peevish noise, but Ottilia's mind veered instantly to the trouble that had been vexing her. If Lord Dalesford was here, then Lizzy had been up to something indeed. She moved to the open door to look out. Francis had met Dalesford at the top of the stairs and stood in low-voiced conference. Anxious, she watched, trying to hear what was said against Sybilla's demands for enlightenment.

"Well, where is he? Why does Gilbert not come in? What has happened? It is not Harriet, is it?"

Ottilia turned and flung out a hand. "Hush, ma'am. He is talking to Francis."

Sybilla banged her closed fist on the arm of her chair. "I won't have it! Do they try to keep secrets from me? Tell them to come in at once."

With an inward sigh, Ottilia slid into the passage. "Francis!"

He turned his head. "One moment, Tillie."

"Sybilla commands you both to come in."

She heard him curse under his breath, but he resumed his low-voiced conversation. Within a moment, however, Francis raised his voice. "Go in, Tillie. We are coming."

Both men moved to obey at last, but Ottilia's fears were by no means allayed. Her spouse's aspect was grave and Dalesford was looking unusually solemn. She threw Francis a questioning glance which he met with a shake of his head, motioning her to go in before them.

Ottilia re-entered the parlour to find Sybilla had risen, facing the door. Ottilia went to join her as the gentlemen walked in and were immediately hailed by Sybilla.

"What is it, Gilbert? What has happened? Do not try to spare me, I beg of you. It is plain you are big with news, and none too pleasant by your looks."

Lord Dalesford grimaced, all the customary humour missing from his features. "It's that girl of mine, I'm afraid, ma'am."

"Elizabeth? Pestilential brat! What has she done now?"

"I am not sure it is entirely her doing, but she is incarcerated in Bridewell, in place of this wretched Meg."

Chapter Eighteen

While Sybilla exclaimed, a cold wind flew down Ottilia's spine. This then was the scheme in the girl's head? A mad scheme. Foolhardy and dangerous. But a sneaking admiration crept in nevertheless. Who would have guessed she might take this method to procure Meg's freedom? Not release, for the authorities were bound to hunt for her. The notion sent urgency pumping through Ottilia's veins.

"How did you find out, sir? Did she send to you?"

Her interruption caused Sybilla to break off mid-sentence, but Ottilia had no attention to spare for her reproachful look. Dalesford turned to respond, with some relief, she thought.

"She sent the maid whom, I believe, you instructed to care for this Meg girl."

"Rose, yes. Did she say what happened?"

"She is downstairs, if you care to question her, ma'am. In great distress, I may say. She went into the cell, it seems, to serve Meg and found instead Lizzy lying on the cot."

Ottilia caught a tight-lipped look from her husband, though he said no word. Her pulse kicked. He blamed her for this too? Well, so he might, for she was culpable.

"How did Lizzy come to be there, did she say?" Not that Ottilia doubted for an instant how it had come about.

"Rose was practically incoherent, but I gather Lizzy accompanied the de Percheval boy there to visit Meg. That is all I know. But my daughter, thank God, had the wit to send to me before it is discovered the prisoner has escaped. I came directly to Francis, for he knows Ingham and I am trusting to that to bring my girl off."

Ottilia looked at Francis. "Do you want me to come? I could talk to Ingham perhaps."

He shook his head. "Gilbert and I will do the business better alone, I think. Besides, he's driving his phaeton and we'd best take Rose too since she is our witness. There won't be room for you." In which case, Ottilia could have no chance to question the maid herself. Pointless, in any event. The priority was to get Lizzy out of there. Francis clapped the earl on the back. "We had better hurry, Gil."

"Yes, indeed. Lizzy has already been in the place several hours." He executed a neat bow towards Sybilla. "Your servant, ma'am."

"Send me word, Gilbert, I charge you!"

"I will, ma'am. Now, Francis, I am with you." He left the room, Francis on his heels.

Feeling shredded, Ottilia's mind roiled with the consequence of Lizzy's crazy action. If the authorities found poor Meg out now, she would be fettered and incarcerated in Newgate, all privileges at an end. There would be no Rose and no comfort. Small chance of swaying any jury in her favour now if she were caught. Branding herself a runaway, she had as well have confessed her guilt. Had Lizzy thought of that? Of course she had not. She had devised her plot without reference to the realities of the case, too young to think of aught but the adventure, the romance of it all. Now indeed Ottilia had cause to regret that she ever succumbed to temptation. Francis was wholly in the right of it to blame her. She had been all too reckless.

The need to right the consequences of her wrong gnawed at her. If she could. If they were to be found. And if she found them? Before the authorities, that went without saying. Then what?

The answer flashed in her head and she almost quailed at it. Get them away. As far away as it was possible to go. And swiftly. Immediate necessities began to revolve in her mind. Had they money? Clothes? What else? Her concentration veered to the most pertinent point. If Meg had escaped with Pierre, where in the world would they go? She spoke without thinking.

"I must make all speed."

She crossed to the bell-pull, hardly aware of Sybilla's protests, her mind busy even as her fears began to multiply.

"Make all speed where? What are you about?"

"I've got to find them, Sybilla."

"Find who? What do you mean?"

"Meg and Pierre. Pray don't try to prevent me. If I don't act, this will spell disaster."

Sybilla was on her feet. "You are thinking she will have runners on her tail, are you?"

"Just so."

"Well, you can scarcely expect Ingham to sit still while his prisoner makes off. You mean to interfere, to flout the authorities, do you? I know you won't think of taking her back to Bridewell."

"Take her back? What, and condemn her for certain?" Only half knowing what she did, Ottilia began to pace again. "No, Sybilla. They must be hidden, but where?"

"Not here! I forbid you—"

"Of course not here. This is the first place Ingham will look. Hush, I beg of you, I must think!"

She was spared more protests as Gipping appeared. "You rang, my lady?"

Ottilia cut in fast before Sybilla could say anything. "My carriage, Gipping. And pray inform my steward Hemp that I require his attendance." She called after him as he was about to leave the room. "Oh, and tell Joanie to fetch my cloak and gloves and bring them to me directly."

"I wish you would not be so impetuous, Ottilia," grumbled Sybilla, as the butler went off on these errands. "Sit down, for the love of God! You are fidgeting me to death."

Too beset to argue, Ottilia resumed her seat and Sybilla did likewise. Aware of the black gaze fixed upon her, as anxious now as she felt, Ottilia struck her hands together.

"Where? Where would they go?"

"The fellow's lodging?"

"Too risky, but I might try to gain news of them there."

"Ingham knows Pierre's direction, no doubt."

"If he does not, it will not take that runner Grice long to discover it."

"What about the Pargeter female? The stepmother? Or is that a thought too obvious."

"Much too obvious. Nor do I suppose for a moment Pierre would take Meg anywhere near her father. He must be planning to leave London."

"And go where? They cannot travel far in a day. Unless the fellow hires a chaise."

"If he can afford it, which I take leave to doubt. Moreover, if I know anything of Ingham, he will have his runners explore every road out of London, along with the stage coaches."

Pierre had been out of action for some days. Who knew what resources he had to draw upon? Unless he was to borrow what he needed? Startled by a thought, Ottilia uttered it aloud. "Lezayre! Would he stop to take leave of his friend? Ask him for money perhaps?"

Sybilla waved a dismissive hand. "Not if he has any sense. He would do better not to advertise such a felonious act."

Another possibility leapt in Ottilia's mind. "Violette?"

"What, and risk running into Randal? Where have your wits gone begging, Ottilia?"

Balked, Ottilia sighed and rose again, impatient to be gone. Except there was no sense in going without a destination in mind. "They must have found help somewhere."

Who else was there? One of Pierre's gambling cronies? Aldreth was rich. And a bonhomous type who had no scruples about wasting his funds. He might well be an option. Redlingfield she dismissed. He was not the type to aid in such a cause without enquiring deeply into the matter, if only from ingrained curiosity. Very well then. Aldreth it must be. Only how would she find him? Mrs Stark would know his direction. The revelation whipped across her mind. "Starkey!"

"I beg your pardon?"

Unheeding, elation soaring, Ottilia swept on. "Why did I not think of her at once? Who better? Starkey helped Meg before, she knows her story and she is as well acquainted with Pierre as anyone."

"You are not talking of that brothel keeper, are you?"

"Yes, I am." She threw out a hand. "No objections, I pray you." Her spirits were already dropping. If she had thought of Mrs Stark's, Ingham would assuredly do the same. Indeed, it might well be the first place he sent the runner Benjamin to investigate. Urgency engulfed her. "Where is Hemp? I have not a moment to lose!"

Justice Ingham, though plainly furious from the pinched look in his face, spoke with all his usual calm, addressing himself to Rose.

"Come here, girl."

Francis turned from where he stood with Dalesford by the desk and encouraged the maid with a nod. Red-eyed still and shaking, the girl approached. Francis gave place to allow her access.

"What time was it when you left the prisoner? The real one, I mean."

"Miss Meg, sir?"

"Yes, girl, your charge. What time did you leave her?"

Gilbert cut in with impatience. "Of what use to enquire, sir? May we not go to my daughter at once?"

Ingham remained unruffled. "Presently, my lord."

Francis caught Gilbert's eye and shook his head. Dalesford gave an audible sound of exasperation, but thankfully said no more. Antagonising the magistrate was the last thing they needed.

There was a tremor in Rose's voice. "It were after I took in breakfast, sir. I got her up and dressed first, and then I went and fetched her meal."

"Yes, very well, but what time did you leave her and when did you go back again?"

His testy tone flurried the maid and Francis, with his wife's habit in mind, spoke gently to her. "Don't be afraid, Rose. Nobody blames you. Just tell Sir Thomas what you know."

She gave a little sigh. "I'm trying, my lord, only I don't rightly know the time. Might have been nine or thereabouts when I went off."

"And you went back at what time?" he asked, relieved Ingham refrained from interrupting.

"It were past one, I know that, my lord. I always take in a snack and coffee." Her features registered dismay. "I near dropped the tray, my lord, when I saw her ladyship a-lying there instead."

"What did she say?" barked Ingham.

Rose twisted her fingers together. "I don't rightly remember, sir, I were that flummoxed. Not her first words, sir."

"Well, when you understood her at last, what said she?"

"She put a hand to her head, like as if it were paining her or she were muddled up like. She didn't rightly remember, she said. She come with a gentleman to see Meg and next thing she knew she woke up a-lying on the cot and she were locked in."

Dalesford broke out at that. "The villain! When I get hold of that boy—"

"A moment, if you please, my lord."

But Gilbert's alarm got the better of him. "For what do we wait, sir? My daughter has been attacked and left in situ. She languishes there while we waste time in pointless questions."

Ingham, rather to Francis's admiration, refused to be hurried. He held up a hand. "The matter must be sifted, my lord. Your daughter will be none the worse for waiting a little longer."

"But will you release her?"

Ingham's brows rose. "If she is innocent in the case, I must obviously do so."

Francis cut in before the incensed earl exploded. "She is certainly innocent, sir. She was sorry for de Percheval, who suffered a beating from the Reverend Pargeter in her sight, and I have no doubt she sought only to assist him by going to the prison in his company."

"Assist him how, my lord Francis?" The sceptical note was pronounced. "What need had de Percheval that he would bring a genteel young woman to a place of that kind?"

In truth, Francis — and indeed Gil as he knew from their hurried discussion — was just as suspicious as Ingham. But he must not show it. He chose prevarication.

"You had better ask her, sir, had you not?"

Gil chimed in. "Precisely. Rose here has no knowledge of the matter. She was not there. Pray let us go at once to this prison and you may question my daughter in person. But hurry, man! She sent to me in great distress."

Justice Ingham was silent for a moment, lips pursed. Then he motioned to his clerk. "Send for Grice, will you? I will see him when I return from the prison." He came out from behind the desk. "Let us go, my lords."

Francis breathed again as Ingham made for the door and opened it, motioning them to go before. Dalesford went out with alacrity, but Francis held back.

"Come, Rose. We may need you too."

The maid scuttled out but Ingham detained Francis as he reached the door.

"How did you come here, my lord?"

"In Dalesford's phaeton."

"Then will you accompany me in a hackney instead?"

Francis hesitated. "For what purpose, sir?"

The fellow's lips twisted. "I have heard nothing from your lady wife, my lord, yet I doubt she has been idle."

With an inward curse, Francis agreed to the arrangement, wondering just how much he ought to reveal. What purpose would it serve to mention this Josh fellow now the bird had flown?

It did not take many minutes to institute the new arrangement, Dalesford agreeing to follow the hack called up by one of the lads abounding in the Bow Street office. Francis got in and took his seat, a trifle wary as Ingham joined him and the door was shut.

"Well, my lord?"

"Well what?"

A faint laugh came from the man beside him. "Come, come, Lord Francis, you know precisely what I wish to hear."

Opting for simplicity, Francis snorted. "If there was anything pertinent, Sir Thomas, you would have been informed."

"Not necessarily." The dry note could not but irritate. "Did you think me unaware Lady Francis filters what she tells me?"

"My wife will scarcely trouble you with unimportant details, sir. She knows your time is precious."

"I am obliged to Lady Francis," came the curt response, "but I should be still more so if she did not keep me completely in the dark as to her activities. What, for instance, is this business of the Frenchman receiving a battering from my prisoner's father?"

"A side issue, sir, of which my wife was ignorant at the time."

"Ah, but how does it come about that I am ignorant of this father having been contacted at all?"

"That is easy, sir. The man is a zealot and half mad. He refused to have anything to do with his daughter once he heard she was in prison. Well for Meg. He is a violent man and she fears him."

"That does not preclude her seeking asylum at his parsonage." He drummed his fingers on his knee. "What else, sir? Be plain with me, I beg of you."

Francis passed a rapid mental review over the past days and decided there was no harm in relating Ottilia's hunt for the perpetrator of the attack, provided he left out the discovery of Helen Pargeter and this Josh of hers. By the time he had gone over the meetings with Redlingfield, Aldreth, Lezayre and Pierre himself, the hackney was drawing up beside the shadow of Bridewell.

Once through the gate, Francis found it a depressing place, known to house apprentices as well as vagrants, prostitutes and petty felons. Tall buildings with windows barred all around loomed over them as they followed Ingham across the open yard, encountering the curious stares of those privileged few permitted to wander freely. They entered an outer office where a man seated at a rough desk leapt up at sight of the justice.

"Lead me to the female accommodations, if you please."

"Yes, sir. At once, sir." The lackey looked with some awe upon the cavalcade, but produced a bunch of keys and proceeded to unlock a barred iron door with a corridor beyond.

Dalesford spoke in Francis's ear. "What a damned place! Lizzy must have windmills in her head to be coming here with that wretch of a Frenchman."

Francis merely nodded, reflecting that Lizzy likely had all too cogent a reason for venturing thus far. He would wager Tillie thought so too. He knew her too well to believe she would sit tight while her protégée fled to a doubtful liberty. He chafed at the thought of what she might do and trusted she would at least take Hemp. He could be relied upon to keep her safe, though the steward would not take it upon himself to prevent any hazardous undertaking.

His thoughts faded as the lackey unlocked another door to a small chamber and Francis caught sight of a brawny female standing at the door to a large room and shouting for quiet. She turned her head upon the opening of the outer door, showing a violence of displeasure in a broad and humourless face. As she caught sight of Ingham, her expression altered.

Surprise was followed on the instant by a servile twist of the lips, more a grimace than a smile.

"You here, yer honour? Gracious goodness, what a surprise!"

Ingham's tone took on severity. "You are destined to be yet more surprised, Mrs Lount. Your prisoner would appear to have escaped from under your nose."

Shock, disbelief and dismay chased one another across the woman's face. "Escaped, yer honour? I'll stake my life none here can have gorn off without my say so."

"I am reliably informed you are mistaken, Mrs Lount." Ingham gestured towards a closed door to one side. "Open up the prisoner Pargeter."

Mrs Lount, protesting the while, fumbled for a bunch of keys at her waist and produced the one needed. She unlocked the door and threw it wide, throwing out an arm.

"There, yer honour. She's in there right and tight, you'll see."

But at this moment, a light footstep sounded and Lady Elizabeth Fiske appeared around the edge of the door. She cast one glance at the assembled company and shrieked. "Papa! Thank heavens!"

"Lizzy, you wretched child!" Dalesford thrust through to the front as Lizzy, wholly ignoring the stunned gaoler, pushed past her bulk and flung herself into her father's arms, bursting into incoherent sobs.

While he petted and soothed, Francis watched how Ingham dealt with the female now staring open-mouthed at the reunion.

"Well, Mrs Lount? That is not the prisoner Pargeter, I think you will agree."

Mrs Lount's gaze came back to him. She closed her mouth, swallowed once, twice, and then turned swiftly into the cell from which Lizzy had emerged. Ingham followed and Francis, his curiosity aroused, went to the door and glanced about Meg's bare and barred prison. The gaoler was looking about her, evidently unable to believe her prisoner was gone. A flash of amusement came as she bent down to lift the quilt upon the wooden framed cot, as if she thought to find the errant Meg underneath. Then she turned back to Ingham, who was awaiting, with arms folded, whatever she might have to say.

"Yer honour, I'm fair flummoxed, I confess it."

"You are, are you? Did you never think to check upon your prisoner?"

The woman fidgeted. "Well, I — well, yes, yer honour, 'course. Night and morning I do. And I lets the girl in when she come and lock her in too."

"And after she's had a visitor? Did you think to check on her then?"

It was plain from the woman's expression that this precaution had been neglected. But she was not silent for long, finding means to place the blame elsewhere.

"What about that there maid, yer honour? She never said nowt. She must've seen as the prisoner weren't in here. Why didn't she say? I'd have raised the alarm in a twinkling, if she'd said."

Ingham lost not one jot of his calm. "It is of no use to try and palm your offence off on the maid. She is not responsible for the security of the prisoners, Mrs Lount. That is your province, and you have failed in it this day." The woman opened her mouth to speak and he held up a hand. "No, say nothing more. We will speak of this again. I will send someone to relieve you and then you may attend me at my office."

With which, he stalked from the cell, Francis hastily removing into the antechamber. Dalesford, an arm about Lizzy, took Ingham up at once.

345

"I would remove my daughter from this place instanter, sir."

Ingham for the first time took stock of the substitute for his prisoner. "I have questions for her ladyship, my lord, but I think we may remove to a more suitable location."

"Your office?"

"I should prefer to prosecute my enquiries before we leave this place. There is a room we may use." He turned to the lackey. "The Governor's office, if you please."

Ottilia refused to wait in the opulent parlour and insisted upon remaining in the hall while the doorman went to enquire. Time hung heavy as Mrs Stark failed to appear and Ottilia's nerves grew taut.

Impatience claimed her at last. "Where is the woman? Hemp!"

Her steward, ever watchful, was waiting by the door. "Milady?"

"Pray follow where that man went and see if you can—" She broke off as footsteps sounded from beyond the stairwell. A woman unknown to Ottilia came hurrying through. A little bird of a woman dressed plainly in dark garments, with a breathless voice and an air of utter disarray.

"Oh, my lady, is it? You are wishful to see Starkey? I am sorry to keep you waiting. Oh, I forgot. I am Merry. Her assistant, you know."

This must be the female Mrs Stark had spoken of and described as useless, but had kept her in any event and given her the post out of the kindness of her heart.

"How do you do? Where is Mrs Stark? The matter is urgent."

"Urgent? Oh, yes, I see. But I'm afraid … you see, she is otherwise engaged just at this moment. Could you come back later perhaps?"

The conviction she had gauged the matter right grew as Ottilia strove for calm. "Later may be too late. I must see her at once."

The woman Merry wrung her hands, looking helpless and anxious. "Oh, dear. You see, she can't just now. She's ... she is engaged upon — well, I cannot say, but her business is quite as urgent, you see."

Her suspicions gathering to full bloom, Ottilia threw caution to the winds. "Miss Merry, let me be frank. Has Mrs Stark given refuge to Meg Pargeter and her swain?"

A horrified look passed over the woman's face. "Oh! How did you—? But you must not... Oh, I don't know what to do!"

Ottilia summoned her best authoritative manner. "Take me to them, Miss Merry. At once."

The woman hopped from foot to foot, her hands writhing one within the other, dismay written all over her face. Ottilia softened her tone.

"We are here to help, not hinder, Miss Merry. No harm will come to them from my intervention. Do you not know it was I who aided Meg in the first place?"

The anxiety lessened and Merry's agitated shifting ceased. "Oh, I see. In that case... But Starkey won't like it at all. She'll give me pepper, she will."

"Have no fear. I will assure her that I forced your hand. Lead me to her."

The woman hesitated no longer, muttering under her breath as she turned and took off with her peculiarly bird-like gait in the same direction she had come.

"Wait here, Hemp. I will be in no danger."

But her steward remained at her back. "I am coming, milady. It is what milord would wish me to do."

There was no arguing with that. Ottilia gave it up, speeding after Merry. The deep-lying fear rose up as the little woman led the way down the same corridor Ottilia recognised from the previous occasion. Were the truants then in Starkey's parlour? But the party passed that door and continued on, arriving at a narrow back stair, up which Merry trotted in a speedy fashion that suggested long habit. Ottilia grasped the bannister and followed at a slower pace.

The passage above proved dingy and narrow, subject to an icy draught from somewhere undetectable. Likely the place was in use by servants only. They passed several doors before their guide stopped at one near the end. She did not at once knock, but put her ear to the woodwork. Ottilia thought she could hear murmuring within and was about to demand entry when Merry straightened, turned the handle, and carefully opened the door. A voice from within hit Ottilia with instant recognition.

"Did you get rid of her?"

She did not wait for Merry to respond, but raised her own voice in reply as she moved towards the door. "No, she did not, Mrs Stark. Pray allow me to enter."

An exclamation sounded and the madam appeared in the aperture before Ottilia could reach it. Belligerence was in both face and tone.

"What do you want? I'm busy."

Ottilia faced her down. "I am come to see the fugitives you are harbouring, Mrs Stark." She threw up a hand as the other's expression showed both surprise and fury. "Oh, you need not fear me, ma'am. I have not brought the runners."

Merry, her restless feet hopping again, ventured a squeak. "She came to help, Starkey."

The madam ignored her, tossing her head at Ottilia. "I might have known you'd stick your oar in. How did you think to come here for 'em?"

Ottilia flashed a smile. "Once I could think straight, it became glaringly obvious. Which, I may say, it will be to Justice Ingham. That is why I came. We must get them away from here at once. Have the goodness to allow me to enter."

Mrs Stark pushed the door open behind her, but paused, an eye on Hemp. "He can wait here. There's not enough room for so many."

Hemp's deep tone came. "I will remain in the passage, milady. Call if you need me."

He stepped back and Ottilia was at last able to go into the room, following Starkey and Merry, who had slipped through ahead.

The bedchamber, as it proved to be, was larger than she had expected but seemed cramped by the press of persons. Meg was sitting on the cot bed, an open valise beside her together with a jumbled pile of clothing she had evidently been folding. Starkey had clearly supplied her again. She looked up and her mouth formed an O of surprise as she caught sight of Ottilia. There was, to Ottilia's instant consternation, no sign of Pierre.

"Where is Pierre, Mrs Stark?" She lowered her voice. "Don't dare tell me he has abandoned her again?"

"Lady Fan!"

Ottilia turned to find Meg on her feet. She looked a trifle shaky and not a little bewildered, but it was plain she was happier than Ottilia had ever seen her. Crossing to her, Ottilia took her hands.

"My dear Meg, I am very glad to see you away from that horrid cell, though I am fearful for you too."

Meg returned the pressure of her hands and then freed herself. "Pierre came for me. I never thought he would."

Did she not understand her peril? Ottilia did not mince her words. "I am happy he cared enough, Meg, and I am sorry to cast a blight over your happiness, but you are in grave danger now. It is imperative that you remove from here without delay."

Starkey cut in. "Pierre knows it well enough. It's this one as has her head in the clouds."

Meg's smile was a picture. "I had rather live there than where I have been. If I have Pierre, I don't care about anything else."

Ottilia drew an unsteady breath. "Then there is little point in my pursuing this. I will address myself to Pierre instead."

Meg sat back down and resumed folding clothes in a matter-of-fact fashion that had nothing to do with the woman Ottilia had last seen. She was transformed.

"Pierre is taking me to America."

"America!"

"That's what he says," said Starkey. "Going to make a new life there."

Flaws and questions found their way into Ottilia's questing brain. "Has he money enough for a passage? From where can he sail? Does he know? And where in the world is he?"

A new voice spoke from the doorway.

"He is behind you, milady."

The French accented voice startled her and she turned. Pierre de Percheval stood in the aperture of the doorway, dressed utterly unlike his customary point de vice appearance. He wore a rough-looking greatcoat, a slouch hat pulled low over his brow and his face half muffled in a scarf.

"Heavens, I would scarcely have recognised you, Pierre!"

He grinned, removing his hat and beginning to unwind the scarf. "It is a disguise well served, no? This hat was given to me by this man of Starkey who guards the door. And Marguerite has the cloak of Milady Elizabeth."

Ottilia breathed more readily. "I am relieved to know you are alive to the dangers, Pierre. Meg seems oblivious."

She turned back to the bed and saw that Meg was gazing at him with undisguised adoration. Undeserved perhaps, but no doubt it would serve them better than recriminations.

"My Marguerite is *aux anges* to be free."

Ottilia's urgency resurfaced. "She is not free yet, Pierre. You cannot remain here."

"Soon we will go."

"Where?"

Starkey took this. "Sending them down to my sister's place. No one outside of my close associates don't know nothing of it."

"It will not serve, Mrs Stark. I know Ingham's runners of old, especially the fellow Grice who came here, as I understand it. He is a ferret of a man. He will find them out in no time."

"Well, they'll be safer there than here. Besides, they don't mean to stay beyond the one night."

Pierre took it up. "Have no fear, madame. I am well used to be hunted, and I am pledged to keep Marguerite safe."

Ottilia grew frantic. "If you set off from here you will leave a trail."

Starkey gave a snort. "You can say that of anywhere, ma'am."

An idea surfaced and Ottilia fairly leapt with triumph. "Not if it is a place of which Sir Thomas Ingham knows nothing." She seized Pierre's arm. "You must entrust yourselves to me. I know just how to bring you off."

Chapter Nineteen

The Governor's office, though sparsely furnished with chairs chosen for utility rather than taste, was sumptuous in comparison with the cell. Lizzy sat at her father's urging in one near the fire, glad of the warmth but wary. Her heart beat fast, for she must act a part alien to her nature, one of weak femininity. Her tears had been genuine, for the long wait for rescue had played upon her nerves and the relief of seeing Papa could not but overwhelm her for the moment.

"Now then, my lady Elizabeth, I will be obliged to you if you will answer a few questions."

Justice Ingham, to whom she had been formally introduced by Lord Francis, had taken a pose no doubt intended to intimidate, standing close enough that he towered a little over Lizzy. She looked up, cultivating a breathy tone that she hoped blended apprehension with willingness.

"Of course, sir. I will tell you anything you wish."

She cast an imploring glance at Papa, who had brought a chair and set it beside her. He sat down at once and took her hand, holding it hard.

"You have nothing to fear, my love."

She smiled at him, but as she turned again to Ingham, she caught a look on her uncle's face that very nearly overset her. He knew! Or guessed? Confident he would not betray her, she brought her gaze to bear upon Justice Ingham.

"I should like to know first why you felt it incumbent upon you to accompany Monsieur de Percheval to this place."

Lizzy breathed more readily. She was prepared for this. Indeed, she had rehearsed it while she waited. "You see, Pierre was terribly afraid Meg would not wish to see him. He said he was conscious he had done her a great wrong and he could not blame her if she hated him."

"He employed you as a go-between?"

"Employed? Why, no indeed. He begged me to go in before and pave his way. I shuddered at the thought," suiting the action to the word as artistically as she could, "but how could I refuse such an appeal? How could I guess he meant to do me a mischief?"

Here she deemed it appropriate to conjure a few sobs and turn her face into Papa's shoulder. She felt him patting her, though a whisper reached her ear. "You little rogue, you."

Lord, he did not believe her either! But Ingham was again speaking and she was obliged to sit up again, biting her lip against the threatening laughter.

"Will you tell me what exactly occurred, Lady Elizabeth?"

Lizzy gathered her forces, releasing her hand from her father's grasp and embarking upon the speech she had put together. "Well, I went in first and explained to Meg that Pierre was outside and wanted to speak to her."

"She was willing?"

Lizzy sighed. "Not at first, but I persuaded her he was truly repentant, for that is what he told me. Then he came in and I waited by the door while they talked."

Ingham had rocked back on his heels, but he leaned forward again. "Did you hear any of their conversation?"

"Oh, no, sir, for they talked in low murmurs." She put her fingers to her face, feigning embarrassment. "I felt a little de trop and wondered if I should leave them, but that woman had said we must knock on the door when we were ready to go and I was afraid to ask her if I might wait in the antechamber."

The justice appeared impatient of this side issue. "Then what happened?"

Lizzy took two very audible breaths as if she struggled for calm. "I am not quite sure, sir. I remember that Pierre got up. He said... I think he said it was time. Yes, 'it is time', he said. Then he came towards me and he said something about being sorry." She put a hand to her head. "And then ... then I felt something strike me and ... and I remember nothing more until I awoke." She let her hand fall to her breast and gazed up at the justice. Was he convinced? He leaned back on his heels and folded his arms across.

"You say you were struck, my lady, but I can see no bruise."

Lizzy was ready for that. "Oh, yes, sir. You cannot see anything under my hair, but you may feel the lump." She turned her head and put her fingers on the spot at one side, still sore to the touch.

There came an audible gasp from Papa and she caught a change in Lord Francis's expression just before she turned away. Justice Ingham looked to her father. "If you permit, my lord."

But Papa's fingers were already feeling in her hair, pushing her own out of the way.

"Good God, there is a lump! Here, you may feel for yourself, Ingham."

Lizzy submitted to the investigation, feeling triumph grow in her breast. Had she not known this would clinch it? A necessary precaution, though it had been painful to bear.

Ingham stepped back. "I am sorry you were subjected to this assault, Lady Elizabeth."

"Assault indeed! How dared that fellow do this to you? After all the assistance we rendered him too. It is an outrage."

354

Was Papa acting a part? Or had her bruise convinced him? Ingham was looking a trifle baffled, she thought, but his words were a shock.

"Be sure the perpetrator will be brought to justice."

Apprehension leapt in Lizzy's bosom. Was it all in vain? "Why, sir, what do you mean?"

He evaded the question. "One thing more, if you please, ma'am. Why did you not at once raise the alarm when you found yourself incarcerated?"

Now genuinely alarmed for the errant Meg and Pierre, Lizzy had no need to feign the distress she might have been supposed to feel. "At first, I did not understand what had happened. I was dizzy and only half myself. But it dawned on me at last that I was alone, and cold, and ... my cloak was gone." She struggled for her rehearsed words, her mind churning meanwhile. Had she given them enough time? "I think that must be how he managed it." Would they get far enough away? "My cloak, I mean." Was Ingham intending to send after them? Oh, of course he would. Why had she not anticipated as much? "I suppose she ... she was wrapped in my cloak and ... and that woman, the gaoler, thought it was me." Heaven send Pierre had the sense to head immediately out of London.

"But this does not tell me why, ma'am, you waited for the maid here to arrive before you spoke up."

Lizzy glanced across at Rose. "I didn't know she would come, sir."

"Why did you not hammer on the door and inform Mrs Lount of your predicament?"

"I don't know. I was afraid." She must drag her mind under control. She was failing badly. "I was too dizzy at first to think straight."

Ingham became testy. "Come, come, ma'am, this will not do. You were there for some hours."

"I won't have you bully my daughter, sir. Has she not suffered enough? She naturally thought first of her father when it came to rescue."

Ingham did not back down, though he moderated his tone. "Yet she did not know the maid was due to arrive. How did she think to send to you, my lord?"

Lizzy sought refuge in agitation, not wholly pretence. "Sir Thomas, I don't know how long I was unconscious. I felt dreadfully ill. I should have called out, or knocked on the door, but I didn't think of it. I thought only that I was in the deepest trouble. To tell you the truth, I was afraid of that horrid female. And then, when Rose came in, I was so thankful. I could not think what might happen to me if I was found there. I begged her to go for Papa, for I knew he would come." She reached to seize her father's hand. "Papa would never fail me, and I wanted him so badly." She gave a dry sob.

Her father's arm came about her as he leaned down. "Don't take on, Lizzy. Hush, now."

At which point, Lord Francis took a hand. "I believe I know your mind, Ingham. It would seem to be the natural thing for someone in Elizabeth's situation to sue at once to be let out. However, I think you make no allowance for the irrational agitation of the moment. Especially," with a somewhat wry look at Lizzy, "when it comes to the distaff side. Women, Sir Thomas, are rarely open to logic."

Ingham's gaze swept her uncle. "I am surprised to hear you say so, Lord Francis, considering the extreme logic of your wife's conclusions."

A smile lit Lord Francis's eyes. "Ah, but my wife is an exceptional woman, sir. I did say it was rare, did I not?"

For a wonder, a bark of laughter escaped Justice Ingham. Lizzy took the part of prudence and remained silent. He turned back to her.

"Very well, ma'am, I will accept your assertions." She breathed again, but he raised a warning finger. "For the moment. I need scarcely tell you that to aid in the escape of a prisoner constitutes a serious felony."

Lizzy shrunk back. "Oh, no! How could you think I would— ? Papa!"

"Enough, Sir Thomas!"

"My lord, it is a warning and I stand by it. I have no more time to waste upon the matter, but I must tell you I am far from satisfied."

"Well, I don't know why you should be. My daughter has been perfectly frank. There can be no arguing that she has suffered an injury, for you felt it yourself."

"I did, my lord."

"She has gone through a severe ordeal and I take it very ill that you suggest she has been instrumental in this business."

Ingham held up a hand. "Make yourself easy, my lord. I may have my doubts, but I have better things to do at this moment than to pursue the matter further."

"Then my daughter is free to go?"

"Certainly. I must go myself. The turnkey is outside the door. He will show you out." He turned to Lizzy with a small bow. "I thank you for your cooperation, ma'am."

The ironic inflexion provoked a twinge of conscience in Lizzy, but she thanked him as prettily as she could. "I am sorry I could not help more, sir."

He nodded, took a cursory leave of the two gentlemen and was gone. Her uncle Francis was the first to express the general relief.

"Thank the Lord that's over."

Her father clapped him on the back. "I am glad you were with us, Fan. The fellow gave me a bad moment there. I feared he might be thinking of indicting Lizzy."

"Highly unlikely. Even if he is suspicious, Ingham must know he cannot prove anything against Lizzy. Merely because she failed to raise the alarm? It would not hold and he knows it."

To Lizzy's consternation, her father turned on her with a severe look. "Tell me the truth, child. Did you have a hand in setting that girl free?"

Lizzy opened her eyes wide. "Papa! How can you ask me?"

"Don't try to evade the issue, my girl. I know you. Until I felt that bruise, I thought precisely as Ingham did."

Lizzy sighed, choosing a spurious candour. "Well, I can see why, Papa. I know I've been foolish in this whole affair, but I would scarcely go so far as to commit a crime."

"Indeed? Are you sure you understood it was a crime?"

Lizzy shifted her shoulders. "I did not think of it at all. My only thought was that Pierre wanted to make amends and I knew poor Meg must be lonely and anxious in here. It seemed the right thing to do." She glanced as she spoke at her uncle and detected a faint frown between his brows. Her tongue betrayed her as she challenged him. "Do you not believe me either, sir?"

"I didn't say I don't believe you," protested her father. "And I am quite sure Francis is of the same mind."

One of his wry smiles quirked Lord Francis's lip. "We are fully of one mind, I don't doubt."

But did that mean he thought her guilty or innocent? Hard to tell. But it was over and she felt decidedly deflated, especially now it had become obvious a pursuit was to be prosecuted.

What would happen to Meg and Pierre if they were caught? It was too much to bear and she felt like weeping, all her triumph in ruins.

"Papa, may we not go home? I am so hungry and I hate this place."

The vicinity of The Silver Moon was as quiet as Ottilia remembered. She leaned to the window as Hemp came to report.

"The door is open, milady."

"Is the coast clear? I mean, can you see anyone about? I don't wish them to be seen to enter the place."

Her steward looked up and down the little street. "It is empty at this moment, milady."

"Very well, then." As Hemp opened the door and let down the steps, she turned to the couple occupying the forward seat, Pierre sitting alert and attentive, his arm about Meg, who had eyes for none but her cavalier. "Come. We must slip in as swiftly and quietly as we can."

"Go first, madame. We will follow."

Ottilia stepped down and followed Hemp directly to the side door through which Helen had disappeared upon the previous occasion. Although logic dictated none could have followed her carriage, she could not shake the disquiet attendant upon such nefarious proceedings. She had acted fast enough, she hoped, that Justic Ingham could not have set his runners onto the chase before her arrival at Maiden Lane, and it had not taken long to extract the fugitives.

Little conversation had taken place during the relatively short ride through streets both busy and deserted, Williams taking a circuitous route upon her instructions. Only once had Pierre queried her intention.

"Where do you take us, madame?"

"To someone nearly concerned with Meg's welfare."

At this, Meg whimpered. "Not him…"

"*Du calme, ma petite.* Milady Fan does not mean your father."

"Assuredly not."

"Then who, madame? Who cares for Marguerite, it is only Helen."

"It is not Helen, although it is through her agency that this haven may be available to you." Unequal to explaining the situation fully, Ottilia turned the subject. "You spoke of America. Have you means to get there? From where can you sail?"

"Ah, this? I have all in hand, madame. I have made enquiries these many days. I have waited only to see Marguerite before."

His confidence passed Ottilia by as she seized on this last. "Then you did not plan this escape? It was a spur of the moment decision?"

"It is done, madame. The way of it is unimportant."

Ottilia's opinion of him rose at this evidence he would not betray Lizzy. She concentrated on the urgencies. "You have some notion of a ship already?"

"*Oui,* madame. The *Mercury* leaves for Boston on Friday."

"Where from?"

"Portsmouth. We must travel there tomorrow."

Then there was no time to lose. She was hopeful of persuading Josh to house them, if she had to use blackmail to do it. How to smuggle them down to the South Coast port became the next hurdle, occupying her thoughts for the rest of the way.

The moment the pair gained the narrow and dusty hallway, Pierre burdened with a portmanteau and Meg's valise, she turned to her steward. "Tell Williams to turn into another street and wait there until you come to him. Then go into the inn through the main door, if you please, and find Josh."

"What shall I tell him, milady?"

"Only that I am here to see him, Hemp. Pray don't mention the others."

He was gone with a nod and Ottilia closed the door behind him with a whoosh of relief. She ushered the fugitives into the little parlour Helen had led her to before and bade them make themselves as comfortable as possible. Easier said than done, for it was mustier than she recalled, and there was no candle alight this time. A bubble of merriment rose up as it struck her how the gloom of the place was so much in keeping with her activities.

Pierre, having urged Meg into a chair, was setting the luggage down on the wooden settle. He turned, a note of disapproval in his tone. "You are amused, madame?"

"Oh, I am merely overwrought, Pierre," she returned guiltily, beginning to hunt for the spills Helen had used to light the candles in the wall-sconces. "Forgive me. It is a habit of mine to be merry at the wrong moment."

A small fire glowed in the grate. Was it Helen's day then? Fortunate if it proved so. She might take a light from the fire, if she could only find the spills. The abortive search made her fretful.

"I cannot find them. I shall have to use one of the candles."

"What do you wish, madame?"

"I am trying to light the candles, that is all."

She was already removing a candle from one of the sconces when Pierre came up.

"Permit that I do this, madame."

She relinquished the candle into his hand and moved to take a chair opposite Meg. Presently light sprang up about the walls and Pierre found a chair and took it to Meg's side, taking her hand as he sat.

"Will you now tell me where we are, Milady Francis?"

Ottilia suppressed a sigh. The moment had come. Reluctant as she was to reveal Helen's secret, there was no alternative. Pierre at least, she guessed, would make the connections, even if Meg did not.

"You are at The Silver Moon public house. Helen has a friend who lives and works here. He is the man who attacked you that night, Pierre, and struck instead at Lord Coveney."

Pierre had barely time to utter a curse when Josh appeared in the doorway, looking decidedly unwelcoming.

"My lady? What can I—?" He broke off, his gaze shifting to the pair at the table. He retreated a step or two. "Who's this with you"?

Ottilia rose and went towards him. "Do you not recognise either, Josh?"

His head poked forward and a shocked gasp escaped him. "It's him, is it? And Meg? She here? It can't be!" Then his eyes lit with hope. "Lordy me, has she been set free?"

"No, Josh." Ottilia grasped his arm to bring him back into the room. "She escaped with Pierre."

"Escaped? Escaped from Bridewell?"

"Yes, but never mind exclaiming over it, Josh. Meg is in the gravest danger and we need your help."

He shrank back. "But Helen said … she promised!"

"She promised you need not testify, Josh, but that is all behind us now. Pray believe me, in this predicament, you are our only hope."

It was late by the time Ottilia arrived at Dalesford House, prompted by the urge to discover the outcome of Lizzy's call for rescue. She had likely missed dinner at Bruton Street in any event, but she could not suppose her niece would be out after the happenings of the day.

The butler disclosed that she was indeed at home and Ottilia breathed out, conscious of a barely heeded relief to know Lizzy was safe.

"Will you conduct me to Lady Elizabeth, Snade?"

The man looked dubious. "Her ladyship went early to her chamber and dined in her room, my lady. She is resting. Allow me to announce your ladyship in the small parlour. Both Lady Dalesford and Lady Candia are within."

But Ottilia had no wish to run the gamut of Harriet's likely distress. Nor could she face Candia with the knowledge of having conducted the object of her affections to a potential future with Meg Pargeter, if all went well. Besides, she had come for a tête-à-tête with Lizzy which ought not to be delayed.

"No, I thank you. Lead me to Lady Elizabeth's chamber." For a moment it seemed as if the butler might refuse, but Ottilia was not to be thwarted after all she had been through today. "At once, if you please."

Snade bowed and turned to lead the way upstairs. Ottilia dismissed him at the bedchamber door and tapped upon the panel.

"Come in."

Ottilia opened the door and entered to find Lizzy not only up, but clearly in a state of agitation. She took one look at her visitor and gave forth a little shriek.

"Aunt Ottilia!" She came forward as she spoke, hands held out. "Oh, I am so glad to see you! I have been frantic with worry."

Ottilia grasped the hands. "Yes, I can see that. You look perfectly dishevelled, child. Have you not had an opportunity to tidy yourself?"

Lizzy released her hands and wafted this aside. "What does it matter how I look? I have been wracking my brains to think where Pierre could have taken Meg and I cannot fathom anything."

"Softly, Lizzy, softly." Ottilia urged her towards the bed and obliged her to sit, taking her place beside her. "I have been with them and all is in train."

"Where are they? Are they hiding somewhere?"

"I cannot tell you that."

"But they are safe?"

"For the moment."

A little sob escaped the girl and she put a hand to her bosom. "Oh, thank heaven! I had begun to think I had served poor Meg an ill turn." She then gave a gasp and clapped the hand to her mouth, an almost comical expression of guilt leaping into her eyes.

Ottilia regarded her with a mixture of amusement and exasperation. "As if I had not guessed. Come, Lizzy, did you suppose I would not? I knew well you had some scheme afoot from the way you spoke when I asked you for Pierre's direction. You did not think of the consequences, did you?"

Lizzy dropped her hand and her eyes too. "Not until I was questioned by Sir Thomas Ingham. I confess it never occurred to me there would be a pursuit. You will say I am stupid and naïve, and you are perfectly correct."

Ottilia had to smile. "I won't say that. You are impulsive rather, too inclined to leap before you look."

"It's true. And you told me to think of the consequences. I thought only of the good ones, of how Meg might be free and happy. Of how Pierre would make amends and take care of her and the baby. I thought I was doing the right thing, Aunt Ottilia, I swear it."

There could be no doubt of her sincerity, and Ottilia's conscience writhed. She spoke without thinking. "I wish I had known you better before I involved you, Lizzy."

"Don't say that, Aunt. You mean you would never have said anything if you had known what a wretched creature I can be." The girl looked ready to weep, moisture rimming her eyes.

Ottilia set a hand on one of hers and shook it. "You are an innocent, my poor child. I should not have involved you in any way and that I did is far more my fault than yours. When one is young one is apt to act without forethought. I did myself until I learned discretion."

Lizzy's tears spilled over but she dashed them away. "I'm not going to turn into a watering pot like the ninny I had to make myself today."

This caught Ottilia's interest. "Did you manage to convince them?"

Lizzy grimaced. "They were all suspicious until I had them feel the bump on my head."

With dawning horror, Ottilia watched her touch fingers into her hair, half of which had escaped its moorings, errant curls licking the girl's shoulder.

"You made Pierre strike you?"

She hissed a breath as her fingers found the spot. "I asked him to, but he refused. It still hurts a trifle."

Ottilia, her guilt soaring to new heights, looked at her with foreboding in her heart. "Lizzy, what in the world did you do? Do you tell me you inflicted this injury upon yourself?"

Lizzy's chin came up, her tone staunch. "I had to. You must perceive that, Aunt Ottilia. No one would have believed me without it."

Barely able to get the word out, Ottilia put her burning question. "How?"

"Well, I tried knocking it against the wall, but that only stung a little. I banged it on the edge of the wooden frame. It was horribly painful to tell the truth and it made me a little giddy so that I had to lie down, but it did the trick."

Ottilia had no words. Unable to determine whether such an act was courageous or foolish beyond permission, she yet could not help a surge of something akin to admiration, tinged though it was with an edge of despair. Lizzy was undoubtedly a girl after her own heart, but she lacked common sense and was plagued with a streak of insouciance which led her to tackle serious matters with too much lightness. Or perhaps she was lucky not to suffer the pangs of deeper knowledge.

Her confession over, Lizzy reverted to the fate of the runaways. "But are they safe indeed, Aunt? It would be dreadful if I had undergone it all for nothing."

Ottilia dragged herself out of her difficult thoughts. "There is every hope they will succeed in evading capture." Although she knew she would be on tenterhooks until Friday had come and gone with no dread news.

Lizzy's eager tones cut into the revival of her anxiety. "Pierre spoke of America, but can they go quickly enough?"

Trying for a light note, Ottilia gave only the gist. "Assuming the winds are fair and they can sail on Friday, and we have heard nothing to the contrary, we may assume they are away and free."

Consternation entered Lizzy's features. "And if not?"

It was plain she had not recognised Meg's danger even now. "I will hear of it if Meg is recaptured."

"And Pierre?"

"I imagine he would be arrested as an accessory."

"Oh, no. Would they put him in prison?"

"Probably."

"And Meg?"

"The law will have no mercy, I fear, Lizzy. You see, they will think she confesses her guilt by running away."

Dismay clouded Lizzy's features. "That is what you meant by consequences, isn't it?"

Ottilia nodded, but felt obliged to reassure. "We must hope it will not come to that." She did not add her own deep-seated fear of the runner Benjamin Grice's proven powers of locating errant suspects.

Chapter Twenty

"But how was this fellow willing to house them, Ottilia, when he would not come forward before?"

Ottilia set down her fork. She was still too wound up by the day's events to do justice to the platter of cold chicken pie, slices of ham and pickled beans cobbled together by the cook and sent up on a tray to the dowager's parlour.

"He was most unwilling at first. At least, he was too shocked to think clearly."

"And reluctant to be involved?"

"Indeed I think so, Fan. And Pierre's attitude did not help matters."

Pierre had taken it in snuff that he must trust to his would-be assassin for succour. In vain had Ottilia explained Josh had meant only to talk to him on Helen's behalf when he waylaid the pair that night.

"This may be, madame, but I do not put myself in the hands of one who has done to me this thing."

Ottilia became tart. "I don't think you have much choice, Pierre. You do realise you committed a felonious act when you extracted Ingham's prisoner from Bridewell?"

"*Oui, mais*—"

"And that if you are caught, you will undoubtedly be imprisoned and Meg will surely hang."

Meg's shuddering response to this had effectively silenced Pierre's protests, but his stance towards Josh was less than friendly, and utterly devoid of gratitude.

"Then how in the world did you persuade the man to do as you asked, Ottilia?" demanded Sybilla.

Ottilia cast a mischievous glance at her spouse. "I was most unscrupulous."

"You have no need to tell me that, you rogue. I suppose you told him he owed it to Meg because he refused to come forward to testify."

"How well you know me, dearest." She handed him her tray. "I am glad you did not wait dinner for me."

"Certainly not. I knew I should have starved else." Francis took the tray and rose, moving to set it down on a side table by the wall. "The moment Mama told me you had driven off to the rescue, I had little hope of setting eyes on you again for an age."

"I wonder you did not come after me, Fan."

"The wonder is you came back at all tonight!"

Sybilla clicked her tongue. "He would have gone after you, Ottilia, but I stopped him."

Her husband returned to the chair next to Ottilia and took her hand, squeezing it hard. "Mama pointed out that I might jeopardise whatever scheme you had in your head, so I had nothing to do but to kick my heels and hope."

Ottilia sighed. "I wished for you several times. It was a piece of work to make all safe, I promise you. Only when Helen arrived did I breathe more easily."

Josh, taking fright, had sent his son off to the parsonage with an urgent message.

Ottilia was at once intrigued. "Your son?"

"My Jack. It's how we keep up, my lady. Helen gives him odd jobs now and now to keep him coming and going, so's he can run errands."

Ottilia had been momentarily distracted from the current problem. "You are married then, Josh?"

"Was, my lady. Widowed these ten year. She died giving my boy life."

Helen had arrived at length, out of breath and astounded to find her stepdaughter and swain on the premises. The reunion was both tearful and poignant, but the outcome proved happy.

"You'd best find them a room, Josh. There's that one your sister keeps for emergencies, up in the attic. They won't be seen going up that back stair and they can stay in here otherwise, for meals and such. Speaking of which, I'll warrant you're both hungry. We'll get you fed in short order. Coffee, Josh! Why have I got to think of everything?"

"She bustled the poor man unmercifully," Ottilia related. "But it gave me a chance to talk to Helen alone while Josh showed them up to this attic room."

Sybilla rapped on the arm of her chair. "What I want to know is how the woman managed to escape the eagle eye of that ghastly parson?"

Ottilia had to smile. "By good fortune, Mr Pargeter is laid up with a streaming cold."

Francis snorted. "Ha! Serve the wretched fellow right. I dare say he caught it in that blasted draughty church of his."

"And a good thing too. A judgement on the man. I hope he may die of it!"

"Sybilla, that is scarcely a Christian sentiment. Not but what it would clear the way for Josh and Helen."

"For pity's sake, don't put that notion into the woman's head, Tillie! The next thing you know, she will be making sure of the parson's never recovering at all."

"What did she have to say for herself?" demanded Sybilla.

"She proved highly efficient and determined to ensure Pierre got Meg safely away. I think she feels it that she did not allow Josh to come forward."

Ottilia did not think it incumbent upon her to relate all Helen Pargeter's distressful sayings.

"I've not done right by my Meg and that's a fact, ma'am. But I've a chance to make up for it now. Aye, and for all the suffering she's been through all these years. Nothing will serve to change my mind about that rogue who served her as he did, but he's willing to do right by her now and that's all that matters."

Ottilia brushed this aside. "I am glad of that, Helen, but here's the rub. Pierre knows of a ship that leaves for America on Friday, but they have to get to Portsmouth. Without being caught by the runners, who you may be certain will be hunting them up and down the country. As yet I can't think how it is to be done, but—"

"Leave it to me, my lady. I'll get Josh to hire the chaise, then there'll be no record of Pierre's name for the runners to find. I'll fetch Meg more clothes and give her one of my veils to wear."

Helen had run on, weaving plans competent enough to allay most of Ottilia's fears, even to the point of delving into her housekeeping to provide her stepdaughter with funds.

"I've a tidy sum put by, ma'am, for I'm frugal as can be. I'll give her all I can spare."

Ottilia had refused an invitation to dine, contenting herself with a cup of coffee before making her farewells, urgent to discover how Lizzy had fared. She'd had hopes of reckoning, from the time of her niece's rescue, just when Ingham had put the pursuit in train. Not that knowing it lessened her anxiety.

It was salutary to her nerves to relate her doings to Francis and Sybilla, but the respite proved temporary. All through Thursday she could not keep her imagination from painting dreadful images of the chaise being stopped and the fugitives apprehended. She slept ill, in despite of all Francis could do to soothe her, and no amount of coffee served to allay her fidgets when Friday came.

Had they succeeded in reaching Portsmouth unmolested? No word had come from Bow Street, which was a hopeful sign. But there was no saying Ingham would see fit to inform her even if his men found the truants. Worse yet, Sybilla could not refrain from complaint about Pierre's supposed attack upon her granddaughter.

"If I am glad of Ottilia's success it is for that girl's sake and not for his, the dastard, hitting Elizabeth over the head as he did. I never heard of such a thing."

The truth of this was the one aspect Ottilia kept to herself, fearful of exposing Lizzy to her grandmother's wrath. Nor could she bear to enlighten Francis, plagued as she was by conscience. She must bear the blame for Lizzy's involvement, despite the hope of a happy outcome if the runaways made it to Portsmouth without being intercepted. Hard indeed to remain quiet in the face of Sybilla's distress.

"All I can say is, I hope to high heaven Ingham's fellows don't run that pair to earth, for if one thing is more certain than another, Ottilia will be moving heaven and earth yet again and driving us all demented."

"For pity's sake, ma'am, have done! Let her be." Francis came up behind Ottilia where she stood at the window, murmuring low. "Pay no heed, my dear one. She is querulous only because she is concerned for you."

Ottilia strove for calm. "I will be well when this day is over, assuming we hear nothing ill."

Sybilla's voice, on an aggrieved note, came again to interrupt them. "Don't stand there whispering, the two of you, for I can't bear it."

Francis moved back into the room. "What is eating you, Mama? You have been tetchy all morning."

"I have been tetchy? Hark at the pot!" Sybilla's tone changed, softening. "Ottilia, child, come here."

With a sigh, Ottilia suppressed a sharp retort and went across to the fireplace. She took one look at her mother-in-law's black gaze, read concern there, and covered her eyes with one hand, sobs rising to her throat. "Don't, Sybilla, pray."

"Don't what, my dear?"

Francis was at her side. "Now look what you've done! Don't weep, sweetheart."

For a moment Ottilia allowed herself to sink into the safe haven of his arms and the urge to cry her heart out receded. She heard Sybilla's words through a haze.

"What have I said? Ottilia, you know my bark is worse than my bite. What ails you, child?"

Ottilia straightened, and looked into her spouse's troubled features. "Thank you, Fan. I am all right now."

"Are you sure?"

She let out a tiny laugh. "No, but I will do my best to keep my countenance."

He guided her back to her chair and she sank down, wishing she might instead keep pacing. But with Sybilla's eye upon her it was foolhardy. Best to try for an appearance of calm. There was blessed quiet for a space as Francis brought a chair next to hers and took his seat, gazing at his mother very much in the manner of a dog guarding a bone which afforded Ottilia a flash of merriment.

Sybilla's delicate brows flew up. "Now you are laughing? Francis, she is growing hysterical."

"I am not indeed, Sybilla. Pardon me. It was just Fan's look." She stretched a hand to her husband's and curled her fingers around his. "I am lucky to have so faithful a guardian."

She received a rueful smile from Francis, but Sybilla snorted.

"Faithful enough to protect you against his own mother." She wafted a hand. "Oh, you need not look daggers, Fanfan. Your first duty is to your wife, but if you can keep her from driving the rest of us into frenzy too, I will give you a medal."

To Ottilia's relief, her spouse took the part of prudence and refrained from answering, avoiding, as did she, Sybilla's black gaze. The ticking of the bracket clock on the mantel grew loud in Ottilia's consciousness, and the sound of wheels on some passing carriage outside in the street penetrated into the room. She became aware there had been also the clopping of hooves when they abruptly stopped outside the house.

Her stomach dropped. In a bang, she was up again, fairly running to the window, only half hearing both her relatives break out behind her.

"What in the world—?"

"Tillie, what is amiss?"

Ottilia peered into the street below. A coach had stopped and the door was opening. A man jumped down without waiting for the steps to be let down. Recognition hit.

"Ingham!" Her pulse thrummed as she turned. "He has come, Fan!"

"Oh, dear Lord!" Francis was up, moving to her. "It need not mean the worst."

"What else? He has no other reason to come here."

Sybilla's voice cut in. "Do you say Ingram is here? Oh, heavens, has he caught them?"

Ottilia moved into the room, for once ignoring her mother-in-law. "Fan, I am beyond frustrated! To be so close…"

He took charge as he always did. "Sit down, Tillie. Take yourself in hand. You cannot meet him moved like this or he will smell a rat."

Ottilia dragged in a breath and let it out, striving for her customary control as she allowed him to usher her back to her chair. "You are right. Back me up, Fan, for heaven's sake!"

"You know I will."

He took up a stance at the mantel, his eyes on the door. Ottilia concentrated on preserving her calm, though the apprehension on Sybilla's face almost threw her back into panic.

"I rely on you to support me also, Sybilla."

"You know me well enough for that, my dear, rats notwithstanding. Besides, I am in it to the hilt since I knew what you meant to do."

"You are a worthy conspirator, Mama."

In spite of all, fear flooded Ottilia as she became aware of footsteps on the stairs. She listened to their approach, feeling as if time itself held its breath. It was almost a relief when Gipping entered.

"Sir Thomas Ingham, my lady."

The justice stepped into the room. One glance at his countenance was enough to inform Ottilia that he was distinctly out of temper.

Sybilla rose to the occasion. "Ah, Sir Thomas, in a good hour. We have been anxious here. You have news of the escapees?"

She gave no clue, to Ottilia's deep satisfaction, in which direction their anxiety tended. Afraid to speak at all for fear her voice would quiver, she looked enquiry instead as Ingham's gaze turned upon her.

"I have little doubt you are hoping for a different outcome than I, Lady Francis." He held up a hand as Sybilla let out a hasty exclamation. "I am making no accusations, ma'am, despite that I cannot help but harbour certain suspicions."

Ottilia preserved her silence as he paused. His glance swept the other two faces, quite as blank, and his mouth twisted. Almost a smile, but not quite.

"Very well. This case has scarcely been my finest hour, but let that pass."

Francis quirked an eyebrow. "I take it your fellows have not yet found them?"

"And will not." Ingham pursed his lips. "It was a close run thing."

Then they had reached their goal? They were away? Ottilia's pulse flurried into life for a space and then steadied. She managed to infuse puzzlement into her tone. "I do not understand you, Sir Thomas. I admit I have been fearful for Meg's future once you had her back in your custody."

Ingham's gaze took on an odd light though he spoke plain. "With good reason, ma'am. As you no doubt surmised, any lawyer worth his salt would have a jury condemn her in a heartbeat."

"It would be taken as an admission of guilt?"

"Exactly so, my lord. Not, if I am to be plain with you all, that there was much doubt of her being found guilty in any event."

Ottilia exchanged a brief glance with her spouse. Had she not said as much over and again? Francis turned back to the justice.

"You said it was a close run thing, Sir Thomas?"

Ingham's features clearly showed his dissatisfaction. "Grice was sure he had them."

"He located their whereabouts?"

Ingham seemed to lose a little of the trappings of his office in a stir of enthusiasm. "One of my best men, Grice. I knew, if anyone could sniff them out, it was he. He drew blank in the obvious places, but he guessed at the Frenchman's mind and very soon lit upon a trail."

Ottilia was sorely tempted to ask how, but refrained. She had not underestimated the skill of the runner Grice, it would seem. He must have targeted Starkey's as she had supposed. If he drew blank there, how else might he find a trail? What did it mean that he guessed at Pierre's mind? He could not have known anything of The Silver Moon.

Sybilla took a hand. "This is your runner, I take it? He followed this trail?"

"Like a bloodhound. It took him to Portsmouth where Benjamin had reason to believe they intended to board a ship."

Ottilia's heart flipped despite the assumption the ship had sailed. Francis, to her relief, pursued it.

"A ship to where?"

"According to certain enquiries made at various shipping merchants, de Percheval was intending to try for America. Where, as he no doubt realised, he must be immune from pursuit."

"You would not send after them there?"

"We have no jurisdiction in that country. Nor have I funds to support the prosecution of a fruitless search through its vast territories."

Impatience caught at Ottilia and she was thankful when Sybilla put forward the vital question.

"But did they board a ship or not, sir?"

"Not at Portsmouth. The Frenchman was cannier than I guessed. The trail proved false."

Startled, Ottilia's gaze flew to Francis. She could not help the interjection. "False, Sir Thomas? In what way?"

Ingham's expression turned grim. "With reluctance, I admit de Percheval outwitted us. He must have planted the trail to Portsmouth deliberately with these enquiries he made for ships leaving from that port. Grice was in time to board the *Mercury* before she sailed for Virginia and prosecute a search, even though her captain protested he had no such passengers and had seen neither hide nor hair of either answering to the descriptions given."

Francis spoke Ottilia's thought. "Then they did not sail after all?"

Ingham snorted. "Oh, they sailed all right. Yesterday. From Poole. It took Grice a full day and a half to chase down the truth. By the time he reached there, the *Hercules* was long gone. Our truants are well en route to Philadelphia by now."

Elation soared in Ottilia's bosom. Then they must have left The Silver Moon that same evening, travelling through the night to arrive at Poole in time to catch the *Hercules*. Pierre had kept her ignorant of his true intent. Bravo, Pierre! He had won his lady well this time.

She was obliged to curb her enthusiasm as Ingham turned to her.

"With reluctance, Lady Francis, I must deem the case closed. As a courtesy, I thought it right to inform you, considering your investment of interest in securing the Pargeter woman's release."

"By lawful means, Sir Thomas."

Ottilia shot the words at him but he did not flinch. His lip twisted once more.

"Naturally. I had not credited you with the foolhardiness obtaining in another member of your family."

Ottilia cast an apprehensive glance at her mother-in-law, but Sybilla thankfully held her tongue though her eyes looked daggers. Her husband, however, batted it out into the open.

"Are you at that again, sir? I should have thought the wound Lady Elizabeth sustained must convince even you of her innocence in the matter. Have you not just spoken of de Percheval's cunning? It is plain he concocted the scheme. Lady Elizabeth was an innocent victim."

Ottilia bit her tongue on denial, her conscience rising once more to plague her. The quick suspicion kindling in Sybilla's face sent her spirits plummeting. The dowager would not let this alone.

Ingham inclined his head. "I must bow to your better knowledge of Lady Elizabeth, my lord. There is, in any event, no future in pursuing the matter." He turned once more to Ottilia, a hint of a reluctant smile in his eyes. "I hope you will not take it amiss, ma'am, if I express the hope there may be no more murderous doings on my watch when you are by."

Ottilia had to laugh. "I take it that is not meant for a compliment?"

His features relaxed at last. "I fear another fall with you may undermine my authority altogether, ma'am." With which, he took his leave and Ottilia, listening to his retreating footsteps, waited in some degree of trepidation for Sybilla's inevitable questions. Sybilla chose instead to break out against the departed magistrate, addressing herself to Francis.

"Do you mean to tell me that fellow had the gall to suspect my granddaughter of engineering this escape?"

"Frankly, Mama, we all did," said Francis, moving back to his chair. "Including her own father."

Sybilla eyed him with a narrowed gaze and Ottilia was relieved not to be the target of that shrewd look.

"Reckless child she may be, but would she go so far?"

"Gilbert was certain she had until Lizzy showed him the wound de Percheval inflicted. It was quite a bump."

"So I understood from Harriet's note." Sybilla's frown did not abate. "She was utterly overset to think of her daughter being attacked. Apparently even Candia's partiality suffered a dent, which is all to the good." Her gaze shifted and Ottilia found herself under scrutiny. "You say nothing, Ottilia. Have you no opinion?"

The rhythm of her heartbeat went out of true as Ottilia met the look. She prevaricated. "Of what use to speak, ma'am? I know well you blame me for Lizzy's involvement."

"I have done, perhaps unfairly. In other circumstances, she might have learned well of you."

Ottilia forced herself to hold that penetrating gaze. "Flattery now, Sybilla? I fear my credit as a mentor for any young female is utterly destroyed."

"Not so. You have a great deal of common sense and when you do not have the bit between your teeth—"

"Enough, Mama!"

"I am complimenting the girl."

"A backhanded compliment." Francis was on his feet again. "I will say it once more. Ottilia is not responsible for anything Lizzy may choose to do. Yes, she may have drawn her in, but she did so for the best of motives. I was also furious at the outset." He glanced back at Ottilia as he spoke. "But I have since come to recognise that Elizabeth Fiske is a force to be reckoned with. I did not know my own niece as well as I do now, ma'am. And if I did not, how the deuce might Ottilia know she was playing with fire?"

Past all bearing, Ottilia rose too. "Oh, stop, Fan!" She moved to him, setting a hand to his chest. "My darling, you are too generous. I admit I did not know what Lizzy meant to do, but I knew she had some scheme afoot."

"You knew?" He grasped the hand and held it tightly. "Why did you not speak of it? We might have prevented—"

"No! It was a hazy notion only. I did not confess it, but the night Sybilla came back from Harriet with a tale of that clandestine meeting, I slipped out — don't scold, Fan, for I took Hemp! — and went to Lizzy to find out what she had been about. Also, for I was desperate enough by then, to ask if she had Pierre's direction. When we spoke, I thought she was keeping something back. I warned her to think before she acted if she had some plot afoot but she denied any intention other than writing a note to tell Pierre how to find Meg in Bridewell. She had been meaning to come to me for the information."

"But you saved her the trouble."

"Yes. She would have done what she did regardless." She released herself, unable to meet the reproach in her husband's eyes. She dared not look at Sybilla, deadly in her silence. Pacing away, she turned to face them. "I did not mean to say a word of this, but it hurts me to keep anything from you, Fan."

He threw out a hand. "My loved one…"

"Oh, don't. Be angry with me if you will, for I deserve it." She looked from one to the other, the guilt swelling in her heart. "I have tried to acquit myself, but how can I? You are right, Sybilla. You too, Francis. I led Lizzy into this and without me she would never have thought to do what she did."

Sybilla was looking bewildered now. "But the bump on her head. Do you tell me she persuaded de Percheval to strike her?"

Francis made a derisive sound. "I would believe anything of that Frenchman after what Ingham told us. Devious and duplicitous is what he is."

Ottilia sighed. "So he may be, but he was gentleman enough to refuse Lizzy's request. She knocked her own head against the edge of the wooden frame around the bed." Blank astonishment succeeded her revelation. Ottilia took advantage of it to hurry on. "Lizzy is truly penitent, for she had no notion how bad a turn she was doing Meg if she were to be recaptured."

Her spouse found his voice at last. "If Lizzy is capable of doing herself a mischief in such a cause then she is capable of anything. Dear God, she might be your copy, Tillie!"

"Except," put in Sybilla, "that she has none of Ottilia's insight and foresight." She struck her hands together. "It seems to me we have all of us neglected that child in favour of Candia since Emily's untimely demise. Well, that must change."

Francis turned a face of undisguised horror upon his mother. "How? I trust you do not expect us to take on the re-education of that hurly-burly girl? I have had enough of dealing with the vagaries of my siblings' offspring, I thank you."

Sybilla snorted. "I am not thinking of you, Francis."

"Nor Ottilia, I hope."

"Nothing of the kind. I mean to take Elizabeth in hand myself. Harriet has no control over her and Gilbert is far too indulgent. Let her come under her grandmother's jurisdiction and she will learn a thing or two, I promise you."

Ottilia could not but feel a rush of sympathy for poor Lizzy, but she could not argue with her husband's dictum.

"I wish you joy of her, Mama. Though I suspect Lizzy may be found to be match even for you."

Alone at last with Francis as they climbed into bed that night, Ottilia admitted to feeling in a state of nervous exhaustion.

Francis was resting against the banked pillows. "As soon as Teresa gets back, we are leaving."

Ottilia settled next to him. "I should be glad of it. Only we have scarcely performed Sybilla's role for us."

"Yes, we have. Or you have. Pierre is out of the picture, which leaves Candia safe. And I don't see that Violette's success creates difficulties for her in any way." He turned to her, leaning on his elbow. "Moreover, I won't have you dragged into this nonsensical notion Mama has about Lizzy."

"Poor child. I pity her."

"Yes, that is all very well, but I know Mama. Blame you she might, but that won't stop her demanding your intervention when Lizzy proves obdurate, as she will do without doubt."

Ottilia touched a hand to his cheek. "I don't care about anything, Fan, except to know you forgive me."

His smile was wry. "For what? Being yourself? You are the woman I fell in love with, Tillie. For better or worse, remember?"

He leaned to kiss her and she returned his embrace with fervour, snuggling into him as he slid down and drew her head to rest on his shoulder.

"And another thing. The sooner you are out of range of that Pargeter woman the better."

A ripple of dismay attacked Ottilia and she pushed up to look at him in the light of his candle still burning on the bedside table.

"You are not thinking she will do something foolish? She is a strong and determined female, I know, but—"

"But nothing. She has that appalling fellow in bed and at her mercy. For two pins, I'd wager she will put a pillow over his head and come bleating to you to save her from the gallows. What's more, you wouldn't blame her."

Indignant, Ottilia struck him lightly on the chest. "How can you say so? A premeditated murder? Most certainly I would blame her."

He caught her hand and held it, a serious look in the dark eyes. "But you would still try to save her, wouldn't you?"

Beset with a tangle of emotions, Ottilia gazed into the beloved features, for once bewildered. "What are you saying, Fan? I am too much at the mercy of my sympathies? Too ready to be worked upon by unscrupulous persons?"

His face softened, a wry smile forming and his free fingers stroked her cheek. "I am saying, my dear love, that you have a big heart, all warmth, and a conscience that drives you to champion the weak and vulnerable. You would take on the world for justice, if you felt the need."

Ottilia's heart flooded and she turned her face into his hand, wetting it with her tears. Her voice shook. "You m-make me s-sound like a s-saint, Fan. It's not f-fair."

"What isn't fair, sweetheart?" He sat up and scrabbled under the pillow, producing a handkerchief.

Ottilia took it and blew her nose. "That I force you to share me with these people. I meant to be a devoted wife to you and instead all I do is rush about like some crusading lunatic, saving all and sundry."

Francis gave a shout of laughter. "That is the silliest interpretation of what I said you could have come up with, Tillie."

She paid no heed, clutching the damp handkerchief and seizing his hand. "Well, no more, Fan. From this moment, I am all yours. Let murderers do their worst, if they will. I shall leave it to the authorities to — how dare you laugh like that, Fan? You sound like a constipated horse!"

Francis fairly gasped, almost doubled up. "I can't help it, you idiotic female."

"But I mean it, Fan. Truly."

"I know you do. At this moment, in any event." His merriment died off at last and he put a finger to her lips. "No more, Tillie, I beg of you. It's useless to make such promises."

"But I—"

"Uh-uh, be quiet, woman!" He pulled her into a rough embrace. "I don't want a wife fawning all over me, I thank you. The one I have is just what I need."

Ottilia sniffed. "She is not. She's—"

"Don't argue with me, madam wife, or I shall take a lesson from Pargeter."

That made her laugh and he kissed her. He blew out the candle and Ottilia allowed herself to be pulled down into the bed. Guilt still niggled but she thought better of saying any more. Presently her mind drifted. She was on the edge of sleep when Francis spoke again.

"I'll tell you one thing, Tillie. If Mama holds by her resolution, we've not heard the last of Lady Elizabeth Fiske."

A NOTE TO THE READER

Dear Reader

To be honest, I had a lot of trouble writing *The Mortal Blow*. It was one of those stories that didn't flow easily. Partly because I had a couple of long breaks, once when I was in the US for a month, and then I moved from a house to a small flat. Downsizing is complicated. This kind of stop/start is not conducive to successful plotting.

Then I ran into legal complications. I wanted the young woman Meg to be in danger of losing her life. This meant I had to find out what would stand in a court of law and whether a jury would be inclined to be lenient. Capital punishment was so common at the time, and for what we would consider minor offences. There was no mercy for someone pronounced guilty of murder. However, it turns out that juries could be persuaded to be sympathetic, and this gave Ottilia hope — as well as her relieved author!

And then I was faced with how to resolve this situation? How to get Meg released? I wrote and discarded several potential plot lines trying to figure this out. By good fortune, Lady Elizabeth Fiske had insinuated herself into the story. Much to my astonishment, I may say. Characters have a way of turning things about to suit themselves, throwing said author into total disarray. This is not a myth. Ask any novelist and they will tell you that characters quite often take over a story.

The truth of this is that we write from a place below the conscious level. Once the scene takes off, the conscious mind is only concerned with adjusting words and phrases that haven't come out quite right. It really has no control over what the characters do and say. I call this the Inner Writer. Quite often she seems to be a completely different individual! I never know what she's going to come up with.

But I digress. Having found myself with this Lizzy prominent in the story, I was able to use her in several ways that helped the plot along. Which made things a little easier. Or so I thought. But, no. More potential plot lines. More discards. Once again the Inner Writer baffled me. I started scenes with the intention of getting from A to B, and found myself instead at P or Z! Another plot point down the drain.

Eventually, it sorted itself out and all the ends got tied up. Phew! It took a few more edits to lick the story into shape, but it was a glad day when I finished the first draft.

Despite all this, I have to say it has become a pleasure to write the scenes between Ottilia and Francis. And the dowager slots in readily too. This couple are so much a part of me now that I feel I know them through and through. I don't have to think beyond where the scene is going because these two write themselves the moment I bring them onto the stage together. It's a treat for me when readers tell me how much they enjoy the development of this relationship, and the fact that the affection between them is so strong. Really, that's not my doing. That's just how it is with Tillie and Fan.

If you would consider leaving a review, it would be much appreciated and very helpful. Do feel free to contact me on **elizabeth@elizabethbailey.co.uk** or find me on **Facebook**, **Twitter**, **Goodreads** or my website **www.elizabethbailey.co.uk**.

Elizabeth Bailey

Sapere Books is an exciting new publisher of brilliant fiction and popular history.

To find out more about our latest releases and our monthly bargain books visit our website: **saperebooks.com**